Praise from the U.K. for *After You'd Gone*

"Harrowing, profound, and beautifully written."
—*Independent on Sunday*

"Incredibly affecting...a devastating debut."
—*The Face*

"O'Farrell is blessed with a tender, solicitous intelligence...honest, moving, and wise beyond its author's years."
—*Time Out*

"O'Farrell's clean, pellucid prose makes this an effortless read...such emotional delicacy really distinguishes this compulsively readable and accomplished first novel."
— *Independent*

"A poignant tragedy punctuated only with happy moments from a brighter past. Girl in a coma, a love affair tragically aborted, a religious tangle and a disturbed relationship between mother and daughter all add up to a gripping and emotionally engaging novel."
—*Sunday Express*

"For a debut novel this has a startling sense of completeness. The way that O'Farrell convincingly manages her web of coincidences and chance events alongside an ensemble cast of characters marks her out as a novelist with a real gift for storytelling. Multiple viewpoints, a difficult plot and an acute emotional pitch may in the hands of a lesser talent show up inadequacies in the writing; in this case they highlight the strengths, showing O'Farrell to be a writer of rare insight and intellect with a real feel for language that renders her love story both tender and tragic without resorting to mush."
—*Financial Times*

after you'd gone

Maggie O'Farrell | after you'd gone

VIKING

VIKING
Published by the Penguin Group
Penguin Putnam Inc., 375 Hudson Street,
New York, New York 10014, U.S.A.
Penguin Books Ltd, 27 Wrights Lane,
London W8 5TZ, England
Penguin Books Austrailia Ltd, Ringwood,
Victoria, Austrailia
Penguin Books Canada Ltd, 10 Alcorn Avenue,
Toronto, Ontario, Canada M4V 3B2
Penguin Books (N.Z.) Ltd, 182–190 Wairau Road,
Auckland 10, New Zealand

Penguin Books Ltd, Registered Offices:
Harmondsworth, Middlesex, England

First American edition
Published in 2001 by Viking Penguin,
a member of Penguin Putnam Inc.

1 3 5 7 9 10 8 6 4 2

PUBLISHER'S NOTE
This is a work of fiction. Names, characters, places, and incidents
either are the product of the author's imagination or are used
fictiously, and any resemblance to actual persons, living or dead,
business establishments, events, or locales is entirely coincidental.

LIBRARY OF CONGRESS CATALOGING IN PUBLICATION DATA
O'Farrell, Maggie, 1972–
After you'd gone / Maggie O'Farrell.
p. cm.
ISBN 0-670-89448-6
1. Coma—Patients—Fiction. 2. Suicidal Behavior—Fiction.
3. London (England)—Fiction. 4. Scotland—Fiction. I. Title

PR6065.F36 A68 2001
823'.92—dc21   00-043898

This book is printed on acid free paper. ∞

Printed in the United States of America
Set in Perpetua
Designed by Peter Ward

To my mother
for not being like Alice's

ACKNOWLEDGEMENTS

My thanks to: Alexandra Pringle, Victoria Hobbs, Geraldine
Cooke, Kate Jones, Barbara Trapido, Elspeth Barker,
William Sutcliffe, Flora Gathorne-Hardy, Saul Venit, Ruth
Metzstein, Georgie Bevan, Jo Aitchison, Ellis Woodman,
John Hole, Morag and Esther McRae

Whatever has happened, happens always

ANDREW GREIG

The past falls open anywhere

MICHAEL DONAGHY

prologue

The day she would try to kill herself, she realised winter was coming again. She had been lying on her side, her knees drawn up; she'd sighed, and the heat of her breath had vaporised in the cold air of the bedroom. She pushed the air out of her lungs again, watching. Then she did it again, and again. Then she wrenched back the covers and got up. Alice hated winter.

It must have been around 5 a.m.; she didn't need to look at her clock, she could tell from the glow behind the curtains. She'd been awake most of the night. The weak dawn light cast the walls, bed and floor in greyish-blue granite, and her shadow as she crossed the floor was a grainy, unfocused smudge.

In the bathroom, she twisted the tap and drank straight from it, bending over and pushing her mouth into the pressurised, icy flow, gasping with the shock of the cold. Wiping her face on the back of her hand, she filled the toothmug and watered the plants on the bath edge. It had been so long since she'd cared for them that the parched soil didn't absorb the water, and it collected on the surface in accusing, mercuried drops.

Alice dressed quickly, putting on whatever clothes she found discarded on the floor. She stood at the window, looking down into the street for a moment, then went downstairs, slinging her bag over her shoulder, closing the front door behind her. Then she just walked, head bent, coat pulled around her.

She walked through the streets. She passed shops with drawn-down, padlocked shutters, street-cleaning lorries scrubbing the kerbs with great circular black brushes, a group of bus drivers smoking and chatting on a corner, their hands curled around polystyrene cups of steaming tea. They stared as she passed, but she saw none of this. She saw nothing but her feet moving beneath her, disappearing and reappearing from under her with a rhythmic regularity.

It was almost fully light when she realised she'd reached King's Cross. Taxis were swinging in and out of its forecourt, people milled through its doors. She wandered inside, with a vague idea of buying a cup of coffee, perhaps, or something to eat. But when she entered the white-lit building, she became mesmerised by the vast expanse of the departures board. Numbers and letters flicker-flacked over each other; city names and times were being arranged and rearranged in letters caught on hidden electronic rollers. She read the names to herself – Cambridge, Darlington, Newcastle. I could go to any of these places. If I wanted to. Alice felt up her sleeve for the bulk of her watch. It was too big for her, really, its face wider than her wrist, but she'd pierced the scuffed strap with extra holes. She glanced at it, then automatically lowered her arm again before realising that she hadn't in fact taken in what she'd seen. She raised the watch to her face again, concentrating this time. She even pressed the little button at the side that illuminated the tiny grey screen – where constantly shifting liquid crystal displayed the time, date, altitude, air pressure and temperature – in a bright peacock-blue light. She had never worn a digital watch before this. It had been one of John's. His watch told her it was 6.20 a.m. And that it was a Saturday.

Alice turned her face up again to the departures board.

4

Glasgow, Peterborough, York, Aberdeen, Edinburgh. Alice blinked. Read it again: Edinburgh. She could go home. See her family. If she wanted to. She looked to the top of the column to see the train's time — 6.30 a.m. Did she want to? Then she was walking fast towards the ticket office and signing her name in cramped, cold-handed writing. 'The Scottish Pullman to Edinburgh' the sign said as she got on, and she almost smiled.

She slept on the train, her head resting against the thrumming window, and she was almost surprised to see her sisters waiting at the end of the platform in Edinburgh. But then she remembered calling Kirsty from the train. Kirsty had her baby in a sling and Beth, Alice's younger sister, had Annie, Kirsty's daughter, by the hand. They were straining up on tiptoe to find her and when they caught sight of her, they waved. Kirsty hitched Annie on to her hip and they ran towards her. Then she was hugging both of them at once and although she knew their boisterousness masked concern and she really wanted to show them she was all right, she was fine, the feel of both her sisters' hands pressing into her spine meant that she had to turn her head away and pick up Annie and pretend to be burying her face in the child's neck.

They hustled her to the station café, divested her of her bag and placed in front of her a coffee adorned with white froth and a sprinkling of chocolate. Beth had done an exam the day before and she related the questions she'd been asked and how the invigilator had smelt. Kirsty, trailing nappies, feeding bottles, jigsaws, Plasticine, held the baby, Jamie, in the crook of her arm while expertly harnessing Annie into a pair of reins. Alice rested her chin in her hands, listened to Beth and watched Annie cover a piece of newspaper with green crayon. The vibrations of Annie's strenuous efforts travelled across the table and up the twin violin-bow bones of Alice's forearms to reverberate in her cranium.

She got up and went out of the café to find the toilet, leaving Kirsty and Beth discussing what to do that day. She crossed the waiting room and pushed through the steel turnstile into the station Superloo. She couldn't have been absent from the café table where her sisters and niece and nephew were sitting for more than four minutes, but during that time she saw something so odd and unexpected and sickening that it was as if she'd glanced in the mirror to discover that her face was not the one she thought she had. Alice looked, and it seemed to her that what she saw undercut everything she had left. And everything that had gone before. She looked again, and then again. She was sure, but didn't want to be.

She bolted out of her loo, shoving her way through the turnstile. In the middle of the concourse, she stopped still for a moment. What would she say to her sisters? Can't think about this now, she told herself, just can't; and she slammed down on top of it something heavy and wide and flat, sealing up the edges, tight as a clam.

She was walking fast back through the café, reaching down beside her chair for her bag.

'Where are you going?' Kirsty asked.

'I have to go,' Alice said.

Kirsty stared at her. Beth stood up.

'Go?' Beth repeated. 'Go where?'

'Back to London.'

'What?' Beth sprang forward and seized hold of the coat Alice was pulling on. 'But you can't. You've only just got here.'

'Have to go.'

Beth and Kirsty exchanged quick looks.

'But . . . Alice . . . what's happened?' cried Beth. 'What's wrong, what's wrong? Please don't go. You can't go like this.'

'Have to,' Alice muttered again, and walked off to find the next London train.

Kirsty and Beth gathered up the children, their bags and the baby clutter, and hurried after her. There was a train just about to depart, Alice found, so she ran to the platform, her sisters following behind her, calling her name over and over.

On the platform, she hugged both of them. 'Bye,' she whispered. 'Sorry.'

Beth burst into tears. 'I don't understand,' she wailed. 'Tell us what the matter is. Why are you going?'

'Sorry,' she said again.

Getting on the train, Alice felt suddenly malcoordinated. The gap between the train step and the platform edge down to the tracks seemed to yawn wide into a huge, uncrossable crevasse. Her body didn't seem to be getting the right spatial information from her brain: she reached for the handle to pull herself across the crevasse, but missed, swayed and lurched backwards into a man standing behind her.

'Steady,' he said, and took her elbow to help her on.

Beth and Kirsty crowded into the window when she sat down. Kirsty was crying too now, and they waved frantically as the train moved off, running beside her for as long as they could before it picked up speed and their strides flagged. Alice could not wave back, she could not look at them and see their four blonde heads running beside the train, captured by the frame of the window as if on a reel of flickering Super-8.

Her heart was jumping in her chest so hard as she travelled that the edges of her vision pulsed in giddy sympathy. Rain screed back along the window. She avoided the eye of the reflection whizzing along beside her in another, reversed, tilted ghost carriage that skimmed over the fields as they hurtled towards London.

The air in the house felt icy when she got back. She fiddled with the boiler and thermostat, reading aloud to herself the incomprehensible instructions, peering at the diagrams bristling with arrows and dials. The radiators coughed and gulped, digesting the first heat of the year. In the bathroom, she stuck her fingers into the compost of the plants. It felt damp.

She was just about to go back downstairs, she thought, when she just sat down where she was – on the top step. She looked at John's watch again and was astonished to see it was only five in the afternoon. She checked it three times: 17.02. That definitely meant five o'clock. Her trip to Edinburgh seemed unreal now. Had she really gone all that way and then come back? Had she really seen what she thought she saw? She didn't know. She clenched her hands around her ankles and let her head fall on to her knees.

When she raised it again, the rain had stopped. There was a peculiar stillness about the house and it seemed to have got dark very suddenly. Her knuckle and finger joints ached, and as she flexed them they made sharp, cracking sounds that echoed round the stairwell. She hauled herself up by the banister and went slowly down the stairs, leaning her weight against the wall.

In the sitting room she stood at the window. The street-lights had gone on. Over the road a television flickered behind net curtains. The roof of her mouth felt swollen and bruised, as if she'd been sucking boiled sweets. Lucifer, appearing from somewhere, leapt noiselessly on to the window-sill and began rubbing his head against her folded arms. She smoothed the velvet of his throat with her fingertips, feeling the rumble of his purr.

She snapped on a light and the cat's pupils narrowed, like the closing of a fan. He jumped to the floor and circled her ankles, mewing loudly. She watched him as he prowled the room, casting sideways looks at her, swishing his long black tail. In the overhead light it was possible to see the ghost of a tabby in the monochrome sheen of his fur. Some recess of her mind told her: he's hungry. The cat needs feeding. Feed the cat, Alice.

She went through to the kitchen. The cat raced ahead of her through the door and began leaping at the fridge. There was nothing in the cupboard where she kept his food but a tired-looking cardboard box of cat biscuits and the brown rust-rings of tins long since eaten. She tipped out the box. Three biscuits fell on to the lino. After sniffing at them for a time, Lucifer crunched them delicately.

'Have I been neglecting you?' She stroked him. 'I'll go out and buy some catfood.'

Lucifer followed at her heels, aghast that she seemed to have changed her mind and wasn't going to feed him after all. At the front door, she got her keys and wallet from her bag. The cat slipped out of the door with her and sat on the doorstep.

'Back in a minute,' she murmured and clicked the gate shut behind her.

Maybe it was something to do with the rhythm of her steps hitting the tarmac or maybe it was being out among crowds of people again rather than in the cool, hermetic interior of the house, but as she walked down Camden Road to the supermarket it all started coming back to her. She could see herself in that white melamine cubicle, walls inscribed with skewered hearts and legends of love. She could see herself washing her hands again at the stainless-steel basin, sprayed with silver beads of water. She tried to stop herself thinking about this. Tried to fill her mind with other things, think about Lucifer, about what else she could buy in the supermarket. She had leant on the gleaming soap dispenser; lurid pink soap had coiled into her wet palm, lathering into oiled bubbles under the water. Behind her in the cubicles, two teenage girls had been discussing a dress one of them was going to buy that day. 'Do you not think it makes me look a bit kind of flouncy?' one had shouted. 'Flouncy? Well, now you come to mention it.' 'Fuck off, fuck off!' What had happened then? What had occurred a few moments later was so disorientating, it was hard to order things in her head . . . Did she need anything else? Milk, maybe? Or bread? . . . Alice had turned then towards the hand-dryer and pressed the chrome button, passing her hands over each other. It had one of those little mirrors stuck to the front. She has never really known why they do that. You're supposed to be able to dry your hair if you turn the nozzle around, or something, but she's never found the need to dry her hair in a public toilet . . . What should she do when she got back? Maybe she could read something. She could buy a paper. How long is it since she read a paper anyway? . . . The whole place had seemed reflective – the shining porcelain tiles, the steel basins, the mirror above them, and the mirror on the hand-dryer . . . Maybe she should call Rachel. She couldn't remember when she last spoke to her. Rachel was probably cross with her . . . The girls' voices had been bouncing off the walls. One of them had raised herself up on to the top of the cubicle and was looking down on her friend. Alice had, for some reason – why? why did she do that? – stepped closer to the hand-dryer, and the new angle made something behind her appear in the tiny square mirror . . . Perhaps Rachel wasn't talking to her. That would be strange. They'd never fallen out before. Perhaps she would get a basket at the shop, or a trolley, yes, a trolley would be good. She could fill it with everything she needed. Then she wouldn't have to go again for a while. But how would she carry it all home? . . . Still with her hands under the hot jet of air, she had stared at the mirror and then, ever so slowly, so slowly that it seemed to have taken minutes, turned towards them.

Alice was by now standing at the pedestrian crossing. The green figure, legs parted in a purposeful stride, was illuminated on the traffic-light opposite. Over the road, she could see the supermarket; figures cruising through the neon-lit aisles. It seemed to her that her life was narrowing down to a vanishing point. People flowed around her, crossing the road, moving on. But she stayed still.

Someone nudged her in the back and she was pushed towards the edge of the pavement. The green figure was blinking on and off. Final stragglers were dashing across the road before the lights changed. The stationary red figure appeared and there was a moment of suspended calm before the waiting line of cars gunned their engines. As they powered past her, hurling fumes up into her face, their solidity seemed enviable to her — edgeless, slick constructions of steel, glass and chrome. The soles of Alice's shoes peeled away from the tarmac, and she stepped off the kerb.

part | one

The only bit Alice can see of her father is the soles of his shoes.
They are a faded brown, striated with the grit and terrain of the pavements he has walked. She is allowed to run along the pavement outside their house to meet him coming home from work in the evening. In the summertime she sometimes runs in her nightie, its pale folds catching around her knees. But now it's winter — November, maybe. The soles of the shoes are curved around the branch of a tree at the bottom of their garden. She tips back her head as far as it will go. The foliage rustles and thrashes. Her father's voice swears. She feels a shout welling like tears in her throat, then the coarse orange rope lowers itself, slightly coiled like a cobra from the branches.

'Got it?'

She seizes the rope's waxed head in her mittened hand. 'Yes.'

The branches shake as her father swings down. He lays a hand briefly on Alice's shoulder then bends to pick up the tyre. She is fascinated by the meandering rivulets that wander through its tread and the weft underneath its heavy black rubber. 'That's what holds it together,' the man at the shop had told her. The sudden scraped bald patch in the middle of the meanders makes her shudder but she doesn't quite know why. Her father winds the orange rope around the tyre and makes a thick, twisted knot.

'Can I have a go now?' Her hands grip the tyre.

'No. I have to test it with my weight first.'

Alice watches as her father jounces on the tyre, testing to see if it is safe enough for her. She looks up to see the branch shake in sympathy and looks quickly back at her father. What if he were to fall? But he is getting off and lifting her on, her bones as small, white and bendable as birds'.

Alice and John sit in a café in a village in the Lake District. It's early autumn. She holds up a sugar cube between finger and thumb, the light behind it making its crystals the massed cells of an intricate organism under a microscope.

'Did you know,' says John, 'that someone did a chemical analysis of sugar cubes in café sugar bowls and that they found strong traces of blood, semen, faeces and urine?'

She keeps her face serious. 'I didn't know that, no.'

He holds her deadpan gaze until the edges of his mouth are tugged downwards. Alice gets hiccups and he shows her how to cure them by drinking out of the opposite side of a glass. Beyond them, through the window, a plane draws a sheer white line on the sky.

She looks at John's hands, breaking up a bread roll, and suddenly knows she loves him. She looks away, out of the window, and sees for the first time the white line made by the plane. It has by this time drifted into woolliness. She thinks about pointing it out to John, but doesn't.

Alice's sixth summer was hot and dry. Their house had a large garden with the kitchen window looking out over the patio and garden so whenever Alice and her sisters were playing outside they could look up and see their mother watching over them.

The freakish heat dried up the reservoirs, previously unheard-
of in Scotland, and she went with her father to a pump at the
end of the street to collect water in round white vats. The
water drummed into their empty bottoms. Half-way between
the house and the end of the garden was the vegetable patch
where peas, potatoes and beetroot pushed their way up from
thick, dark soil. On a particularly bright day that summer,
Alice stripped off her clothes, scooped up clods of that earth
and smeared it in vivid tiger stripes all over her body.

She scared the pious, nervous children next door by roaring
at them through the hedge until her mother rapped on the
window-pane and shouted at her to stop that at once. She
retreated into the undergrowth to collect twigs and leaves
to construct a wigwam-shaped lair. Her younger sister stood
outside the lair and whinged to be let in. Alice said, only if
you are a tiger. Beth looked at the soil and then at her clothes
and then at their mother's face in the kitchen window. Alice
sat in the moist dark with her stripes, growling and gazing at
the triangle of sky visible through the top of the lair.

'You thought you were a little African boy, didn't you?'

She sits in the bath, her hair plastered into dripping spikes,
and her grandmother soaps her back and front. The skin
of her grandmother's hands feels roughened. The water is
grey-brown, full of the garden's soil, lifted off her skin. In
the next room she can hear the thrum of her father's voice,
talking on the telephone.

'Don't cover yourself in soil again, will you, Alice?'

Her skin looks lighter under the water. Is this what skin
looks like when it's dead?

'Alice? Promise me you won't do it again.'

She nods her head, spraying water over the ceramic sides
of the yellow bath.

Her grandmother towels her back. 'Wee angel wings,' she says, patting Alice's shoulder-blades dry. 'Everyone was an angel once, and this is where our wings would have been.'

She twists her head around to see the jutting isosceles triangle of bone flex and retract beneath her skin, as if preparing for celestial flight.

Across the café table, John looks at Alice who is looking out of the window. Today she has pulled the weight of her hair away from her face, giving her the appearance of a Spanish *niña* or a flamenco dancer. He imagines her that morning brushing the shining mass of her hair before clipping it at the back of her head. He reaches over the empty coffee mugs and cups the large knot of hair in his palm. She turns her eyes on him in surprise.

'I just wanted to know what it felt like.'

She touches it herself before saying, 'I often think about getting it all cut off.'

'Don't,' John says quickly, 'don't ever cut it off.' The aureoles of her eyes widen in surprise. 'It might contain all your strength,' he jokes feebly. He wants to free it from its silver clasp and bury his face in it. He wants to inhale its smell to the bottom of his lungs. He has caught its scent before. The first time he met her, she was standing in the doorway of his office with a book in her hand, and her hair swung at her waist so cleanly that he fancied it almost made a bell-like note. He wants to edge along its byways and curves in the dark and wake up in its strands.

'Do you want another coffee?' she says, and as she turns to look for the waitress he sees the shorter hairs springing from the nape of her neck.

Sometime after that coffee, John stretched his arms across the table and pressed her head between his hands. 'Alice Raikes,' he said, 'I'm afraid I'm going to have to kiss you.'

'You're going to have to?' she said levelly, although her heart was hammering in her ribcage. 'Do you think now would be a good time to do it, then?'

He made a great show of pretending to think about it, rolling his eyes, creasing his forehead. 'I think now is probably OK.'

Then he kissed her, very gently at first. They kissed for a long time, their fingers entwining. After a while, he pulled back and said, 'I think if we don't go soon, we may be asked to leave. I doubt they'd appreciate us making love on the table.' He was holding on to her hand so tightly that her knucklebones were beginning to hurt. She floundered with her other hand for her bag under the table, but encountered only his legs. He wedged her hand between his knees.

She began to laugh. 'John! Let go!' She struggled to release both her hands but his grip only tightened. He was smiling at her, a puzzled look on his face.

'If you don't let me go we can't leave or make love,' she reasoned.

He released her immediately. 'You are absolutely right.'

He fished her bag off the floor himself and hurried her into her coat. As they walked out of the door, he pressed her to his side, breathing into her hair.

The curtains in the sitting room of their house were of a heavy dark mauve damask, insulated on the outermost side with a thin membrane of yellowing sponge. As a child, Alice took against these curtains. She found it incredibly satisfying to peel away great swatches of the sponge, leaving the mauve material threadbare with light shining through it. One Hallowe'en, after they had scooped out the soft moss of a pumpkin's innards and scored square eyes and a jagged mouth into its skin, Beth and Alice were left reverently gazing at its flicking, demonic glow. Kirsty had eaten too much of the pumpkin scrapings and was being administered to somewhere else in the house. She couldn't say whether she actually planned to burn the curtains but she somehow found herself standing beside them, holding a lit match in a thin-fingered grip, training its curling flame to the curtain's edge. They caught fire with astonishing speed; the damask fizzled away as the flames tore upwards. Beth began to scream, great tongues of flame were licking across the ceiling. Alice jumped up and down in delight and exhilaration, clapping her hands and shouting. Then her mother burst into the room and dragged her away. She shut the door on them and the three of them stood wide-eyed and frozen in the hallway.

Ann runs down the stairs two at a time. Beth's screams are getting louder. They are real screams, full of terror. The sitting room is filled with smoke and the curtains are on fire. Beth hurls herself sobbing at Ann's knees and grips both her legs tightly. Ann is for a moment immobilised and it is then that she sees Alice. She is gazing at the flames, rapt, her whole body contorted and twisted with delight. In her right hand is a spent match. Ann lurches forward and seizes her daughter by the shoulder. Alice struggles in her grasp like a hooked fish. Ann is shocked by her sudden strength. They tussle, Alice spitting and snarling until Ann manages to grip both her hands and drags her kicking to the door. She shuts all three of her children in the hall and then runs to the kitchen for water.

John has fallen into a deep sleep. The rhythm of his breathing is that of a deep-sea diver. His head is resting on Alice's sternum. She sniffs his hair. A slight woody smell like freshly sharpened pencils. Some kind of shampoo. Lemon? She inhales again. A vague overlay of the cigarette smoke of the café. She places her hand on his ribcage and feels the swell and fall of his lungs. The whispering tick, tick of her own blood sounds against her eardrums.

She eases herself out from underneath him and hugs her knees to her chest. She is tempted to wake him up. She wants to talk. His skin is tanned a light golden brown all over, except for his groin which is a pale, vulnerable white. She cups her hand over his penis, curled against his leg. It twitches in response. She laughs and covers his body with her own, burying her nose and mouth in the curve of his neck. 'John? Are you awake?'

The fire was put out by my mother dousing it with water. The black sooty streaks were to scar the ceiling for years. Although my parents often talked about redecorating the room, the fire was never mentioned, never discussed. Not once did they ask me what had prompted me to set fire to the curtains.

Ann scrabbles on her bedside table for her cigarettes. As she strikes the lighter, she glances over at Ben to see if he has been disturbed. He is sleeping with a slightly surprised look on his face. She draws on her cigarette and feels the bitter smoke filling her lungs. A dream about the boarding-school she was sent to has woken her and now she can't sleep. She is again seven, standing in uncomfortable lace-up shoes at the door of the school, watching her parents' car recede down the gravelled driveway, too shocked even to cry. The nun standing next to her extracts the small suitcase from her fingers. 'There we are now,' she says.

Ann doesn't know who she means by 'we': she has never felt more alone in her life. I can never forgive you for this, Ann thinks, and in that moment her love for her parents sours irreversibly to something that will come close to hate.

She spends the next eleven years at the boarding-school, where the nuns teach her how to eat fruit correctly at a dinner table. Twenty-seven girls line up with twenty-seven apples and twenty-seven fruit knives to watch Sister Matthews deftly pare the tight apple's surface into a snaking coil of green that falls to the waiting plate. They line up again outside in the yard where the nuns have a perfect half of an old car to learn how to get out of a car without showing your slip. When Ann gets in she is unnerved by the gaping hole to her right; the car's body ends just short of the seat she is sitting on and beyond is the damp and misty expanse of Dartmoor. Sister Clare raps on the window. 'Come on, Ann. Don't take all day about it.'

Ann glances at herself in the rear-view mirror. Her way isn't rebellion, but inner defiance. She hoists herself from the seat gracefully, her skirt falling at the desired angle into the correct folds.

'Good, Ann. Girls? Did you see Ann?'

Ann stops before she reaches the back of the queue. 'Sister Clare? What happens if you are sitting in the driving seat? Is it the same method?'

Sister Clare is nonplussed. What a question to ask. She thinks for a moment, then brightens. 'Don't worry about that. Your husband will be driving you.'

The nuns hand out heavy books, and the girls balance them on their heads. Anyone wearing their hair up is scolded. They must parade across the gym in a figure-of-eight. Ann hates this more than anything else; she resents the restricting symmetry, of ending up where she began. Nevertheless, she volunteers to go first and executes a perfect turn. The nuns applaud and so do the other girls, though less enthusiastically. She removes the book and while the other girls are performing, Ann opens it and begins to read. The book is full of diagrams and cross-sections of plants. Ann follows with her fingertip the path of water through the plant up from the spread of roots, through the stems, to the petals. She reads on and learns about how plants fertilise. She is heartened by the gentle brushing of pollen against stamens and hopes that it is like that for men and women and not like the whispers that go around the dormitory. She has spent hours poring over a forbidden copy of *Lady Chatterley's Lover* and found herself none the wiser. Was it not all about flowering and seeds anyway?

To the complete surprise of her parents, the nuns, the school and Ann herself, she did well in her final exams and gained a place at Edinburgh University to read biology. Edinburgh suited Ann; she liked the tall, dignified buildings of grey stone, the short days that sank into street-lamped evenings at five o'clock, and the dual personality of the city's main street, which on one side had glittering shops and on the other the green sweep of Princes Street Gardens. She liked the small flat she shared with two other girls, which overlooked the Meadows; it was at the top of a tenement block with a cold, windy central staircase leading up to it and an equally cold sitting room where they sat and drank pots of tea in the evenings.

University life did not suit her. Every day just seemed to uncover more and more things she didn't know. She found lectures bewildering and tutorials humiliating; she was one of the few women in her year for biology and the men either patronised her or ignored her. They found her reserved and old-fashioned, preferring the company of the more liberated nursing students. She was too bored and too proud to ask for help from any of the academics. On the day she got her results, Ben Raikes asked her to marry him.

She'd known him for exactly six months. Two days after they first met he'd told her he was in love with her; it had been a surprising and, as she would later find out, uncharacteristically impulsive admission. She didn't know how to answer him, so didn't. He hadn't seemed to mind, just smiling at her as they stood together in the square outside St Giles's Cathedral. He started taking her to dances – she'd never been before – holding her firmly with his hand in the small of her back, his jawline against her hair. He was inclined to improvise on the dance steps taught to her so rigorously by the nuns. It made her laugh. He had limpid blue-green eyes and a nice smile. Once, when he had called on her at the flat, he had brought her flowers

– yellow roses, the petals curved and pleated together into tight yellow mouths. After he had gone, she'd snipped off the ends of the stalks underwater and placed them in a jam-jar on her desk. Whenever she entered the room, their yellow-yolk brightness pulled her eyes to them.

He asked her to marry him on the Meadows. As she was saying yes, she was aware that she was doing so only because she could not face going to live with her parents. Since meeting Ben Raikes, she had realised that there was some vital part of her that seemed absent, that she could never be wholly activated by love. He held her hand and kissed her and said his mother would be pleased. She fingered the imprint of his kiss as they walked back. The ring he gave her cast a shoal of light-flashes on to the ceiling when she lay awake at night

The telephone rang shrilly. From some depth of sleep, Ben felt Ann sliding from the bed. Later he will try to convince himself that he tensed, listening out for what was being said. But he'll know that he sank into sleep again because he'll remember waking with Ann's palm on his chest, her fingers touching his throat. His eyelids pulled up like portcullises. He couldn't see her face, the gloom smudging her features, but words reached him as individual sounds, devoid as yet of meaning: 'Accident,' Ann was saying to him, over and over, 'accident', and 'Alice'. Alice is his daughter. Accident.

'Wake up, Ben, we have to get up. Alice is in a coma. Ben, wake up.'

Is this my voice I can hear? It is as if I'm living in a radio, floating up and down on airwaves, each with their different voices – some I recognise and some I don't. I can't choose the bandwidth.

This place feels clean. The smell of antiseptic crackles in my nostrils. Some voices I can distinguish as outside myself, those that sound farther off, as if through water. And then there are those within – all kinds of spectres.

Why isn't life better designed so it warns you when terrible things are about to happen?

I saw something. Something awful. What would he have said?

Ann cups Alice's chin in her hand and scrutinises her face. Alice, unused to this treatment, looks up at her mother, attentive.

'Where did you learn that song?'

Alice had been singing while she searched the garden for flowers for a miniature garden that she was creating in an old shoebox.

'Um. I don't know. I think I heard it on the radio,' she improvises, nervous. Is she going to get told off?

Her mother continues staring. 'It's a song on a cassette that

I only bought yesterday. There is no other way you could have heard it.'

Ann appears to be talking to herself now. Alice fidgets, impatient to get on with her tiny garden. She wants to steal some cocktail sticks for a runner-bean row.

'I have a feeling, Alice, that you are very musical. My father was a great musician and you must have inherited it.'

An unusual, effervescent feeling is creeping into Alice. Her mother is smiling at her admiringly. Alice flings her arms around her middle and hugs her.

'We'll have to get you some lessons and nurture that talent of yours. You mustn't let it go to waste. Do you know, my father could name any note that he heard? He had perfect pitch and played with many orchestras all around the world.'

'Did you go with him?'

'No.' Ann eases Alice's arms off her abruptly. Alice wanders off down the garden, her shoebox garden forgotten. She is musical! What does it matter that she isn't pretty like her sisters? She has something that sets her apart, makes her different. Perfect Pitch. Nurture. She rolls the new words around on her tongue.

Her grandmother comes out into the garden to take in the washing and Alice skips over to her. 'Granny, guess what? I'm musical! I'm going to have lessons.'

'Is that right?' Elspeth says. 'Well, don't go getting above yourself now.'

I was sent once a week to a woman down the road to have piano lessons. Mrs Beeson was tall and incredibly thin with long grey hair that was usually looped into clips on top of her head or sometimes spread in a greasy grey curtain over her shoulders. She wore long orange crocheted cardigans. Spit collected in the corners of her mouth when she talked. Throughout the lessons in her dark front lounge, her large, mottled cat would lie across the piano, purring.

I learnt how to hold my hand on the keyboard as if I had an orange in my palm and how to translate the black dots on the page to the smooth, flat white keys or the thin, finger-like black ones – every good boy deserves favour, all cows eat grass. I learnt the flamboyant Italian phrases and how to alter my touch accordingly.

I practised hard. The piano in our house was right next to the kitchen and my mother would open the door to hear me play. My fingers became strong and muscular, I kept my nails short, I held in my head the precise number and types of sharps and flats in each key, at times of stress I would drum out the fingering for different scales on any available surface.

I did exam after exam, toiling over the same three pieces for months to perform them in a musty church hall to a glazed-faced examiner. I think I did believe that I was talented: my certificates, framed by my mother, said so, didn't they?

Alice had been at the party three-quarters of an hour. Mario had kept her clamped to his side for the first half-hour but as soon as he became drunk enough she had extricated herself and escaped to the corner of a room. It was a second-year's room, covered in posters of the Stone Roses and the Happy Mondays and crammed with people; the bed was sagging under the weight of six people and a girl in a tight white catsuit was dancing on the desk, shouting at a few of the goggle-eyed boys to look at her.

Alice found the boys here odd: they were either incredibly introverted, with an excess of knowledge in an esoteric subject, or stunningly arrogant, but yet completely unsure of how to talk to her. It was the first time she'd mixed with large numbers of English people. On her first day a boy called

Amos had asked her where she'd come from. 'Scotland,' she'd replied.

'Ah, how many days did it take you to get here?' he'd asked, in complete seriousness.

She looked around the smoky room and told herself she'd give it another five minutes and then she'd leave. Mario waved from the other side of the room, Alice drained her mug of warmish, syrupy wine and smiled back thinly.

Mario was an Italian-American from New York, very rich and very beautiful. He was at the university for a year, courtesy of his father. When Alice had asked him how he'd arranged an exchange year from America, he said, 'My father opened his cheque book,' and roared with laughter. She had met him in her first week while wandering the corridors of the university library. She'd seen him smiling at her and had asked him for directions to the North Wing. He'd offered to show her and led her instead to the tearoom where he'd bought her tea and cakes. He sent her flowers that soaked her room in a heavy, sweet scent, he called on her at all times of the night and day. He wanted to be an actor and would recite great chunks of plays to her in public places. He had long, wild, curly black hair that reached almost to his well-formed shoulders. She'd met no one like him in her life and he seemed large and colourful compared to the bland, well-brought-upness of most of the people she'd encountered so far. Aside from that, she was flattered by his attentions: Mario had so many women after him.

Last night, they had been walking through the deserted streets of the town centre after seeing a film. Mario suddenly pressed her up against the metal framework of an empty market stall and kissed her hard. She was amazed. His body was hard and hot and his hands travelled over her body. He was pushing his pelvis into her, making the metal pole behind her press into her back.

29

'God, Alice, I have the largest boner ever,' he breathed into her neck.

'Boner?' she managed to say.

'Boner. You know, erection. Do you want to see it?'

She laughed incredulously. 'What? Here?'

'Yeah. Why not here? There's no one around.' He pulled open her shirt and started biting her breasts.

'Mario, don't be ridiculous. We're in the middle of town.'

Alice felt him start hitching up her skirt and feeling for her pants.

'Mario!' She wriggled and pushed him away. 'For God's sake.'

He grabbed her by the hips and went to kiss her again, but she struggled free. 'What the hell's the matter with you?' he shouted, his face red with exertion.

'Nothing is the matter with me. We're in the middle of town. I just don't want to get arrested, that's all.'

She started walking away but Mario caught her by the arm and swung her round. 'Jesus Christ, I'm only human, Alice. Don't you think I've been patient? I bought some condoms today, if that's what you're worried about. I assumed we might get around to it at some point.'

'You assumed, did you?' she scoffed. 'Well, you assumed wrong.'

'For fuck's sake, honey, anyone would think you were a fucking virgin or something.'

They stared at each other, Mario panting and Alice rigid with anger. 'Well, for your information, I am,' she said softly and walked off.

Mario caught up with her outside the darkened windows of a bookshop. 'Alice, I'm so sorry.'

'Go away.'

'Alice, please.' He caught hold of her and wrapped his arms around her, suffocatingly, preventing her from walking any farther.

'Leave me alone. I want to go home.'

'Alice, I'm so sorry. I was a jerk to say those things. I had no idea. I mean, why didn't you say?'

'What do you mean, why didn't I say? What was I supposed to say? Hello, I'm Alice Raikes, and I'm a virgin?'

'I just had no idea. You seem so . . . I don't know . . . I mean, I couldn't tell.'

'You couldn't tell?' She was angry again. 'How do you usually tell?' She struggled but he held her fast. 'Let go of me, Mario.'

'I can't.'

She felt that his whole body was shaking and she realised in horror that he was crying. He hugged her and sobbed loudly into her hair. 'Alice, I'm so sorry. Please forgive me. Please forgive me, Alice.'

She felt a mixture of disgust and guilt. She'd never seen a man cry before. There were people walking past, staring at them. She put her hands up to his shoulders and shook him. 'Mario, it's all right. Don't cry.'

He released her at last and, holding her at arm's length, gazed at her searchingly. His face was desperate and tear-streaked. 'God, you're beautiful. I don't deserve you.'

She fought an impulse to laugh. 'Mario, come on, let's go. People are staring.'

'I don't care.' He flung himself against the wall. 'I've upset you and I can't forgive myself.'

'Mario, you're being ridiculous. I'm going.'

He seized her hands. 'Don't go. Tell me you forgive me. Do you forgive me?'

'Yes.'

'Say, "Mario I forgive you."'

'Don't be stupid.'

'Say it! Please.'

'All right. Mario, I forgive you. Right. I'm going now. Goodbye.'

She walked down the street, leaving him slumped against the wall in an attitude of profound grief. Just as she was about to turn the corner, she heard him shout her name. She turned. He was standing in the middle of the road, his arms flung wide in an expansive theatrical gesture.

'Alice! Do you know why I got so upset tonight?'

'No.'

'Because I'm in love with you! I love you!'

She shook her head. 'Good night, Mario.'

The next day, Alice was reading some critical theory when he knocked on the door. He smiled at her radiantly and offered her a bunch of wilting chrysanthemums.

'Mario, I told you I couldn't see you today. I've got work to do.'

'I know, Alice. I just had to come over. I've been up all night, just walking by the river.' He clasped her around the waist and kissed her deeply. 'I meant what I said last night, you know.'

'Oh. Right. Mario, you have to leave. I've got an essay to write.'

'That's OK. I won't disturb you, I promise.' He ran his hands down her sides.

'You're disturbing me already.'

He walked to the other side of the room and sat down on the bed. 'I won't do it again. Promise.'

She carried on reading. He made a cup of tea in the tiny kitchen in the corner of her room. He flicked through a couple of her books and put them down with a slap. He fiddled with her stereo, looked through her CD collection and then began doing press-ups.

'Stop that.'

'What?'

'That panting. I can't concentrate.'

He rolled on to his back and looked up at her. 'You work too hard, you know.'

She ignored him. He began stroking her ankle. 'Alice,' he whispered.

She kicked him off. He grabbed her ankle. 'Alice.'

'Mario. You're really getting on my nerves.'

'Let's go to bed.' He ran his hand up to her thigh and buried his head in her lap.

'Right. That's it. Get out.'

'No. Not before I've got what I came for.' He smiled wickedly. 'Do you know why I came here today?'

'No. Frankly I don't.'

'I came,' he paused to kiss her left breast, 'to take away your virginity.'

I had both my hands clasped around the last banister and was swinging from side to side. I was not allowed to do this as it weakened the woodwork but my mother had a visitor and I was eavesdropping.

'My father was very musical,' she had her social voice on, 'and it was always my greatest wish that one of my girls would inherit his talent.'

'And they haven't?' the visitor enquired.

'I used to think Alice had. She plays the piano, but she is not particularly talented. She tries hard but her playing is average, really.'

I left the hall and walked through the kitchen. With my right hand I was testing the springiness of my little finger. It felt frail, brittle. I could have broken it with one cruel flick.

It was as if a large bowl of warm liquid I had been carrying around inside me had sprung a leak. All that warmth was draining away. I was furious with myself for being so gullible and with my mother for planting such ideas in the first place only to dash them by idle chat with some tedious neighbour. It was almost dark outside but I tore around the garden in a rage, ripping leaves off plants until my hands were bleeding.

My grandmother happened to come into the bathroom with a pile of clean towels while I was bathing my hands in tepid water. She put down the towels on the side of the bath when she saw me and began stroking my hair, tucking loose strands behind my ears. 'Alice Raikes, why is it that you rail against life so?'

I said nothing. Bitter-tasting tears were rolling rapidly down my cheeks.

'Can you tell me what it is that's making you cry? Or would you rather not? Did something bad happen at school today?'

I looked up, so that my face and hers were framed by the mirror. 'I'm just so ugly and horrible,' I burst out, 'and I'm no good at anything.' My sobs were beginning to choke me.

'Well, my dear, I have to say that I've seen you look-ing better.'

I looked at my face and laughed. My eyes were swollen and bloodshot and my cheeks streaked with mud and the green ooze of leaves. My grandmother squeezed my shoulders with her powerful hands.

'Do you not know how bonny you are? Is it blonde curls like your sisters that you want?' I hung my head. 'I see it is.' She turned me round to face her. 'Alice, I'll tell you a secret. In here,' she pressed her hand against my solar plexus, 'right here, you have a reservoir of love and passion to give someone.

You have such a huge capacity for love. Not everyone does, you know.'

I listened solemnly. She tapped me on the nose. 'Just you make sure you don't give it all away to the wrong man.' She turned to pick up the towels. 'Now, away up to bed. You'll be worn out with all that crying.'

I didn't give up. I still went once a week to Mrs Beeson's flea-infested front room to be drilled in my scales and touch. Somehow my mother's proclamation released me. I stopped galloping through exams and played what I wanted. Mrs Beeson phoned my mother to report that I had lost my motivation and that I could be a 'nice wee player' if I tried a bit harder. But I had no interest in that any more.

Alice looked down at Mario's flushed and grinning face. She had already made up her mind that she was going to sleep with him at some point, but was convinced that it wouldn't be good for his already considerable ego for them to do it whenever he decided the time was right. Right now he had his hands inside her shirt and he was struggling with the clasp of her bra. She tried to get hold of his arms. They grappled.

'Mario, stop it. I am not going to sleep with you today. I mean it.'

He smacked his head with his palm and shouted, 'Then when? I have to sleep with you! I must!'

'I have to work. I've got this essay to write.'

He cast himself face down on the floor and began rolling about, groaning.

'I am going to sleep with you,' Alice noticed that Mario was suddenly still, 'but not now.'

'OK. Just make it soon. I've got balls like watermelons.'

She laughed and turned back to her books. After a while

she realised Mario had gone to sleep. Later they went out to the party.

John took the stairs two at a time. Trust Alice to have an office on the top floor of a five-floor building. When he got there he could see through the glass door that the room was deserted, apart from Alice. She was sitting, straight-backed, with her hand on the telephone, as if she'd just finished a call. He strode in, slipped his arms around her shoulders and, lifting the heavy plait of hair, kissed her neck. 'I was wondering if you'd like to have lunch with me,' he whispered.

She felt stiff in his arms. Her profile was pale and set.

'What's wrong?'

She said nothing. He came around to crouch beside her and grasped her hand. 'Alice? What is it?'

She looked at him for the first time. Her pupils were so dilated that her eyes were almost black. He stroked her hand and kissed it. 'Tell me.'

She dug her nails hard into the back of his hand, gathering strength to speak. 'My grandmother has died.'

He put his arms around her. 'Alice, I'm so sorry,' and he held her as the first tears splashed on to her desk.

Alice had forbidden John to take up the invitation that she knew her mother would issue after the funeral.

'But I want to see the house where you grew up,' he had protested.

'Tough,' she'd said grimly.

So when Ann pressed John to come back to the house he knew to make the excuse that they had to get back to their B&B. But Alice's precautions hadn't prevented her mother from buttonholing her in the crematorium toilet. 'John seems very nice.'

'Yes. He is.'

'Have you been seeing him long?'

'A couple of months.'

'Where's he from?'

'London.'

'I mean originally.'

'Originally? What do you mean, originally? He was born in London.'

'He could be Italian or Greek or something. He's so dark.'

'Dark?'

'In colouring.'

'Well, so am I, in case you hadn't noticed.'

'Is he Jewish?'

Alice exploded, 'What the hell has that got to do with anything?'

'So he is,' Ann said calmly.

'Yeah, he is. Do you have a problem with that? You are so hypocritical sometimes. You call yourself a Christian, putting on that ridiculous performance in there when you know Granny didn't even believe. Aren't Christians supposed to be tolerant and love thy neighbour?'

'Alice, there is no need to fly off the handle. I was merely asking.'

Another woman came into the toilets and went into a cubicle. Alice washed her hands in the scalding water and her mother handed her a paper towel.

'I'm just worried that it may cause you problems, that's all.'

'What do you mean?' Alice hissed. 'What problems? There are no problems. You're the one making problems.'

'Do his parents know about the relationship?'

Alice made a fatal hesitation. 'His mother's dead, for your information.'

37

Ann rolled her eyes. 'Does his father know, then?'

Alice was silent.

'Has he told his father he's seeing a Christian?'

'I'm not a bloody Christian!'

'Alice! Don't swear in here!' Ann turned round to see if the other woman might have heard. 'A Gentile, then,' she whispered.

'No. He hasn't.'

Ann pushed her face close to the mirror to check her make-up. 'I see.'

Alice was sullen, defiant, her mouth drawn into a tense line. Ann sighed and, in an unaccustomed gesture, clutched her daughter's hand. 'Alice, I'm not getting at you. You can see who you like, as far as I'm concerned. You should know that by now. I just can't bear to see you letting passion impair your judgement. Don't ever let all this being in love stuff obscure your sense of self-preservation.'

'What *are* you talking about?'

'I just don't want . . . I don't want you to get hurt.'

'I'm not going to get hurt. John's not like that.'

'You don't know that. Men don't have the decisiveness of women. And Judaism is notorious for putting pressure on men not to marry out.' Ann wanted to impress this on Alice but didn't know how to do it without angering her further. 'Notorious,' she repeated lamely. 'Ask anyone.'

'What would you know about that?' Alice scoffed. 'And, anyway, I've only been with him for two months. We're not planning to get married or anything.'

Beth came through the door. 'Who's getting married? Not you, Alice?'

'Oh, my God,' Alice clutched her head dramatically, 'no, I'm not getting married.'

'John is Jewish,' Ann told Beth with emphasis.

'So?' Beth was nonplussed.

'There!' said Alice. 'You see? Not everyone reacts like you.'

Beth looked from her sister to her mother and linked her arms through theirs. 'Come on. This isn't the time to argue about this.'

They went out through the doors. John was standing with Ben, Kirsty and Neil.

'John, I've been trying to convince Alice to come back to the house and she's being very stubborn. You will come, won't you?' Ann pressed John's arm.

'It's called the Law,' Alice said.

'The Law? That's a funny name.'

'Sometimes it's known as Berwick Law. It's a volcanic plug, one of three, the other two are Arthur's Seat and the Bass Rock. They're all made of the same volcanic rock.'

'Hey, I've heard of the Bass Rock.'

'It's very famous. There's a large gannet colony there.'

'Can you see it from here?'

'Usually you can see it easily, but today it's a bit misty.'

They strained their eyes and she pointed out to John the outline of a craggy column of rock that reared up out of the sea.

'Is the white stuff rock or bird shit?'

She gave a short laugh. 'I don't know. Probably shit, I think. In the summer you can get a boat out there from the harbour.' She swivelled round forty-five degrees. 'That's my school.'

John looked down at the grey and brown buildings clustered at the bottom of the Law, the large white Hs of rugby posts staked into the neighbouring field. 'It's tiny!'

She laughed. 'Do you think so? Well, it's hardly a North London comp. There are about six hundred pupils, I think, not all from North Berwick. The people from other towns and villages near here send their kids here too. That smaller building is the primary and the larger is the secondary.'

'Did you go to the primary school as well?'

'Oh, yes, and Beth and Kirsty.'

They carried on slowly up the grassy slope, Alice clutching the urn containing Elspeth's ashes. Seagulls swung on invisible trapezes in the foggy, salty air. Ben had agreed quite readily to Alice's proposal of scattering them on the Law. Ann had been less inclined to believe that Elspeth had told Alice that was her wish and was more in favour of fertilising a rosebush with them. But, for once, Ben had asserted that if that was what his mother had wanted then that is what she should have. The sisters had been surprised. John had chosen that moment to converse with an elderly and, as he rapidly found out, deaf friend of Elspeth's in another corner of the room.

'OK. Here's a good place,' she said and stopped. She handed him the lid and peered for the first time into the urn. John watched her face.

'It looks just like sand,' she said flatly, not really knowing what she expected. She pushed in her hand.

He felt in his pockets for the small trowel that the undertaker had given them. 'Here. You can use this.'

'No,' Alice said fiercely, steeling herself.

The wind was strong so she didn't have to throw it, as she had feared. She just loosened her fingers and the breeze snatched it away.

'The wind's heading north!' she cried. 'Towards North Berwick! That's where she was born!'

She released fistful after fistful of ashes to the wind. John watched her from a distance, surrounded by a veil of ash and dust. Her solemnity had gone; she was excited, almost dancing, as she sent Elspeth back to where she had come from.

Mario stumbles from the bed and starts scrabbling around in his trouser pockets.

'I have one here somewhere,' he mutters. 'Christ. Where the fuck is it?'

Alice lifts her head a fraction from the pillow and looks down at her body, almost as if she'd never seen it before. When she lies on her back like this her hipbones jut out like bookends and her breasts splay outwards, nipples pointing to the ceiling. Mario storms about the room, tearing his hair, throwing items of their scattered clothing about, his erection fading. He can't possibly have forgotten it, can he? He's been carrying one for weeks. Alice puts one hand behind her head and one on her stomach, feeling the murmurings of her digestion. When they were little, Beth used to beg to be allowed to press her ear to Alice's stomach and listen to her 'plumbing'. Alice wonders vaguely how Beth is and then stops wondering because Mario is climbing into bed beside her. 'God, these beds weren't made for this, were they?' he complains.

'Well, this is a women's hall of residence. Fifty years ago, if you had a male visitor the janitor used to come round, take the bed out of the room and put it in the corridor.'

Mario laughs. 'That's not true, is it?'

'Yes, it is. And women weren't allowed to have degrees either.'

He decides that this is neither the time nor the place for one of Alice's diatribes on feminism and puts his arms around her. She realises with a jolt that he's completely naked. 'Did you find a condom?' she asks, a little nervous. She doesn't entirely trust Mario.

'That's all taken care of.'

'I didn't see you put it on,' she says, lifts the sheets and looks down. 'You're not wearing it.'

They both survey Mario's flaccid penis.

'You have a lot to learn, haven't you?' He sighs. 'If a guy has to stop and look around the room for a condom, it's not unusual for him to lose his erection. You can't put a condom on without an erection.' He grasps her wrist and guides her hand towards his groin. 'So what we have to do is make it come back.'

They start kissing again. She feels his penis swelling in her hand. She pulls away and laughs. 'That's amazing.' She pulls back the sheets to examine it and laughs again.

'What's so funny?'

'It's like one of those speeded-up nature films, you know, when you see flowers growing in about five seconds.'

Mario stares at her. 'What were those boys in North Berwick thinking of? How come you missed out on this when everyone else was doing it?'

She shrugs. 'I don't think people were. Doing it, I mean. North Berwick's not like that. It's not exactly New York. Everyone would have known and probably told my mother if they'd seen me holding hands with a boy. There was no one worth the trouble, to be honest.'

She grips his penis and turns it this way and that, as if inspecting it for defects.

At her touch, Mario feels his abdomen contract with desire. Alice is wearing only a pair of black pants and is bending over his groin, her hair tickling his thighs, her breasts hovering over his body. He hurriedly splits open the condom packet with fumbling hands and rolls it down over his penis. She leans back on her haunches and watches with that same expression of scientific interest. Mario grabs her by the arm and pulls her down. 'OK, Alice.' He is lying on top of her now, his hands gripping her buttocks. 'Just relax.'

She is finding it hard to breathe. Mario suddenly seems incredibly heavy. He is grappling with her knickers, pulling them down. His hands seem to be everywhere, while hers are pinned to her sides. She wriggles to try to free herself a little. He groans. 'Oh, Alice.'

His breathing is fast and rasping and she suddenly feels his latex-covered penis pushing at her. She flinches in shock. He is gripping her shoulders as if pulling himself up on to a high wall. His penis, slippery and hard, jabs and thrusts at her groin.

'Mario.' She tries to speak but her mouth is muffled by his chest. She twists her head to the side with difficulty. 'Mario!'

Immediately his face is there and his mouth is covering hers, hot and panting. She manages to free one of her arms and pushes at his shoulder. He pulls her even closer, then seizes her pelvis in both of his hands and angles it up off the bed. She grabs a fistful of his hair and pulls it. 'Mario, stop it, please.'

Suddenly she feels him thrust right inside her and a second later a sharp bolt of pain shoots through her lower body. She thrashes and hits out at him. 'Mario! Don't! Please can we stop? You're really hurting me!'

'Don't worry. It always hurts first time round. Just relax, honey. You're doing fine.'

With every dry and rasping thrust, his shoulder rams into her chin. Her groin is throbbing with pain and her legs ache from being forced apart. Alice's mind goes a blank white. She begins counting the punching thrusts to try to block out the consciousness of this heaving, panting body thrashing about on top of hers. At number seventy-eight, she feels his back arch and at seventy-nine, he does a kind of prolonged rigid shudder and collapses on to her, breathing hard.

For a good five minutes, they remain like that, then Mario raises himself on his elbow, smiling beatifically. He notices that Alice looks a little white and wide-eyed but reassures himself that this is normal for a girl's first time. He begins to wonder why she isn't looking at him, then he thinks of something. 'Did you come?'

Alice reached for John's hand on the way down. It felt cold and she chafed it between her palms. The sky was turning a darker, inkier blue and the lights of North Berwick were coming on below them.

'You never cried again after that time, did you?' John said.

'She didn't like me to cry.'

Dr Brimble peered at the student over her desk. She really should go and have her eyes tested. The girl didn't look too bad, a little tired, perhaps. 'What seems to be the trouble . . . er . . .' she consulted the notes before her '. . . Alice?'

The girl looked dead ahead, avoiding her eye. 'Last Friday I had sex for the first time and I've been bleeding ever since.'

'I see. Do you have a burning sensation when you pee?'

The girl nodded.

'Have you had a temperature?'

'I don't think so.'

'It sounds like honeymoon cystitis. It's very common but unpleasant, and unfortunately, if you've had it once you're very prone to have it again. I'd better have a little look. Could you go behind that screen, take off your skirt and pants and give me a little shout when you're ready?'

Dr Brimble was satisfied that there was no serious internal damage but she was rather disconcerted by the amount of bruising on the girl's hips and thighs. She glanced again at her rather tense, mute face and stole a surreptitious look at her watch. She was running ten minutes late as it was. Once the girl was dressed again and sitting at her desk, she decided to frame her question delicately. 'The person you had intercourse with,' she began, 'he was . . . ?' and waited for the girl to finish. Alice looked at her, blankly.

'Was he a boyfriend?'

The girl seemed to consider this for a moment and then said, 'Yes.'

'Right.' Relieved, the doctor handed her a prescription. 'This course of antibiotics should clear it up. Any problems, come back.'

When Alice got back to her room later that afternoon, there was a note from Mario pinned to the door saying where the hell was she and he'd be back in two hours. She sat for a few moments on her bed, then got up and dragged her rucksack down from the wardrobe. Within an hour she was on a train to Scotland.

Elspeth took a deep breath. 'Ben, that's wonderful, but when am I going to meet her?' She hoped her voice sounded more sincere than she felt. Wasn't this a bit sudden?

'Soon, I'll bring her out to North Berwick some time for tea.'

'Good.' She felt calmer now, her voice under control. 'I'm looking forward to it already. What's her name?'

'Ann. She's English.'

'Right. Well, I'm so pleased, my dear. Very many congratulations. How are you fixed for Thursday?'

'I'll ask Ann and call you again tomorrow.'

'Fine. I'll speak to you then. Bye-bye now.'

Elspeth replaced the receiver in its black Bakelite cradle and smoothed her hair with a quick hand. This was very unlike Ben, who was the younger and more cautious of her two sons. But Elspeth could recognise that resonance in his voice that meant he was happy. If they are coming on Thursday she should begin baking a cake today, which would give her time to strain the fruit in muslin first. She went down the flagstone steps into the kitchen, checking her appearance in the drawing-room glass on the way.

Elspeth was born in North Berwick, a small seaside town east of Edinburgh, in 1912; the year the *Titanic* sank. Her father was a Church of Scotland minister and they lived in a small, dank manse on Kirkports, one of the narrow, winding streets near the beach. It was North Berwick's heyday as a fashionable holiday resort for the rich, and large new houses were springing up on the town's fringes. Her mother took her for walks along the seafront on warm days and on Sundays they went to the church in the middle of the High Street to hear her father lift his voice into the rafters. She went to the primary school down by the sea and every day her mother would be waiting for her at the gates to take her home. They would often walk back along the East Beach and Elspeth would beg her mother to tell her about the time when the vast whale had been washed up on the sand. Her father had taken her on a trip to the Chambers Street Museum in Edinburgh to see the skeleton of the whale, which hung suspended like a huge grey kite from the museum ceiling. He had held her over the balcony edge to touch it; it felt warm and crumbly and she couldn't equate those dusty bones with the immense beast that had been thrown up by the sea and covered the whole beach.

When she was seven her parents were sent as missionaries to India. Whether it was their idea or whether they were acting on the advice of another Elspeth never knew, but they decided that it would be best for the child if they didn't tell her they were leaving. They dressed Elspeth in her best clothes and took her out for a walk on the beach, each holding one of her hands. While she was playing with the pebbles and seaweed on the blustery seashore, they slipped away and when she turned round they were gone and in their place was the upright figure of a housemistress for St Cuthbert's School for Girls, who took her by the elbow and led her up the beach and on to a train for Edinburgh and boarding-school. She didn't see them or North Berwick again for seven years.

'It's such a shame that Kenneth, Ben's brother, couldn't make it. He did so want to be here to meet you, Ann.'

Ann nodded and helped herself to another slice of Elspeth's cake.

'His job seems to keep him so busy.' There was a pause in which Elspeth hoped Ann would speak. She had barely heard her voice. 'He's a doctor,' Elspeth volunteered.

Elspeth felt puzzled by this woman and hoped that her face didn't show it. Ann was pretty in a fragile, English way with slender wrists and nice manners. Her hair was a smooth, flaxen white-blonde and her skin pellucidly pale. She had light, light blue eyes fringed with delicate lashes. Everything about her was fragile and small. When Elspeth had shaken her by the hand, she had felt as though she could crush the younger woman's finger bones with one slight squeeze. Next to Ben's sandy-haired, healthy ruddiness, she looked of a different race. She was obviously a bright girl but Elspeth couldn't work out whether her silence stemmed from shyness, which didn't seem likely. Ann was self-assured, sitting upright in the chair, giving Ben clear instructions on how she took her tea, looking about her with barely veiled curiosity.

'Where is it that you stay, Ann?'

'I beg your pardon?'

Ben interjected, 'She means, where do you live.' He patted her small pale hand and laughed. 'You'll have to get used to Scottish idioms. We say "stay" when we mean "live".'

'Oh. I see. Well, I live near the Meadows, Mrs Raikes.'

'Please call me Elspeth. Everybody does.'

Ann gravely inclined her sleek blonde head.

'Tell me,' said Elspeth, appealing to them both, 'about the wedding plans. When is it to be? What do your parents think, Ann?'

She saw an uneasy look pass between the two of them. Ben

cleared his throat. 'Ann hasn't told her parents yet.'

Elspeth was aware of her face registering surprise and tried, unsuccessfully, to alter her expression to one of mild interest. 'Oh, I see.'

'We don't really want a long engagement, do we?' Ben turned to Ann, who had brought her hand up to her face and was pressing it to her mouth in an odd gesture. That this woman did not love her son became suddenly apparent to Elspeth. She felt a sharp stab of pity for Ben, who so obviously adored Ann. 'So we thought we'd get married in the autumn,' Ben was saying, 'October maybe.' He laughed with evident excitement. 'I start at the university in September and there's no point in waiting, is there?'

'Have you thought about where you'll live?'

Ben's face clouded. 'No, not really. Somewhere small. A university wage isn't much.'

'I've been giving it a bit of thought,' Elspeth began, 'and, you see, this house is far too big for just me. I don't know how you'd feel about living out in North Berwick but the train only takes about an hour. I'd love you both to come and live here, I really would, but only if it's what you want.'

Ben hesitated, looking at Ann. 'I'm not sure . . .'

'This is a beautiful house, Mrs . . . I mean, Elspeth. How long have you lived here?' Ann said.

'Most of Ben's life. It belonged to my parents-in-law. When my husband died, the boys were still very small, Ben was only a year old, and they asked me to come and live with them.'

'How did your husband die?'

Elspeth smiled to show that she didn't mind such a direct question. 'It was malaria. He was a missionary, like my father, and we were living in Africa. Everybody got malaria out there and there weren't the drugs then as there are now. I think he must have had a particularly bad strain. He died two weeks later. It was not a good position for me to be in. We'd only been married two years and I had two wee boys to bring up and nowhere to go. I was very lucky that Gordon's parents offered to take me in.'

'What about your parents?'

'My father was a missionary, as I said. They didn't earn a great deal, as you probably know, and my mother and father couldn't have afforded to keep the three of us. Not that they would have turned us away, mind, but life would have been very difficult. Gordon's parents were so good to us, even though to begin with they didn't approve of our marriage.' Elspeth laughed.

'And you never married again?'

Ben shifted in his seat, wondering whether his mother minded Ann's frank questioning.

Elspeth was just pleased that Ann was talking at last. 'No, dear. Gordon was the only one for me.'

'So Gordon's parents left you the house?'

'That's right. They left it to me in the hope that I would pass it on to the boys, which I will do, one day.'

'Well, I would love to live here.' Ann smiled, and Elspeth felt relieved.

'Well, that's settled, then. Do you think you'll like North Berwick?'

Elspeth's overriding recollection of boarding-school was of being hungry or cold, or often both. St Cuthbert's comprised mainly the daughters of well-to-do Edinburgh families, who would all go back to their homes in Morningside or the Grange at the end of the day. The boarding-house was just behind the school where there were twenty boarders from the ages of eight to eighteen. Elspeth remembered always having a cold, her cardigan sleeves stuffed with damp hankies embroidered with 'E. A. Laurie'. Her parents loved her, she was sure of that, and wrote to her once a week, sending her scraps of brightly coloured silk, carved ebony elephants or sepia picture postcards of dusty streets. She never asked when she would see them again or why they had never told her they were going.

The most difficult part was the holidays. Even the other boarders, miserable, thin girls, had places to go during the breaks, but Elspeth's parents could never have afforded to bring their daughter out to India. She spent her first few holidays hoping and expecting a kind letter from her grandmother or aunt in Glasgow, but it never came. They disapproved of Elspeth's mother's marriage and by default the daughter that came of it.

She missed her parents and North Berwick desperately. The climate of Edinburgh was so different from that of North Berwick, although they couldn't have been more than twenty-five miles apart. Edinburgh was steeped in a coagulating damp and mist; whenever Elspeth tried to conjure her childhood there she envisaged wet, slicked streets at dusk, veiled with sheets of feathery rain and grey buildings. Every winter she was plagued by asthma and lay awake, struggling for breath, imagining herself back in the crisp, dry sea air of her birthplace.

Elspeth became a peculiarly independent and resourceful child, immune to the slights to which the other, richer girls subjected her. When, in her third year at St Cuthbert's, a school outing to Kirkcaldy was organised, Elspeth wore her school uniform while the other girls were dressed in bright sweaters and matching hats. On the train, a girl called Catriona MacFarlane started a whisper that Elspeth Laurie had no other clothes apart from her school uniform. Catriona was queen bee in their year, so even girls who liked Elspeth were obliged to join in the giggling and nudging. Elspeth stared resolutely out of the window at the rain-smudged outskirts of Edinburgh. Catriona became incensed by Elspeth's lack of response, began whispering more and more ostentatiously and eventually stood up in the aisle and roughly pulled the sleeve of Elspeth's regulation red cardigan. 'Elspeth, why are you wearing your school uniform? Don't you have any other clothes, Elspeth?'

Elspeth turned to face her. 'No, I don't.'

Catriona was thrown. She had expected denial or silence. The other girls watched, tense and silent.

'Why don't you have any other clothes, Elspeth?'

Elspeth turned her gaze out of the window again. 'My father is a missionary and he doesn't have much money.'

'How come you can afford to go to this school, then?'

'The Church pays for me.' Elspeth's voice was quiet, and they had to strain to hear her.

Then a teacher, Miss Scott, came bustling down the aisle. 'Catriona MacFarlane, what are you doing out of your seat? Sit back down again please. We are nearly there.'

Elspeth invites Ann to see the garden.

'Ben tells me you are a biologist,' Elspeth says, as they step outside the back door. 'What part of biology is it that you specialise in?' Elspeth is hoping that now they are alone, Ann might open out a little more. Elspeth likes women. She finds their minds and lives interesting, and enjoys their company, especially that of educated, bright young women. She is always saddened that she could not have had a daughter after her two boys.

'Plant life, I suppose. My thesis was more to do with botany than biology.'

'How marvellous. You must get stuck into this garden when you live here. It's far too big for me to manage, as you can see.'

The garden is indeed huge, with lush green grass sloping down to Westgate and a croquet lawn to the left of the house. The broad horizon of the sea glints through the gaps in the trees. Ann wanders away towards the bottom of the garden. The bright white of her dress hurts Elspeth's eyes. She notices Ben hovering in the kitchen window and pretends not to see.

'Where is it that you are from, Ann?' she calls.

Ann speaks without turning round. 'My parents live in London now, but I grew up mostly in a boarding-school in the middle of Dartmoor.'

'I spent a large chunk of my childhood in a boarding-school for young ladies in Edinburgh. It's surprising the number of people who did. Did your parents live abroad?'

'My father was a musician and my mother used to travel the world with him.'

'Ah. Are you musical yourself?'

Ann shakes her head. 'The school I went to didn't teach you anything apart from social skills.'

'I see. Boarding-schools are funny things. I refused to send the boys away, even though Gordon's parents wanted me to. I wanted them to grow up here in North Berwick.'

'People who send their children away to boarding-school should never have had them in the first place,' Ann says bitterly, stripping the branch she is fingering of its leaves. Elspeth begins to understand a little more of her prospective daughter-in-law.

Ben and Ann were married in what had once been Elspeth's father's church in the High Street in North Berwick. The whole town lined the pavement opposite to see Ben Raikes's pale bride emerge from the red sandstone church in her scandalously short and tight wedding dress. It had been chosen by Ann's mother in an attempt to inject some style into her daughter's wedding. Ann had refused to get married in a register office in London and had insisted on having the ceremony in this godforsaken windswept village in the middle of nowhere. During the photographs, Ann's mother clung to her collapsing beehive hairdo, eyeing Elspeth's severe undyed hair and lace-up shoes. Ann's father attempted to light a cigarette in the brisk October breeze and tried to ignore all the curious onlookers across the street.

They had a week's honeymoon in the French Alps, where Ann's hair was bleached a dazzling white. Ben couldn't quite believe his luck and while she slept he would sit above her and trace with his fingertips the network of violet rivers frozen just beneath her skin.

Ann wanted children straight away and Ben didn't argue with her, as he would never argue with her about anything. During the first couple of months of marriage when Ann failed to conceive, she didn't worry particularly. But when six months of trying to get pregnant had gone by, she began to fret. 'Don't worry, darling,' Ben said, when he saw her reach despondently into the cupboard for the sanitary towels that she clipped to a looped belt around her waist. 'It takes time, you know.'

Ben left the house at around eight and Elspeth would usually be out and about in North Berwick for most of the day doing her charity work or seeing her innumerable friends. Ann would wander from room to room of the house that was supposed to be her home but in which she never failed to feel like a guest who'd long outstayed her welcome, pressing her lower stomach with clenched fists, as if willing it to miraculously gestate. If she had a child, she told herself, she'd feel like she had a right to live in this echoey house with upright chairs, leather-backed books and watercolours of seabirds.

Nine months into their marriage, Ann became passionate and cool by turns. Sometimes when Ben came home from the university she would be waiting for him upstairs on the bed, glowing with desire, wearing nothing but her slip. Downstairs, Elspeth would turn up the wireless while Ann would seize him with hot palms, pressing herself against him, and pull him towards the bed. When they had finished, Ann would hold on to Ben, wanting him to stay in her as long as possible, and lie completely motionless, imagining the sperm writhing up inside her. But every month without fail she would feel the aching cramps in her back and the slow, dropping heat between her legs. Then she would turn away from Ben in bed. Confused, he would tentatively caress her stiff back and kiss her impassive, taut face, murmuring to her, 'Ann, my love. Please, Ann. Don't be upset, my love.'

This went on for a year. It was Elspeth who finally cracked. One morning at breakfast when Ben had left, she took one look at the pinched whiteness of Ann's face and said, 'Things can't go on like this, can they?'

Ann said nothing but Elspeth saw something she had never seen before: a single, silver tear, coursing down Ann's porcelain cheek.

'I think we should make an appointment to see the doctor.'

A hoarse sob broke from Ann's thin frame. 'I can't. I can't bear it.'

'Can't bear what?'

'I can't bear to be told that I can't have children.'

Elspeth took Ann in her arms for the first and last time of their lives together. Ann stiffened momentarily then pressed her face into Elspeth's shoulder and sobbed.

'There, there. You cry. Let it all out. Crying never did

anyone any harm,' Elspeth kept saying. 'We'll sort it out. Don't worry.'

The family doctor took Ann's pulse and blood pressure, palpated her stomach through her skirt, asked discreet questions about her menstrual cycle and 'marital relations', making notes all the time in deft, neat handwriting. 'There is nothing wrong with you or your husband, Mrs Raikes. I am quite certain that you will conceive in no time. Take exercise, get some fresh air.' He also gave her a prescription.

In the chemist's on the High Street, Elspeth scrutinized the prescription, holding it close to her face. 'What are these?' she asked the pharmacist.

'They're just pills,' he said cheerfully, but Elspeth was not to be put off.

'I know that, sonny, but what are they for? What do they do?'

The man consulted the piece of paper again, 'They're tranquillizers.'

Elspeth's mouth thinned. 'In that case, we won't be needing them. Come along, Ann. Good day to you.'

Through Kenneth's medical contacts and Elspeth's determination, Ann and Ben got an appointment to see Scotland's leading gynaecologist, Douglas Fraser. For five months, she travelled to Edinburgh once a week and was punctured for blood, probed with cold, slim metal instruments and interrogated on her diet, medical history, menstrual cycle and sexual habits. She and Ben had tussled and fumbled like teenagers behind impervious white screens to produce a sperm sample, while Elspeth sat a few metres away reading magazines. Then, almost two years after they had first married he called them for a final diagnosis. They sat on red leather chairs and watched while Dr Fraser shuffled papers on his desk. He was a large, kindly man with watery eyes. As he faced them, he was struck by how young they looked, and felt it almost indecent that he was discussing their having children.

'There is nothing wrong with either of you. Both of you are normally functioning, fertile human beings.'

Ann sighed tearfully and Ben asked, 'Then why is it we've been unable to conceive?'

'The problem lies in the combination of the two of you. The fact of the matter is that you, Mrs Raikes, are rejecting your husband's spermatozoa.'

Ann tossed her head. 'What do you mean "rejecting"?'

'You are – if you like – allergic to Ben's sperm. Your body has an allergic reaction and gathers all its immunity against it and – rejects it.'

Ann looked at the doctor. 'So you are saying if I had, say, married another man, there would be no problem?'

'Well, you could put it like that. What's happened to the two of you is a one in a million occurrence. And, yes, if you'd married a different man there probably wouldn't have been a problem. It is just an incompatibility of yours and Ben's individual antibodies.'

'But what can we do about it?' asked Ben, reaching for Ann's hand.

'At the moment, there is no proven treatment,' Dr Fraser said carefully, 'but there is something that I would like to try on you both. I can't see why it won't work.'

'What is it?'

'What I propose to do – and this is something that has been researched for some time now – is take a section of your skin from here,' and he indicated Ben's upper arm, 'and graft it on to here,' and he indicated Ann's upper arm. 'Ann's antibodies will assimilate themselves to the new graft and stop rejecting your sperm. It's as simple as that.'

Their faces reflected, just as he'd expected, a mixture of astonishment and hope.

'It will be a very straightforward operation. You won't even have to stay in overnight.'

'But it sounds so . . . so . . .' Ann groped for the right word.

'Medieval? Yes, I know. But a basic physical problem requires a basic physical solution. Saying that, I'm not promising anything.'

'Is this . . . is this the only solution?' Ben asked.

'Yes,' Dr Fraser said gently, 'it's your only hope.'

Elspeth picks them up in the car from Edinburgh General Infirmary. They are holding hands as they cross the car-park and have matching bandages on their left arms. Ben is left with a puckered, translucent scar and Ann, a two-by-two-inch square of slightly darker skin that soon grows and breathes as if it has always been a part of her. She also becomes pregnant within a month.

Ann's first was a long and difficult birth. She began to understand the true semantics of the word 'labour'. For a day and a half the dome of her belly contracted and raged and she saw the heartbeat of her child echoed in an undulating red electronic line. When the line went flat and the machine cried out a monotonous bleep, they cut her with one slash and dragged the baby out by the head with cruel steel forceps. Seconds later they were staring into each other's eyes in shock. She never strayed far from Ann. In time she would bear a daughter and give her Ann's name.

In the second hour of her second daughter's life, Ann wrapped her baby tightly in a shawl. She thrashed her red, angry limbs until she was free, her tiny starfish hands clenched in defiance. They called her Alice – a short name that never seemed to contain her character. The word starts deep in the back of the mouth and ends with you expelling air from your lips. She had black hair and black eyes from the moment she was born. People bending over her pram would glance at Ann and at the cherubic older child and then back at the baby with olive-black eyes. 'She's like a wee changeling, isn't she?' said one woman. Ann's fingers tightened around the pram handle. 'Not at all.' When Alice was still young enough to seem like a child to Ann, she left to travel the world. She waved goodbye from a train window, beads looped and plaited into her long black hair, rainbow skirts trailing the ground. She returned crop-haired, in tight leather trousers, an Oriental dragon rampant on her shoulder-blade. 'How was the world?' Ann asked. 'Full,' she replied.

Her third daughter was watchful and loved. She drank in the sights of her two older sisters and was like both of them at once, and so not like either of them at all. She saw, copied, emulated. She was cautious, made no mistakes because they'd made them all for her. When Ann visited her, she made her tea from the herbs that grew in her window-boxes.

Jamie screams and batters the tray of his highchair with his plastic trainer cup. Annie joins in the wailing gleefully, letting her cornflakes get soggy and unappetising in the milk.

'Quiet!' Neil roars from behind the *Scotsman*.

The children ignore him. Kirsty crams a spoonful of baby rice into Jamie's mouth, hoping to thwart the noise. 'Eat up your breakfast, Annie, or you'll be late for playschool.'

'I hate playschool.'

'You do not. You liked it last week.'

'I hate it today.'

'You haven't been yet so how do you know you hate it?'

'I just do.' Annie swishes her spoon around her bowl, making the milk skirl around the rim.

'Don't play with it, just eat it,' Kirsty says. Jamie chooses that moment to spit out his rice which spatters Kirsty's shirt. 'Oh, bloody hell,' she exclaims, jumping up for a cloth.

'You swore! You swore!'

Neil appears from behind the paper. 'Eat that up at once, young lady,' he thunders at Annie.

'No, I won't, I don't like it!' she shouts.

Neil smacks her hand. 'Do as I say!'

Annie begins to scream in earnest. Over the racket, Kirsty hears the telephone ringing. 'I'll get it.'

She picks up the receiver with one hand, wiping down her shirt with the other.

'Hello?'

'Kirsty, it's Dad.'

'Hi, how are you? Listen, can I call you back? It's feeding time at the zoo here and as you can probably hear, things are getting out of hand.'

'I'm afraid I've got some rather bad news.'

Kirsty turns her back on the kitchen and clutches the receiver with both hands. 'What is it? Is it Mum? What's happened?'

'Your mother's fine. She's here with me. It's Alice.'

'Alice?'

'She was hit by a car. She's in a coma.'

'What? But when?'

The kitchen has become deathly quiet. Annie is holding her spoon to her chest, staring open-mouthed at her mother. Neil comes across the room and stands behind Kirsty, listening. Jamie, sensing a change for the worse in the atmosphere, begins to snivel.

Ben listens to his daughter's sobs down the telephone. Ann moves in and out of the room, putting things into suitcases.

'It was last night. They called us early this morning. We thought we'd wait until now to call you. There seemed no reason to wake you all up.'

'But, but . . . I don't understand. I only saw her yesterday.'

'Yesterday?'

'Yes. She came up to Edinburgh on the train. Completely out of the blue. Beth and I met her at the station. She seemed fine. For a bit anyhow. But then she went all peculiar and said she had to leave. And then she just got on a train and left.'

'Really?'

'Oh, my God, oh, my God, this is so awful. I can't believe it.'

'I know, love, I know,' Ben says. 'Your mother and I are going down there today. I asked if she could be transferred to a hospital in Edinburgh, but they said there was no way they could move her.' Ben's voice catches for the first time. There is a pause in which he tries to collect himself. He doesn't want to upset Kirsty even more by crying himself. 'The other thing is that we have to contact Beth.'

'What? What do you mean?'

'Well, I rang the payphone at her halls of residence, but she doesn't seem to be there. I don't want to just leave a message saying . . . this.'

'Of course, of course.'

'It's so difficult to get in touch with her sometimes.'

Neil takes the receiver off Kirsty. 'Don't worry about that, Ben. You and Ann just get yourselves down there. I'll sort Beth out.'

'That's very good of you, Neil. We're going to catch a train now. I'll call you again tonight.'

part | two

The sun is burning off the mist, revealing the snaggled rocks that rear up at intervals along the sand. On the beach is an odd, broken assortment of my family – my older sister is away at college with the man she will eventually marry, my grandmother is off visiting friends in Glasgow, and Mario is with us.

I left without telling him and offered my parents no explanation as to why I had arrived home a week before term ended. Mario turned up on the doorstep the next day, having charmed the address from the housing officer. My family have accepted his arrival with unexpected and unprecedented equanimity and here we all are, playing happy families on Gullane beach.

My mother has nested herself down beside a rock with the *Scotsman on Sunday* keeping the water that the sand holds from seeping into her skirt. Arranged around her are a black snakeskin handbag, her shoes, laces tucked in under the tongue, my father's book on seashore birds and a number of white plastic boxes protecting the picnic Beth and I made earlier. Beside her, in a deck-chair, my father sleeps with his mouth open.

Beth is twisting her hair into silky, flaxen coils and snipping off her split ends with nail scissors from my mother's handbag.

The scissors flash with light and she gives Mario long, sideways glances as he resolutely chews his way through sandwiches he picks from the boxes by my mother. He eats with a concentrated seriousness, his jaws slapping open and snapping closed. He is not speaking. His eyes scan the slowly appearing horizon. In about two hours' time I will tell him that I don't ever want to see him again and he will return to America. But we don't know this yet. For the moment, there is only the beach and the gulls going schree-schree over our heads.

The bruises on my thighs and hips have faded to yellow and I have only just stopped bleeding. Above my left breast is a round, red bite mark, pitted deep into my skin. Every night, blanching, I dab it with acrid-smelling witch hazel, but its bright colour refuses to dwindle. I am thinking about this when my mother catches my eye. I look away.

My father wakes and starts asking my mother what time it is. She ignores him and he reaches for the paper instead, crushing its pages into a methodical square before reading it.

'Have you had enough to eat, Mario?' my mother asks, in a way so barbed it makes me look up. His name puzzles her. She can't say it without frowning. He nods with a mouthful of food and gives her a thumbs-up. Beth titters. I stand up. 'Shall we go for a swim?' I ask Beth.

She jumps to her feet and helps me unzip the back of my dress. We begin struggling out of our clothes and flinging them into an untidy heap – we have our bathing costumes on underneath. Mine is black and hers is white with blue stripes. I readjust the straps, pinging the elastic into place against my skin. I see my mother looking at the bruises on my legs, her face collapsed in confusion. I turn round. 'Race you to the sea.'

We run together towards the sea, leaving Mario with my parents. The hard ridges of the sand push up painfully into the soft parts of my feet. Behind me, Beth shouts at me to slow down.

I stop short at the sea edge, stunned, panting: it is full of jellyfish, their viscous bodies palpitating like breathing hearts, their fringed tendrils ready to hook and sting. There is not a square foot of the water that does not contain a shivering mass of clammy glue, and it seems malevolent, as if these creatures have spontaneously generated from its elements.

'I'm not going in with them in there,' Beth says, and pokes at one with a stick. It convulses in shock, draws in its threads and shoots itself away with surprising speed. I clutch her and pretend to push her in. She screams and wriggles, laughing, and I am momentarily blinded by her hair, which streams into my face in the wind.

We lie on our stomachs in a shallow pool, our feet cutting swathes in the sand. I rest my chin on my knuckles. Final swirls of fog roll slowly up the beach. Beth twirls her hair and whistles. I am conscious of something pressing on me that I want to say to her, but when I open my mouth to speak I realise that I don't know what it is. A dog passes, red-rag tongue lolling from his mouth. He eyeballs us briefly, but lollops on, too busy to stop.

'Yooooo-hooooooo.'

Our mother's voice reaches us through the cries of the birds. I turn my neck and look under the crook of my arm to see her running in the way only women of her age can – awkwardly modest, with her knees together, as if she'd rather be walking. She is brandishing a camera. Beth and I smile dutifully into the sun as the shutter clicks. I will keep that photo on my wall at college until my final year, when I have a party where it disappears, either trodden underfoot with cigarette butts or stolen by someone who likes the look of us.

My father joins us hastily, not wishing to be left alone with

Mario. Mario trails behind. He has taken off his shirt. His chest is tanned. He flexes his arm muscles. If I keep him out of the edges of my vision, I could almost pretend he isn't here. At the top of the beach my mother's newspaper wheels across the sand.

'Are you going swimming or not?' He looks at me hard.

I stand up. My costume is damp, cold and crusted with sand.

'There are too many jellyfish,' Beth tells him.

Mario closes his hand around my wrist and runs towards the sea, dragging me behind him, my wrist bones cracking and bending under the pressure. Spumes of water spray up under my flailing legs, the jellyfish are swirled about in the agitated water and I hear a screaming that isn't the seagulls. He stops dead, the icy water lapping at my ribcage and placing his hands on my shoulders, he forces me down. My knees buckle and water closes over my head. I twist and thrash under his grasp, lashing out at him, swallowing great gulps of bitter water. My skin is prickling, alert with the panic of sensing the stinging brush of jellyfish trails. Through his fingers I can feel the shudder of his laughter. Suddenly I am released. My head soars and breaks the surface and sunlight rushes in on me. The sound of the beach roars in my ears and I gasp for air, gagging and coughing. I wipe the water from my eyes with shaking hands and we stare at each other for a split second before I am pushed down again into the silence of the sea. This time I keep my mouth closed. The water is swinging with light. His fingers are pressing small circular bruises into my shoulders. The jellyfish hang in clusters just below the surface like parachutes. Beyond them, I can make out the figures of my parents, distant and blurred, standing at the shore.

I know where I am. I know more than they think. Earlier today someone with an officious voice said, close to my ear, 'It is touch and go as to whether she will ever regain consciousness.' Touch and go. Makes it sound like a children's game.

Today I am bothered about the story of King Canute. (I say 'today' from habit – I have no idea if it is night or day or even how long I have been here. The strangest thing is that I sometimes have difficulty in remembering the names of things. Yesterday, or whenever it was, I couldn't remember the word for the wooden structure for sitting with four legs. I trawled through my memory and found I could recall de Saussure's semiotics theory, large chunks of *King Lear* and the recipe for Baked Alaska, but had no recollection of the word whatsoever.) But I was talking about King Canute. The story is, of course, that he was so arrogant and despotic a leader that he believed he could control everything – even the tide. We see him on the beach, surrounded by subjects, sceptre in hand, ordering back the heedless waves; a laughing stock, in short. But what if we've got it all wrong? What if, in fact, he was so good and great a king that his people began to elevate him to the status of a god, and began to believe that he was capable of anything? In order to prove to them that he was a mere mortal, he took them down to the beach and ordered back the waves, which of course kept on rolling up the beach. How awful it would be if we had got it so wrong, if we had misunderstood his actions for so long.

Maybe it would be a good thing if I don't come back. But if I don't, I'll never get to find out anything, ask anyone any questions. But, then, do I really want to know?

'Would you mind holding the line a moment, please?' Susannah pushed the hold button on the phone. 'Alice, it's some bloody journalist. Can you talk to him? I've got a thousand things to do today and it's the last thing I need.'

Alice, on top of an aluminium step-ladder with an armful of books, shoved the books haphazardly on to a shelf. The Literature Trust was having a big crisis: not only were they in the process of moving from a cold, outsized, crumbling Georgian house in Pimlico to a compact terraced building in Covent Garden, but they heard yesterday that their main funding body was cutting their grant and sacking their director. A new director had already been appointed and would start tomorrow. Alice and Susannah, while still trying to absorb the news, were unpacking all the boxes from Pimlico.

'Oh, no,' Alice groaned, 'the vultures are circling already. What does he want? Did he say?' She wiped the palms of her hands on the overall she was wearing, leaving thick stripes of dust snaking up her legs.

'No. He asked for the press office.'

'The press office?' Alice repeated. 'Who does he think we are? Can you find out what it's about? Maybe I could call him back.'

Susannah returned to the line. 'Sorry to have kept you waiting. Our press office is a bit tied up at the moment . . . She's up a ladder . . . Yes . . . Can I ask what it's regarding?' Susannah grimaced at Alice as the voice on the other end rattled on tinnily, like a trapped bee. 'OK. Fine. Hold on, please.' She put the phone on hold again. 'Alice, it's John somebody or other, the arts correspondent for . . .' Susannah named a national broadsheet. 'He says he wants to do a profile on us – the new-look Literature Trust. Why we've moved, what our plans are now, blah, blah, blah.'

'Yeah, right,' said Alice, as she climbed backwards down the rickety steps of the step-ladder, 'I'll bet you my body weight in chocolate he's just digging dirt.'

I'd been working at the Literature Trust for two months and

I loved it. Which was lucky because nothing much else was going right. I was living in the top flat of a converted Victorian terraced house in Finsbury Park. The area was pretty rough and the rent cheap – literature charities do not pay high salaries. The house would have been beautiful once and its existence was testament to the fact that the area had been prosperous at one time or another. But somehow the street had declined and all the other houses, save this one terrace of nine or ten houses, had been replaced with sprawling seventies estates. The terrace looked abandoned and forlorn, an island of gentility among shabbiness and depression.

I had just left Jason, a music teacher I had been living with for a year or so, and I moved there because I had nowhere else to go. It was the first flat I'd seen, after days of poring over the tightly spaced columns of *Loot*. The landlord was a mean-spirited bastard, never answering my calls when the cistern flooded the tiny bathroom or when I demanded some furniture for my so-called furnished flat. For months I had no curtains and no chairs in the kitchen. I got used to eating standing up with my back leaning against the humming fridge.

There were three flights of stairs up to my door. I was on the top floor in what would have once been the servants' quarters, but were now renovated, partitioned and divided beyond recognition. In the whole time that I lived there, I never once saw any of the other people who lived in the building. Because I hated being in the flat, I arranged to be out every night. I led a frenetic social life where I would be out with my friends in Soho or Covent Garden or organising literature events and would return and fall into bed, exhausted, after midnight, only to rise and leave the flat at eight in the morning. I knew other people were living there only by the bass-lines of their music and the rhythm and frequency of their orgasms. The whole building was, in truth, a death-trap. The front door was always bolted and double-locked to prevent burglary, which was all too common in the street; there were no fire-exits and I was a hundred feet off the ground. If there had been a fire, I would have died, unable to escape. I used to lie in bed at night after my evenings out and wonder about the people living in the floors below me. Were they the sort of people who smoked in bed, or who lit candles and forgot about them, or who left their gas rings on by mistake? They kept me awake, these faceless people and their imagined pyromaniacal exploits; I had inadvertently trusted them with my life.

'Hello, this is Alice Raikes.' Alice fiddles with a paperclip as she speaks. From across the room, Susannah pulls a face. Alice ignores her.

'Hello, Alice Raikes.' He sounds amused, cocky. Alice dislikes him instantly. 'This is John Friedmann.'

'Can I help at all? You're doing a profile on us, I believe.'

'Yes, I am. Are you speaking to me from up a ladder or have you come back down to earth now?'

'Er,' she experiences a stab of irritation, 'we have just moved, you know.'

'So I hear. How do you like your new offices, Alice?'

'They're just fine, thanks,' she says impatiently. 'I didn't know yours was such a caring, sharing newspaper. If I'd known, I'd have asked you to come and help lift a few boxes for us.'

He laughs. 'Right. OK.' She hears him scuffling about in his papers. 'I don't know if your colleague mentioned anything but I'd like to do a piece about the Literature Trust – your move, your new aims, and so on.'

'Fine. What would you like to know?'

'Well, I was wondering if we could go over your plans for the next year . . .'

'OK.'

'. . . and also . . .'

'Yes?'

'. . . whether you could confirm for me that your grant's been stopped and your director's been booted out.'

Alice sighs. 'I was wondering when you'd come round to that,' she says.

'Can you confirm it for me? Has your director been given the sack? Why was he sacked? Do you—'

'People like you really piss me off,' she interrupts him.

'Pardon?'

'The Literature Trust has been doing public arts projects for almost fifty years now. Did you know that? Were you at all aware of that before you phoned me up?'

'Yes, I was.'

'I don't believe you,' Alice retorts. 'You're an arts correspondent, aren't you?'

'Ye-es,' he says.

'Then name me one project that we've done in the last year. Go on. Just one.'

There is a silence from the other end of the phone. 'Look,' he says eventually, 'this is hardly the point, is it? I just want to know—'

'I know what you want to know and I'm not going to tell you.'

'Why?'

'Because we're a national arts organisation and you're a national arts correspondent and you can't tell me one thing we've done. When we do important and effective things like creating workshops in prisons and schools, or bringing Commonwealth writers to tour Britain, or creating a national competition for new writing you lot don't give a damn. You're only interested when something goes wrong.'

'Listen, I understand that you feel passionately about—'

'I don't think you do understand. I don't think you understand at all. If you really do want to do a profile on our aims and objectives – like you said at first – then, fine, I'll help you. But if you're just calling me to dig dirt then I won't. I hate to say it, but you journalists are all the same.'

'Is that right? In what way?'

'You just rehash scandal – all of you, tabloid, broadsheet, it's all the same. It would be so good if someone came up with a new approach. Or if someone actually thought about what the Literature Trust does or even what literature does before calling me with predictable questions about things that don't really matter in the long run.' She stops. She's out of breath.

'I see,' he says. 'A new approach. Like what?'

'If I wanted to be a journalist I'd have got a job on a newspaper. I'm not writing your article for you. The approach is up to you. I'm just here to respond to your questions – predictable or otherwise.'

There is an appalled silence, both from the other end of the phone and from the office. She realises that everyone is staring at her, horrified, and she turns away from them to face the wall.

'Right. Right. I see. That's how it is, is it?'

'Yes,' says Alice recklessly. 'If you can't be bothered to do your research, then you don't get your interview.'

There is another pause. She hears him exhale. 'I see, I see . . .' He tails off. She waits. 'Um . . . in that case, I'll . . . I'll call you back. OK?'

'OK.' She hangs up.

'Well,' says Susannah, rifling through her in-tray on her desk on the other side of the room, 'he'll think twice about calling us again. What was he like?'

'A complete wanker.'

Today Alice had that familiar, tight, bulging knot of crossness in her stomach. If she tried to unravel it, it would crack and splinter her fingernails. She didn't like herself.

What she couldn't fathom — and wouldn't ever be able to, as she would find out — was the fickleness of people: how people can like you one day, but the next, because of something as random as telling the teacher how you were growing cress on a wet tissue on your window-sill, you were no longer in favour.

There was a thick haar rolling in from the sea. It hung heavy over the town and had even reached up the hill to the school. The yard was cold, hung with mizzling rain. The Law, right next to the school, looked huge and dark, its top hidden. Alice tried hard not to look over at where her friend — her former friend — Emma was playing skipping with four or five other girls. The rope was getting wetter all the time; it slapped the damp concrete and at each apex of its turn sent off a spray that soaked the skippers' hair. Emma was jumping up and down in perfect rhythm with the turning rope, her knee socks edging lower. 'You can't play with us,' she'd said, her voice made nasal with scorn that Alice had even asked. She was now singing along with the others: 'Greeeeeen gravel, greeeeeen gravel, growing up so high, why did the sweetheart that I loved, why did he have to die?'

Alice looked around for Kirsty and Beth. They were usually easy to spot, the bright white-gold of their hair gleaming among the other children's. There was Kirsty, leaning against the playground wall, talking with two of her friends. Beth was over at the sandpit bossily admonishing a small, frightened girl who had dared to throw a handful of wet sand into the air.

In Alice's pocket, wrapped carefully in hard, shiny, pallid paper was the head of a fish. She shuddered at the thought of the juices from the raw, wet amputation seeping slowly into a dark patch on her duffel coat. If she squeezed its cheeks, the mouth opened. Its tongue was narrow, grey and grizzled. But its eyes – its eyes! – perfectly round, luminous silver orbs. They swivelled in their sockets. She tested her own eyes – did they swivel? To her left was the shadowing bulk of the school, to the right the shelter wall; ahead were figures squiggled carelessly on the rainy playground by a wide-nibbed pen. She wished her eyes were silver.

She pulled down her hood over her eyes and mouth until the neck of the coat hung on the crown of her head and the hood bagged out loosely beneath her face. The school, the shelter and the figures were all gone. She heard their noise as if through water – far off and distorted. It was just her and the fish now, alone in the liquid dark.

Five minutes later the phone rings again.

'I was wrong! I was wrong!' Susannah shouts and waves the receiver at Alice. 'It's John the Journalist!'

Alice groans and picks up the phone. 'Hello? Is that John? Don't tell me – you've found out all you need to know about literature and the Literature Trust in five minutes. I'm impressed. Are you always such a fast worker?' Alice is suddenly conscious of the unintended double entendre and feels an unaccustomed blush fire her face. She's fervently thankful he can't see her.

'I have a proposition for you, Alice . . .' He is laughing. Bastard. '. . . fast worker or not.'

'What is it?'

'I'll do my homework on the Literature Trust if you'll do an interview in person.'

Alice is silent for a moment, then says, 'Where?'

'At the Literature Trust offices. Where else did you have in mind?'

Alice feels her face heat up again. Damn him. 'This place is in a real state. I wouldn't dream of letting a hack like you in here. We've got boxes and dust everywhere. Look, I've got to be in the Docklands tomorrow anyway. I could come to your offices. You're in Canary Wharf, aren't you?'

'That's right. Well, that's fine with me. When's a good time?'

'I'm quite busy at the moment. How about lunchtime? Then we could eat and talk at the same time.'

'I was always told that was bad manners.'

'Well, I don't mind about bad manners.'

'Really?'

For God's sake, she tells herself, this is getting ridiculous, hang up at once.

'Right,' she almost snarls, 'I'll see you tomorrow at one,' and hangs up without waiting for an answer.

Ann and Ben take a taxi from the station. It's an uneven journey, the taxi travelling swiftly at first, tarmac rumbling beneath them; then they hit a traffic jam where they sit for what feels like ages, the engine churning over, the back of the cab filling with sour fumes, the red meter flicking. Ann sits bolt upright, the tendons in her neck visible beneath her skin, staring out of the windscreen as if intending to make the road blockage disappear by telekinesis. Ben shifts in the leather seat. His clothes have wrinkled under him during the train journey. He hardly ever comes to London and always forgets how brash he finds it. He cranes his neck out of the window to see the obstruction, and the whitish, level light of the street makes his eyes smart. The sun – much warmer here than in Scotland – seems harshly bright, picking out people's outlines, making the colours in their clothes shout. He feels the heavy air around his head churn and a cyclist whizzes past, his face obscured by a pollution mask and mirrored visor, the tread of his wheels crunching as he weaves in and out of the stationary cars. Ben brings his head back into the cab and winds up the window. He will never understand why Alice left Scotland to come here.

They could have taken the tube. Maybe it would have been quicker. But the tube to both him and Ann is a fearsome thing: a horrible machine into which you get sucked, dragged down by crowds and escalators, spat out on to blackened platforms where trains arrive and leave with alarming speed, and all you have to find your way is a map of tangled, coloured wires and strange-sounding names. In his breast pocket is the address of the hospital and the name of the doctor. They dictated it to him down the phone that morning. He puts his hand to the pocket, listening out for the crack of paper to reassure himself, and as he does so, the taxi eases its way into a moving lane of traffic.

They begin speeding through streets, almost without stopping. Ben gets the sensation they are heading uphill. Fragments of shouts, conversations, music, car horns are snatched from the air and whirled into the cab. And the view is changing – large Edwardian houses with railings, trees with gleaming cars parked outside have replaced the ramshackle streets around King's Cross. Ben has no idea where they are. His knowledge of London is limited to two trig-points – the station and Alice's house in Camden Town. He's been to Alice's office in the centre of the city, and to the National Gallery, which must have been close by because they walked there after she finished work one Friday. Once, maybe even on the same visit, she'd taken them to a park in north London where people were swimming about in a brackish, algae-ridden lake. Alice swam: he has a distinct memory of her dark head, sleek as a seal's, bobbing up some distance away from where he was sitting on the bank. He has never lost that father's instinct when any of his daughters swim, to check that when they dive down they come up again. John swam too that day, Ben now remembers, taking running dives off a slippery wooden duckboard. Was that park anywhere near here? Ben cannot grasp how these locations – disparate in both geography and time – fit together.

The hospital is large and grey, crouched on a hill. Even before they get out of the taxi, when Ben is still counting change

79

into the man's hand, he can hear the muted roar of its workings
– air-conditioning, electrical generators, incinerators. Going up
the steps, they hold hands like they did when they were first
engaged. Ben is holding a roll of newspaper unnaturally high
against his chest. In it, the heads of some late-flowering yellow
roses nod to the rhythm of his walk.

Inside, the artificial light casts everyone in a greenish pallor.
It is not like the hospitals he's been in before – slightly shabby
places with curling floor tiles and fading wall paint. This one is
new and modern, and reminds Ben of an airport. Ann speaks
to the receptionist, bending over to make her voice heard
through the hole in the Perspex screen. A nurse with the
flat London vowels Ben finds hard to understand leads them
down a corridor, and then they are in a strange, echoey,
sub-lit labyrinth. They take a left, then another left, then a
right and then Ben loses count, following instead the rubber
ridges of the nurse's shoe soles, which squeak on the pink
lino. Pink like the insides of things. They pass heavy wooden
doors on silent hinges, rows of people seated on plastic chairs,
a canteen, lifts, staircases, a glass walkway, beyond which is a
tiled pond circled by two orange goldfish, racks of folded-up
wheelchairs, a noisy corridor filled with people and shouting,
a ward with bright cartoon characters painted on the walls
where blank-faced children sit cross-legged on beds, a young
man holding a paper cup underneath a water dispenser, sending
balloons of bubbles up into the inverted bottle. Then they pass
though a pair of swing doors. There is silence here, and a room
with a large window on one side, framing trees and cars and sky.
Alice is there on a bed. The initial thought that jumps into Ben's
mind is that he'd forgotten how tall she is. Her body seems so
long and thin as to take up the whole length of the bed.

He walks round and lays the newspaper cone of roses on
the bedside table. He looks up to thank the nurse for bringing

them here, but she seems to have gone. Ann is biting her lip, which Ben knows means she's trying not to cry. Their eyes meet across the bed. Both of them are afraid to touch her, Ben realises. He reaches quickly for one of Alice's hands. It is limp, yet warm, the fingers loose and bendable, entirely without resistance or energy. If he let it go it would just drop back to the bed. Ben runs a fingertip around the white dent at the base of her fourth finger. She has stepmother jags around her nails, which are cut neatly into white crescents. How long is it since he held his daughter's hand?

He places it back beside her hip, curling the fingers into her palm, and moves around the bed towards Ann, puts his arm around her shoulder and kisses her hair. Alice's hair is gone; shaved so close to her head that the white of her scalp shows through.

'Do you remember when she returned from Thailand with that tattoo?' Ben says. 'We were so angry.'

Ann gives a coughing laugh through her tears. 'She didn't care, though.'

There is a thin, transparent tube running into Alice's mouth, held on to her face by a strip of elastic. The ventilator machine sighs profoundly at regular intervals. Another, thinner tube runs from a clear bag held high on a stand into Alice's arm. Ben leans over her. Her lips are pale and bloodless. Bruising shadows most of the left side of her face and one of her eye sockets, and there is a scraped graze on her cheekbone. He notices that tiny violet veins run in branches over her eyelids. Beneath them, her eyes are still, as if mesmerised by an image printed on the inside of her lids.

Almost in unison, Ben and Ann reach for a chair and they take opposite sides of the bed, their elbows on the mattress. The bed is an odd height and Ben feels like a child at a high table.

'Hello Alice. It's us,' he says, feeling a little self-conscious, like he does when he talks to very small, very shy children. 'Your mother and I have come to see you.'

Ann strokes her cheek. 'I'm almost afraid to touch her in case I set one of these machines off,' she whispers. 'Do you think she knows we're here?'

Ben isn't sure what he thinks yet, but he nods decisively for his wife's sake. Then they both look back at their daughter. It occurs to Ben that they have expended so much thought on the logistics of the journey and getting themselves to the hospital that neither of them have really thought about what they would do when they got here.

Ann fills the sink. The water flashes and throws icy darts of light up to the ceiling. It is a clear, bright, crisp afternoon – the best weather for North Berwick. She might go down to the beach later on where the wind will be freezing and scalpel-sharp. From the window, the island of Craigleith is defined clearly against the navy-blue sea. The sea is Ann's weathervane; she can see it from practically wherever she is in the house. Its colour and texture change by the hour and can be anything from a forbidding airforce blue on stormy days to a deep green on cloudless August days. She doesn't hold with forecasts, although she does find a certain rhythmic calm in listening to the shipping forecasts. Years ago Ben, thinking she would be interested, bought her a map of all the places – Faroes, Fairisle, Northutshire, Fisher, Forties, Cromarty. He hadn't understood that she didn't care where they were – and why on earth would she, for heaven's sake? – that it was precisely because it was meaningless to her that she enjoyed it. Ann sighs. She had pinned up the map so as not to hurt his feelings, of course. Then one of the girls had torn it when flouncing out of the back door in a teenage tantrum – probably Alice. In fact, it was definitely Alice. Ann had been secretly glad that she could take it down, folding it into itself so that the northern Hebrides gently kissed the Isle of Wight, jagged coastlines rubbing up against each other in the rubbish bin.

A sudden crash from the room above makes her jump. She looks up at the ceiling, listening out for Elspeth's footsteps. The moment stretches, her hand in the cooling water in the sink. Nothing.

'Elspeth?' Her voice sounds strident, still unmistakably English after all these years. 'Elspeth! Are you there?'

Ann wipes her hands on a flowered dish-towel and goes through the sitting room, up the stairs. The door to Elspeth's room is shut. Elspeth has kept on living in the front bedroom. Ann feels periodically irked by this; the room she and Ben have had since they were married is smaller and faces Marmion Road. If you leant out of the side window then you could admittedly see a square patch of sea but it was nothing like the the long line of horizon, broken only by the jutting rocks of Craigleith, Fidra and the Lamb, that dominated the whole of one side of Elspeth's room. 'My view', as Elspeth rather unnecessarily referred to it.

Ann taps at the door with her nails. 'Elspeth? Are you all right?' Her voice quavers a little. She presses down the handle.

Elspeth is lying stretched out on the carpet, one hand flung above her head. Her body forms a perfect parallel to the line of the horizon which, Ann notes, is beginning to darken. Ann lets go of the door handle, which springs back with a loud ping, walks over and stands above Elspeth. Her face is grey, twisted. The position her body has fallen in is an oddly seductive, starlet pose; one arm above her head, the other draped over her chest, her legs drawn up. Ann bends over at the waist. There is no sign of any breathing at all.

She straightens up and tiptoes back across the room.

Half-way, she wonders why she's tiptoeing. She leaves the door open deliberately and goes back down the stairs.

In the kitchen she empties muddied potatoes from a brown paper sack into the sink. They fall against each other in the water and the soil dissolves slowly, sinking into a gritty sediment at the bottom. When a pile of wet peelings has developed at her side, she realises that she won't be needing as many potatoes as she'd thought she would, but doesn't stop peeling.

Later she hears Ben come in and shout, 'Hello!' He treads upstairs and she hears the lavatory flush, the water rushing though the house, him going into their bedroom. She's never realised before how heavily he walks. She waits, listening, her hands resting on the draining-board. There is a short silence. She picks at a loose jag in her thumbnail, reaches for an emery board, but puts it back. Then Ben shouts her name three times, 'Ann, Ann, Ann!' and she waits, turning her head to the doorway, arranging her face into an expression of wide-eyed concern.

I'd never been to Canary Wharf before. I'd seen the tower, of course. It's difficult to miss its flashing pyramidical top in the smoggy London skyline. But despite having always disliked it, I did feel a little awestruck when I stood beside it and tilted my head back to see its sheer height soaring into the sky.

At the security desk I filled in a form saying where I was from, why I was here and who I was seeing. I have gone over in my head so often that moment where I first wrote his name, where the muscles and tendons in my fingers, hands, arm and shoulder conspired to form the curves, spikes, strokes and dashes that spelt out the name 'John Friedmann'. Did I feel anything?

I don't believe in fate. I don't believe in cushioning your insecurities with a system of belief that tells you, 'Don't worry. This may be your life but you're not in control. There is something or someone looking out for you   it's already organised.' It's all chance and choice, which is far more frightening.

I'd like to think that as the lift swooped up the floors I sensed that something important was about to take place, that my life was about to split away from my expectation of it. But, of course, I didn't. Who ever does? Life's cruel like that – it gives you no clues.

Alice rises towards the surface of sleep. The phone is ringing. How long has it been ringing for? It is strangely quiet and she realises that the main road that runs past their front door, whose roar she hears unconsciously all day, is silent and empty. She can picture it – the miles of deserted tarmac, leached of colour by the overhead orange street-lights. The phone rings and rings and rings. She strains to hear if her housemates are stirring to answer it.

As soon as she was conscious of the first ring – maybe even before – she knew it was Mario. Who else would phone in the middle of the night and for so long?

It is the first term of Alice's second year at university. She has moved out of the grey university corridors into a house with her friend Rachel and two other girls. The house is small, with no central heating, a rickety narrow staircase, and no kitchen, just a Baby Belling in the corner of the sitting room. They like it, though. It smacks of freedom and independence, giving them a hint of life beyond exams and parents and rules. Their friends still living in university rooms come round and sit in the mismatched armchairs and watch as Alice or one of the others brings a saucepan of pasta to the boil on the tiny white box of a cooker.

In a sudden surge of decisiveness (she's been avoiding his calls for weeks and the others have become adept at lying to him about her whereabouts) she rips back the blankets and jumps up from her bed – a mattress on the floor. The cold hits her and she feels as if she's entered a wind tunnel. She runs down the stairs on her bare tiptoes and snatches up the receiver. There is a silence. She doesn't speak.

'Alice?'

'Mario, do you know what time it is here?'

There is a fault on the line. The wires have crossed like chromosomes and Alice can hear her own voice echoing back, disconcertingly close to her own ear.

'Shit, honey, I know, I just had to call. Did I wake you?'

'Of course you bloody well woke me. What do you want?'

'You know what I want.'

'Mario, I've told you before. It's over. You've got to stop ringing me.'

Her voice sounds thin and frayed relayed back to her. She shakes the receiver in frustration.

'I know you don't mean that. We can sort this out, I know we can. It is difficult when we're so far apart, I realise that. I want you to come to the States over Christmas. I'll pay. We just need to see each other and talk.'

Alice stares at the boisterously patterned carpet at her feet and conjugates possibilities   I don't love you, I won't love you, I never loved you.

'No.'

'What do you mean "no"? Alice, I can't live without you. I love you. I love you so much.'

He is crying now. The sobs and gulps coming through the phone sound somehow obscene to her. She feels interested in the fact that his crying has no effect on her whatsoever. What happened with Mario seems so far away it's like something she read or heard about – it wasn't her. She can barely even remember what he looks like. She can't conjure much about him at all – the intimidating size of his presence when he was near her, yes, but not much else; not his smell, or the feel of his weight or his hands, or anything.

His crying is reaching a crescendo of which, as an actor, Mario ought to be proud. She is perched on the arm of a chair, shivering in her thin pyjamas. She wishes she'd put socks on before she came down.

'Mario. This has got to stop. I mean it. It's over between

87

us. You have to face up to that and get on with your life.'

'I can't!' He is shouting now, getting into the swing of things. 'I need you!'

She sighs angrily. 'No, you don't. Forget it, Mario, it's over. Just leave me alone. I never want to talk to you again. I'm really tired and really cold and I'm going back to bed now.'

'This can't happen. I won't let it. I won't let you say it's over.'

'Mario . . . just . . . just fuck off.'

There is a stunned silence from America.

'Fuck off? Did you just tell me to fuck off?'

'Yes, I did, and I'll tell you again. Fuck off.' Alice slams the phone down.

John looks up at the sound of a rap at the glass door of his office. Standing in the doorway is a young woman with long dark hair swinging gently down her back. She's holding a book pressed to her chest.

'Hi. I'm looking for John Friedmann.'

'That's me.' John stands. 'You're Alice? Come on in.' She crosses the room and instead of sitting in the chair he indicates for her, goes to the window. He is a bit stunned: he was expecting an earthy-looking, earnest, blue-stocking type with specs and shapeless flowing clothes, and is a little disconcerted by the appearance of this tall, striking woman in a short skirt, knee-high boots and black and green striped tights.

'What an amazing view.'

'It is, isn't it? It's the only compensation for working out in this godforsaken place.' John is also discomfited by her vague familiarity: he feels certain that he's seen her somewhere before but can't place her. It puts him at a disadvantage, somehow. The rather aggressive banter they had over the phone seems impossible now. 'There was the most incredible rainbow

88

yesterday – it must have been just after I'd spoken to you on the phone – arching all the way over east London.' He cuts a swathe through the air, describing its curve. 'It lasted for ages. You see quite a few from up here. It must be the height or something.'

'So there's a pot of gold in Leytonstone somewhere.' She turns her eyes on him.

Is that a flirtatious look? No. She seems to be assessing him. Her eyes are dark, like her hair, with flecks of amber around the pupils. John forces himself to look away, and strides manfully towards his desk. What on earth is the matter with him? The minute some attractive woman walks into his office he goes to pieces. 'You don't look like someone who works at the Literature Trust.' He hopes she'll laugh. She doesn't.

'And what are people who work at the Literature Trust supposed to look like, according to you?'

'I don't know.' He ducks out, angering her further.

'Yes, you do. You think we're all dusty academic types with glasses. Why not say it, if that's what you mean?'

'No! Not at all.' He busies himself in saving the work displayed on his computer screen. She sits down opposite him. 'Anyway,' he says feebly, 'you have just as many sweeping opinions on journalists, it seems. You think we're all just writing different versions of the same preconceptions.'

She puts her head on one side and narrows her eyes. Beautiful eyes. Lovely neck. For God's sake, get a grip on yourself.

'I'm prepared to be convinced otherwise. That's the difference between us.'

Her words hang in the air. The computer's hard drive hums. They stare at each other. John thinks he has never liked the word 'us' better in his life and has a speedy headrush-fantasy where an omniscient camera lens zooms out above them and it seems that Canary Wharf, and indeed the whole of London, is empty apart from this room where they are sitting opposite each other. This leads to him trying to remember a quote from a John Donne poem. Something about love making one little room an everywhere, or was it an anywhere?

She is looking at him with faint alarm. Has he been staring at her? He searches wildly for something to say and in a moment of heaven-sent inspiration, catches sight of the book she was carrying when she came in. She's put it on the desk in front of her and has her hand over part of the cover. He can still make out the title. *The Private Memoirs and Confessions of a Justified Sinner.*

'That sounds a bit of a heavy book.'

She smiles for the first time. 'It is, I suppose. I'd never say I have a favourite book, but this is one I have read over and over again. I wanted to look at something in it so I brought it with me to read on the tube.' She hands it to him. It has a gloomy painting of an evil-looking boy as its cover.

'What's it about?'

'It's hard to say. You'd have to read it, really. It's the most terrifying book I've ever read. A boy gets followed and tormented by a protean devil called Gilmartin. It's set in Scotland and Gilmartin pursues him all over these bleak, barren landscapes. You're never quite sure whether the devil is real or just a projection or externalisation of his own evil side.' She shivers and then smiles again.

'Oh,' he says, a little bemused. He gropes for a suitable and non-vacuous response, coming up with: 'You're Scottish, aren't you?'

'Yes. I only discovered it when I went to university, though. We had this reading room in the main library with a vast, domed ceiling. You were forbidden to talk and got shouted at if you breathed too loudly. It was always full of rows and rows of serious academics with obscure, out-of-print tomes propped up in front of them. I was reading this one day, in late afternoon when it was just getting dark outside. I'd just reached a particularly scary bit – where they are digging up this ancient body that's still intact – when I felt a hand grip my shoulder from behind. I screamed really loudly and the noise echoed and bounced around the huge ceiling. People were horrified. It was only a friend asking me if I wanted to go for a cup of tea. I frightened the life out of him too.'

It has clicked for John – that description of the reading room. 'I was there too!' he shouts.

'Where?'

'The library . . . I mean, the university . . . I mean, I was at university with you!

She is immediately suspicious. 'Were you?'

'When did you leave?'

'Um . . . five years ago. No, four.'

'I knew it! I knew it!' He feels like getting up and dancing around the room. 'I knew I'd seen you somewhere before! I graduated six years ago, which must have been . . .'

'My first year, or the end of it,' she finishes for him and, scanning his face, says bluntly, 'I don't remember you at all.'

'No, well, I don't really remember you. Not properly. You just look vaguely familiar. I probably saw you around the library or something, although I don't think I heard you scream.'

'You're not going to put that in your article, are you?' She looks genuinely worried.

'No. It will go no further – famous last words of a journalist.'

There is a pause. John leans back in his chair, lacing his hands behind his head.

Alice looks about her. 'So . . .' she says eventually, 'Are we going to do it here?'

'What?'

'The interview.'

'Of course, of course. The interview. I thought we might go up to the canteen. Is that OK with you?'

She nods, getting up.

The strangest thing about this is that a thought can go on and on circling your mind, that you can't stop obsessing over it, that there are no brakes to apply to things you no longer want to think about. In normal life, you distract yourself – pick up a newspaper, go out for a walk, turn on the television, phone somebody up. You can throw your mind a sop, trick yourself into thinking you're all right, that the thing that's been haunting you is resolved. It won't work for long, of course – an hour, two hours if you're lucky – because nobody's that stupid and because these things always come back to you when you're once more idle and distractionless. In the small, dark hours of the night, when you're being rocked into blank-mindedness on a bus.

The problem with being like this is that you are constant prey to these exhausting cycles of thought. Just now, I am getting no rest from how terrible it is that he doesn't know.

He who knows me better than anyone else has no idea of this. No inkling. We think we know everything there possibly is to know about each other. And then suddenly I discover this massive thing that alters the whole path of my life.

It's like those kitsch religious cards you can buy in Catholic countries; the ones with a ridged, plastic finish that just look strange and lurid and three-dimensional until you tilt them and discover another picture behind the first. You can make it look as if Mary is bringing her hands up to pray, or Jesus is blessing you, or that the angels are crying. To me it feels as if everything has been tilted to reveal this whole other picture which has existed, just out of sight, all along.

I keep trying — over and over, because I can't switch it off, can't fool myself into numbness with meaningless activities — to imagine what he would say; how he might have reacted if I had come back to a house with him in it, and said, 'John, I saw the most terrible thing today. You won't believe what I saw, let me tell you what I saw.'

'Hold still, Alice,' Ann scolds, gripping Alice's shin between her knees. Her mother has placed her up on the kitchen counter. She's trodden on a bee and got stung in the soft, blue part of her foot. Yet again. 'How many times have we told you not to go barefoot in the garden? How many?'

Alice shrugs, sobbing. It's the shock more than the pain, really. Although the pain is quite astonishing, shooting up way beyond her knee, making her foot swell up so that the ankle bones disappear into the flesh like raisins into cake mix.

Alice would really prefer Elspeth to be doing this, but she's not sure where she is. As soon as it happened, she'd started screaming, Kirsty had run into the house shouting, 'Mummeeeeeeee, Alice has stepped on another beeeeeeeeeeee!' and Ann had come rushing into the garden, scooped her up and deposited her here in the kitchen.

'Put your foot in the water.' Ann had filled the basin next to Alice with cold water. Alice, for a reason unfathomable both to her and to Ann, refuses. 'Put it in, Alice.'

'Where's Granny?' she manages to say between sobs. She sees her mother's face fall slightly, twitch downwards. Then Ann rights herself, seizes Alice's ankle and forces her foot into the water. Alice lets out a piercing shriek and thrashes her foot about. Both of them get soaked. They grapple and

Ann manages to pin both of Alice's arms to her sides. When Alice is fully immobilised, Ann says, through gritted teeth, 'If you don't put your foot in the water, the swelling won't go down. If the swelling doesn't go down, we can't get the sting out. If we can't get the sting out, it won't stop hurting. Why do you never do as I ask?' Alice struggles again in her mother's arms. Ann squeezes her all the tighter and leans all her weight on the child's body. 'You won't be told, will you? You're just like your bloody father.'

The words, barely audible, are vicious and fly from Ann's mouth like hornets. Even aged eight, Alice is surprised. She looks out of the window at her father's silhouette, bending over, digging holes in the flower border down the side of the house. He is trailed by the diminutive figure of her younger sister, who drops bulbs into the holes from a brown paper bag held in their father's hands. 'Good girl,' he is saying to Beth, 'that's very good.' Alice feels a heat emanating from her mother's face, clamped to hers because of their fight, and she turns to see her mother pressing her teeth down into her lip, a rush of sudden blood staining her pale cheeks.

Ann lets go of her, but she sits still, not crying now, letting her mother search her footsole for the sting. Alice is aware something has happened, but she doesn't know what exactly. Is her mother upset because she asked for Elspeth? She wants to ask her mother this but can't think of the right words to say it. Ann is silent, her head bent, her hands gentle now. Alice gets a funny, liquid feeling under her ribs. She wants to say she's sorry, she's sorry for being naughty, she's sorry for asking for Granny. She would like her mother to press her hands to her hot, clammy face.

Ann straightens up triumphantly. 'There!'

She lifts Alice down and holds out the sting for her to see. They peer at it together. It is tiny, spear-shaped, brown and brittle. It clings to the whorls and ridges of her mother's finger. Alice is amazed that something so small could cause that amount of pain. 'Can I have it? Can I have it?'

'No.'

'Please!'

'What on earth do you want it for?'

Alice can't think of a reason, but she knows she wants it. She wants to hold it, to look at it for a long time. She hangs off her mother's arm. 'Please! Please can I have it?'

Uncharacteristically, Ann relents and, bending down, transfers it from her finger to Alice's. She then goes from the room and Alice hears her walk quickly upstairs and close her bedroom door. But Alice isn't thinking about this at the time, she is holding the bee-sting in the crook of her middle finger, where she carries it for the rest of the day.

Afterwards, he walked with her to the lift. It seemed to take a long time for it to come and Alice couldn't think of anything to say to him.

'You don't have to wait with me. I'm sure I can find my way out.'

'No, no. I don't mind.'

An overweight man in a loosened tie breezed through the lobby and said, 'All right, John?' and, casting his eyes appraisingly over Alice, winked at him. She pretended she hadn't noticed. John was furious, she could tell. A vein pulsed in his temple.

'Have you got a lot to do this afternoon?' she asked him, to break the silence.

'Yes, as usual.'

'When did you become a journalist?'

'Straight after university. I did an MA at City University and then had various smallish jobs. I've been here for a year now.'

The lift arrived with a computerised ding.

'Well, thanks for lunch. When's the article due out?'

'Next Thursday, I think. I could phone you to let you know, if you want.'

She went into the lift. 'Oh, don't worry about that. You've probably got enough to do.'

'No, it's not a problem . . . Alice!' He thrust his foot between the closing doors, which crashed open again. 'Shit . . . that hurt.'

'Are you OK?'

He massaged his foot, leaning on one of the lift doors to stop them closing. 'Just about. It's not funny, you know, I could have lost a foot and it would have been your fault.'

'I hardly think so. Anyway, it would have been an industrial accident, wouldn't it? You'd have got millions in compensation.'

At that moment a grim-faced woman walked into the lift.

'I was wondering if . . . whether you would like to . . .' he faltered, as the woman fidgeted pointedly with her watch. '. . . Er . . . I wondered if I could borrow that book.'

She was taken aback. 'Well, yes. Do you really want to?'

'I'd love to.'

She reached into her bag and handed it to him. He took it and stepped back. 'I'll give it back to you.'

Alice was about to say that there was no need but the doors closed.

Rachel had just returned from an early lecture and was knocking on Alice's door. 'Alice? Are you awake? Are you dressed?'

Alice was sitting in bed with a book propped up on her knees. The curtains were open and the mid-morning sunlight formed triangles of light on the carpet. 'Yes, come in. How was the lecture?'

Rachel appeared in the doorway still in her coat and scarf, clutching a parcel. 'Boring, actually. Guess what came for you in the post.'

'What?'

'It's from New York.'

Alice put her hands over her eyes. 'I don't want it! Take it away!'

Rachel sat down on the bed and tossed the parcel into Alice's lap. 'Open it, go on. It could be something nice, something expensive.'

Alice turned it over in her hands. There was no return address but the handwriting was unmistakably Mario's. It was an ordinary brown padded envelope and what was in it was light, bulky and squashable, giving easily to the pressure of her fingers. What was it? Clothes?

'You open it,' she said, pushing it into Rachel's hands.

'No. It's addressed to you. You open it.'

Alice peeled back the Sellotape on one end of the envelope and held it upside down, shaking whatever it was into her hand. What came out was so shocking that things registered in reverse order in her mind. Hair. A lot of hair. Black hair. Curly, tangled hair. Familiar hair. Hair cut in one hack from someone's head. Hair she'd felt between her fingers before. Mario's hair.

Both girls shrieked loudly and leapt from the bed. From the other side of the room they clutched each other, Alice frantically shaking loose strands from her fingers, and looked at it, nestling in a black clump on the bedclothes, like some overgrown rodent.

'Jesus Christ, the man's a psycho,' Rachel muttered.

Alice jumped up and down, rubbing her hands on her

pyjamas, 'Uuuuurrrgggh! Yuk, yuk, yuk! It's horrible. God, what a thing to do.' Having it in her hands, feeling again its ravelled spirals and curves, brought back with a slamming force the time she had slept with him. It was as if he was there in the room with them, not thousands of miles away across an icy Atlantic. She looked about despairingly. 'What do we do with it?'

'We throw it away.'

'I can't. I'm not touching it again.'

Rachel picked up Alice's waste-paper basket and marched over to the bed, brandishing it before her. She swept the hair into it and carried it downstairs. Alice heard her emptying it into the wheelie-bin at the front of the house.

'Thank you, Rachel,' she called.

'Any time.'

But for weeks, Alice would find stray strands hooked into a teacup, coiled around the soap or clinging to her tongue, making her spit and hiss.

John prowled around the lobby, banging himself on the head with the book.

'You fucking coward, you fucking, fucking coward.'

This was the last thing he needed.

When Alice got back to the office later on that afternoon, Susannah was beaming at her across the room.

'What's up with you, Cheshire Cat?' Alice said, as she sat down at her desk.

'You've had a call,' Susannah said, and was then distracted by something on her computer.

'Who from?'

'That man,' Susannah said absently, peering closely at her screen.

John Friedmann, Alice thought irrationally, and was immediately cross with herself. She started flicking through her card indexes. 'Which man?' she said, as if she didn't really care.

'That man. Whatshisname. You know.'

Alice stopped flicking. 'Suze, do you think you could be a little more specific?'

'Sorry.' Susannah turned to face her, concentrating on her now. 'That man from the organisation in Paris.'

'Oh.' Alice fought a feeling of intense disappointment. 'That man.' This was ridiculous. She couldn't be getting all hung up over that journalist. Could she?

'Isn't he the one you've been trying to get through to all week?' Susannah was looking at her, puzzled by her unenthusiastic response.

'Yes. Yes, he is.'

Alice, for something to do, opened her diary.

'But he's called you back. This is good news, isn't it?' Susannah persisted, 'I mean, it probably means he wants to do the project with you, doesn't it?'

'I hope so. I'll call him back in a minute.'

There was a pause. Alice, feeling that Susannah was still looking at her, kept her head bent over her diary, filling in needless appointments.

'How was the interview, by the way?'

'Oh . . . fine . . . all right . . . yeah, great. Well . . . it was . . . fine, actually.'

At the sound of the bell jangling on its wire, Elspeth comes out of the back room of the Oxfam shop to see her afternoon replacement already taking off her coat at the till: a largish, florid-faced woman in a turquoise plastic mac.

'You're early today,' Elspeth remarks.

'Yes,' the woman tells her, 'it's good to get out the house early on a day like today.'

Elspeth feels uneasy about this woman. Always has. She wears those glasses that react to the light. In today's bright sunshine, you can't see her eyes at all. Can't trust someone who won't show you their eyes. And she always brings her dog into the shop. It's a nice enough dog, but it smells. Puts folk off.

Outside the shop, Elspeth hesitates. She needs to go to the supermarket to buy something for the girls' tea when they come home from school, but she does have this extra half-hour to spare that she hadn't bargained for. On an impulse, she turns away from the direction of home and walks towards the end of the High Street, saying hello to various people on the way. She turns right at the chip shop down Quality Street and crosses over to the Lodge Grounds.

She doesn't come here often, but it's one of her favourite places in the town. She likes the way its cultivated prettiness is caught midway between the wide, flat sweep of the beaches and the gorse-covered cragginess of the Law. Even though it's a weekday, people with buggies and prams are wandering up and down the uneven, winding concrete paths, looking at the plants or just enjoying the sun. Passing the aviary, she shudders. Elspeth has never seen the attraction of caged birds.

At the brow of the hill, she sees a small gaggle of teenagers in the red and black uniform of the High School. A quick scan of the group assures her that neither Kirsty nor Alice is among them. It was last year that she came face to face with a shame-faced Kirsty and two of her friends down by the harbour at eleven o'clock on a Wednesday morning. Elspeth had promised to say nothing if Kirsty gave her her word that it wouldn't happen again.

Elspeth, still feeling a little like a child let out of school early herself, sits down on a green bench with the crazy golf course behind her and the town and the sea in front of her. It was at about this spot that she and her then fiancé Robert had been walking when they met a man to whom Robert introduced her as Gordon Raikes. Elspeth knew of the Raikes family, their large house on Marmion Road and their golf-club factory on the outskirts of the town, but she had never met their youngest son, Gordon. He'd been away at school and then at St Andrews University, Robert told her, as she and Gordon looked dumbly at each other. As she always told him later, she might as well have taken off Robert's engagement ring there and then. She and Robert had walked away together and as they went round a corner to go down the slope, Elspeth had turned and seen him, still standing there beside the privet hedge, looking after them. It must have been here. There were no concrete paths then, of course, only dust-soil ones that turned to churned mud in the rain.

She'd met him again a week later on the blustery High Street, both with their mothers, both weighed down with parcels of food. He'd winked at her while their mothers chatted and she'd surprised herself — and him too, no doubt — by winking back. It was only a few days after that that she'd been standing by the harbour, watching the fishing boats coming in, and he'd appeared from round a corner. 'Hello, Elspeth,' he'd said, and stopped to look down into the boats with her. Caught fish slipped and slithered about on the decks, their tails flicking, their parched mouths opening and closing. The fishermen threw creels and baskets up on to the harbour with a regular thud, thud, thud.

'Do you always get called Elspeth?' he'd asked.

'Not always. Some people shorten it to Ellie.'

'I bet you don't like that,' he'd said, leaning his elbows on the railing next to her.

She'd shaken her head. 'No, I don't.'

'I thought so. You don't suit a shortened name.'

He'd taken her out on to the point beyond the swimming-pool and she'd sat with her arms around her knees, slightly nervous of the swell and fall of the waves that slapped the rocks so close below them and the stiff breeze that whipped her hair around her face, listening to him tell her how he wanted to go into the church and be a missionary.

'My father wants me to go into the family business, but I just don't think it's for me. I don't see how I could be happy doing that. That's what should be your priority, shouldn't it, Elspeth?' He'd stopped tossing pebbles into the greenish sea at that point and looked at her. She'd said nothing, her mouth dry, thinking only, what on earth will my parents say?

'Don't you think, Elspeth, that you should always be as happy as you possibly can be?' he'd asked again.

She'd raised her chin to meet his insistent gaze. 'Yes. Yes, I think you should.'

He'd squatted down on his haunches, so that he was on a level with her. 'Are you really going to marry Robert?'

'I don't know.'

'Don't marry him. Marry me,' he'd said. Then he'd crawled over the rocks and did something that Robert had never done – kissed her full on the lips.

Elspeth shades her eyes from the sun and turns her head to look east out to the Bass Rock. Farther off down the path, where the trees and undergrowth were thicker, she sees an unmistakable flash of blonde hair and a familiar, petite figure. Ann. Elspeth feels a slight stab of confusion. Didn't Ann say she was going into Edinburgh today? But Elspeth sits forward on the bench, raises her hand to wave and draws breath to call her name – but the shout never comes.

With her arm still raised, she watches as a dark-haired man she'd assumed to be just a passer-by pulls Ann towards him. Sunlight is eclipsed between their bodies and they kiss. Elspeth lets her hand fall to her lap and looks down at the ground. Was it here that she first met Gordon? Or was it farther towards that oak tree? She looks back down the path again. Their bodies are parting now. There is sunlight between them again. They are talking. Ann cups her hand around his jaw. It is a gesture so familiar to Elspeth: she has seen her do it to the children, to Ben.

The man walks off quickly, away from Elspeth. Ann sets off in the other direction. Elspeth watches her daughter-in-law walk more slowly down the winding path within a hundred yards of her, then disappear out of the Lodge gates. Elspeth looks again at the receding back of the man, then she stoops as if she's experiencing physical pain, pressing the ball of her fist into her closed eyes. An even worse thought has suddenly occurred to her.

Two days later Alice answered the office intercom in the middle of the morning.

'I'm here to see Alice Raikes.'

The line crackled and the sound of traffic in the street came booming down the line. She couldn't place the voice. 'Who is it?'

'My name's John Friedmann.'

She slammed down the handset at once. 'Oh, shit.'

Everyone in the office looked up. Then she pressed the button to let him in. 'Oh, shit, shit.' She tore open her bag and seized her hairbrush and began sweeping it through her hair in long, urgent strokes.

'Who on earth is it?' Susannah shouted across the office. Anthony, the new director, appeared out of his room.

'What's going on?' he asked mildly. 'Why is Alice running around?'

'Oh, God. Don't ask . . . bugger . . . What am I going to do? How do I look?' Alice appealed to Susannah.

'Completely mad.'

She galloped down the first flight of stairs then slowed her pace so as not to appear red in the face and panting when she saw him. He was standing at the bottom of the stairs, reading one of the literacy posters stuck on the wall.

'Hello.'

He turned and smiled as if he'd been caught doing something wrong. She tried to ignore her stomach, which was trying to cram itself up into her throat. 'Hi,' she said, leaning in what she hoped was a casual manner on the banister. 'What are you doing here? Did you forget to ask me something for the interview?'

He shook his head.

'Did you read the book?'

'No. Not yet.'

There was an agonising pause. She fiddled with her hair and put a strand of it into her mouth.

'I was just passing through Covent Garden and . . .' He stopped, sighed and cast his eyes up at the ceiling. Then he slung his bag to the floor, looked at her and said, 'I think we both know that's a lie.'

A curious thing happened to Alice's face. The muscles around her mouth, the ones that controlled her smile, seemed to go into spasm and she had to bite her lips so as not to appear to be grinning in a rather brainless way. She looked at the floor. A taxi rumbled past outside. He rubbed his hand against the weft of his stubble. 'You have to come and see a film with me tonight.'

Her smile disappeared immediately. 'What do you mean, I "have to"? Aren't you supposed to say things like "please" and "would you like to"?'

'No. Why should I when it's perfectly obvious to me that you are a witch and that you've put some evil spell on me?' He came towards her. Oh, my God, was he going to kiss her? Right here? She panicked and backed into the stand holding poetry competition leaflets. He came so close that she could feel the sweep of his breath on her neck: she was sure that he would be able to hear her heart pounding. She forced herself to hold his gaze without smiling. 'I love it when you're angry,' he whispered.

Her laughter burst out of her like water from a dam and she thumped him hard on the chest. 'You are the most infuriating man I have ever met. I would never go to the cinema with you! Never! Not even if . . . if . . .' she floundered for the most outrageously hurtful situation '. . . not even if it was my favourite film playing for the last time ever and you had the last spare ticket. Not even then!'

John rubbed his chest where she'd hit him. 'Every time I see you I get injured in some way. But I'm optimistic. Not even a witch can do much damage in a cinema.'

'I'm not coming!' she shouted.

'Yes, you are,' he shouted back.

'I'm not! I'd never go anywhere with you.'

She sees him first, outside the cinema in Shaftesbury Avenue, his head bent over a newspaper, frowning slightly. He glances up the street in the opposite direction to the one she's coming in. She sees that he's resting one foot on the bridge of the other, that he's quite tall, and the anxiety in the curve of his neck as he cranes to see up the crowded pavement.

'Hey,' she says, tapping the newspaper, 'you're off-duty, you know. You can put that away now.'

Relief floods his face as he turns towards her. They don't touch, but stand apart. 'You're late, Alice Raikes. I thought—'

'I'm always late.'

'I'll remember that . . .'

She sees that he was about to say 'next time' but stopped himself.

'Do you want to go in, or shall we just stand and smile at each other all evening?'

He laughs. 'We could, but I'm afraid you'd get bored. Let's go in.'

Alice walks beside him, her hands in her jacket pockets, talking about the film. When she is emphasising a point she turns her body towards him and says, 'Don't you think?' She is wearing close-fitting, dark navy jeans and heavy-soled boots with metal heels that flash in the neon signs of Soho. Outside a Japanese noodle bar she stops and inhales, closing her eyes.

'What is it?' he asks.

'I love that smell.'

John sniffs but can only smell the bitter-sweet stench of rotting vegetables and the acrid, burnt smell of stir-fry.

'It really reminds me of Japan,' she says.

'You've been there?'

'Yeah. I spent about a month in Tokyo.'

'Really? When?'

'During one of my university holidays. I did lots of travelling then – those long holidays were the best thing about being a student.'

'Did you like Japan?'

'I loved it. It was very exciting. I was ready to leave when I did, though. Tokyo's such a frenetic city. We went straight from there to Thailand, and spent a few weeks recovering on a beach.'

We? John thinks.

'Who were you with?' he says casually.

'An ex-boyfriend of mine.'

He has to swallow hard to stop himself from shouting, who was he? did you love him? how long did you go out with him for? when did you split up? do you still see him?

'What would you like to do now?' he asks instead.

'Don't know. Got any ideas?'

'I've got a problem, rather than ideas.'

'What?' She looks at him sideways through her hair which she must have loosened sometime during the film. When she arrived earlier, it was knotted at the nape of her neck. Sometimes he finds her gaze a bit unsettling.

'Well, because I spent quite a lot of my day running around Covent Garden in a state of teenage angst about some woman . . .' he looks at her carefully; she has bowed her head and the curtain of hair has slid further over her face '. . . I got no work done. I have to have a two-thousand-word article about independent American cinema in by nine tomorrow.'

'I see.' She shakes back her hair. 'That is a bit of a problem.'

'Mmm. At least I can kid myself that I was doing research for it tonight.' He nods in the direction of the cinema.

'We-ell,' she rocks back and forth on her boots, 'I think I'll head home, then.'

'Where is it you live?'

'Finsbury Park. How about you?'

'Camden. Can I give you a lift?'

'You've got a car?'

'Yes. It's my one luxury in life. I need it to get to assignments, or that's what I tell myself. Do you disapprove?'

'Not at all. It's pure envy.'

'Would a lift help you with your envy, or make it worse?'

He sees her hesitate, unsure. 'Alice, don't worry, I haven't been drinking. I'm not a mad axe murderer and I solemnly promise not to molest you.' Unless, of course, you want me to, he adds mentally.

She lets herself get as far as closing the car door before she says, 'Do you want to come in for a minute? If you need to get off, then maybe—'

He is out of the car in seconds and even takes the keys out of her hands and opens the door for her. 'Up here?' he asks, heading for the communal staircase.

'Right at the top.'

He waits by the flat door for her. 'Do you live on your own?' he asks, only a little tensely.

'Yeah. I prefer it. I shared with some friends for a while but found I never saw them apart from when we met to argue over whose turn it was to clean the bathroom. Then I lived with my boyfriend, my ex-boyfriend I should say, which didn't exactly work out.' She says this avoiding his eye, feeling his interest crackling between them. 'This place is only supposed to be temporary, but I've been here five months already.'

She is surprised at how curious he is, poking his head into each room of the tiny flat.

'It's a bit grim, isn't it?' she shouts.

'It's OK. I've seen worse.'

He comes into the kitchen. 'Is that you?' He is peering at a photo of her and Beth on a beach. They are in swimming costumes, lying on their stomachs in a rock-pool.

'Oh, God, don't look at that.' She comes to stand behind him, looking over his shoulder. 'I was about eighteen, I think. That's my younger sister, Beth. I always liked that photo of us and I lost the only copy I had ages ago. Beth sent me this reprint last week. It's funny, I never thought then that it was one of the last times I'd be living at home with my sisters. I was desperate to leave home, but didn't really notice when I did. It just kind of happened.'

He has pulled it off the wall and is holding it close to his face in one hand; in his other he rolls the Blu-tack that held it to the wall. 'Have you always had long hair?' he asks.

'Not always. Not when I was little, and I cut it soon after that picture was taken.'

He turns to her and she realises how close they're standing. The atmosphere changes in that instant.

'How long did it take to grow again?' he murmurs.

'Er.' She can't remember anything at all right now. 'About four years,' she hazards.

He puts out a hand to touch her hair and slowly winds a strand of it around his finger. She shivers.

'Are you cold?'

'No.'

He bends towards her, curling his fingers around the back of her neck. His mouth brushes hers very gently. It feels surprisingly soft and warm. She allows herself to lean into him, bringing her arms up to the small of his back to press him closer. She can feel the thud of his heart through his jumper and she closes her eyes.

'Shit,' he says, with a sudden violence, and pulls away. She is unbalanced, both by his movement and the shock. She nearly falls and puts out a hand to steady herself, catching the soft mound of flesh at the base of the thumb on the corner of the table. Her hand begins to throb all the way up to her elbow and she raises it to her mouth.

John has hurled himself, rather over-dramatically, Alice feels, into the kitchen chair and is clutching his head between his hands, elbows resting on the table. She is determined not to speak first. When his voice does come, it is muffled: 'Alice, I'm so sorry.'

She cannot answer and stands there, her hand pressed to her mouth. He looks up. 'Did you hurt your hand?'

He reaches out but she steps back. He flinches. They

stay like that in silence for a minute or two – Alice standing and John looking at her imploringly. He takes a deep
breath: 'The thing is . . . the problem is . . . This sounds
so awful . . . I'm kind of . . . with someone else at the
moment . . .'

She nods, but feels as if her body is beginning a sickening,
giddy slide down a steep incline.

'It means nothing to me, Alice . . . It's not what you
think . . .'

'Please don't. Let's . . . let's just forget it.'

'It's not what you think,' he repeats urgently, 'I guarantee you.'

'And what is it that I think, according to you?' she asks.
The words sound odd to her – over-enunciated, clipped.

'That I'm a two-timing bastard,' he says. 'It's not that. The
thing is—'

'Forget it,' she interrupts him, 'just forget it. It doesn't
matter. You've got a girlfriend. Let's leave it at that.'

He pushes his hand through his hair. 'Sophie's not my
girlfriend . . . not really . . . and the point is . . .'

'Please,' she turns and walks to the window, 'I really don't
want to hear about it.'

Four floors below, cars zoom past, their headlights sweeping over John's car, parked just outside her flat.

'I think you should leave now,' she says.

If she stays here with her back to him, he'll go and she'll
never have to lay her eyes on him again.

'You don't mean that,' she hears him say behind her, and
she whirls round to face him.

'I certainly do mean it. Get out of my flat. Now.'

He doesn't move from his seat at her table. Alice stares at
him, incredulous, meeting his gaze for the first time since –
when was it? – he'd been touching her hair and they'd been

about to kiss. Time seems to have splintered and it feels as if that was hours ago.

'I want you to leave,' she says, with deliberate slowness, as if explaining something to a foreigner. 'I don't allow anyone to fuck me about.'

'You have to believe me,' he says, 'I'm not fucking you about. I really am not. Just let me explain—'

'Explain?' she demands. 'What explanation is there? That things aren't going too well with your girlfriend so you thought you'd try it on with me instead? Well, don't worry. Nothing's happened. There's nothing you're going to have to lie to her about.'

He is looking down at the table top now. He lays his hands on the fake teak surface, palms down, fingers splayed out. 'How many times do I have to tell you? Sophie's not my girlfriend. She's nothing to me. She doesn't really give a shit about me, it's just—'

'Sex?' Alice suggests.

'No.' He looks up, outraged. 'I wasn't going to say that.'

He stands and comes across the kitchen towards her. She looks away from him and folds her arms across her body.

'And how can you say,' he says, 'that nothing has happened here tonight?'

She pushes past him, strides down the hallway and wrenches open the door. 'Get out. I'm not going to tell you again.'

She sees him hesitate, then reach for his keys on the table and come towards her. He has to pass very close to her to get out of the door, and as he does so, he clasps her arm and goes to kiss her cheek. She pulls away as if he's burnt her, bumping her head on the door edge. He puts his hand over hers, presses it to the side of her forehead. 'I'm sorry,' he whispers, next to her ear.

Alice feels tears rising to the surface, and she pushes his hand away.

'Just go. Please,' she says, looking down at his feet.

'I'm going to sort things out and call you tomorrow, and then I'll explain everything, OK?'

She shrugs.

Then he is gone and there is a cold draught blowing through her open door. She shuts it, listening to his feet drumming down the stairs. Then the front door slams and it's only after she hears his car start up that she moves away from the door.

She walks into the bathroom and turns the hot tap on full. The pipes gurgle and cough out tepid water. She keeps her hand under the flow, and when it feels hotter, she pushes the plug into place. As the room fills with steam, she stands in front of the mirror.

You'll never see him again, she tells herself. The places where he touched her — her neck, her lips and her arm — seem raw, almost painful. She looks herself right in the eye, daring herself to cry. Then she presses her hand against her shirt, over her heart, and says, in what she thinks is a strong yet offhand voice, 'I never want to see you again.' She can detect only the slightest quickening in her heart's beat, only the faintest tightening of her throat. She'll have it perfect by tomorrow.

Ben is finding it difficult to concentrate on what the doctor is saying. Behind him, illuminated on lightboxes, are cross-sections of Alice's brain. He can see her eye sockets, her cheekbones, her forehead, her nose etched out in ghostly greyish photo-negative. The brain itself is a swirled, ridged confusion of dark patches, dips, valleys, folds.

'There's really nothing more I can tell you at this stage,' the doctor says, spreading his hands as if finishing a magic trick.

'But . . . but is there anything we should be doing?' Ann asks.

'You can talk to her, play music that means something to her, read aloud. It's important to try to jog her out of this state.' The doctor stands at this point, screwing up his face as if short-sighted, pacing up and down behind his desk. 'You know,' he begins, 'the police and some of the witnesses are saying that . . . the accident . . . may have been . . . a deliberate attempt on Alice's part to . . . to take her life. We don't know this for sure yet, but . . .'

Ben's throat is filled with a taste of straw. Out of the corner of his eye, he sees Ann uncross and recross her legs, lean forward: 'You mean . . . suicide? Alice was trying to commit suicide?'

'It's a possibility. They're not certain. But it is something we have to take into consideration.'

'Into consideration?' Ben repeats, dazed. 'In what way?'

'It's crucial to keep stimulating her.' The doctor sighs. 'What I'm saying is, she's not going to wake up if there's nothing to wake up for, is she?'

They sit at Alice's bed without speaking. Ann's hands are twisted into the strap of her handbag. Ben fingers the small clear zip-lock plastic bag containing the things Alice had on her at the time of the accident. The doctor had given it to them. Ben imagines that the doctor had been there as the things were pulled or cut from Alice's torn, bloodied pockets: the wallet with exactly £2.80 in coins, half a packet of spearmint-flavoured chewing-gum (sugar-free), a platinum wedding ring and a key-ring with three serrated-edged latchkeys and two chunkier deadlock keys. Nothing more. Attached by its mouth to the key-ring is a small enamelled fish, tarnished with a mineral green, articulated with brass joints so the tail can flick from side to side. It's Japanese, Ben knows, but can't remember how he knows this. Did Alice tell him at some point? He extracts the wedding ring from the bag and holds it up to the light between his thumb and index finger. It feels light and warm. There is no inscription.

'I don't believe it,' Ann says suddenly. 'I don't believe it. Alice wouldn't do that.'

'Do you think so?'

'Absolutely. They've made a mistake. She just wouldn't do it. I mean, it used to cross my mind sometimes that she might. After John and everything. But it's not Alice somehow, is it? She's much too . . . defiant.'

'Mmm. Maybe.' Then Ben remembers something: 'Kirsty said Alice was in Edinburgh yesterday.'

'Edinburgh?'

'Yes. I meant to tell you. Kirsty told me this morning on the phone.'

'Alice was in Edinburgh yesterday?' Ann is frowning, as if she thinks Ben is lying. 'When yesterday?'

'I don't know. Alice phoned from the train, I think, and Kirsty and Beth met her at Waverley.'

'Waverley?' Ann's voice cracks. 'What time?'

'I don't know,' Ben says again. 'Alice stayed for about five minutes, Kirsty said, and then just got on a train back to London.'

Ann stands up so quickly that her bag falls to the floor. Purse, paper, comb, hankies, cigarettes, lipsticks, keys skitter over the tiles, under the bed, between the chair legs. She ducks down to pick the things up one by one, clutching them to her middle.

'Are you all right?' Ben asks, stooping to help her.

'Yes. Of course I am. Why wouldn't I be?' Ann goes to the door and pulls it open. 'I think I might go for a cigarette.'

'Right,' Ben calls after her. 'See you later, then.'

'Alice, it's me. Listen,' his voice is trembling, 'everything's sorted.'

She curls her fingers more tightly around the receiver, but says nothing.

'Alice? Are you there?'

'Yes.'

'Then say something.'

'I don't know what to say.'

'Just . . . just tell me I didn't blow it last night.'

'John, there's nothing to "blow", as you put it. You're with someone else and you did an interview with me and we went to the cinema. Nothing happened.'

He is silent. She can hear the office behind him; the buzz of telephones and the gentle cacophony of keyboards clicking.

'Alice,' he says, with difficulty, 'I'm not with someone else. I wasn't before, not really, and I'm certainly not now.'

She doesn't answer. He tries again. 'Alice, please . . . you can't say that nothing has happened . . . Look, I'm in trouble here . . . I don't go around doing this all the time . . .'

She removes the receiver from her ear. Her hand hovers. Hang up on him, she tells herself, hang up. To give herself strength, she tries to recall the sliding, slippery feeling of the night before when he pulled away from her.

'Don't hang up! Please don't . . . Alice? I know you're there. Please say something or . . . or . . . I'm going to go mad.'

'Don't be melodramatic.'

'Oh, hello there. I thought I was on my own for a minute. Why are you being so stubborn?'

'I'm not being stubborn. I just refuse to let you mess me about. Why should I? What about Sophie? What did she—'

'Fuck Sophie,' John interrupts vehemently. 'You must listen – she was nothing to me, I was nothing to her. She wasn't the problem.'

'Then what was?'

He hesitates. 'I can't tell you now.'

'Why not?'

'I just can't.'

'Why? Because you're in the office?'

'No, it's not that. It would just take too long to explain. Alice, please, just give me one more chance. Just one – that's all I ask, and if I fuck up again I swear I'll never darken your phone line again. I'm so sorry about last night. Just give me a chance to explain myself. Please.'

Her mind is whirring through possibilities – it's not his girlfriend, he can't talk about it in the office, it takes a long time to explain. What can it be? If it's not another woman, then . . . no . . . surely not.

'John?'

'Yes?'

'This problem of yours . . .'

'Alice, I told you. I can't explain now. I need to see you and then I'll tell you everything. I promise.'

'It's not . . . You're not . . . ?'

'What?'

'Are you . . . ill?'

'Ill?' he repeats.

She sighs with exasperation. 'Are you HIV positive? Because if it's that, then you might as well just tell me now.'

He gives a short laugh. 'God, no, nothing like that. No, I'm in perfect physical health, though I'm not sure about mental right at this moment.'

'Oh.'

There is a long and strained silence. She scribbles furious, spiky doodles on the notepad in front of her in black biro.

'Look,' John says, 'we can't talk about this over the phone. Have you got a pen there?'

'Uh-huh.'

'OK. Write this down: Helm Crag Hotel. That's two words, H-E-L-M and crag, C—'

'I know how to spell "crag", but why   '

'Just write it. Have you got it?'

'Yes, but what—'

'OK, that's Easedale Road, Grasmere. Now, there's a train leaving Euston at five fifteen. Write that down too. You'll need to change at Oxenholme and get a train to Windermere. From there you can get a taxi to the hotel, which is just outside Grasmere in a valley called Easedale. The reservation's under my name.'

'John, if you think I'm just going to—'

'Now. I've got to review a play in Manchester tonight so I'll be getting there a bit later on. It could be nearer two or three in the morning.'

'What the hell—'

'I know. I'm sorry about that, but it can't be avoided. I'll be driving, you see, all the way from Manchester. But you can have dinner and go for a walk—'

'John! Listen to me!'

'What?'

'I never want . . .' Alice begins the first words of a long speech she rehearsed in the bath the night before, but immediately forgets the rest.

'Anyway,' he continues, as if she hadn't spoken, 'we can spend all of Saturday and Sunday together. I doubt I'm going to be able to take Monday off, otherwise—'

'What are you talking about? There's no way, absolutely no way, I'm coming to some hotel in the Lake District with you. I can tell you that right now.'

'Why not?'

'Why not? What do you mean, "why not?" I hardly know you, apart from anything else. You must be mad if you think I'm just going to drop everything and jump on a train for a dirty weekend with you.'

'Who said it's going to be dirty?'

'There's no point in even discussing it. I've got plans for the weekend anyway.'

'Cancel them.'

'No way. The whole thing's completely out of the question.'

'You must come. Please. We need to talk about things and I think we should both get out of London. It's all arranged. It's the most beautiful hotel ever. You'll love it. It's completely vegetarian.'

'How did you know I'm vegetarian?'

'You told me in the canteen when we did the interview.'

'Did I? I don't remember that.'

'Well, I do. Alice, please come. What do I have to do to convince you? Tell me and I'll do it.'

'You are the most arrogant person I have ever met. Give me one reason, one good reason, why I should cancel all my plans this weekend to spend a weekend, where it will most probably rain, with a man with a . . . a . . . dubious secret.'

'Because,' he says softly, 'I don't know how I'm going to bear it if you don't.'

Molly, the girl on duty that night, woke up at the sound of a car crunching on the gravel outside. She sat up, still dressed in the flowered uniform of the hotel, and groped for her watch. It was 2.24 a.m. She stumbled out of bed, tripping on her shoes that she'd kicked off earlier and pulled on a jumper.

Standing in the hallway was a dark-haired man. Youngish. Good-looking. They didn't get many young guests. They tended to be older people here for the view, or bearded hill-walking types here for the mountains. He was holding a black grip-bag and a portable computer. He smiled when he saw her tiptoeing down the stairs.

'Hi. I'm so sorry to wake you this late,' he whispered.

'That's OK. Mr Friedmann, is it?'

'That's right.'

'Have you had a long drive from somewhere?'

'Well, London this afternoon, but I had to spend the evening in Manchester.'

'Oh, right. On business?'

'Yeah. You could call it that. I had to sit through one of the worst and most excruciating pieces of theatre I have ever seen in my life.'

Molly laughed. 'Why?'

'It's my job. Somebody's got to do it.'

'Are you some sort of a critic or something?'

He nodded.

'Would you like anything to eat?'

'Is that a real pain for you? I don't need anything hot. Just a sandwich would be great.'

'Sure. If you could just sign here,' Molly passed over the registration book, 'and here's your key.'

He recoiled as if she'd handed him some dog shit on a plate. 'Key?'

'Yeah. The key to your room. You could take your bags up while I make your sandwich.'

'You mean this is the key to my room and it's still down here at the desk?' He was gabbling like an idiot now.

'Well, that's where we keep them.' There was something decidedly strange about this guy. He looked like he'd just received the worst news of his life, like she'd just told him his mother had died or something.

'Oh.'

'Is there a problem with that, Mr Friedmann?'

'A problem?' He stared at her for so long she began to feel self-conscious. She began working out how loudly she'd have to shout to get the other girls to hear her. This guy was weird. 'No. No problem,' he said soulfully, and reached down to pick up his bag. 'I'll take this up to my room.'

'Well, you'd better be quiet about it. Your wife went to bed hours ago.'

'My what?' he snapped.

'Your wife.' Did he not understand her accent or something?

'My wife!' he cried, suddenly jubilant. 'She's here? I mean, she's come?'

'Yes. She checked in earlier, had dinner then went straight upstairs.'

'Did she? That's great!' He leapt to his feet, beaming like a madman, seized his bag and started up the stairs, two at a time.

'Do you still want the sandwich, Mr Friedmann?' she hissed after him.

'No, don't worry about that. Thanks for your help. Goodnight.'

Molly began thumbing through the bookings file. How long would he be here for?

When John closed the door behind him it was completely dark and he couldn't see a thing after the luminous light of the corridor. He stood motionless, still clutching his bag and computer, waiting for his eyes to get accustomed to the dark. Somewhere in the room he could hear Alice breathing. He was suddenly seized with an urgent and inappropriate desire to break into hysterical giggles and had to put his bag down and clamp his hand over his mouth. The urge subsided, which was lucky. She probably wouldn't take kindly to being woken in the middle of the night by a cackle of mad laughter. He was then struck by the thought that he couldn't remember the name of the mad woman in *Jane Eyre*. Something beginning with B. Alice would know, but he felt that might be an even worse reason to wake her. Beryl, was it? Beryl Rochester didn't sound right somehow. Beryl . . . Beattie . . . Beatrice . . . Bridget? No. Shit, what the hell was her name? This was going to annoy him all night unless he could remember. His brain carried on helpfully supplying him with women's names beginning with B. Biddy . . . Beth . . . Bridie . . . Shut up, brain. Brain, sit. Lie down. Stay.

He could now discern a glow from behind the curtains. He could make out the white of the bed sheets and — ohthankyougodI'lldoatleastonegooddeedeverydayfortherestofmylifeforthisIpromise — the white of Alice's skin and the black of her hair. She was lying on her side with her back to him, her breathing regular. John sat down on a chair by his side of the bed and unlaced his boots. Did she always sleep that side of a double bed? Did the ex-boyfriend she'd mentioned sleep this side? Maybe he should go round the other side. Oh, for God's sake, John, just get into the sodding bed, will you? He stripped down to his shorts — well, it wouldn't do to appear too presumptuous, would it, he didn't want to frighten the living daylights out of the girl. What was she wearing? He leant over the bed cautiously. It was hard to tell. Her hair was covering her shoulders. Maybe she was naked. The thought made him want to leap straight into the bed there and then. But, hang on, if she was naked and he got into bed with his shorts on, she might think he was a bit of a sad git. Or, worse, a virgin. But if she wasn't and he got into bed beside her completely in the buff, she could get the fright of her life and think he was pulling a fast one. Which he was anyway. He looked helplessly round the room for clues. Her clothes were strewn on the chair beside her side of the bed. He was struck with another thought. Where had he put those condoms he bought in Manchester? He was just about to start rummaging through his luggage when he envisaged a horrible scenario: Alice waking up and turning on the light to see him looming beside the bed dressed only in a pair of jockey shorts, brandishing a large box of condoms.

He pulled back the covers and eased himself into bed. Please wake up now. Go on. It would be perfect. She would wake up slowly and sense him there. Then they could cuddle and maybe — no, for heaven's sake, not yet.

'Alice?' he whispered. He couldn't help himself.

He edged over the bed towards her. She was wearing a nightdress. Thank the Lord. It was some kind of thin, pale, filmy material.

'Alice?' he murmured again. Please wake up, Alice.

John realised in complete and utter horror that he was getting a huge and urgent erection. Shit, shit, shit. For fuck's sake, what a way to wake her up — thrusting a large wanger between her thighs. Hi, darling. Missed me, did you? He broke out in a panicked sweat and moved away from her as fast as he could without bouncing the mattress too much. Oh, Christ, she was stirring and turning over. What the hell was he going to do if she woke up now? Lie on his front and not move? She'd think he was retarded or at least decidedly odd. Hi, Alice. Yeah, I'm fine. Just have to lie here for a few minutes and not move. How was the journey up by the way? She was waking up, John was now convinced of it. Her breathing was distinctly shallower and his erection showed no sign of going down. What the fuck was he going to do? Think of other things, quick . . . er . . . cold showers . . . what else, what else . . . medical examinations at school . . . er . . . times tables. Times tables! One eight is eight, two eights are sixteen, three eights are . . .

He sneaked a look over at Alice. Was she really still asleep or had she woken and was lying there, horrified into silence by the sex fiend in bed beside her? No, she was lying on her back, still fast asleep. John carried on looking. The sheet had slipped to her waist and through the thin material of her nightdress he could see the curve of her breasts and – shit, shit, he was back to the beginning. He was never going to get any sleep tonight and would be a blithering, sleep deprived idiot in the morning. Great company for Alice, who must have had a good five hours already.

Ann pushes through a side door into a garden, swearing as she catches the jutting bone of her wrist on the steel handle. The air feels close; a screen of grey cloud, hanging just above the glistening chimneys of the hospital, seems to press down on the city, trapping in the fumes and stale air.

Ann leans on an ornamental breeze-block wall stippled with sharp plaster spikes. The hospital surrounds her on four sides. The garden in which she is standing is so prefabricated that she can see the lines in the lawn where they laid down the turf sods. It's getting dark already. On her left-hand side is the corridor in which her daughter lies unconscious, shaven-headed, insensible to the world around her, lungs automated to inhale every four seconds.

Ann opens her cigarettes, pulls one out and, gripping it between her lips, searches her coat pockets for her box of matches. She has to strike the match's purple tip against the rasp of sandpaper three times before it catches flame. She holds the smoke in her mouth, watching the tip of the cigarette glow orange in the darkening air, then allows it to curl down into her chest, infiltrating each flower-like alveolus. She counts along the windows of the corridor, working out which one is Alice's.

Ann knows she should grind her cigarette into this wall, get back to the room, sit down next to her husband and daughter. But, for now, she doesn't. She stands, letting her smoke drift away from her on the breezeless air, watching the light blaze out in strips through the metal blind over Alice's window.

Elspeth stands at the bay window at the back of the house, looking out at her granddaughters. On the lawn, Beth turns cartwheels and calls to Alice every now and again, 'Were my legs straight then? Did you see? Watch this time.'

Alice, who has recently razored the ends of her hair into uneven jags and dyed a long streak of it an alarming kingfisher blue, lies on her stomach along the edge of the patio, clad entirely in black, reading. In a flash of skinny legs, white knickers and a rumple of skirts, Beth does another turn. 'That looked great,' says Alice, not looking up from her book.

'Did it?' Beth says, her face flushed with exertion. 'Did it, Kirsty?'

Kirsty, in a bikini, sits in the sun with tufts of cotton wool jammed between each of her toes. She shakes her nail-varnish bottle and, unscrewing the lid, says, 'Yeah. Perfect, Beth.'

'It's an absolute crime,' says a voice next to Elspeth. Elspeth turns to see Ann standing next to her. Three days have passed since that day in the Lodge. It's the weekend and Ben is out playing golf on the links by the sea.

'What is?' asks Elspeth.

'That,' Ann says, exasperated, pointing towards Alice. 'It's a crime to do that to hair as lovely as hers. I don't know what she thinks she looks like.'

Elspeth leans her hand on the window-sill and faces Ann. Above their heads are the black, sooty streaks from when, years ago, Alice inexplicably set fire to the curtains. 'There are worse crimes.'

Ann looks at her, surprised no doubt by the vehemence of her words.

'Don't you think, Ann?' Elspeth persists.

Under Elspeth's fierce look, Ann flushes a hot red. They stare at each other, Elspeth willing herself not to be the first to look away. Ann's head turns back towards the garden.

'Do you know what the Greeks did to adulterous women, Ann?'

There is no answer. Ann presses her hand to her mouth.

'Do you?'

Ann shakes her head without speaking.

'They were strapped to the back of a mare in the middle of a courtyard, filled with the family of the man. A stallion was then let loose and they all watched as the woman was slowly crushed to death as the stallion mounted the mare.'

'Please . . . don't,' Ann says.

'And do you know what else? I always thought what an utterly barbaric thing that was to do to anyone. Until now.'

'Does Ben know?'

'No. And he won't, if you can swear to me that you'll never see that man again.'

They look out, Elspeth at the girls, Ann's eyes focused somewhere on the horizon.

'Do you love him?' Elspeth asks.

'Who? Ben?'

Elspeth gives a short laugh. 'No. Not Ben. I know you don't love Ben. The other one.'

Ann shrugs defiantly. 'I don't really think I have to answer that question.'

'How long has it . . . have you . . . ?'

'Years.'

Elspeth sees that Ann is turning to go. She puts out a hand, grips her tiny, fragile wrist and drags her back to the window. 'People have always remarked – idly, I always thought and now I wonder just how many people do know – how odd it is that we have two small blonde girls and one tall dark one.' Elspeth pulls her round and forces her to look out of the window with her. 'And as I was standing here, I too was just thinking how odd it is. Look. Alice looks like a different species next to her sisters, she could be from a different family. Or a different father, perhaps. Odd, too, how Alice isn't in the least bit scientific like everyone else in this family, how she spends all day reading or playing the piano. Strange that her nature is much more tempestuous and impulsive than anyone else's. I can't think of anyone in my family who's like her. Can you? Can you think of anyone she reminds you of? Anyone at all?'

Ann fights against Elspeth's strong grasp. Elspeth releases her at last. 'Tell me.'

'Tell you what?'

'Is Alice Ben's?'

Ann looks out at Alice through the window. She is standing now beside Beth on the lawn, ready to catch her ankles when she does her handstand. 'Slowly,' she is saying, 'slowly, Beth. Otherwise you'll kick me in the face.' Kirsty is painting her toenails in laborious strokes, her personal stereo clamped over her ears.

'I . . . I don't know . . . I can't be certain . . . I'm almost sure she is.'

'Almost? What does that mean?'

'Exactly what it says.'

Alice wakes with a start. Something is not quite right. She swivels her eyes suspiciously from left to right. It is morning. Sunlight is streaming in through a large bay window. It's very quiet. No traffic. She can hear birds singing. Birds? Her clothes are on an antique chair just in front of her. She moves her head fractionally. The pillow case is white cotton with lace borders. She looks up; she's in a four-poster bed. She looks down; there is a male arm curved around her ribcage. She stares at it blankly. It is strong-looking, tanned, with black hairs. Its fingers are curled round its thumb. Its owner appears to be lying behind her, pressed up against her back.

Before she can investigate further, there is a knock at the door. She opens her mouth to say come in, but no sound emits from it. A few seconds later, she stares in astonishment as a girl with a mass of curly hair wearing a long, flowered skirt comes into view carrying a huge tray. 'Morning, Mrs Friedmann,' she says. 'Here's your breakfast. I'll leave it by the window.'

Alice is about to ask her why on earth she's calling her Mrs Friedmann, when the full truth suddenly hits her. Oh, Christ, oh, God, what is she doing here?

As soon as the door closes, she springs from the bed like a startled antelope, wrenching herself free of John's grasp. He grunts and topples into the dip her body has left in the soft mattress. Alice waits nervously, balancing on one leg. He opens his eyes. 'Hello,' he rubs his face groggily, 'you look lovely.'

She feels that there is a strong danger she's grinning foolishly. He certainly is. 'Breakfast's arrived,' she says, crossing the room to the window.

'Good. I'm starving. I didn't have any dinner last night.'

For something to do, she pulls back the curtains, feeling horribly conscious of the shortness of her nightdress. It barely covers her bum, for God's sake, but it's the only one she's got. She also suspects that against this strong sunlight it's very see-through. When she turns back to face him she can see from his glowing expression that it definitely is.

'What time did you arrive?' she asks him, in a rather formal voice.

'About three, I think.'

'How did you get on last night?'

He looks mysteriously panicked for a moment and then says, 'Oh, the play, you mean. Awful, actually.'

'Do you want some toast?'

'Come here,' he says, and holds out his arms.

'John,' she says, in a strangled voice, 'I can't. It's too . . . weird. I can't cope with all this,' she waves her hand around the room, taking in their bags, their crumpled clothes, the huge four-poster bed, 'before we've even . . . I mean, I haven't even kissed you yet. Not properly, anyway.'

He lets his arms drop on to the bedclothes. 'I know what you mean.'

'And,' she says, 'I've still got to hear about your mysterious secret. I mean, that is why we're here, isn't it?'

John is silent. Alice fidgets with the teacups on the breakfast tray and pretends to be admiring the view of Easedale.

'I'm very glad you said "yet",' he says quietly.

'Pardon?'

'I'm very glad you used the word "yet". You said, "I haven't even kissed you *yet*."'

'Well, I'd hardly be here if I . . . I mean . . .' She comes forward a few paces. 'John?' she says.

'Yes?'

'Are you . . . ?' She starts to giggle.

'Am I what?'

'Are you . . . ?' She giggles again. 'I mean, have you got any clothes on at all?'

He smiles proudly. 'Yes, I have. I kept my shorts on.' He kicks back the bedclothes in an arc and stands up. They stand there, Alice in her nightie, John in his shorts, about three feet apart, regarding each other.

'I think,' John begins slowly, 'that we'd better go out for a walk.'

If this is living, then it's like living in a cave or submarine and having the slenderest periscope reaching up to the outside world; a periscope so slender it picks up only smell and sound — and rarely at that.

Yesterday, last week, this year, a minute ago, this morning, two months ago — it could have been any of these — my nose dragged from the air down to where I am now a certain smell. They say smell is the most evocative of the senses. (I once considered having a relationship with a man who had a very limited sense of smell — I like to think things didn't work out between us because of this. After meeting him once, Rachel pronounced him an emotional retard and she was right. But if I am more charitable, how could he have been expected to develop to full emotional capacity without this associative tool? How could anyone live without that crucial link between immediate physical environment and interior recollection?)

As soon as this smell reached me, I was thinking of car

journeys as a child – stifled, sicky, bare legs glued to the seat covers, Beth's elbow pressing into my side, the three of us pleading for a window to be opened and our mother refusing because the breeze would mess her hair – and of a wardrobe we were forbidden to open, filled with immobile dresses strung by their shoulders from padded hangers. It was my mother's perfume, sprayed once a day on the pulse of her jugular vein and again on her wrists, and allowed to air before she puts on her clothes. It's a smell that trails behind her like a tail, bites into the air of any room she has been in, any clothes she has worn.

It can only mean one thing: my mother has been summoned. I feel somehow at a disadvantage in this – she can see me, but I can't see her. Is she there now, right now, this minute – whenever 'this minute' is? It's a horrible notion, that she could be there, sitting just outside my skin and I am crouched in here, waiting. She is somewhere up there, with my sisters, perhaps, and maybe even my father as well.

Alice and John walk around Easedale Tarn on a narrow path of stones and compacted earth. The terrain changes under her feet constantly, from dry, grassy turf to sodden, lurid-green marshy areas that cling, sucking, to her feet when she lifts them to step forwards. People pass at regular intervals. Alice says hello cheerfully, and so does John, but less cheerfully. He is walking about three paces behind her, mostly in silence, and has taken off his sweater and tied it round his waist. She is waiting for him to begin some sort of confession or explanation, but none has been forthcoming so far. She feels a tide of frustration gaining momentum within her, and knows that if he doesn't come out with it soon, she is likely to do something drastic.

As if to put this thought out of her head, she stops and looks about her. High ridges surround them on three sides and ahead of them is the wide, mirror-still, slate-grey expanse of water. She is unnerved by the flatness of the lake: there is no wind and the only movement on its surface are the lines drawn by the ducks, who glide in fussy, noisy groups around its edges.

John has come to stand close beside her. Rather too close, she decides, considering that he's made her wait for this bloody revelation for a good hour now. Suddenly she feels him take hold of her hand. She looks down in surprise. He is sliding his fingers between hers while looking out over the lake, as if unaware of what his hand is doing. This is most definitely not on. Alice extracts her hand from his and walks on. Behind her, she hears him mutter, 'Fair enough,' to himself in a faintly surprised tone.

'Alice,' he says, more audibly, 'do you want to sit down here for a bit?'

She turns and, with one hand resting on her hip, looks back down the path at him. 'All right.'

But when they sit he is silent, swigging water out of a bottle. What can be this serious? Alice wonders. He is sitting with his elbows hooked round his knees, facing the lake. He looks desperate, as if he's about to tell her something awful.

'So,' she says decisively.

'So,' he replies, turning to her, half smiling. Their faces are very close. She is looking at his mouth and finds herself imagining what it would be like to kiss him. Really kiss him. She is remembering the feel of his mouth on hers and beginning a private fantasy of them together on this damp turf beside the lake when she realises that her spine is beginning to bend involuntarily towards him. Her brain slams on some emergency brake and she sits bolt upright again. She incants Rachel's advice, given last night via a British Rail phone on the train: do not sleep with him until he tells you whatever it is. Do not do it, Alice, you're not allowed. She feels a little frightened all of a sudden: what can be this bad? He rests his hand on her wrist. 'Alice, how do you feel . . . about me?'

She shakes her head. 'I'm not telling you that when you're about to tell me you've got a wife and twelve children, or that you're about to emigrate to Australia, or that you're a convicted criminal who's starting a life sentence next week, or that you've recently decided you might be gay.'

He laughs.

'Am I close?' she asks.

'Not even remotely.' He lapses into silence again, his fingers stroking the branch of veins at her inner wrist. She looks up into the sky and sees a bird wheeling about in wide, sweeping circles. She looks down and, at that second, its reflection hits the lake surface on one of its downward curves. That's it, she thinks, I've had enough of this. She reaches down and starts unlacing her boots.

John realises in alarm that Alice is unbuttoning her jeans and peeling them off. 'What are you doing?' he says, looking around to check that no one else can see them. What on earth is going on? He was in the middle of telling her and suddenly she starts stripping off.

'I'm going in,' she says, as if he's asked her a really dense and unreasonable question.

'In . . . ?'

'In there,' she replies, pointing at the lake.

'But . . . it'll be freezing. Alice, don't. Come back.'

She ignores him, her feet making small plopping sounds as she steps gingerly into the dark water, her arms held out for balance. She lifts one foot out of the water, her toes splayed.

'It's so cold!' she exclaims, and then wades in much more quickly, leaving a trail of bubbles in her wake.

Utterly nonplussed, he stands and comes down to the

water's edge. She is now quite far out, up to her knees. 'Alice, please come back,' he bleats foolishly, 'you might slip and fall in. You'll get hypothermia.'

'It's fine, once you get used to it.'

'Stop pretending you're in an Arthurian legend and come out, please.'

Her laughter bounces towards him across the water's surface. He sees a middle-aged couple sitting farther along the bank, the wife pointing at Alice and the husband, John suspects, having a look at her – clad only in a skin-tight T-shirt and a pair of lacy knickers – through his binoculars. Alice shrieks and John sees her lurch to one side, struggle to regain her balance and then turn round to face him. The water reaches her thighs.

'Right, John Friedmann,' she calls across the water, cupping her hands around her mouth, 'this is your last chance.'

The middle-aged couple and several others who have stopped on the path look back at him expectantly.

'What do you mean?'

'If you don't tell me what the problem was the other night, I'm going to swim to that bank,' she points to the bank opposite them, 'and you'll never see me again.'

John looks over at it. He estimates that she could probably swim it faster than he could walk all the way round to it. Is this some kind of test, a dare? Does she expect him to go in after her?

'You want me to tell you right now?' he asks, playing for time.

'Right now,' she says, then adding maliciously, 'now or never.'

'Alice,' he attempts to reason, 'can't we talk about this . . .' he gestures towards the people watching '. . . a little more privately?'

She shakes her head. 'You've had all morning to talk to me privately. I can't wait any longer. Tell me now.'

He looks at her across the water, her head on one side, her hands clasped behind her back, shivering in the icy water. Would she swim away if he didn't tell her? He couldn't risk it.

'I'm Jewish,' he shouts back at her.

There is a pause. She looks as if she's waiting for him to elaborate. He shrugs helplessly. The collective gaze of the people on the bank is fixed on Alice, waiting for her reaction.

'That's it?' she says.

'Yes.'

'So why's that a problem?'

'Because . . . you're not.'

She seems to be considering this, looking up at the sky, then back at him. There is a pause for a good few minutes, Alice standing in the lake, John in an agony of suspense on the bank, flanked by spectators. He is just considering removing his own boots and trousers and going in after her, when she speaks again: 'So you don't think you can get it together with me because I'm not Jewish? Is that it? That's why you . . .' she pauses, selecting her words, presumably in view of the audience they have '. . . stalled the other night in the kitchen?'

'I didn't think I could,' John corrects. 'I thought I'd decided that non-Jewish girls were out of bounds.'

'And now?'

'Now . . . I think I don't care about that any more.'

She doesn't reply. He waits, agitated, shifting from foot to foot.

'Alice, please come in now.'

'I'm thinking.'

'OK. Sorry.'

He turns round to glare at the people, who dissemble and make a pretence of walking on. When he turns round again she is wading back to him, a very serious look on her face. He stretches out his hand for hers, and when he manages to grasp it, it's blood-stoppingly cold. He pulls her in and hugs her to him. 'God, you're freezing,' he exclaims and, touching them with his fingertips, says, 'Your lips are turning blue.'

She pulls away and gives him a very level stare. 'We need to talk about this,' she says.

'I know.'

Alice takes the sugar cubes out of their bowl one by one and builds them into a tiny wall, cantilevering out the edges so that it wobbles precariously on the Formica surface of the table. John watches her. 'It must sound ridiculous to you,' he says after a while.

She is in the process of adding a fifth layer to her wall. While she reaches for another cube, she curls her hand around it as if protecting it from the danger of strong draughts. 'No,' she muses, 'not ridiculous.' She wedges it into a small gap, but the structural tension is blown by one cube too many and the whole thing collapses with a loud clatter on to the table.

'Damn,' she says, and sweeps them all back into the bowl. She brushes the loose granules from her fingertips, glancing at the waitress's disapproving stare from behind the safety of the cappuccino machine, then rests her elbows on the table edge and looks at John, concentrating properly on him again. 'Not ridiculous,' she repeats, 'more strange, I suppose. Outdated. I mean, I've heard of it happening before to people but I think I thought it only really happened in extremist religious sects. I'd kind of worked out you were Jewish, what with your name and the fact that you don't exactly look Aryan, but it never even occurred to me that it could be a problem.'

'The thing is,' he says, 'it's not so much about religion. It's hard to explain. It's more to do with . . . with . . . social identity than God. It's more race than belief. I mean . . . I went to Jewish classes three times a week and . . . well . . . all this has been drummed into me from a very early age.'

'I see,' she mumbles, a little out of her depth now. She looks out of the window. Tourists wander up and down Grasmere's main street. A woman wearing a long red mac over shorts and wellingtons stops right beside her on the other side of the glass to read the menu displayed just above Alice's head. Alice stares at her, feeling how odd it is that a stranger thinks they can stand that close to you just because there's a pane of glass between you. The woman looks down and sees Alice looking at her and steps back. Her face is annoyed, embarrassed, and she tries to read the menu at her new distance, screwing up her eyes with effort.

'So Sophie was . . . ?'

John laughs and bites his lip. 'Sophie was a bit of a disaster area. She's a family friend. A nice Jewish girl, as my father would say. I think I thought . . . I think both of us thought it would be really good if things magically worked out between us, but they didn't, of course. I was going to finish it last weekend, but I didn't get a chance to see her and then I met you and that kind of took everything over. My father is so desperate for me to meet a Jewish girl . . .' He lapses into silence, his chin cupped in his hand.

Alice watches him, waiting for him to elaborate.

'He's not going to be too happy about this, but . . .' he gives a dismissive shrug '. . . that's his problem. It's all been made worse, you see, because my mother died and my father came over all religious,' he finishes abruptly.

'Oh,' says Alice, jarred, 'I'm sorry. About your mother, I mean.'

At that moment, the waitress appears, giving them what Alice feels to be a rather sinister smile. Alice's next sentence is halted in her throat and they both lean back into their seats as the waitress places more coffee in front of them. She seems to spend an age piling their used plates and cups on to her tray, and while she is scraping the crockery over the table surface, Alice takes a cautious look at John. He is looking at her and she is so discomfited – by what he's just told her, the question over what will happen now, whether he's changed his mind, whether she's changed her mind – she feels a maddening heat diffuse over her face. She looks away, starts blowing on the surface of the scalding coffee in front of her, fiddles with the spoon in her saucer.

'Alice, when I say that my father won't be too happy about it,' John says hastily, once the waitress has gone, 'I'm not automatically assuming anything . . . I mean, I'm not taking it as read that we're going to . . . get . . . involved or anything. I mean, it depends on what you think . . . I don't want to jump the gun . . .' He grinds to a halt.

Alice lifts the spoon and looks into it. On one side is her face, distorted, all mouth and nose, and on the other is the room behind her, the waitress stretched like an inverted comma, walking on the ceiling. Alice drops it back into the saucer. She allows her eyes to focus on the man in front of her – on his hands, inches from hers on the table's red Formica, on his shoulders, on his eyes, his mouth. How could she ever think she might have changed her mind? She feels shy suddenly – not a feeling she is used to. It seems harder to touch him now, sitting in this café, than when they'd been beside the lake. She feels unable to reach out for him but almost scared to move in case any movement is interpreted by him as a move of rejection.

He stretches his arms over the table and presses her head

between his hands. Moments later, they are kissing and kissing as if there is no one else in the room with them; people at neighbouring tables look for a moment, then look away; the waitress tuts and rolls her eyes heavenwards; others on the pavement outside nudge their companions, pointing.

On Sunday, at about nine o'clock in the morning, John comes out of the bathroom in one of the hotel's robes.

'Do you know what?' says Alice from the bed.

'What?' He sees that she is wearing one of his jumpers and gets a little lift of pleasure from this. She's lying on her stomach reading a book with her feet waving in the air. She looks about fourteen.

'We might as well have stayed in London. I mean, it's not as if we've seen much of Easedale or the Lake District.'

'How can you say that, when we've got this spectacular view?' He throws open the curtains with a dramatic flourish. 'You urban philistine.' He sits down at the table in the window, where he's set up his computer, and begins towelling his hair violently.

He hears her bare feet thudding over the floor then feels her hands on his. 'John, if you carry on doing that, you'll be bald by the time you're thirty.'

'I need some blood to my brain if I'm ever going to write this article. And anyway,' he says, from under the towel, 'there's no danger of me going bald. I come from a long line of men with full heads of hair.'

'Are you sure about that?' She whips the towel off his head like a barber then runs her hands down inside the robe, kissing the back of his neck.

'Alice . . . no,' John says, meaning, Alice, yes, carry on and do what you like. 'I have to . . . er . . . I really should . . .' He watches her fingers starting to untie the knot at his waist like a man paralysed. Where is the synapse that orders his hands to get hold of hers and stop them removing the robe? Where has it gone? Has she destroyed it? Maybe his brain is melting. Oh, God, he thinks, as she sits astride his knee, her hands and mouth working their way down his body, he'll never work again.

With a supreme effort, John tips her off. 'Enough. Stop tormenting me. I have to write this sodding theatre review or I'm in deep shit. Stay away from me, do you hear?'

She laughs and goes into the bathroom. He hears the sudden hiss of the shower being turned on. His notes from Friday night are practically illegible – pages and pages of biro scrawl. He sighs and looks out at the mountains for inspiration. She has begun to sing something. Sounds Scottish, or Irish maybe. She has a good voice. John turns in his seat towards the bathroom. She'll be in the shower now, all wet. Covered in soap maybe. He glances back at his notes. He could just . . . no. He has to finish this. He puts in his earplugs resolutely and switches on the computer. 'To concede and labour the obvious, Friday night's performance was . . .' he begins, and then stops. Was what? He skim-reads his notes again and tries to summon up a general feeling about the production he saw. The only general feeling he can summon up at the moment is an explosively effervescent happiness with an underlying glow of lust – neither of which has anything to do with the Manchester Playhouse's *Peer Gynt*. He deletes what he has written and starts again: 'Ibsen's *Peer Gynt* is not a play in which you can afford to skimp on strong acting sense.' OK. Right. Now we're getting somewhere.

Suddenly she's there, under the table between his knees, pushing the robe apart. He jumps in surprise and 'akdjneuskjnlkfhakew' appears on the computer screen. He pulls out his earplugs just as she takes his penis in her mouth. The effect is immediate: it's as if all his blood abandons the other parts of his body

and rushes to stiffen it. His head swims with the shock.
'Oh, Christ.'

Her mouth is soft, pliable and incredibly hot. He can feel
the ridges of her palate pushing against him and, every now and
then, the slightest graze of her teeth. He releases her hair from
the clip she'd put in it for the shower and it spills over his thighs
and her shoulders. The only time in his life when he thought he
was going to ejaculate prematurely was last night when she bent
over him in the dark and wound its length tightly around his
penis. He takes hold of her arms and pulls her towards him.

Table seven in the window is still empty and it's almost the end
of breakfast time. Who's missing? Molly casts her eyes swiftly
round the dining room. The young couple from London, of
course. The rest, older and more used to staying in hotels,
have come down on time and are solemnly eating their fruit
salad and maple-syrup pancakes, barely talking. Molly peers at
her watch. She wants to get off early today, if possible. Her
boyfriend, who is working in the Wordsworth museum down
in the village, is coming up to see her this afternoon. They are
going rowing on Grasmere.

Her feet ring as she walks across the polished (by her)
floorboards to clear a vacated table. The family, leaving by
the door, smile at her.

'I think autumn is coming,' the father says.

Molly remembers feeling an imperceptible edge in the air
when she put the rubbish out earlier this morning. 'I think
you're right.'

'It must be beautiful around here, with all the trees.'

'It is, I'm told, but I won't be around to see it. I'll be
leaving here in a few weeks.'

John grips her, lifts her up and staggers towards the bed.

Giggling, they crash on to it rather more precipitately than he'd planned.

'Are you OK?' he says, concerned.

'I think so. It's not often I get eleven stone of male flesh landing on top of me at such a speed . . . Oh, shit.' Her voice becomes strangled and she bites his shoulder. 'What are you doing to me?'

He eases himself up on to his elbows to look at her. She is frowning concentratedly, her eyes focused somewhere past his head. He touches her face. 'Hello. Are you all right in there?'

She laughs and stretches her neck to kiss him.

Molly and Sarah, the other girl, have cleared the whole of the dining room apart from the one unused table.

'What shall we do with this?' Sarah asks, gesturing towards it.

'Don't know. They may come down at any minute.'

'Then again,' Sarah says, 'they may spend all day in bed like yesterday.'

Molly laughs. 'Shush, they might hear you. Anyway, that's what I'd do if I came here.'

Sarah snorts and throws her a duster, which cracks in the air like a whip. 'That would depend on who you were with.'

They work on, wiping the table surface first, then smearing it with beeswax polish. Molly rubs in fast, circular motions until her face rises up before her in the burnished wood.

He knows she's close: her breathing is shallow and urgent and she's gripping him tighter all the time. Their bodies are slippery with sweat. John runs his tongue up Alice's neck to her ear, tasting salt. Her body jolts and arches. 'Oh, Jesus fucking Christ, fucking, fucking hell!' she shouts. He has to turn his head away to prevent being deafened, at the same time laughing incredulously at her string of expletives. She is clutching the back of his neck, sobbing or laughing, he can't tell which. After a few minutes, he starts to withdraw, but she tightens her arms around him. 'Don't go just yet.'

'Well, believe me, I'd love to stay, but I've got the population of China down here.'

Alice tiptoes down the stairs. The hotel seems deserted. She rings the bell at reception, guilty at how loud it sounds, but no one answers. She pokes her head tentatively around the swing door into the kitchen. There's no one there either. The cooker is off, cooling with its door open. Tin foil covers various pots and trays. Lentils soak in a big glass bowl, releasing slow bubbles to the water's surface. The clock above the dishwasher, showing the time to be a quarter to one, ticks loudly.

Alice can hear voices coming from somewhere. She walks towards the front door, the bright sunlight making her eyes smart. On the steps in front of the hotel sits the curly-haired girl with a boy. They are eating sandwiches from white plates balanced on their knees. The boy has his arm around the girl's shoulders. They are laughing about something, and with his other arm, the boy is wiping his eyes on the edge of his T-shirt. 'I don't believe it, I just don't believe it,' he is saying. At the sound of Alice's footsteps on the gravel, the girl turns her head then gets to her feet.

'Hello,' Alice says.

'Hi.'

Now she's standing, Alice sees that she's wearing shorts, heavy-duty boots and a big woollen cardigan.

'I'm sorry — you're off-duty, aren't you? I didn't realise.'

'That's OK. Did you want something?'

The boy is half turning to look at her. Alice remembers

having seen him earlier, walking across the lawn, his head tipped back towards the sky.

'No, don't worry. I was wondering if we could get something to eat before we drive back to London. We missed out on breakfast, you see.'

'Yes, I know. We don't usually serve lunch here, but I'm sure I could find something for you.'

Alice shakes her head. 'No, no. I wouldn't dream of it. We can go into the village. You enjoy your lunch. I used to work in a hotel so I know how annoying it is when people like us don't eat at the proper times.'

Molly looks relieved. 'Well, if you're sure . . .'

'I am.' Alice turns to go. 'Have a nice afternoon.'

Alice prowled round the edges of the walled garden at Tyningham, a large country house open to the public on Sundays. It was hot. She was wearing her black Victorian frock coat. 'It's your father's birthday, put on something nice for God's sake,' her mother had hissed, when she'd come downstairs. Elspeth had told Ann to 'leave her be'. So she couldn't take it off now.

In places, the red-brick wall was covered with a grey-green lichen. Borders ran along the walls, planted with roses, herbs and bright orange flowers that Alice didn't know the name for. At one end was a small, murky pool with a stone griffin spouting a weak trickle of water from its mouth. There was a lawn, hemmed in with low, myrtle hedges. In the middle, on white wrought-iron garden furniture and under a parasol, sat Alice's family.

The waitress, carrying a large tray, was advancing over the lawn. Alice walked back over and took her seat between Elspeth and Kirsty. Elspeth and Ben were having a conversation about Kenneth, Ben's brother, and his new medical practice. Alice half listened, watching the waitress unload the teacups from the tray. Beth was pestering their mother to go and visit the horses after this. 'Can we, can we, can we?' Beth said, bouncing up and down in her seat. 'Please?'

Ann extracted each saucer one by one from the pile the waitress left them in, balanced a cup on each and filled it with a stream of hot brown tea. Then she handed them to Kirsty, Elspeth, Ben and herself. 'I ordered juice for you,' she said to Alice. 'We'll see,' she said to Beth, and handed them both a tumbler of orange liquid.

'Happy birthday, Ben,' Elspeth said, toasting her son with her teacup.

The night before, Alice had wrapped up a compass, the dial of which was suspended in a globe of water. On one end it had a big, transparent sucker. Ben had moistened it with his tongue and stuck it to the windscreen of the car. 'It's a wonderful present, Alice,' he'd said, turning round to smile at her. All the way from their house to Tyningham, it had swivelled, readjusted and shifted, marking the slightest increments in their changes of direction.

'I need a glass of water,' Ann announced, apparently to no one. Ben stood and ran after the disappearing waitress. 'It's hot,' Ann said, fanning herself with her hand. 'Don't you want to take your coat off, Alice?'

Alice didn't answer, but sucked the lurid-coloured juice up through a straw. Saccharine-tasting liquid passed through her mouth, coating her teeth. She fished from her coat pocket a pair of sunglasses and put them on, plunging into shade her family, seated around her, and her father coming towards them over the lawn carrying a glass of water that was glinting in the sunshine. Her mother pursed her lips. Ben placed the glass in front of her. Barely turning to him, she said, 'Ben, can you fix the parasol? I'm too much in the sun.'

'Like Hamlet,' Alice muttered.

Ben twizzled the white plastic stick that speared through a hole in their table. The parasol shade spun round above them.

'What did you say?' Ann peered at her daughter as if she was very far away.

'I said, like Hamlet. He said to Claudius and his mother that he was "too much i' the sun". Like you did. Just then.'

'Oh. But why——' Ann broke off. 'Ben, not like that. This way. Over here, towards me more.'

Elspeth pushed back her chair and walked away, as if to go and see the griffin dribble water over the Victorian grotto. Alice saw this. Alice saw her father sit down again and reach to the ground for Ann's fallen cardigan. She saw him place it over her shoulders. She saw, as if for the first time, her father performing all these small tasks for his wife. And she saw him, at the end of it, place his hand on Ann's knee, smiling round at his three daughters on his forty-fifth birthday. And Alice saw, a few moments later, her mother move her chair ever so slightly, but just enough for Ben's hand to fall into the space between them.

As they near London, they stop talking. The tape playing finishes and John doesn't put on another. Alice leans her head against the car window, counting the infinity of orange lights and occasionally watching them reflected in the lenses of John's glasses.

'What do you need to wear glasses for?' she asks suddenly.

He takes his eyes away from the road for a moment to look over at her. 'You make it sound like a crime. I need them for driving, going to the cinema and theatre – that sort of thing. Long-distance stuff. Working at a computer eight or nine hours a day has done it.'

'So you're going to go blind as well as bald.'

'Blind, maybe, but not bald.'

He moves his left hand from the wheel on to her leg. She smooths the hollow of her palm over the back of his hand, listening to the changes in sound as it moves over his knuckles, tendons and fingers.

'When was it your mother died?' she asks.

'It was the end of my first year at uni. I was nineteen. You would have been a sexy seventeen-year-old.'

'A stroppy seventeen-year-old, more like.' She curls her fingers around his. 'How did it happen?'

'She had breast cancer. Initially, anyway. She found the first lump the day after my A levels finished and she was dead by the following summer. It had spread everywhere – pancreas, lungs, bowels, ovaries, liver. At Easter they opened her up, intending to operate on her liver, and when they saw all the tumours, they just sewed her back up again and sent her home. They told us she wouldn't last the month out, but she did, and two more as well.'

'John, that's terrible.'

'It was, yes.'

'How did your father take it?'

'Pretty badly, as you'd expect after twenty-six years of marriage.'

'And how is he now?'

'Well, you see, now he's turned religious. Really religious. I suppose it's not that surprising, when you think about it. But he's worried a lot of people.'

'Why?'

'Because his new-found faith has such a . . . desperate . . . obsessive quality about it. My mother was very religious and he was always cynical about it. Used to tease her a lot. I mean, he'd have been the first to describe himself as a Jew, but he would have been claiming it as his race, rather than his religion. He referred to my barmitzvah as "life insurance". She tried to make us all keep kosher but he wasn't having any of it. Anyway, since she died, he's become a real religious monomaniac. He won't even eat at my house – even if I buy the right food – because I don't keep a kosher kitchen. He has separate plates for milk and meat, he's even got two dishwashers. He observes all these obscure laws and I keep forgetting. He gets really annoyed if I do something like phone him on a Saturday. It's pretty . . . difficult at times. He seems to have this twisted logic that unless he perpetuates my mother's belief – the belief he himself used to mock – he's somehow being untrue to her memory. He's always been very pro the idea of me marrying a Jew but now he's obsessed. It's been hard. I wish sometimes he would meet someone else, just so there'd be someone else for him to focus on.'

'Apart from you, you mean?'

'Yes. I don't think he will, though. I can't imagine it.'

John takes back his hand abruptly and puts it on the wheel again. His face looks shuttered up and gloomy. Alice is silent and the warmth his hand has left in hers fades rapidly. She clasps her hands together over her knees, drawing them up to her chest.

As they are driving through Crouch End, he says, 'Alice, I've had the most brilliant weekend.'

'So have I. I loved that place.' She stretches out her legs. 'Am I going to see you again?'

His shoulders jerk in surprise and the car swerves dangerously. 'What do you mean? Don't say things like that. Are you going to see me again? Well, of course. I mean . . . don't you want to see me again? I thought . . . What are you talking about? Was this just some little fling for you?'

'No, of course it wasn't. You know that. There's no need to get angry.'

'Yes, there is a need to get angry when you say things like that. Tell me what you mean, Alice.'

'What I mean is, the Jewish thing.'

He doesn't say anything. When she plucks up courage to look over at him he is gripping the wheel, his shoulders hunched. She sighs. 'John, I'm not angry with you. I don't want to give you a hard time. I couldn't give a shit what religion or race you are, you know that. But it does matter to you, you can't deny it. I just want to be realistic.'

'Realistic?'

'Yes. I don't want to get hurt by you. You have to decide what you want.'

'This is what I want,' he thumps the wheel, 'I told you that.'

She says nothing, unconvinced.

'You don't believe me, do you?'

'It's not that. I believe that you believe what you are saying here and now, but I also believe that you could change your mind.'

'I won't.'

'You might.' She spreads her hands over her eyes and temples. 'Look, this is all getting a bit heavy. We have only just met. Why don't we agree to just take it easy and see what happens?'

He grunts non-committally. 'I don't see why you just can't believe me.'

'John, let's not spoil the weekend by arguing over something that hasn't and might never happen. This is all so speculative.' She sees a signpost for Holloway flash past. They are heading towards the outskirts of Finsbury Park. 'Could you drop me off at my flat, please?'

He looks instantly panicked. 'I thought . . . I mean, would you like to come back to my house? You haven't seen it yet.'

'I'd love to come and see it another night, but I need to unpack and get ready for work tomorrow.'

'Oh. I feel . . . I'd really like you to come back. I feel like we'd be parting on a bad note.'

She shakes her head. 'We're not. I promise.'

'Come round for dinner, then. Tomorrow night – no, shit, I can't make tomorrow. How about Tuesday?'

'Tuesday's fine. What time?'

'Eight o'clock? At my house.'

The car has drawn up at the end of the terrace outside Alice's flat. John jumps out of the car and comes round the other side just as she is getting out. He puts his arms around her and they kiss for a long time.

'I'm so sorry for being arsy earlier. I'm an idiot.'

'No, you're not, and it's fine.'

He traces her cheekbone with his thumb. 'I wouldn't ever hurt you, Alice.'

She turns her head and bites his thumb. 'You'd better not.'

He laughs, lifts her off her feet and spins her round. 'I'll see you Tuesday, then.'

'Yes. There's just one small problem with that.'

'What?'

'I don't have your phone number or address.'

He puts her down. 'For God's sake. I'd better give it to you.' He scribbles furiously on a piece of paper, then they kiss again. 'Are you sure you don't want to come back?' John says, after a while.

'Yes. You'd better go now before I change my mind. Be off with you.'

Alice waves after his receding tail-lights. It's only after his car has disappeared round the bend that she looks at the piece of paper he's given her. On it is written his phone number, his address and then the words 'love John xxx'. She bounds up the steps to her flat door.

She lets herself in, awkwardly clutching her bag in one hand and struggling with the lock and handle with the other. Dropping the bag to the floor, she stands with her back against the door for a while, still holding her keys. Then she moves through the flat, putting on a CD, drawing the curtains, filling the kettle. Her room is full of evidence of her hurried packing on Friday afternoon – clothes strewn all over the bed, books in sliding heaps on the floor. She feels strange looking at all this. Was it really only two days ago that she'd thrown those things there? It feels like another age, that the whole flat belongs to a different person. She flops on to the bed. She can unpack in the morning. In the flat below, rhythmic music starts up and muffled voices are raised above it. She lies on her stomach, propping her chin up on her hands. John's note is curled in her palm. She smooths it flat on the duvet. A train rattles through the night, making the house shudder. Somewhere across the city he is swinging his car into his street.

'I've seen your type before,' the man said, as he approached Ann.

Ann brought her cigarette to her lips and inhaled. The man was vaguely familiar to her, and it wasn't impossible that she could have seen him in and around the town, but it was probably only because there were hundreds of men in this town who looked like him – thinning ginger hair, the beginnings of a paunch straining at his shirt buttons, a suede-panelled cardigan, fawn slacks. Ann breathed out the smoke, watching as the man's eyes began to water. He had a rim of beer froth stuck to the ends of his thick, ginger moustache.

'Have you?' she said.

'You're English, aren't you? Oh, yes.' He answered himself, so Ann didn't bother to make any response. 'I know your type.'

'Really? And what's that?'

Ann had been standing alone in the front room of a large brick house on the eastern edge of North Berwick. All around her youngish married couples like her and Ben talked and ate and drank and flirted with each other. It was the party of someone Ben had been at school with. He was now a dentist, Ben told her, as they walked up the driveway. Ann had been standing by the fireplace, having slipped away from Ben ages ago when an earnest-looking man with a Labrador-dog tie started asking him what car he was thinking of buying this year. And now this man had appeared from the kitchen, bearing — ominously — two glasses of beer.

'Petite,' the man said, 'blue eyes. Blonde.' He gave the word a revving up like a motorbike.

'Married,' Ann added, holding up her hand to show him the gold band encircling her finger.

'Aha!' he said, focusing on it with difficulty. 'A challenge! I like that! Lemme see.' He slammed his beers down on the mantelpiece and got hold of her hand, stroking it flat on his own. 'Now, you might not think it, but I am a very respected palm-reader.'

'Is that so?' Ann drew on her cigarette once more.

'Oh, yes, oh, yes. You're very passionate, very responsive. But there's something that life isn't quite giving you, something that leaves you with a deep but hidden dissatisfaction.'

Ann pulled at her hand, but the man had her wrist in a tight, sweaty-fingered grip.

'What's this?' he asked, running the tip of his finger along a jagged, colourless scar that bisected her palm, making her fingers jitter compulsively. 'Nasty cut that must have been. How did that happen, then? Husband did it, did he?'

Ann removed her cigarette from her lips. 'Let go of my hand,' she spat the words out one by one, very clearly, 'you ugly little troll.'

The man let her wrist slither from his grip, astonished. Ann flicked the butt into the fire grate and walked away through people whom she knew were looking at her, but she didn't care.

She wanted Ben. Where was he? It felt like hours since she'd left him with the boring man. In the hallway, she saw the woman whose house it was, standing next to an arrangement of hideous blue dried flowers whispering with another woman Ann didn't know. 'Have you seen my husband?' Ann asked.

'Ben? He was in the dining room, I think, last time I saw him. Bit worse for wear, I'd say. But, then, as I'm always telling my Peter, if you can't let your hair down once in a while, what can you do?'

'Yes.' Ann plucked at the hem of her blouse. 'In here, did you say?'

'Right through there, on your left. Can't miss it.'

'Thanks.'

Ann pushed her way down the corridor, through various people lining the walls with drinks and cigarettes in their hands. Women's bodies were softer; they moved to let her pass. Men's didn't yield but inquisitively held their ground, remaining rigid to her as she tried to slide past them. I am thirty-one years old, Ann thought, my three little girls are asleep in their beds, what am I doing here?

In the dining room, a woman in too-tight trousers was sitting on the smoked-glass-topped table fondling a tabby cat. Two men were standing in front of her.

'The thing about the Edinburgh schools,' one of them was saying, 'is, of course, that you are guaranteed that your child will be mixing with others of alpha-type intelligence.'

'You just don't get that guarantee with the High School,' the woman said.

'You just don't,' the second man agreed.

'Excuse me,' Ann said, stepping towards them, 'you haven't seen Ben, have you?'

'Ben who?' asked the woman. The cat circled her hips, tail in the air, displaying the neat circle of its anus.

'Ben Raikes.'

'Ooooooh,' the woman exclaimed, and held out her hand. 'You're Ann, aren't you? I can't believe we haven't met before.

I'm Gilly. This is Scot and this is my husband Brian.' They all shook hands. 'My Victoria's in the same year as your Kirsty.'

'Right.'

'We were just having that old state school–private school debate. Where do you and Ben stand on that?'

'Er, well, Kirsty's only seven and Alice has only just started at the primary, so—'

'Wee Alice! I know that one! Seen her coming out the school with Kirsty. Gorgeous – the both of them. Alice is awfully dark, is she not?'

'No,' Ann started backing away, 'I mean, yes. Yes, she is. Well, I must find Ben. Nice to meet you all.'

They watched her go, faintly surprised.

Ann made it back to the doorway of the front room and stood on tiptoe to see if Ben had appeared in there. The troll-man was now playing drinking games with another, taller man. Just as she was about to step out into the hallway again, a sandy-haired man with smooth, tight-fitting skin seized her by the waist. 'We need to start the boogying.'

'No.'

'Why don't we get the ball rolling? You and I?'

'No. Please.'

'Oh, come, come, give it a whirl, eh? We're only young once.'

Ann pulled herself away from him, the side of her handbag striking a radiator, which gave out a long, low note like a cello. Ann pushed her way into the hall. She wanted Ben so badly she thought she might cry. She knew that he was somewhere in this house, but she couldn't get to him. Standing under the stairwell, she felt an urge to wail his name at the top of her voice and shout, I'm here, please come to me.

Seeing the troll-man lurch out of the door, Ann sprinted up the deeply carpeted flight of stairs and locked herself into the bathroom. She lowered the lid and sat down, her handbag dangling on to the floor, her thumb moving rhythmically over and over the ridge of her scar. The woman of the house had decorated her bathroom in green paint. Tiles adorned with three-dimensional seahorses, conches and starfish lined the walls. Ann was astonished to see that a diaphragm, dusted and ready for use, lay in its case on the side of the bath. She stood, saw her face in the mirror, and wondered if she was about to throw up. Then she realised that it was just that her skin was catching the reflection of the nausea-green paint on the walls.

Ann heard someone on the stairs. 'It's a day's drive to Dover, straight down the A1,' a woman's voice was saying, 'then the night ferry, then it's about two days' drive to the Alps. Or so Dennis tells me.'

'Well, I hope it's not too hard going, what with the kids and all.'

Ben. It was Ben's voice. Without a doubt. Ann sprang to the door and pulled it open. The corridor and stairs were bare.

'Ben?' Ann went down a few stairs and saw the sea of party faces filling the hallway. She turned and rushed back up. 'Ben! Ben!'

Where in God's name was he? He couldn't have got far – she knew that.

'Ben? Where are you? Ben!'

Then she heard his voice, somewhere, surprised: 'That's my wife.' She cocked her head on one side, trying to ascertain where it came from. 'Ann?' she heard him call. Upstairs somewhere. Definitely upstairs.

'Yes!' She scrambled up the stairs, two at a time. 'Ben! I'm here! I'm here!'

She pulled open the first door she came to, but it was dark, a cupboard of some sort, smelling strongly of teak and varnish.

She heard herself expelling a small noise like the beginning of tears, and she slammed the door shut. Then he was behind her, his hand on her arm. 'Hello there,' he was saying, 'were you calling?'

'Ben.' She pressed her face into his shoulder, relief closing her throat so she couldn't say anything more. He tried to move back from her so that he could see into her face but she wouldn't let him go. He was laughing, embarrassed and pleased.

'Are you all right?'

'Where were you? You'd gone . . . I didn't know where you were.'

'What do you mean? I was here all the time.'

Ann rubbed her forehead against the nap of his jacket, pushed her mouth up to his neck. 'Can we go home?' she whispered into his ear. 'Please.'

She felt him turn his head to see if anyone could see them, and she pressed herself closer. 'Let's go home,' she whispered again, 'let's go now.'

He was still trying to see into her face, but she buried her head further into his shoulder. 'If that's . . . if that's what you want.'

'I do.'

'I'll get our coats.' He tried to move away, but Ann still wouldn't let him.

'I'll come with you.'

'OK.' He encircled her waist with his arm, supporting her as if she was injured. 'Let's go, then.'

Ann curls her feet around the top rung of the stool. These stools have been built for tall men; Ann finds them dizzying and frightening. Once on them, she cannot easily get off, and the slightest inequality in the lengths of their legs means they can tip alarmingly, making her clutch at the rim of the wooden bench.

She is sitting in the university laboratory. Its silence calms her. It's different from that of the library, where the air is leaden with concentration and crammed with typed, black words. Here people talk, but in low tones. The conversations are never flippant, but always about work and test results and apparatus. Nobody talks longer than they have to, or asks you any personal questions. It's insulated, safe: you know that everyone comes here to do their experiments, and then they leave.

In front of Ann on the bench lie a scalpel, a dissection board made from dark, hardened wood and a bundle of plant stems, the petals of the flowerheads broken and crushed. She is, she knows, supposed to be conducting an experiment with the xylem vessels, cutting the stems open, staining them with a dark blue dye and placing them on sharp-edged slides under a microscope.

When the tutor announced last week that they had to do this experiment, Ann sat with her pen poised above her notebook. All through the lecture the people around her had filled page after page with notes and diagrams. But Ann hadn't been able to separate the flow of sounds coming from the tutor's mouth into coherent words. She has no idea why she has to fill the xylem vessels with blue dye, or study them under a microscope, or even what she's supposed to be looking for when she does.

Ann shakes the wisps of hair off her face, straightens her back, holds her knees together and picks up the scalpel. She can do this, she can, she really can. She presses the tip of the blade into the base of the stem, its tight, turgid breadth splitting easily, oozing succulent whitish juice. With barely any pressure, she slits the stem into two exact halves. Lilac petals fall, scattering the bench top, and she places them next to each other on the dissection board. Ann breathes again. She can do this. She can do this. She is doing this.

She picks up the next stem and holds it between thumb and forefinger in her left hand. Sun is slicing into the lab through the high-up windows. Because the windows are so widely spaced, the benches are alternately illuminated by this white, midday light: one bench in shade, the next in sunlight. Ann's is in a bright, almost biblical shaft, with all the apparatus around her given black, clearly outlined shadows. She can see her own elbows on the bench, hands raised, ankles crossed under the stool, and she can't believe that she casts such a distinct image because she feels so insubstantial, so matter-less, so lacking in any kind of density or form or shape.

She turns back to her hands and watches with something like interest as the scalpel she is holding presses into the skin of her left palm. Her fingers holding the stem spring open, but the scalpel presses harder. A glittering red bloom appears from her hand and flows in a fast stream over the mound of her thumb and down her wrist. There is no pain. But she can hear that clean sound like a blade through grass as the scalpel travels across her palm, bifurcating her lifeline. Her fingers curl back into themselves. She lets the scalpel drop. Her sleeve feels wet all the way up to her elbow.

It's as if her lens on the world has been twisted into a new focus: everyone looks very close to her all of a sudden. She can hear the whisperings of two men at the other side of the room, discussing the amount of ethanol contained in a pipette, which one of them is holding up to the window above her head. They don't look at her. At the front of the lab the stick insects in their perforated glass box rustle, scratch and rub their thin, articulated legs against each other as they transport themselves around their closed-in, simulated world of heat and leaves; dust motes whirl in the shafts of light; a Bunsen burner three benches away roars like a waterfall.

Ann slides off the stool until her feet touch the ground. The dissection board has drunk up the blood that has fallen on to it like a thirsty plant. Ann finds that distasteful, and all she knows is that she wants to get away from it, that blood-filled slab of wood, and get away from here. The beam of her vision moves around the room like a searchlight: basins with high-arched taps, orange rubber tubing running from gas taps to burners, which make the room behind them swim with heat, the two men who are now bending over their elaborate construction of glass piping, a fair-haired man sitting at a microscope, slowly wheeling the lens up towards his eye, a woman shaking something in a test tube, another man taking off his jacket and placing it squarely on a peg, the shelves with the jars and jars of formaldehyde-soaked lizards, rubbery piglets and shut-eyed foetuses.

Ann walks down the centre pathway towards the door. She passes the woman with the test tube, who doesn't look up. As she approaches the man peering down the microscope, she must have shaken her head or flicked back her hair again because one of her hairpins falls out of her carefully constructed chignon. It must have been loosening itself for hours from the position in which Ann shoved it that morning, the forces of gravity tugging away, and in that instant it drops to the tiled floor, making a twang like a highly pitched tuning fork. It is a strange noise for the laboratory – a minuscule note of intimacy among all those sounds of boiling and cutting and condensing and growing. Ann hears it and puts her good hand up to her hair, feeling a strand of it falling down to her shoulder. The microscope man hears it, and it makes him glance up from his slide. His eyes rest on Ann for a microsecond and he is reflexively looking back down the tunnel of light to his vision of cells seething in iodine when he leaps up from his stool. 'Christ Almighty.'

He seizes Ann by her uninjured arm and, producing a low chair from somewhere, guides her on to it. Ann is relieved. The crown of her head is feeling hot, her leg muscles tired of holding her upright.

'Where is it that you're cut?' he asks, in a low, very calm voice, bending over her. 'Can you show me?'

Ann tries to open her fingers, but suddenly hot arrows of pain shoot up to her shoulder. She gasps, shocked, tears start into her eyes and spill down her cheeks. The man holds her hand over a basin and runs the tap over it. Blood is sluiced away from it, swinging into the white curves of the porcelain and away down the plughole. Under the water, they both see a red gash, running diagonally across her palm. The man examines it, frowning. 'Fine,' he says, 'you're doing fine.'

Then he crouches and starts removing one of his shoes. The other people in the lab have stopped their activities and gathered round the little drama. And they all watch, puzzled, as the fair-haired man struggles with the knots in his lace. Ann's arm is stretched out limply on the bench top as if it no longer belongs to her. He rips the lace from his shoe and, holding Ann's arm above her head, his face tense with concentration, wraps it around her wrist and tugs it tight.

Ann winces. 'That's too tight,' she says, crying again, 'it hurts.'

'I know. I'm sorry. But you've cut through the blood vessels,' he explains, in the same soft and patient voice, 'and I think most of the tendons, so we have to stop the blood-flow to your hand.' He reaches into his pocket, drawing out a white handkerchief, and, before Ann can draw back in surprise, he is pressing it, folded, to her wet cheeks. 'There,' he says. Then he turns to the people staring at them. 'I'm going to phone

for an ambulance. Can one of you stand here holding her arm
up like this until I get back?'

When the ambulance comes, he steps into it with her. He
is called Ben, he tells her, Ben Raikes, and is doing his Ph.D.
He loves Edinburgh, especially the Botanical Gardens, and is
not from the city but a small town on the sea, east of here. He
wants to know her name, where she's from, if she's travelled
much in Scotland, how she likes biology, how her hand is, how
did she come to cut it that deeply anyway, does it still hurt her,
is there anything he can do. But Ann is feeling strange now.
How did she come to be here in the back of an ambulance
with a garrulous Scottish man who has her blood on his shirt
and, in his pocket, her tears on his handkerchief? She feels as if
her life has been somehow diverted: where would she be now
if she hadn't cut her hand, or if her hairpin hadn't fallen out,
or if it hadn't fallen out as she happened to be walking past
Ben Raikes, making him look up? This is all so unexpected
and she doesn't like that, doesn't like the fact that this man
has taken care of her like this, that her hand is cut and messed
and throbbing, and that she wants him to please, please take
hold of her hand again in his gentle fingers, like he did back
there when her blood was seeping out of her veins.

Her hand is bandaged, stitched up, hurting less and held
to her chest in a sling when, the next morning, she finds a
small envelope in her pigeon-hole. It has 'Anne' written on
the outside in blue ink. Strong, squarish letters. The misspelling
makes her sure, makes her heart thud, makes her hand ache in
a strange excitement. It has to be him. Ann's never had a love
letter before. Never wanted one before. In the library, she slits
the top of the envelope open with a steel ruler. But out comes
not a letter with love held in its folds or steeped in its ink,
but lots and lots of paper squares, each with a letter on them.
Ann stares at them, confused and disappointed, lets them fall

through her fingers. Then she sees that in the corner of each square is a number.

Electrified, she spreads them out before her like a croupier, turning over any that are face down. People around her circle the shelves, or turn over pages of books, or scribble lines of writing on paper. But Ann is forming words out of cut-up squares, looking frantically for the next number, the next letter, blood pounding through her body: C a n ' t s t o p read the first two. Can't stop, can't stop, Ann chants to herself, as she searches the slough of white paper squares in front of her. He can't stop. Can't stop what? t h i n k i n g a b o u t . Then: y o u . M e e t m e a t t h e H e a r t o f M i d l o t h i a n , s o o n a s y o u c a n , B e n.

Ann jumps up. Then she sits down. Then she sweeps all the letters back into the envelope. Then she goes over to the nearest person. 'Excuse me, do you know what the Heart of Midlothian is?'

Ann has never been to the cathedral, never noticed that in front of it, set into the cobbles, is a stone heart. She is worried, as she walks as fast as she can up the Royal Mile, that she won't be able to find it among the chaos of the cobbles, that she might miss him, that he might think she never came, that he might have gone. But as she turns round the corner of the blackened cathedral, she sees him sitting on a bench, hunched into his coat, a book in his hands. Seeing her, he stands and gives a little wave. She thinks: he is smaller and thinner than I remembered. She thinks: my hand hurts. She thinks: do I love him? She thinks: he tied his shoelace around my wrist to stop me losing blood. She thinks: I wonder how long he's been waiting.

There are times when I am there and times when I am not – when I am elsewhere, blocked off, blocked in. But there are times when I am closer than others and I can hear and smell and feel the things I cannot see outside myself. It's like a tide that bears my body up, taking me closer to the light and sound.

Now that they are here, I am glad.

My father used to tell us the story of how he met our mother ('I looked up and there she was, red blood running down her arm and on to the floor'), and we used to get her to show us the scar, white like a fork of lightning across her palm. Sometimes she would – opening her hand for us like a plant reacting to light – and sometimes she wouldn't.

Throughout my life, I have imagined it over and over again – I have a perfectly constructed image in my head of the laboratory and how it looked; and my mother with the scalpel that slipped and sliced through her hand; and her walking through the room; and my father being the only one to jump up and help her; and him climbing into the ambulance with her. I see them so clearly: young, my mother's hair long, pinned up; my father with one laceless shoe slack around his foot, and a linen handkerchief washed and ironed by Elspeth.

But today, in this state I'm in, I'm somewhere up near the ceiling, looking down into the laboratory as if into a dolls' house: I see my mother advancing towards my father, her sleeve stained red. And just at the point when he hears the hairpin drop and is looking up to see her for the first time, I want to take them up like Plasticine figures, lift them out and press them tightly together with the palms of both my hands.

The only light now was from the fire which someone must have built up – a hissing roar leapt into her ears, Alice found, if she tilted her head towards it. The faces beyond it dissolved and reformed in the heat haze it threw up. Beyond them, she could still just about make out the line of the horizon and the shoreline. If she tilted her head the other way, away from the fire and the whirling, hard-edged, jangling music thudded out by the sound system, she could hear the rhythmic suck and crash of waves.

She stood up, brushing the sand off the back of her long black skirt. Where was Katy? She'd disappeared down the sand dune a while back to find them something else to drink, making Alice promise to wait for her. Alice peered down into the gloom, scanning the faces, searching for the blaze of Katy's red hair. She would go down and look for her. She flicked the trailing end of her feather boa over her shoulder and set off down the dune towards the fire and the main bulk of the party where bodies were standing about or gyrating to the music. Her boots sank into the soft sand and her feet were carried faster than she intended by the momentum of the slope. The sudden speed thrilled her and she held out her arms against the rush of air: she seemed to be whizzing past groups of people, her feet moving beneath her involuntarily, her hair and the ends of the feather boa flying out behind her. Giggling to herself, she came to a halt by crashing into someone at the bottom. Whoever it was had to grab hold of her by both arms to stop themselves from falling over.

'Sorry,' Alice said breathlessly, 'sorry, I couldn't stop.' The person didn't let go of her. She screwed up her eyes in the semi-dark. It was a boy, taller than her. Did she know him? 'Sorry,' she said again, expecting him to let go. The boy pulled her round to face the fire and both of them were staring into each other's faces by the demonic, orange glow of the flames. She knew who he was – Andrew Innerdale, in Kirsty's year at school. He had a brother in the year below Alice, or was it two years below? Their father, the kind of arty, ex-hippie type that stood out a mile in North Berwick, owned the antiques shop on the High Street. Still with his hands curled around her upper arms, he said, 'I thought it was you.'

Alice felt incensed, curious and flattered all at the same time. His face was very close to hers and she could smell the tang of beer on his breath. His eyes raked over her face in the semi-dark: there was something about his gaze that unsettled her. She put her hands flat against his chest and shoved him away from her. He staggered back a step, uttering a small, mewing cry of surprise. She turned and drifted away through the crowd of people, searching for Katy, nestling deeper into the mass of feathers coiled about her neck.

She had found the feather boa at the back of Elspeth's wardrobe. She had been half-heartedly groping in its dark depths for a cardigan her grandmother had asked her to fetch, when her fingers brushed against something soft, silky and springy. She'd snatched her hand away in surprise, examining it as if expecting it to be injured by what she'd just touched. Then she'd ducked down so her eyes were on a level with the shelf and cautiously inserted her hand again. This time she didn't draw back her hand when she'd felt its imperceptible brush, but gripped it carefully and drew it out towards her. It uncoiled like a cobra from its resting place at the back of the wardrobe and, within seconds, a long spray of blackish-green feathers was travelling past her astonished eyes. On and on it came and when she finally placed it around her neck, its ends almost reached the floor. She looped it round and round her neck then surveyed herself in Elspeth's mirror.

The feathers, piled up to reach her ears, were the sleek, oiled black-green of a starling's throat. At the centre of the boa, where they were woven into some invisible cord, they were gossamer soft before frothing out into the firm, spiky feathers with hooked filaments that caressed her cheeks like blades. Alice had never seen anything so beautiful and she had never wanted anything so badly: it made her weak with longing, the will to possess this thing. Why did her grandmother have it? Why had she never seen it before? Where had Elspeth worn it and would she let her have it?

Alice had stood for a few moments in front of her mirror, her fingertips stroking the outermost feathers. Then she had picked up the cardigan Elspeth had wanted and gone downstairs, the end of the feather boa trailing down her back like the tail of a sea monster.

Elspeth had, of course, given it to her, and tonight's beach party was its first outing. She was being careful not to let it touch the sand, as she wove in and out of groups of people. The idea of wet sand among the sleek feathers made her shudder.

Suddenly an arm was being passed around her waist. She whipped round, but it was a grinning Kirsty, materialising out of the dark. 'Hello, girlie,' Alice said, throwing an arm around her sister's warm neck, 'how are you doing?'

They walked on together through the crowd of people, arms round each other, Kirsty leaning heavily against her.

'Just fine. How about you? Having a nice time?'

'Mmm. I've lost Katy. You haven't seen her, have you?'

'Um, no. Don't think so.'

Someone behind them shouted, 'Kirsty! Kirsty!' and Kirsty

slipped out of Alice's grasp, back into the gloom. 'Have to go,' she said, over her shoulder. 'See you later.'

'OK. What time are you going home?' Alice called after her, but Kirsty didn't hear.

Alice climbed to the top of the other dune and, shivering in the stiff breeze that always returned at night, looked around again for Katy. She couldn't see her. If she went home she'd be better to walk some of the way following the seashore, rather than take the more direct route over the golf course: it was too dark now and she'd be sure to fall into a bunker. She knew the way via the beach much better. She made her way down the slope, gripping handfuls of marram grass for balance this time, and walked off down the beach. A few people called after her. 'I'm going home,' she called back, her voice carried by the breeze, 'bye-bye.'

Without the contrast of the fire, it was easier to see down by the sea. The foam of the waves caught what little moonlight there was filtering through the thick cloud. Five hundred yards or so away from the party, she turned and walked backwards for a few steps, watching the small black cut-out shapes and the glow of the fire's embers. Then she turned and faced the direction she was walking in. The first chill of nerves at the darkened, empty beach ahead of her passed over her skin. She crossed her arms, pushing her hands up into her sleeves and walked quickly, her head down, her boots slopping through the wet sand of the shoreline, the hem of her skirt absorbing salty water, sand, seaweed and tiny flakes of shell. When the jagged rocks of Point Garry appeared out of the pitchy black, she began to relax. She breathed into the feathers around her neck and began to sing to herself in a whisper a song that had been playing on the sound system at the party. Not far now.

Alice stopped, her breath catching in her throat. On the rocks in front of her was a person, just standing there. She could

171

see their outline, darker against the sky. She cleared the hair from across her face and called out, 'Hello? Who's that?'

Whoever it was didn't answer, but jumped down from the rocks and started walking towards her.

'Don't!' she shrieked. 'Don't come anywhere near me! I'll scream! Tell me who you are!'

The person stopped and held up its hands in a supplicant posture. 'Sorry.' It was a boy. 'Don't be scared,' he said. 'Is that Alice?'

'Maybe,' she said, still angry. 'Who are you?'

'It's Andrew,' he said, advancing forward on the sand again.

'Andrew Innerdale?' she demanded.

'Yes.'

'Well, you scared the fucking life out of me, Andrew Innerdale,' she said, and marched on. She could sense him somewhere behind her, hear his breath coming in shortened gasps as he caught up with her.

'I'm sorry. I'm really sorry. I didn't mean to scare you.' His voice was even, very close to her ear.

'Well, you did.'

They walked on in silence for a bit, then Alice stopped and said, 'I'm going to cut across the golf course here.'

'I'll come with you.'

She hesitated. Blood was pounding past her eardrums. This male shape in the dark beside her made her nervous and excited and confused. What was it wound up behind his eyes that frightened her?

'All right,' Alice said.

Over the golf course, they could see a necklace of sulphurous yellow street-lights. She felt more composed as they neared them, and they both gradually emerged from the gloom. He was tall and skinny, wearing thick-soled boots like hers.

'You're Kirsty's sister, aren't you?' he said.

'Yes.'

'You don't look like her.'

'I know.'

The manicured lawns of the golfing greens rolled under their silent feet and they bobbed in and out of the small artificial hillocks of the course.

'Are you doing your Highers this year?' he asked.

'Yeah. What about you? Are you doing CSYS like Kirsty?'

'Uh-huh.'

'What will you do then?'

'Don't know yet. My mum wants me to be a doctor, but I want to go to art college. Like my dad.'

'Do it, then. It's your life, not hers.'

'Yes, I know.' He sounded miserable. Alice started to feel a bit sorry for him. He turned to her with a grin. 'You don't like hockey, do you?'

'What?' She stared at him. 'No, I don't. How do you know?'

'I have double history first thing Friday morning, and you have games. I'm in the history block, here,' he demonstrated with his hand, 'and you're on the playing-field here,' he put his other hand next to it, 'right beside the window.' He grinned again. 'I sit by the window. You always look well pissed off.'

She laughed. 'I am. I hate it.'

'I could tell,' he said. Then he stopped walking and took her elbow. 'Alice . . . um . . . why don't we stay out here for a bit?'

She shifted uneasily, pushing her hands up farther inside her sleeves. 'I don't know. I should be getting back, I think.'

'You can stay a bit longer.' He put his arms around her tentatively. She felt his body pressing against hers, felt various points meeting with the corresponding points of hers – his chest against her breasts, his thighs against the length of her own, the gentle bulge of his groin pressing against hers through his trousers and the thin material of her skirt. His arms were whiplash thin, but strong as he held her more and more tightly to him.

She stood still, unsure. He began to speak. 'I really like you, Alice. I've watched you at school and I think you're really . . . you're really . . . nice. I know you're a bit younger than me and everything, but I think it would be OK, don't you? I mean, what do you think?'

Unease slithered in her stomach. The feathers of her boa crushed between them cracked and pricked her through her clothes.

'I don't know,' Alice said, and wriggled away from him. 'I don't know.' She began walking towards the town again.

He caught her by the arm again. 'Alice, will you kiss me? Please? Will you?'

She looked at him in wonder. Where did this passion come from? His face was suffused with embarrassment and urgency. She thought he might cry. He bent towards her and she found herself again looking straight into his eyes. An awkward, nameless fear leapt within her and she planted the heel of her palm in the centre of his chest. 'No,' she said, pushing him away. 'No.'

Then she turned and, drawing her feather boa about her, ran towards the houses at the edge of town and didn't stop running until she got home. As her feet thudded rhythmically on the tarmac pavements and her ragged breath burnt in her chest, she replayed over and over in her head what she thought she'd seen. His eyes – they were the same dark brown as hers, with lighter flecks at their centres. Looking into his eyes gave Alice the sensation that she was looking into her own.

Dr Mike Colman pushes a fifty-pence piece into the thin slot of the coffee machine and waits. A plastic cup is ejected forcefully into the metal tray and topples on to its side. Scalding brown liquid squirts out of the nozzle, over the fallen cup, down the side of the coffee machine and on to his shoes. 'Oh, for fuck's sake.'

He feels his temper fraying at the edges and takes a deep breath, inserting another coin into the slot. In the corner a woman flicks violently through magazine after magazine, ignoring her companion, an older woman, who asks over and over again, 'How did you think he looked? I thought he looked better. How did you think he looked?'

Two nights ago, Mike had got back well past midnight, desperately needing sleep, and had met Melanie on the landing, sobbing into the worn neck of her teddy bear. The nanny's door had been resolutely shut and he'd lifted her back into bed. 'Why can't Mummy live with us any more?' she'd demanded between hiccuping sobs. He'd stroked her hair — 'We've talked about this before, Melanie, do you remember? Mummy lives with Steven now and you can visit her whenever you want' — when what he really wanted to do was throw back his head and howl like her. She'd gone back to sleep eventually, her hair tangled and her thumb hanging slackly in her mouth.

But then, of course, he couldn't sleep. Fucking Steven – his so-called best friend.

Mike swills the acrid coffee around his mouth, wincing as he swallows. The older woman has subsided into silence and is staring up at the yellow strip-lights. He hates waiting rooms, especially at night. The tiny mathematics of human life. But nothing, nothing was as bad as the period between three and five a.m., when all visitors and day-workers have gone, most of the patients are asleep, and a terrible, breathing hush descends on the wards and corridors. It's during those hours that most deaths in hospitals occur. Mike hates that shift more than anything.

He makes his way back to Intensive Care through the winding white corridors. He never has to think about which turning to take, or read the signs: his sense of direction is good. There are people who've worked here longer than him who still get lost. Mike's method, not that he would ever tell anyone this, is not to think about it, to let his subconscious take over, to occupy his mind with something else while his body and instinct take control. He has a suspicion that if he stopped and thought about which direction to take he'd forget and fumble and lose his way.

In the room, sitting beside the bed, Mike finds a woman in a red dress with streaked blonde hair. 'Hello,' he says.

She shifts in her seat, swivelling her upper body to face him. 'Hi. I'm Rachel.'

Her shoes are high and black, with painfully narrow toes. A briefcase rests on the floor beside the chair. He can tell from the chafing around her eyes that she's been crying. Mike says nothing, but checks the machines and the drip. He presses his thumb to Alice's inert wrist, counting the number of times her heart sends blood hurtling past his touch. He peels back her eyelids, shines a beam into her pupils, one of which is fixed, dark and wide like a sea anemone, the other small, quivering and black. He can feel Rachel's wide-set green eyes watching his every move.

'How is she?' she asks. Her voice has the volume and directness of someone used to getting answers to all her questions.

'How long have you known her?' Mike enquires.

'Years. We met at university.' She tilts her head to look at the figure on the bed. 'She's my best friend, I suppose.' She stands, walks to the window and looks out into the velvet black. 'We lead very different lives now, but we're still close, I'd say.'

'Did you see her parents today?'

'No,' she says, and he can tell without turning round by the way her voice reverberates off the wall in front of him that she's moved from the window and is somewhere at his back, watching him again. 'I think I must have just missed them. I had to work later than I thought tonight.'

Mike adjusts the breathing tube and the cone of plastic strapped to Alice's face. Its edges have made red welts in her skin

'So,' Rachel says as she comes round the bed and returns to the chair, 'how is she doing?'

'There's no change.'

'Is that good or bad?'

'It's neither.'

They both look at Alice. Mike notices for the first time that the cuts to her face are hardening into scabs, that her bruises are turning a dark purple-black. He feels again how strange it is that such a major part of the body's working can break down and yet simple things like the healing of skin can just carry on as normal. There is something oddly calming about watching her – maybe it's the rhythm of the ventilator or that she never moves, apart from the artificial rise and fall of her torso. He lowers himself on to the side of the bed.

'You know, they say it may have been deliberate. A suicide attempt.'

The ventilator sighs once, twice, Alice's chest rising and falling in sympathy. Mike glances at Rachel.

She seems unsurprised, biting her thumbnail with emphatic nips of her white, rather childishly shaped teeth. 'Yes,' she says simply, after a while. 'It had crossed my mind.' Rachel leans forward and runs a finger down the thin skin of her friend's temple. 'Alice, Alice,' she whispers, 'why did you do it?'

'No, no, not like that at all,' Alice says, in a lowered voice into the receiver, trying unsuccessfully to suppress her laughter. The office is quiet today, everyone's back bent over their computer screens, and their ears, Alice imagines, tuned into her conversation.

'Well, what, then?' Rachel is shouting at the other end. She's on her mobile, the connection between them fuzzing, the movement of her walking juddering her voice. The line cuts out for a second then returns: '. . . in bed, or not?' she is saying.

'Rach,' Alice reminds her, 'I'm in the office.'

Rachel sighs. 'OK. You can tell me later. So what about the deep dark secret? Did you manage to get it out of him or didn't you do that much talking?'

'He's Jewish.'

The sound of hooting and car engines comes down the line, then Rachel's voice, suddenly still, as if she's stopped walking. 'How Jewish?'

'What do you mean, how Jewish? Are there degrees of it?'

'Of course there are.'

'Well,' Alice doesn't know what to say, 'he's . . . he's . . . er . . . he said he's worried about what his dad will think.'

179

'I see.'

'It's weird, isn't it?'

'Not really. It's not as if it's uncommon or anything.'

'Oh.' Alice is surprised. 'Isn't it?'

'For God's sake,' Rachel says, 'I forget this about you sometimes.'

'Forget what?'

'That you've spent most of your life holed up in some Scottish village in the middle of nowhere. Of course it's not uncommon. It happens all the bloody time. Is it just a problem with his dad or is it him as well?'

'Um, I'm not sure.' Alice thinks back. 'Both, I think.'

'Hmm,' Rachel says. 'Look, I'm going to have to go. I've got to be in court in two minutes. Just . . . just be careful, that's all. Don't get too involved before you know what's what, OK?'

Alice makes her way from Camden Town tube station with her *A-Z* held in front of her. John's street is a narrow, short one that on the map isn't even long enough to contain its own name, held in the fork between Camden Road and Royal College Street. She wends her way up Camden Road, past the World's End pub on the corner where people have spilled out on to the pavement with their glasses in hand. At the lights outside Sainsbury's, she crosses the road and buys a bottle of wine from a small Algerian shop with banks of exotic vegetables and cacti outside. The man wraps it for her in a twist of moss-green paper and calls after her to 'have a lovely evening, darling'.

After walking up and down a few times, peering at the houses' numbers in the twilight, she decides his house must be near the far end of the narrow street. It is one of a typical north London Victorian terrace. The front door is blue and there are lights on in every window. At the door she can feel the vibration of loud music coming from the house. She rings the bell and he opens the door so quickly that she wonders if he was waiting behind it. He looks dishevelled, his shirt all untucked and his hair standing on end. Then they are locked together and he has wrapped his arms around her so tightly she can hardly draw breath. She doesn't know how long they stay like that; it all seems already so familiar – the smell of him and the way her head fits into the curve of his neck, the way he cups his palm around the nape of her neck when he is kissing her. She pulls back to look at him, running her fingertips over his mouth and cheeks. 'It's so good to see you,' she says unnecessarily.

He reaches past her and shuts the front door. 'Come on in, he says, pulling her by the hand through the hallway into a big high-ceilinged sitting room. Two rooms have, at one time, been knocked together, forming a sweep of floorboards from a bay window at the front to a back door opening out on to a small garden. The walls are painted a dark paprika red, with one whole side of the room taken up with bookshelves. In the corner is a messy-looking desk with his computer and a fax machine that winks and blinks at intervals. There are two scruffy, comfy sofas at right angles to each other and a table, piled high with magazines, papers and books.

John is standing behind her, his arms around her waist. 'Well?' he murmurs into her hair.

'Well what?'

'What do you think?'

'John, it's so beautiful. What an amazing house.'

'I'm very lucky. I bought it with the money my mother left me. I often think I ought to get a housemate, or get a friend to move into the spare room or something, but I've got used to the luxury of living alone. I wouldn't ever want to live anywhere else. I love it. I live in this room mostly. The rest of the house is pretty bare. I never seem to have the time to do anything to it.'

She walks across the room to the bookshelves, runs her hand along the spines of the books lined up and turns around to face the room. 'I like it,' she says decisively.

'Come and see the rest.'

She follows him out into the hall and watches his thigh muscles moving inside his jeans as he climbs the stairs. At the top he turns to see her smiling to herself. 'What are you grinning about?'

'Nothing,' she says, trying to straighten her face but starting to laugh.

'What is it?' He seizes her and presses her up against the landing wall. 'You'd better tell me.'

'It's nothing,' she gasps, giggling. 'I was just thinking about . . . about the weekend . . . you know.'

'What part of the weekend, in particular, would that be, then?'

'Oh, I don't know.' She curves her hands around his buttocks and pulls him towards her. 'This part maybe.'

They kiss. She feels a sudden, stabbing desire for him. She wants him; she wants him so much it gives her a physical, prickling, longing ache. She wants him here, right here on this darkened landing with only the light from the sitting room downstairs, and she wants him now. He is unbuttoning her shirt, bending his head to kiss her throat and chest. She fumbles with the buttons to his shirt, but this desire has made her clumsy and they refuse to slide through the material. She tugs at them desperately. 'Bugger,' she says.

'What's the matter?' His voice sounds thick and muffled.

'Can't get your shirt undone.'

He steps back briefly, grips the back of the collar with both hands, shrugs it over his head and flings it to the floor. She holds

out her arms for him. She loves the feel of his smooth, warm
skin, the hard springiness of his torso. She runs her hands up
his back and along his arms, pressing her mouth to his neck and
shoulder. Then she stops. Something is not quite right, there is
something uneasy, a niggling something registering somewhere
in her consciousness. She attempts to sort her fuddled mind into
a coherent thought. Smell. She has begun to smell something
ominous.

'John?'

'Mmm?'

'I can smell something burning.'

He raises his head and sniffs the air like a bloodhound.
'Shit.'

He hurtles down the stairs two at a time and disappears.
Alice leans against the wall, her breath shuddering in her chest,
heartbeat chasing heartbeat. I'm in love, she thinks, I love this
man, I love him. She explores this feeling, cautiously, like
someone walking on a newly healed limb for the first time,
finding out its limitations, wary of any signs of weakness. Is
she frightened? No. Excited? Yes – incredibly. She wants to
gobble up time, to rush through days and weeks and years
with him, so they can do everything right now. But, at the
same time, she wants to freeze it: she knows enough about
love to be aware of its double bind – that there's no love
without pain, that you can't ever love someone without that
tinge of dread at how it might end.

She tugs at the hem of her skirt and rebuttons her blouse,
feeling at the same time for the light switch along the wall. It
must be here somewhere. She feels almost nervous at going
downstairs again in case, just in case, she sees a casual
indifference in his eyes – but in her heart she knows she
won't. She thinks he loves her or, at least, could love her,
and as she pushes her palm in wide sweeps over the wall,

she wonders absently how long it will be before she tells him she loves him. Her fingers find the switch and she turns on the light.

For a second she is blinded and she stands blinking in the strong, yellow electric light. There's no shade on the bulb. She is standing, she sees, on a small bare-boarded landing. There are three doors off it, all slightly ajar. She pushes one open and turns on the light. It is John's bedroom: surprisingly spartan, with a double futon with a blue cover, a bedside light, and a tower of books next to the bed. There's nothing on the walls, some clothes scattered about. The bay window looks over the street. She fights a compulsion to scrutinise everything in minute detail – to open drawers, flick through books – to glean any information about this man who has walked into her life but she feels voyeuristic; John doesn't know she's in here, after all.

The next room is obviously where he keeps all his junk. It's smaller, at the back of the house and crammed with stuff – two bicycles in different stages of disrepair, an old computer disgorging a tangle of coloured leads, a large chest of drawers, a wardrobe, shelves full of files, heaps of clothes, paper, magazines, newspapers. The third room is the bathroom, painted a rich dark blue. The bath is huge and turquoise. By the loo is another pile of books – some poetry, a complete works of Ibsen and *The Journalist's Handbook*. There is a constant gurgling, bubbling sound that she assumes is the pipes until she turns to go and sees a large tank behind the door. A pump spurts out water in a steady trickle and the tank glows with a fluorescent tube light: illuminated in it are not fish but a strange motionless creature.

Alice approaches the tank. It's like a lizard but all white, and hangs suspended in the water, regarding her with tiny black eyes set back in the sides of its head. She has never seen anything like it: around its head is a spray of fragile, delicately fronded pink gills, which pulsate slightly. Its feet fascinate her: they are like dolls' hands — dainty and pale with tiny meticulous fingers. It looks inexpressibly melancholy. What strikes her most of all is its stillness: it doesn't move even when she bends right down next to it. She wonders how it stays afloat in mid-tank without appearing to move its legs or thick tail. Surely it should sink to the gravelled bottom? As she watches, it moves painstakingly slowly to the edge of the tank, its muscular tail flicking it through the water; when it reaches the side of the tank, its nose bumps the glass and it sinks a few inches in the water, then stops, gazing at her soulfully. She presses her fingertips against the glass. 'What are you doing in there?' she whispers.

It gazes at her with its mournful pinprick eyes. She straightens up and turns to go downstairs.

In the kitchen, John is standing shirtless at the cooker, vigorously stirring something in a pan. 'Hello,' he says, as she enters, 'it's not completely ruined, don't worry.' He leans over and kisses her. 'Have you been having a look round?'

'John, what's that thing?'

'What thing?'

'That thing in the tank upstairs.'

'Oh,' he laughs, 'it's an axolotl.'

'A what?'

'An axolotl. They originate from South America. One of my cousins breeds them. It's amazing, isn't it?'

'But is it a reptile or an amphibian or what?'

'They're the larval form of salamanders. If I let him get used to being out of water, he'd become a salamander. They're the only larval form in existence that can breed.'

'So he's stuck in constant adolescence?' She shudders. 'What a horrific thought. That's so cruel. You should let

185

him grow up into a fully fledged salamander and put him out of his misery.'

'Didn't you like being an adolescent?'

'No! I hated it. I couldn't wait to grow up and leave home.'

'Really?'

'Yeah. I was an awful teenager – horrible to live with and horrible to look at.'

'I don't believe you.'

'It's true. I wore black all the time, did nasty things to my hair and didn't talk to my parents properly for five years.'

'Have you got any photos?'

'None that I'd show you. Anyway, don't avoid the issue: you're trapping that poor creature in that terrible no man's land.'

'Not really. It's more like he's permanently in his twenties – he can breed, he can have relationships, he can lead a happy, normal axolotl life. He never grows old, which is a pretty good deal, I think. The Dorian Grays of the amphibian world.'

'He doesn't look very happy.'

'Not at the moment, but wait and see. He's nocturnal. He's sleeping just now. In a few hours he'll have woken up and will be zipping round his tank, churning up the gravel. Just wait and see.'

John opens the oven door and ducks down to look in. 'Not long now,' he says, and slams it shut.

'Aren't you cold?' she asks, and puts her arms around him from behind, resting her head between his shoulder-blades.

'No,' he says, and Alice hears and feels his voice resonating through his chest. 'I feel fine.'

'There's a good smell.'

'Are you hungry?'

She nods.

I loved being in love with John. Love is easy and strange. I would ponder it on rattling tube trains, on crowded buses, at work – what was it about him that produced this effect in me? I could never decide definitively and had lists of both generalisations and detailed particulars: I loved his generosity, his ability to laugh at himself, his determination, the way he could unequivocally apply himself to any task, his impulsiveness, and how he could find humour in any situation. But yet, I also loved the way he rubbed his hair in a circular motion when he was tired, how his upper lip would stick out when he was cross, that he couldn't go to sleep unless he had a glass of water by the bed, and that he was constantly surprised by how much food he could eat.

I really loved watching him shave. My father, ever since I could remember, had used an electric shaver and so the whole ritual of a wet shave fascinated me: the badger-haired brush given to him by his father, the little pool of water in the sink, the razor to which he would give a quick, flicking shake before applying it to his face. I would sit on the side of the bath watching him work a lather from the brush and his palm, then slather it into a beard-shaped mass on his face. Then the rasp of the silver razor against his stubble and the bizarre faces he pulled to hold his skin taut. Sometimes I would stand behind him and imitate these faces, until one day he laughed so much he cut himself. I loved the way that before his face would be sharp and prickled, leaving red welts on my face and body, and then afterwards it would be so smooth I could run my lips along it. The severed stubble clustered like iron filings around the sink after the water had drained away.

I loved him more than anything else I'd ever known. How was I to know he was a gift I couldn't keep?

Early on a Saturday morning at Alice's flat, the phone starts to ring. John is lying in bed, flicking through the pages of a weekend supplement, a glass of water propped up beside him. Alice is in the bath. John looks across to the phone doubtfully. 'Shall I get that?' he shouts.

'Yes. Could you?' Her voice comes back through the wall.

John leans over and picks up the receiver. 'Hello?' he says.

There is a hollow silence at the end of the line. The narrow acoustics of the bathroom send the sounds of splashing running round the walls of the whole flat.

'Hello?' he says again, louder this time.

'Is Alice there?' The voice, female, is terse and slightly outraged. Alice's mother. Has to be. John puts down the glass of water on the bedside table. 'Yes,' he says, 'she is.' He is aware that, for some nebulous maternal reason, the fact that a strange man has answered her daughter's phone early in the morning means that Alice's mother must automatically dislike him, as well as be as rude as she possibly can.

'Well, can I speak to her, then?'

'I should think so,' he says and then, purely to annoy her, enquires, 'Who shall I say is calling?'

'It's her mother,' she snaps.

He has to put down the phone and rush across the room so she doesn't hear him laughing. 'Alice,' he calls through the bathroom door, 'your mother's on the phone.'

She appears from the steam, a towel wound around her head. John climbs back into bed and watches as she pads across the room and picks up the receiver. Alice is my girlfriend: he tries out the idea. My new girlfriend. The language for these situations frustrates him. 'We are going out together' – he hates that phrase. 'Girlfriend' seems hopelessly teenage and inadequate. What then? 'Partner' is too business like, 'lover' a bit racy for everyday parlance. 'Friend'? Sounds like he has something to hide. 'Special friend' – oh, please. None of these words is enough because what he really wants to say and wants to tell everyone is—

John loses his train of thought at this point because Alice's conversation is gaining momentum and ferocity. It's become a vicious game of verbal ping-pong.

'Who? I'm not telling you.'

A pause while her mother's voice twitters out of the receiver.

'I know what time it is, thank you.'

Another bout of twittering.

'Because it's none of your business.'

And it goes on like this for a few minutes, Alice barking every few seconds: 'Yeah, right . . . What I do is up to me . . . Why don't you just keep out of it?' . . . I know I didn't tell you . . . No . . . No . . . Yes . . . No . . . I think I'm old enough to decide . . . If I wanted your advice, and believe me I don't, then I'd ask for it . . .' Then it ends with Alice shouting, 'Just go to hell!' and hanging up. There is a short silence. Alice stares at the phone, motionless. It starts to ring again. She picks it up as if she knew all along that would happen. 'What?' she snarls.

John starts laughing. This is incredible.

'Why?' she shrieks. 'Why? Because I knew you'd react in exactly the way you are doing . . . Don't start with that shit again . . . I am! . . . No . . . What's the point in being cautious? . . . Love? Love? How can you use that word? You wouldn't even know what it was if it came and slapped you in the face.'

This time there is a monotonous buzzing from North Berwick: her mother's hung up. Alice bangs the receiver down again and starts bouncing round the room like a ball of lithium on water. 'How dare she? How dare she?' she rants. 'God, if she thinks she can just ring up here and start lecturing me about—' She stops, lets out a kind of screeching growl and, ripping the towel from her head, flings its sodden length to the floor.

'Jesus,' says John, from the bed, 'does this happen a lot?'

'This is nothing,' she says, with a grimace, 'we're just warming up.'

'So what was it about?'

'You.'

'Me?'

'Who you are. What you're doing answering the phone in my flat. How long I've known you. Why I hadn't told her that I'm involved with someone again. As if,' she shouts, 'that's any of her business.'

'Well . . .' he ventures '. . . I mean, she is your mother. It is kind of her business, isn't it?'

She looks at him, astonished, as if this had never occurred to her. 'But she's just interfering for the hell of it. She always comes over all weird with me and men. Always.'

'All weird?'

'Yeah, all over-protective and censorious. Goes on and on and on and on about how I should be careful and cautious, not get hurt, make decisions over time, how passion isn't necessarily what's good for you in the long run. Et cetera, et cetera.'

'Isn't she like that with your sisters as well?'

'Not really. But they have sensible, long-term boyfriends and then get married.'

He is tempted to remind her that only one of her sisters is, in fact, married, but doesn't. 'Are you going to call her back?' he asks instead.

'No!'

As an experiment, John goes out of the room. In the bathroom he picks up his toothbrush and the toothpaste. Before he's finished brushing his teeth, he hears Alice dialling and then: 'Mum? It's me.'

When he comes back, she is combing out her hair, bending over, the wet ends almost touching the ground.

'How did it go?' he asks, sitting down on the edge of the bed.

'Oh, fine.' The comb travels rhythmically down. 'It doesn't mean anything, really. It's all just . . . fireworks.'

She shifts position, passing the comb into her other hand.

'Did you mean what you said,' he asks, '. . . about her . . . and . . . love?'

There is a hesitation in the combing. Her face is obscured by her hair. She shrugs, then resumes with twice the vigour. 'Yes.'

'So . . . what about your father?'

'Hmm. I'm not convinced. Sometimes I reckon she just used him as a stud.'

'Stud?'

'For us.'

'Us?'

'Not you and me, John,' she says patiently. 'My sisters. And me.'

'Really? You really think that?'

She tosses back her hair and stands upright, frowning, looking down at him. 'My father would do anything for her, but she—' She breaks off, seeing the expression on his face. 'It's OK, you know. It just makes me more determined.'

'In what way?'

'Not to be like her.'

John is woken by a violent movement in the bed beside

him and a large hank of Alice's hair being tossed across his face.

'Alice? Are you all right?'

'Can't sleep.' Her voice is small, tight and querulous.

He puts out a sleep-heavy arm to feel for her. His palm meets the curve of her hip. She is on her side, on the edge of the bed, facing away from him. He moves over and curls his arm about her. 'What's wrong?'

Suddenly she has shrugged him off and is sitting upright, rigid with indignation. 'It's this fucking futon. It's so uncomfortable,' she bursts out, close to tears.

He blinks in surprise, trying to clear his head and understand why she's so upset. 'Oh.'

'It's so . . . so hard and it hurts . . . my kneecaps.'

He laughs. He can't help himself. 'Your *kneecaps?*'

She thumps him. 'Don't laugh at me,' but then she begins to laugh too. 'It hurts my kneecaps. There's nothing unusual about that, is there?'

'Well, yes. I've never heard of anyone having sore kneecaps from sleeping on a futon.'

'If I lie on my front my kneecaps ache because the mattress is so hard.'

He wriggles under the duvet and starts rubbing her kneecaps.

'Is that better?'

'No,' she says, still obscurely annoyed.

He very gently kisses them in turn. 'Is that better?' he asks again. There is a pause.

'A bit,' she says.

When she arrives the next evening after work, he makes her put on a blindfold in the hallway.

'Why?' she asks. 'What's happening?'

'Wait and see.' He propels her up the stairs before him,

making sure she doesn't trip, fixing her hand on the banister, holding her steady. He stops her in the doorway of the bedroom. 'Ready?'

'Yes, yes. What is it?'

He pulls off the blindfold. In the bedroom, in place of the maligned futon, is a new king-sized bed. She shrieks and leaps on to it. 'John! It's amazing!' She bounces up and down exuberantly. Pillows fly and the duvet rumples under her feet. He watches her, leaning against the door jamb. 'And is it of the desired softness for madam's precious kneecaps?'

She flops down on to her stomach, giggling. 'Yes. It's perfect.' She rolls on to her back and sits up, awkward all of a sudden. 'Thank you so much, John. You didn't have to, you know . . . I mean, not just for me.'

He is aware that they both know the bed is a bit of a sign. Neither of them has, as yet, said anything about the future, and he has been surprised to find that he's a bit impatient about this. 'No, I did, really,' he says, in a serious tone, testing her reaction. She blushes furiously and avoids his eye. OK, Alice, he thinks, have it your way, the time is not now. He comes across the gap between them and sits down on the bed. 'I did have to,' he continues, in a lighter tone of voice, 'to stop you going on at me in the middle of the night.'

She laughs. 'I'm really sorry about that. I just couldn't sleep and I get all cross when I can't sleep. I'm sorry, John.'

'Well,' he says thoughtfully, 'there is one way you can make it up to me.'

She begins to smile that wicked, slow smile that never fails to give him an erection. 'Oh, yes?' she says. 'And what would that be, then?'

'You could shag the living daylights out of me on our new bed.'

Ann stands in the doorway, watching Alice. Her daughter's face is tense, set into that all-too-familiar defiant scowl as she removes that ridiculous, moth-eaten feathery thing that Elspeth gave her and lays it carefully on the bed. It's Elspeth who encourages this kind of behaviour in Alice, not setting a good example, not laying down boundaries, which is what a wayward girl like Alice needs. Imagine being sent home from school for being – what was it the headmaster's letter said? – 'inappropriately dressed for academic study'. Ann watches as Alice buttons up a white shirt of Kirsty's and puts on a skirt of a rather more demure length.

'Tights,' Ann commands grimly, pointing at the hole above Alice's left knee. Alice, simmering with suppressed fury, strips off her tights and pulls a fresh pair from her drawer.

'Tie,' Ann says, holding out at arm's length the regulation red and black striped tie of the High School. Alice shakes her head. 'Tie,' Ann repeats more firmly.

'I'm not wearing a bloody tie.'

'I will not have you using that gutter language to me, young lady. And if I say you're to wear a tie to school, you're to wear a tie.'

Alice shakes her head again. 'No.'

Ann sighs. She actually can't be bothered arguing about this

one. To tell the truth, she's quite surprised at how easily Alice
has given in to agreeing to change. An hour ago she'd come
through the door saying she was never going back to school.

'Right. In the car. I'm going to drive you back.'

'I'll walk,' Alice says sullenly.

'I said I'm going to drive you. In the car. Now.'

Ann decides to make the most of the five minutes she has
her daughter trapped in a confined space. 'Your father and I
are sick and tired of your present attitude. You're difficult,
rude, uncooperative, uncommunicative, unhelpful. You look
ridiculous and I for one am glad to see that the school agrees
with me. I want to see a big change in your behaviour, starting
from now. I think that—'

Ann is momentarily distracted from her flow by a car
lurching in front of her at a junction. It stalls. Ann is forced to
brake suddenly and she almost swears. Luckily, she remembers
just in time that she is delivering a lecture on good behaviour
and stops herself. 'And another thing,' she begins again, less
convincingly, trying to remember where she left off, edging
the car towards the junction outside the school.

'Shut up, shut up, shut up,' Alice mutters, her hands over
her ears.

'Don't speak to me like that,' Ann rasps, warming again
to her theme.

'I don't know what your problem is,' Alice shouts heatedly.
'I get the sodding grades, don't I? That's all you and Dad care
about anyway!'

'I'm not going to warn you again about your language,
Alice. Your grades at school are not the issue here.' Ann is
distracted again, but this time by a boy standing at the school
gates as they pull up. Tall, in a black sweater, his bag slung
over his shoulder. It's his son. Undoubtedly. His eldest. Ann
slams her foot abruptly on the brake and peers through the

windscreen to get a good look at him. Looks like his bloody awful mother. She is aware that next to her Alice is swinging open the car door. It is slammed violently and Alice walks away without saying goodbye. Ann's anger has all drained away, Alice's misdemeanours forgotten, in the face of this morbid curiosity in the boy. He has his father's stature, but his mother's colouring and that dreadful cutesy, curly hair.

Ann watches him. He is gazing at a girl coming towards him, smiling nervously. Ann recognises that smile. She is about to give herself up to a little, maudlin weep when she suddenly realises it's Alice he's smiling at. As Alice reaches him, he pushes himself off the wall he's slouched against and falls in step beside her. Ann stares at them, gripping the wheel. Do they know each other? Are they friends? Are they . . . ? No. Impossible. Why, out of all the three hundred-odd boys at the school, would Alice pick him? Ann sees him reach inside his bag and hand Alice something. He touches her lightly on the shoulder as he does so. Ann's body freezes over in horror.

She cranes her head out of the window. 'Alice!' she shouts hysterically. Several people turn round, but not Alice, who is now half-way across the yard with that boy. 'Alice!' Ann shrieks again. Alice's step falters but she carries on, faster this time. Ann leans on the horn. The sound blares out across the yard. Teenagers and teachers and primary-school kiddies turn round to look curiously at the Raikes sisters' mother sitting red-faced in a car by the school gates, honking the horn. Alice turns and marches at a furious pace back across the yard, her colour high, her eyes flashing fire. The boy follows a few steps behind. Her face appears in Ann's window. 'What are you doing?' she cries. 'Go away, will you?'

'Alice,' Ann clutches her daughter's wrist, 'who is that boy?'

'What?' says Alice, appalled.

'That boy.' Ann jabs her finger at him.

'It's none of your business. Why are you doing this to me? Go away. Please.'

'Just answer my question. Who is that boy? What's his name?'

Alice is looking at her in incredulous fury. 'You are so embarrassing,' she hisses. 'He'll hear you. Why can't you just go away?'

'If you tell me his name then I'll go. I promise.'

Alice stares at her, torn between her need for privacy and her desire for Ann to disappear. 'Andrew Innerdale,' she says.

Ann closes her eyes. She never in a million years expected this. Is this divine retribution? Alice starts to withdraw her arm from Ann's grip. Ann clutches at it with renewed terror. 'Alice, tell me, are you going out with that boy?'

Alice is really furious now. 'Let go of me,' she spits, 'you promised you'd go. You promised.'

'Just tell me. Are you?'

'Why should I tell you? It's none of your business.' Angry tears are springing into Alice's eyes.

'I want to know.'

'No. No, I'm not. We're just friends. OK?'

Ann looks past Alice at the boy who is hanging back, staring at them uncertainly. 'And are you going to go out with him? Does he want to go out with you?'

'Mum, please! Please can I go?' Alice twists her arm in her mother's grip. 'Why are you doing this to me? I hate you, I hate you! You're hurting my wrist.'

'Answer me. Does he?'

'Yes,' Alice sobs, wiping her eyes with her free hand.

Ann lets go. Alice springs back from the car, rubbing her wrist, and runs across the yard into the school building, leaving the boy calling after her, 'Alice! Alice! Where are you going?'

Ann does a U-turn in the road, causing a driver coming in the other direction to gesture at her, and drives at top speed back to the house. She shuts herself in her bedroom, in case Elspeth should come back unexpectedly, cradling the phone on her lap.

She still knows the number off by heart. Of course.

'Can I speak to Mr Innerdale, please?' she says, to his assistant. Then his voice is next to her ear and she is speaking and he is answering and she has to press her nails into her palms several times because she realises that nothing has changed, that despite the silence between them since she ended it – again – almost a year ago and despite the fact that she daily congratulates herself that she has managed to tear out the love she had for him by the roots, nothing has changed. 'I need your help,' she hears herself saying.

'Of course, Ann. Anything.'

'You've got to keep your son away from my daughter.'

'Your . . . ? Which one?'

'Alice.'

There is a pause. She hears him tut, his tongue hitting the back of his teeth.

'You mean my daughter, then.'

Ann stands, still grasping the phone, and begins to walk in tight, controlled steps around the room. 'Now, look, I don't want to go into all that again.'

'Why don't you just admit she's mine? Do you know that sometimes I leave the shop early and watch her walking home from school? I pass her in the street almost every week, sometimes close enough for me to touch her. She looks more like me than my own sons. She's mine and you know it. Why can't you just admit it?'

'What difference would it make?' Ann retorts. 'She's Ben's to all intents and purposes. And for your information, it is also,' she adds haughtily, 'more than likely that she is his altogether.'

'That's rubbish, Ann, and you know it. Of course she's mine. There's no doubt about it. The older she gets, the more obvious it is. Don't you think she has a right to know the truth?'

'I'm never going to tell her about you. Never.'

'You can't cope with it, can you, Ann? You can't cope with this constant, living reminder of what we had – and what we still have.'

'We have nothing.' Ann thinks out these words, sees them as if written on an autocue inside her head, and reads them aloud to him. 'There is nothing between us. It's over. I've told you.'

'I don't believe you.' And he drops to a whisper, 'Ann,' he murmurs, his voice curling out from the telephone, sliding down the secret spiral staircase of her ear, 'come and see me.'

'No.' She is panicked now. She can cope with anything but this. She stops walking about. She feels giddy, as though if she took a step she might tip forward into a terrible hole. If she stays rooted to this spot of her bedroom carpet, keeps her feet neatly together like this, everything will be all right.

'Please,' he urges.

'No.'

'Ann, don't say that. I love you. And I know you love me. You can't waste that. You just can't. Nobody will find out. Ben will never know, I promise you. Liza will never know. We'll be careful.'

'We were careful last time.'

'Not careful enough. Ann, please.'

'No.' Is this her speaking? Is this her voice saying these things? 'I mean it.'

He doesn't speak, doesn't ask her again. And part of Ann is glad, so glad, because if he asked her one more time, she knows she wouldn't say no, if he asked her again, she couldn't say no, she'd be out of this house and down at his shop in minutes. She is so close. Why doesn't he know that, damn him, why doesn't he ask again, just one more time, that's all it would take, my darling.'

After a while, she hears herself speak: 'I need you to promise me you'll keep your son away from her.'

Ask me again.

'Andrew can see who he likes.' His voice is distant this time, offhand and impersonal.

'Please. I need your cooperation on this. You and only you know how . . . wrong it could be.'

'What am I supposed to tell Andrew – sorry, son, she's your sister?'

'I don't care. Tell him what you have to. Make something up. You have to do this for me. Please.'

Please ask me again.

'You do realise that your asking me to do this is tantamount to admitting that Alice is my daughter.'

'I know that,' says Ann softly, 'but what are you going to do about it? Sue for custody?'

I still feel afraid, unsettled. Earlier – some time earlier, I don't know when – I was suddenly aware of this presence. Someone I didn't know was close to me, bending over me maybe. The scent my nostrils relayed to me was unfamiliar, male, tinged with nicotine.

I once watched a buzzard circling its prey from the air. It cruised the sky, searching, and when it found something, it would drop like a plumbline and hang suspended four or five feet above it, wings oscillating rapidly, waiting maybe a full minute before diving down.

This person, whoever it was – It was as if I could hear the crack of beating wings, feel a shadow hovering above me. My mind whirred and clicked: I wanted to scream, reach out and push him away. Is there a worse thing – knowing that someone is there and being powerless to move, speak or even see them?

Alice had been asleep since Newcastle, curled against him, her legs tucked under her, her funeral-black clothes rumpled and creased. She looked pale, with dark crescents under her eyes. John read her copy of *Daniel Deronda* and watched houses, factories, fields and the blank gazes of cattle reel past. Across the aisle a toddler grizzled and jumped up and down on the seats. 'Stop that, Kimberley,' the mother kept saying, without looking up from her magazine. Opposite them, two nuns peeled and ate a red string bag of oranges in silence, piling up the bits of peel on the table in pungent-smelling ziggurats. One of them gave him an oddly beatific smile when he caught her eye. The other looked away sourly. At Peterborough, Alice stretched and opened her eyes.

'Hello, how are you feeling?' John said.

'Um, all right.' She yawned and pushed her tangled hair out of her eyes. 'Where are we? Have I been asleep long?'

'About two hours. We've just left Peterborough.' He closed the book and shoved it in the gap between their seats. 'Your family are great, you know.'

'Hmm.' She stared out of the window. 'I wish you could have met my grandmother.'

He took her hand and squeezed it. 'I wish I could have done too.' He leant forward slightly to see if she was crying, but her face was dry, her eyes unfocused as the dusky scenery slid past them. 'You know,' he continued, 'there is nothing anyone can say that will make you feel better, but do you know this?' He frowned with concentration. '"Love is not changed by death and nothing is lost, and all in the end is harvest."'

'Who said that?'

'Julian of Norwich. Someone sent it to me when my mother died.'

'Julian of Norwich? The mad medieval mystic?'

'The very same, but she wasn't mad, I'll have you know.'

Alice repeated it under her breath, looking at him intently. 'I like it. "Love is not changed by death . . ." I think Elspeth would have liked it too. Her husband died when she was about my age.'

'Really? What of?'

'Malaria. They were missionaries in Africa.' She picked up

the book he had been reading and absently flicked through the pages with her thumb, over and over. 'I'm glad we scattered her ashes on the Law,' she said suddenly. 'Did you scatter your mother's ashes somewhere?'

'No. She's buried in Golders Green.'

'Oh. Burial.' She shuddered. 'I've never liked the thought of that very much.'

'Why?'

'Putting the body of someone you love into the cold, damp earth, and then knowing that under the mound that you visit and tend is still them, slowly decaying bit by bit.'

'It's not really them. Only their body.'

'Yeah, but bodies are important too. In your sense of them, anyway.'

'I suppose so. It's never bothered me. I've never really thought of what lies beneath that headstone as my mother.'

She knelt up on the seat to see if the toilet's engaged sign was on.

'I need the loo. Back in a sec.'

She edged between him and the seat in front; he felt the warmth from her body on his face briefly before she walked down the aisle, steadying herself against the movement of the train by grasping the tops of the seats.

When she got back he saw she'd washed her face and brushed her hair. 'You look better,' he said, stroking the damp tendrils around her face.

'I feel better.' She smiled and swung her legs across his lap.

'What are you doing tomorrow?' he asked. 'Do you fancy an afternoon film at the NFT?'

She screwed up her face. 'I have a feeling I'm doing something, but I can't remember . . . Oh, yes! Of course! I've got a big day tomorrow. I'm looking for a flat. I've decided. I just can't bear that place any more. I'm going to get up really early, buy *Loot* and scour London to find my ideal home. Well, that's the plan anyway. I doubt I'll find one that quickly, but you never know. My dream home is out there somewhere – and I've just got to find it.'

As she talked the idea that had been gradually forming in his mind crystallised into a definite and articulate desire – that she should live nowhere but with him. He watched her fiddling with a plastic cup from the buffet car, and her words reached him in snatches – '. . . one-bedroom flat in north London somewhere, Kilburn maybe . . . about eighty pounds a week or something . . . Willesden is supposed to be nice . . . a quieter road . . .'

'Move in with me,' he blurted out.

She was immediately silent. His words hung in the air between them.

'I mean, if you want to.'

'Do you want me to?'

He laughed and cupped her face in his hands. 'I really, really want you to.'

She circled his wrists with her fingers. Her pupils were very wide, her mouth serious. She's going to say no, he thought. Shit, shit, shit. Damn. Serves you right for hurrying things too much.

'Do you want to move in with me?' he said shakily, and then began to burble: 'I mean, you can think about it. You don't have to decide right now. We could leave things as they are, if you like. Whatever. And if you need your own space you can keep your own flat or if you move in – not that I think you're definitely going to or anything, it's entirely up to you – but we could clear out the spare room so that—'

'John!' Alice put her fingers over his mouth.

'What?'

'I'd love to move in with you.'

His heart lifted with relief and happiness, and he leant forward to kiss her. Just as his mouth reached hers, she said, 'But . . .'

He pulled back to look at her again. 'But what?'

'I think you know what I'm going to say.'

For the next few seconds he ran through everything he could think of. 'What? I've already got rid of the futon. What is it? The decoration? The furniture? The axolotl? Tell me and I'll change it.'

'No, no, it's not the house. If I'm going to move in, we have to tell your father about us.'

John leant back into his seat. Since that drive back from the Lake District almost three months ago, his father hadn't been mentioned at all. He'd been coasting along under a ridiculous illusion that things could stay like this – him perfectly happy and in love and his father suspicious about how he was spending his evenings and weekends, but nothing more. He suddenly saw how difficult it had been for Alice, harbouring the knowledge of this problem but saying nothing to him. He was angry with himself for the level of his self-deception, causing her all this pain and uncertainty while he hid his head in the sand.

She laid her hand on his arm. 'John, the last thing I want to do is to upset things between you and your father.' He saw that her eyes were filling with bright tears and that she was struggling fiercely with herself not to cry. It broke his heart but he was unable to speak. 'But don't you see?' she continued, the tears spilling down her cheeks now. 'How can I move in if he doesn't know? What if he calls round? What if he rings and I answer the phone? He's your father. We can't live together without him knowing, and I can't move in with you if you are denying my existence to him.'

He pulled her towards him and kissed her face repeatedly,

licking the salt from his lips. 'Don't cry, Alice. Please don't cry. I'm so sorry I've been so crap about this. I'll tell him tomorrow. I promise. He'll be fine about it, really he will. Everything's going to be all right.'

When Elspeth returns to the house at four, she can hear the noise from the end of the drive: Alice is screaming at the top of her voice. Elspeth hurries down the path around the side of the house and opens the back door. Ann is near hysteria – clutching the edge of the kitchen table – and Alice, her hair all disarrayed and looking oddly conventional in a white shirt and school skirt, is shrieking. 'Don't you ever, ever tell me what to do!'

Elspeth shuts the door firmly and the noise stops as they both turn to look at her. 'What,' she says, 'is going on? Do you realise that people on the road can hear you, Alice?'

'I don't care!' Alice weeps and storms from the room. She crashes into the sitting room and a few seconds later they hear the piano lid being slammed open and the opening chords of a Chopin waltz banged out violently and very fast.

Elspeth turns to Ann and raises her eyebrows.

'Elspeth,' Ann begins, 'something awful has happened.'

The seriousness of her tone, the whiteness of her face makes Elspeth's heart stall. 'To . . . to Alice?'

'Yes.'

'What is it?' Already Elspeth's mind is running along possibilities – drugs? police? expelled from school? pregnancy?

'Not really to her . . . It hasn't happened yet, at least I

don't think so . . . but the fact is it might . . . and it could be serious . . . serious trouble if it does . . . and I don't know how to tell her without her knowing why . . . I don't know how to stop it.'

'Ann,' says Elspeth sharply, 'what is it that's happened?'

'Alice is . . . his son has fallen for Alice.'

Elspeth is about to ask whose son for God's sake, but the realisation hits her as soon as she opens her mouth. 'I see,' she says instead and sits down at the table.

Ann darts to her side, fidgeting with nerves. 'Elspeth, you've got to help me. You've got to help me stop . . . this happening.'

Elspeth turns and surveys her daughter-in-law. 'Don't you realise,' she says, 'that if you tell Alice not to do something it will more than likely make her go ahead and do it? Don't you see that? Do you understand your own daughter so ill, woman?'

Elspeth goes into the sitting room where Alice is bashing on the piano and takes a firm hold of Alice's hands. 'That's enough of that, missy.'

'Don't you start ordering me about as well,' Alice cries, raising her red, streaked face to Elspeth's.

Elspeth sits next to Alice on the piano stool, and continues to hold both of Alice's trembling hands in her own. 'If you don't learn to curb this temper of yours, Alice Raikes, you'll one day hurt someone you really love,' she says, beginning to stroke her right palm soothingly up and down Alice's taut back. 'What a lot of fireworks over nothing. I'm not ordering you about. That is no way to treat a musical instrument, as you well know.'

The ends of Alice's hair brush the keys as she wipes the tears from her face. Elspeth holds up her left hand – spanned out – palm to palm against Alice's, lifelines crossing, finger to finger. 'Look at that,' she says. Alice looks. Her fingers extend above Elspeth's by the length of a whole metacarpal. 'What big hands you have.'

'All the better to play my scales with,' Alice mutters.

'Tell me,' says Elspeth after a while, 'do you like this Andrew boy? Do you really like him?'

Alice shrugs non-committally. 'He's all right.'

'That's not what I asked.'

'But that's not the point,' says Alice, flaring up again indignantly.

'I would say it's very much the point. Whether he's worth all this anger and energy. Whether you really want him or not.'

Alice says nothing, sullenly jiggling her leg.

'Well?' Elspeth persists.

'He's all right,' Alice repeats.

'And nothing more?'

'No,' she admits finally, 'nothing more.'

'Good.' Elspeth releases Alice's hands from her grasp and says, 'Now play me something nice.'

Alice's hands hover over the keyboard for a few seconds. There is a slight click as her clipped nails hit the ivory keys and then she begins to play.

He leaves at ten in the morning. Alice waves him off from the front door, 'Good luck!' she calls after him. John pulls a face.

Since getting up, they have had a forced jollity about them, both of them joking and chatting as normal, pretending that what John has to do today is not that serious at all, just another visit to his father. After his car has pulled away, Alice clears away the breakfast things, has a bath, takes a long time drying her hair and goes across the road to buy a newspaper. She can't settle at anything: she tries to read a book for a while but the words on the page jump about, and no matter how many times she rereads the opening paragraphs, she cannot muster enough interest in the characters to carry on concentrating. She keeps wondering what's happening with John. He'll have arrived by now. Has he told him yet? Will he tell him straight away or wait until they've been to the synagogue? What will he say? Will he be OK about it? Will he be angry? She flicks through the paper and reads the film reviews. At one o'clock she phones Rachel and leaves a distracted message on her answering-machine. What will he do if his father forbids him to carry on seeing her?

She decides to go out. Leaving John a note on the kitchen table in case he should come back while she's not there, she wanders into Camden Market. The streets are packed with tourists, teenagers with lurid hair and ethnic clothes, and dealers whispering, 'Grass? E? Acid? Anything?' The air is thick with joss-sticks and patchouli oil and the canal banks are full of people sitting in the sunshine, dangling their legs over the water. She watches a young woman with cropped blonde hair have her belly button pierced. She buys a jumper with bright yellow and blue stripes that barely covers her midriff: she wears it home, stuffing the one she came out in into the carrier-bag the stall-holder gives her.

John still isn't back when she finally returns. There is a message on the answerphone from Rachel: 'Alice? It's me. Are you there? Pick up the phone . . . You're not there? OK. Just wondering how the big confession went. Call me soon. Bye.'

She feeds the axolotl, the way John has shown her: dangling a scrap of prawn from plastic tweezers in front of its snubbed nose. 'Come on,' she murmurs to it, 'aren't you hungry today?' It looks straight ahead, mournfully, and just when her arm is beginning to ache seriously, it flashes forward and seizes the prawn scrap from the tweezers in one abrupt gulp.

At about four she hears John's key in the lock. She leaps on to the sofa and affects a relaxed position, as if she's been lying there reading all afternoon.

'Hello?' he calls.

'Hi.'

He comes in through the sitting-room door and gives her a weak smile. He looks exhausted and drained. She gets up, goes over to him and hugs him. He rests his forehead on her shoulder.

'Come and sit down,' she says, peeling his jacket off his back and pushing him towards the sofa. 'Do you want a cup of tea?'

He knits his brows. 'Um. I'd rather have a whisky.'

She pours him a double, spilling a few drops on the table, and hands it to him, standing in front of him. He takes a swig and, putting his arms around her middle, buries his head in her exposed midriff. 'I like your jumper,' he says, his voice muffled.

She strokes his hair. 'I bought it today. I was so worried about you I had to go shopping. How was it? Do you want to tell me now or later?'

'We-ell,' he says slowly, and she gets the feeling he is keeping his face buried in her stomach so that he doesn't have to look at her, 'it was no worse than I thought it would be.'

'That bad, eh?'

He nods, 'Yes. Just about.'

'John, I'm sorry.'

His arms around her tighten. She lets her fingers stray through his hair.

'Alice,' he says, 'you've got to learn that none of this is your fault. You do know that, don't you?'

'I suppose so, but I can't help feeling responsible, can I? I mean, if it weren't for me—'

'He'll come round,' he interrupts, 'once he's had a few days to think about it.'

They're both silent for a moment. Alice cannot bear to see him crushed and hurt like this, and feels incensed. 'But what did he say? Does he hate me?'

'Of course he doesn't hate you. He's going to love you.'

'We're going to meet?' she says to the top of his head, alarmed.

'Well, yes, one day. Not yet, maybe. But when he's got more used to the idea, I'll take you to meet him. He'll love you when he knows you.' He sounds grim, determined to convince himself.

'But what did he say?' she persisted.

'You don't really want to know.'

'Oh.'

She pulls away from him, walks to the back window and looks out into the garden, twining and twisting her fingers. It is beginning to get dark and the trees are being tossed by the wind. The reflection in the window has projected the room into the cold, dark garden. Everything is reversed and in it John is looking at her over the back of the sofa.

'Alice?'

'Yes?' She doesn't turn round, watching him instead in the reflection.

'Talk to me, please. Don't go silent on me. Tell me what you're thinking.'

She shrugs, as if to free herself of a stiffness in her neck. 'I don't know. I don't know.'

'What don't you know?'

'I don't know . . . I don't know if I like not knowing what he said.'

'What do you mean?'

'Well . . .' Alice wonders what she does mean. She feels unbelievably confused, her thoughts all whirled in a tangle. 'I suppose I mean . . . I find it astonishing that it matters to him so much, but how can I ever hope to understand it if you won't tell me?'

He doesn't reply straight away. She sees from the reflection that he sits on the sofa for a few seconds then he stands and comes across the room, slipping slightly in his socks on the bare boards. He takes her firmly by the shoulders and turns her round to face him. 'Alice, I . . .' Then he stops. He smooths his palm over her forehead, then rests it in the curve of her neck. 'It's difficult to explain,' he says, in a lower tone of voice. 'To tell you what he said might be . . .' He stops again and takes a deep breath. 'You see, I can kind of understand, after my lifetime of conditioning, where he's coming from. Do you see what I mean?' he asks her.

She nods impatiently. 'Yes. But, John, why don't you just tell me what he said?'

'Because . . . because I'm afraid it would sound ridiculous and divisive . . . and . . . and extreme to you.'

'No, it wouldn't,' she says indignantly. 'Don't treat me like I'm made of glass. I want to know. Come on. Tell me the worst.' She almost squares her shoulders. 'I can take it, you know, John.'

He bites his lip. 'You want to know the worst?'

'Yes.'

'Sure?'

'Yes! How many times do I have to tell you?'

'OK. My father said that if I were to marry you it would be like letting Hitler win,' he says, in a rush.

There is a pause while Alice attempts mentally to process this statement. 'Letting Hitler——?' She shakes her head. 'I don't understand. What on earth have we got to do with Hitler?'

'Because if I were to marry you, our children wouldn't be Jewish, and he sees that as the extermination of Jews.'

'But . . .' she begins, then is silent. She turns back to the window. Letting Hitler win? Letting Hitler . . . ? It's such an outrageous assertion that part of her wants to laugh. She's not quite sure what the other part of her wants to do.

'Al,' he says, laying a hand on her back, 'it's a dreadful thing to say. I didn't want to tell you. He didn't mean it, I just——'

'What did you say?'

'To him?'

'Yes.'

'I said . . . er . . . I said lots of unrepeatable things, among

which I said that I didn't believe in letting the Third Reich
dictate my love life.'

'Right,' Alice whispers. 'Shit.' She feels she might cry.
Hitler? Not for the first time she tries to imagine John's father.
What kind of a person would say that? She reruns the sentence
in her head, trying it out in different ways, with a variety of
different emphases.

He grabs hold of her round the middle and pulls her towards
him. 'Alice, this is stupid. I can't believe we're arguing about
this. I don't believe in letting my father dictate my love life
either. He's bluffing, that's all. He'll come round. You've got
to understand: he's coming from a very different perspective. I
knew it wouldn't be easy telling him. I knew he'd take it badly,
but I know him. He isn't one to bear grudges. His bark has
always been worse than his bite. Once he's had a think about
the whole thing, he'll be fine.'

'But how do you know? What if it really does mean
being cut off from your family and your background and
. . . everything? I can't let you do that.'

'It won't come to that, I promise.'

'How do you know?' she persists.

'I just know. I know my father – this won't last, I guarantee
you. Let's not argue any more.' He tips her face back so she
is forced to look him in the eye. 'Now when,' he says, with
mock fierceness, 'are you going to move in?'

'I'm not sure,' she says reluctantly, 'when's good for you?'

'As soon as possible.'

'Well, I've told my crook of a landlord that I'll be leaving
the flat at the end of December.'

'Bollocks to the end of December. How about tomorrow?'

'I had no idea you had this many clothes, Alice. When do you have time to wear them all?' John is lying on Alice's bed, watching her trying to force the lid of her trunk shut. She bounces up and down on the lid and attempts to squeeze the lock together, panting with the effort.

'I know, I know. I should really throw some out, but I can't bring myself to do it. I love clothes.'

'Evidently.'

'I've been collecting them for years. In that cupboard, you know—' She breaks off, exasperated. 'John, come here a sec, will you, and sit on this so I can shut it?'

He rolls off the bed, crawls through the debris littering the room and adds his weight to the trunk. The lock snaps shut.

'There!' She flicks her pony-tail over her shoulder and sits back on her heels. 'Now, what next?'

He picks up a fragile, colourful paper Chinese dragon from a box. 'Where did you get all this stuff, Alice?'

'All over the place. That's from Bangkok, I think, or somewhere.' She lifts a box down from the top of the wardrobe, opens it and peers inside. 'God, this is all stuff from uni. When I moved out of Jason's house I didn't sort through anything, I just shoved it all into boxes and got out of there as quickly as I could.'

'Quite right too. The little shit,' John mutters, wandering into the bathroom.

She smiles at his retrospective loyalty and pulls out a handful of old postcards, hairgrips, a bicycle bell, ribbons and photographs. She shuffles hastily through the photos, grimacing at images of herself at nineteen and twenty in a variety of poses with a variety of friends.

'Hey, John, look at this. I've got to show this to Rachel.' She follows him into the bathroom where he is piling all her toiletries into a cardboard box and hands him the stack of photos. On top is one of her and Rachel beside a tent in a field. It is summertime and they have their arms around each other's waists, smiling happily. Alice is wearing a flowing golden-brown kaftan. Her hair is in plaits and she has stars drawn all over her face. Rachel is wearing flared, patched jeans and a flowery halterneck top.

'My God,' says John, peering at the picture. 'What on earth were you doing?'

'We were at Glastonbury, hence the outfits. It must have been second year. After the exams.'

He starts looking through the other photos, sniggering. She has turned to go back to her packing when she hears him say: 'Alice – look at this.'

He is staring at a photo.

'What is it?'

He says nothing but just lowers the photo for her to see. It's a younger Alice at a party. She is smiling, her face turned to one side, her mouth open slightly and her hand raised as if in the middle of saying something to the photographer. 'What?' Alice asks, perplexed. 'It's just me at a party.'

'No, look.' He says, and taps his fingertip on the corner of the frame. 'Who does that look like to you?'

She takes the photo from him and holds it closer to her face. In the background, just behind and to the left of her, is someone who looks suspiciously like the man standing next to her right now.

'No. It can't be.' She shakes her head, moves through to the bedroom and holds the picture up to the window.

John follows her and looks over her shoulder. 'It is me. It's definitely me.'

His face is in half-profile and he is looking sideways at the camera. He appears to be leaning on a desk or table of some sort and has a beer-can in his hand. She recognises unequivocally the curve of that brow, the line of the jaw, the way the hair stands up in tufts. Even though the man in the photo is a lot younger, it is unmistakably John. 'Shit,' she whispers, 'it *is* you.' She turns to look at him. 'How can that be?'

'What party was that? Do you remember?'

She looks at the photo again, hardly able to believe what she sees. She scrutinises what she's wearing, what she can see of their surroundings in the dim background light. She stares at the smudged replica of John's features in a photo she must have seen a hundred times since it was taken.

'It must have been your first year, if we were both there,' he is saying. 'I don't think I ever went to any parties there after I'd left.'

'It was a party in some house beside the river. It was the summer term, I think. Can't remember the name of the person whose party it was, or why I was even there.'

'Richard somebody,' John says.

'Richard?' Alice screws up her face. 'Yes, that's right. He was awful. He did history. He was a friend of a friend, or something.'

'I remember that party now.' He nods. 'Someone was sick on a bed.'

'Well, it wasn't me.'

'And you were there? That is just so weird. I don't remember seeing you there at all. I do have a feeling I used to see you in the English library – all legs and hair.'

'You should have been concentrating on your finals, not eyeing up first-years.'

'Mmm. I had to do something to keep my motivation up.'

'Motivation? Is that what you call it?'

He is staring at the photo again. 'Imagine if we'd met then. Imagine if, at that point in time, you'd turned to your left and said to me, "John Friedmann, in six years' time we will fall in love."'

'You'd have thought I was bonkers.'

'I'd probably have thought, Game on! But why, oh sexy and mysterious woman, must we wait six years?'

'I was too young. I wasn't ready for you then. I still had to go through Mario and Jason. Without them I wouldn't have got to you.'

'What, so I should be grateful to those dickheads?'

'No, what I mean is that it's like an equation, an emotional equation: Mario divided by Jason equals John.'

He laughs. 'Well, thanks for getting around to me eventually.' He tucks the photo into his jacket pocket. When she puts her arms around him later she hears it crackle against the pressure of her touch.

A taxi deposited them on the pavement outside Alice's house, and when they stumbled from its high step, with bags and coats, Ann looked up to see the unbelievable – a light burning in Alice's bedroom window. Her heart jumped in her chest, and while the rational half of her mind knew that her daughter was unconscious in a hospital bed, the other half was shouting, 'she's here! It was all a mistake, she's been here at home all along!' Ben saw it too. His face was upturned, the whites of his eyes glistening in the glow.

Ann groped in her bag for the keys, held together by that fish key-ring of Alice's that Ann had never liked very much. Fish had always given her the creeps – slimy, scaled things with serrated jaws. Resting one hand against the wood of the door, she pushed the key into the lock, turned it, and the door gave.

Then they were jostling in the hallway together, Ben fussing with the bags, Ann fighting a stupid reluctance to look upstairs towards the light. What was she afraid of seeing? The light filtering down delineated the walls and objects in the dark room downstairs. Ann moved into the sitting room on brittle ankles, still in her coat, still holding the keys, and turned on the light. On the coffee table was a book, resting face down, its pages splayed, a glass of half-drunk water and a clump of tissues, crisp with dried-up moisture. Ann took off her coat, laid it over the back of a chair and folded her arms across her chest. Ben lumbered across the room and sat on the sofa, tipping his head to rest on the sofa back. Water leaked from the corner of his eye. Whether it was a tear or not, Ann didn't know, and she was irritated to see that he didn't wipe it away, just kept staring at the ceiling.

Ann walked about, eyeing the room. She pulled open a drawer at random, not really knowing why, and found library cards, a sprig of lavender, old and scratched sunglasses, crumpled bank statements and a fountain pen, choked with dried ink.

In the kitchen a tall, narrow cardboard box of cat biscuits stood on the table. The kettle lid was off, resting beside the kettle on the counter. On the chair in the corner was a half-knitted sweater in bright green wool. Ann frowned. She didn't know Alice knitted. Walking to the window, Ann peered out into the gloom trying to make out the garden. She had just pressed her forehead to the cold of the pane when she saw, on the other side of the glass, just inches from her face, a pair of eyes swivel and flicker. A scream stretched from her mouth as if on elastic and she reeled back into the room, stumbling over the kitchen chair. Ben appeared behind her, his face edgy and strained. 'Ann? What's wrong?'

'There was . . . there . . .'

Inarticulate with fear, she pointed at the window, and as she did so saw black fur brush against the pane as a large rodent-like creature turned and resettled on the window-sill. The cat. Of course. She'd forgotten about the bloody cat.

At once furious and relieved, she marched to the back door, unlocked it and wrenched it open. The cat, hunched on the narrow ledge, regarded her with vertically slitted green eyes.

'Come on,' she gestured towards the kitchen, 'hurry up, if you want to come in.'

It didn't move. Gnats zoomed around it in the pool of light cast from the kitchen window. Ann stood in the doorway. 'Are you coming in or not?'

It remained motionless. Sighing, Ann stepped back and started closing the door. But just before it closed fully, the cat darted, quick as a minnow, through the hand-span gap.

It stood in the kitchen, the very tip of its tail twitching, one of its front feet raised above the lino. Ben held out his hand to it, murmuring nonsensical sounds. It touched his fingers once with its nose, its whiskers prinking the air, cooler now the door had been open. Ann could see its claws, sheathed up inside its paws. She watched as Ben moved his fingers up to its head, touching its ears – strange alert triangles of soft papyrus.

But then the creature seemed to shrug inside its skin, its back bristling up into dinosaur spines, and it started to edge around the room, low to the ground. It looked at them again, opened its red maw of a mouth and began to emit a horrible, yowling cry.

'What's wrong with it?' Ben asked anxiously, ducking down to peer at it, under the table. 'Is it in pain?'

Ann put her hands over her ears. The noise seemed to enter the sides of her head like knives. 'How should I know?' She caught sight of the cat-biscuit box on the table again, and said, 'Maybe it's hungry.' She shuddered. The noise was a hideous cross between miaowing and weeping. She'd never heard anything like it, didn't know cats were capable of a noise like that. 'Ben, it's horrible, horrible. Can't you get it to stop?'

Ben tried to get hold of it, or tried to stroke it, addressing it in low, soothing tones, but it wouldn't let him get anywhere near it. The ululating howl went on and on. Ann couldn't stand it any longer. She pushed her way through the kitchen door to go back into the sitting room and, as she did so, the cat shot out with her, grazing her legs with the fur of its flank, sprinting across the floorboards of the sitting room and disappearing up the stairs.

They waited, Ann in the doorway, Ben standing by the table. The noise had stopped. All Ann could hear was Ben breathing and that monotonous grind of traffic you seemed to be able to hear everywhere in London. They stood together in this sudden calm, side by side, barely moving. Then Ann thought about the light that was still burning in the room above their heads, and realised they were both afraid to go upstairs.

Alice staggers through the door with three bags of shopping, kicking the door shut behind her. She transfers all the bags to one hand and bends to pick up the post with the other. On the way to the kitchen she looks through it idly. A letter for John. A shiny envelope addressed to 'The Occupier' telling them to 'Play and Win Today!' and a postcard for John in sloping black handwriting. She knows even as she starts to read it that she shouldn't be reading it but something goads her on until she's finished. Then she goes back to the beginning and reads it again. Then she reads it again and again and again, after which she puts the shopping down on the table, switches on the kettle, still holding the postcard, sits down, places it squarely in front of her and reads it again: 'Dear John,' it begins, 'It was, as always, great to see you last weekend. Thanks for coming over. I only wish I could see you more often, but you seem so busy these days. Thanks also for sharing with me your dilemma. My only wish is for your happiness, and I know that you cannot be happy in the long term with someone who isn't Jewish. If you want to have affairs with a few non-Jewish girls, it is no concern of mine. But if you marry this girl, or live with her as if you are married, I will no longer be able to think of you as my son. I know your mother would have felt the same. Fondest love, Dad.'

Alice sits for a long time with the card on the table before her. She reaches into the carrier-bags for an apple, which she rolls between her palms, staring at the card for so long that the black letters blur into tiny black dots that jump about like ants. Then she looks away and presses the cool green skin of the apple to her forehead. With her fingertips, she turns the card over: on the other side is a picture of Brighton pier in a distinctively seventies tint, with a violently turquoise sky and lurid orange windbreakers on the beach. She wonders if Daniel Friedmann chose this view deliberately or whether it was the first card that came to hand.

Then she gets up and roots in her bag for her address book, walks over to the phone and dials a number. 'Rachel? Hi, it's me. Listen, I can't talk now, but can I come and stay? . . . No, it's not that . . . Kind of . . . I know . . . Look, I'll tell you all about it later . . . Yes . . . No . . . I just don't know at the moment . . . It won't be for long, I promise . . . No, I know that . . . Thanks . . . See you in a bit.'

She hangs up, goes through the living room and up the stairs. On the landing she pauses, as if she's lost her way, but then she goes into the bedroom and pulls a bag down from the cupboard.

John has been anxious – over-anxious, in her opinion – that she should make as many changes to the house as she needs to make it feel like her home as well as his. He keeps telling her to move whatever she wants, paint rooms, and insisted that they go shopping last weekend to buy furniture for her. She hadn't really thought it necessary – John's house seems amorphous to her; fluid, comfortable, normal. There is nothing that grates on her, nothing that feels alien. But, to keep him happy, they had driven furiously from second-hand shop to second-hand shop, cramming the car and, when no more would fit, strapping on to the roof-rack a chest of drawers, an armchair with a sagging seat and a piled brown cover, a bookcase, another bookcase, a small bedside table. At the cheval mirror, she had tried to persuade him to stop. 'Might come in handy, though,' he'd said, raising his eyebrows at her, 'somewhere in the bedroom. Don't you think?' Alice had burst out laughing. The shop-owner had a fit of coughing.

She pulls open her chest of drawers. It had taken them three goes to get it up the stairs. John's friend Sam had come round in the end to help. Alice had stood on the landing as the two men swore and shunted and cursed as they heaved it up, step by step.

Into her bag she shoves a jumble of whatever comes into her vision – underwear, shirts, a pair of jeans. She can't think logically. She leaves her new chest, bookcases and table and goes into the bathroom, where she sweeps all her things into one of the bag's side pockets. She stands a moment looking at the axolotl hanging as usual in its tank; it gazes back at her morosely, then she clatters down the stairs. If she is really going to leave tonight, she needs to be gone before John gets back: if she sees him, it will be impossible to walk through that door.

It's only when she sits down on the tube that she bursts into tears.

John returns at about nine. The house is dark. He fumbles for the hall light as he wipes his feet and shakes the rain out of his hair.

'Alice!' he calls. No answer. 'Alice?' He listens for her answering voice. Nothing. Was she going out tonight? He tries to remember if she said anything about it this morning, but doesn't recall her mentioning it. The answerphone is on but there are no messages. In the living room he sits down, kicks off his shoes and yawns. He feels a little disgruntled and wishes she was in. He was looking forward to seeing her and bought a bottle of wine on the way home. Was this what life was like before he met her? Returning home, tired, to a cold and empty house? Although she's only been living here permanently for a week, he has become rather hooked to the surge of pleasure he gets from coming back to find her curled up in the bedroom reading, or talking to the axolotl while running a bath, or watering the seedlings she's planted in an old sink just outside the back door. He goes into the kitchen, sees some bags of shopping on the table and is puzzled. She must have been in and gone out again. When he reaches for the kettle to boil water for some tea, he finds it full of still hot water.

He wanders upstairs to the bathroom, fills the basin with water and splashes it repeatedly over his face. As he is humming to himself and lathering his hands with some fancy-smelling soap that Alice has put there, he stops dead. Her toothbrush has gone. His own toothbrush lolls on its own in the mug. He hurriedly rinses his hands and wipes them on his trousers, darting paranoid glances around the room. Don't be silly, he tells himself, she'll have left it somewhere in the house. But her moisturiser has gone, her hairbrush has gone, her towel has gone.

John rushes across the landing and wrenches open the chest of drawers they bought a few days ago from a junk shop on the Holloway Road. Has anything been taken from here? It's hard to tell. There are still loads of clothes here, all neatly folded one on top of the other. He spins round to the bed. All her books are still stacked up on her side. It's OK. She's just out somewhere. And taken all her make-up and her toothbrush with her? But she hasn't gone. She can't have gone. It is then that he sees the top of the cupboard behind him, reflected in the mirror above the bed. There is a large space where she had previously stored her rucksack, the one that had been all round the world with her, she'd told him proudly. He flops down on to the bed. Why, why, why has she gone? He racks his brain to think of anything out of the ordinary that happened that morning. Did he say anything to upset her? They had had breakfast together, like they did most mornings, and she kissed him goodbye before she left for the tube. Nothing awful in that. They had talked about going to the Czech Republic in the summer after she had seen a picture of Prague on the back of a cereal packet. Had he said anything outrageous enough to make her want to leave him?

A note. She must have left a note. Maybe she had had to go away unexpectedly and had been unable to contact him. Maybe one of her family was ill or something. She would never have just left without saying anything, would she? He bolts down the stairs and scours the living room for a piece of paper with her handwriting on it. Nothing. He goes through to the kitchen and searches desperately through the shopping. Perhaps she left a note in there – avocados, pasta, aubergines, yoghurt. Nothing more. It is then that he sees something on the table. He snatches it up and for a moment he is so hyped up that he can't read it. It's a postcard from his father. Why is he sending him a postcard? He never sends him postcards. Ever. He is just about to fling it aside and continue the search for the missing Alice when he catches sight of the words 'non-Jewish'. His heart closes in dread and he reads it through rapidly, his eyes darting across the closely spaced words, one hand clamped to his forehead. For a few moments afterwards he can only stare at it blinking. How could his father be so cruel, not only to him but to Alice? He must have known that there was a strong chance that she would read this.

He lowers himself into a chair and tears the card in two with deliberate precision. He then tears the two halves into two equal parts, and tears those two halves into two and continues in this way until he has a small heap of black, white and shiny seventies Brighton sky-coloured confetti.

He must think about this logically. He now knows why she's gone but the question is where would she have gone to? Out of everyone she knows, who would she have run to? She'll have most likely taken her address book with her, otherwise he could have gone through her friends alphabetically. Who might she call after reading this? Her family! Her sisters! Of course. He starts up and reaches for the phone. 'Raikes,' he mutters, 'Raikes of North Berwick.'

Directory Enquiries gives him the number, which he scribbles on the back of his hand with the biro he has tied to the phone. He is just about to punch in the number when he receives a warning nudge from his common sense. What is he going to say to them? Hi, it's John. You don't know this yet but your daughter has moved in with me. Yes, it's great news, isn't it? Anyway, she's gone missing. I think she's left me. You wouldn't happen to know where she is, would you? No? Oh well, never mind. I'm sure she'll turn up.

John replaces the receiver. She must be somewhere in London. She's due at work tomorrow, after all. For a split second – and a split second only, as he prides himself later – he entertains the notion that she's gone back to Jason. Don't be ridiculous, John. Get a grip.

He paces up and down the living room, as if searching for clues, but all he can think is, Alice has left me, Alice has left me. Is this what happens in a crisis? Your brain offers up only the most mundane information. Who, who, who is she with?

It is only after he has done his fifth circuit of the room that it hits him. Rachel. Who else? All he has to do now is remember her surname and he can get her number from the phone book. Rachel . . . Rachel . . . Rachel . . . who? It's no use. Alice has probably never even mentioned her surname.

He knows she lives somewhere in south London, Greenwich, maybe, but has no idea where exactly. He quells an irrational urge to get in the car and drive through the streets looking for her, and hurls himself despairingly on to the sofa, gazing at the phone. Ring me, Alice. Go on. Pick up the phone, wherever you are, and dial this number. Don't do this to me.

Suddenly he sits up, revitalised with an idea. The last redial button. Surely she would phone whoever she was going to before she set out? Thank God for technology. His hand trembles slightly as he presses the button and he clamps the receiver to his ear, as if desperate not to miss a sound. The other end rings once, twice, three times before he hears the unmistakable click and hiss of an answering-machine. Damn, damn, damn. Then he hears, 'Hi, this is Rachel's machine. I can't come to the phone right now but leave me a message and I might call you back.' Brilliant! He knew it, he knew that's who she'd call. He clears his throat nervously. Whoever's side Rachel was on, it certainly wouldn't be his. 'Hi Rachel, it's John here. I was wondering if you had heard anything from Alice tonight. Could you please give me a call on . . .'

The machine clicked off, beeping angrily as someone picked up the phone. 'Hi, John.'

'Alice? Is that you?'

'No. It's Rachel.'

'Rachel, have you spoken to her? Do you know where she is?'

There was a pause from the other end.

'Rachel, I know you'll know. Please tell me. I'm desperate.'

'She's here. She's fine. Don't worry.'

'Can I talk to her?'

'I'm not sure. Hold on a sec.' Rachel covers the phone but he can just about hear her say, 'Al, it's him. I've told him you're here . . .' There is an unintelligible expostulation from Alice, presumably, then Rachel says, 'Come on, Al, he has a right to know, the poor bugger. He wants to talk to you.'

He can hear the timbre of Alice's voice talking, but can't make out what she's saying. He feels as if every nerve and fibre in his body is straining, on the point of snapping. Alice, please. Come to the phone.

Then her voice, right next to his ear. 'Hello.'

'Alice.'

'What?' She sounds very small and very far away.

'Alice, please come back. Don't do this.'

'I had to.' He hears the slightest quiver in her voice. 'There was a postcard . . .'

'I know. I saw it. I ripped it up.'

They are both silent. John wants to shout come home, come home, please come home.

'How did you find me?' she asks.

'The appliance of science. Last-number redial.'

'Oh.'

Another pause. John winds the springy wire round and round his fingers. 'I also spent a good while running through the list of your friends and family, wondering who you'd be with. I thought of Rachel but couldn't remember her surname.'

'Saunders.'

'Right. I'll remember that next time you leave me.'

'John, I'm so sorry. I didn't want to—'

He cuts across her. 'He doesn't mean it, you know. It's emotional blackmail. Can't you see? He wrote that card because he wanted precisely this to happen.'

She is silent again, but he can feel her listening. 'He wanted you to see it and he wanted you to walk out on me. You're playing right into his hands. It's evil and cruel of him, he doesn't mean a word of it, and please, please, please come back.'

231

'But he said—'

'He said a lot of old shit.'

'But what if he really does mean it? I can't let you do that. I can't . . . I just thought . . .' He hears her suppressing a sob. 'I just thought it would be easier for us this way.'

She starts to cry in earnest and she must be removing the mouthpiece from her face because it's beginning to sound very distant. Is she going to hang up?

'Alice?' He grips the phone so hard his knuckles begin to ache. 'Alice! Are you there?'

'Yes.'

'Give me Rachel's address. I'm coming round to get you.'

'I don't know, John . . . I think maybe—'

'This is absolute madness. I love you.' He hears her sigh heavily and can feel her wavering. At least she's stopped crying. 'He doesn't mean it, I promise you. Look, even if you are going to dump me, we can't exactly leave it like this, can we?'

She laughs and then sniffs. 'I can get the tube back to Camden. It's all right. You don't need to drive over here.'

'Don't be ridiculous. Give me the address. I'll be there as soon as I can.'

'OK.'

Forty minutes later, John is peering at the range of dimly illuminated bells on the front door of the converted town house that Rachel's flat is in. He tries one at random and gets an irritable German man telling him, 'It's the third floor and please would you ask them to label the bell?' Rachel lets him in and he takes the stairs two at a time. On the third floor, Rachel is waiting for him with her door open. Alice's rucksack is propped up next to her on the landing.

'Hi, John.' She gives him a swift kiss on the cheek. 'That was quick.'

'There wasn't much traffic and I was probably breaking the speed limit all the way.'

Rachel smiles. 'It must be love.'

'Yeah. Something like that.' John is impatient, craning to look behind her. 'Where is she anyway?'

Rachel turns round and shouts, 'Alice! Lover boy's here.'

'I'm really sorry about all this, Rachel.'

'Don't apologise. It's completely fine. She's seen me through plenty of crises.'

Alice appears in the corridor, a faint smile on her face, her eyes large and damp. 'Hello, John.'

He holds her to him, kissing the top of her head. Her arms are tight around his shoulders and the warmth of her breath soaks through his collar.

'All right, that's enough.' Rachel says. 'I'm getting cold standing here with the door open.'

Alice gives Rachel a hug. 'Thanks, Rach. Sorry I couldn't stay.'

'Never mind. Next time, maybe.'

'Don't tell me this is going to be a regular occurrence,' John protests.

'Just remember,' Rachel says to Alice, as she's closing the door, 'he knows where I live now.'

In the car, he fits the keys into the ignition. Alice pulls down the mirror above the passenger seat and examines her reflection critically. 'I look awful,' she grumbles, then turns to him, grinning: 'Are you sure you don't want me to stay here?'

John doesn't answer. She sighs deeply and rubs her eyes. 'I am absolutely knackered. Let's go home.'

Alice sits opposite him in the bath, her knees drawn up to her chest, her chin resting on her knees. They study each other through the steam. John scoops up water between his palms and pours it over her shoulders. It trickles in silver rivulets

233

down her arms, her back and over her chest. 'Don't ever do that again, will you?'

She doesn't answer but takes a deep breath, filling out her cheeks, and plunges face first into the water. He jerks back in surprise. Water sloshes violently over the sides and on to the lino. Her fingers fasten on to his ribs and tickle them. Hard. He writhes away from her. More water slops over the side.

'Alice!' He is cross. He grabs her shoulders and pulls her up out of the water. She emerges laughing and coughing, a wet mermaid, her hair and face streaming, her eyelashes stuck into wet spikes. Her face is inches from his and her smile dies when she sees he isn't laughing.

'I'm serious, Alice.' He feels suddenly petulant and incredibly tired. 'Can you imagine what it was like to come back here and find you gone and,' he gestures inarticulately towards the sink, 'find your stuff gone? It was awful. Awful. There was no note. No explanation. I had no idea why you'd gone until I found that bloody card and I didn't know where you were or if you were all right. Don't ever do that again. Please.'

Her brow is puckered and she shakes her head, spraying him with droplets of water. 'John, I'm so sorry . . . I wasn't thinking.' She slides her arms around his neck, her body coming to rest on his. 'I won't ever do it again. I promise.'

Ben twitches the curtains straight and turns to look at his wife in the doorway. 'Ann, we have to sleep here.'

'I know.'

'At least for tonight.'

'I know.'

'There's nowhere else.'

'I know, Ben, I know.'

Ann sidles across the bedroom and pokes at Alice's bed with the heel of her palm as if testing the mattress for softness. She stays bending over it.

'It's too late to get a hotel room.'

No response.

'We could sleep on the sofas downstairs, or there's a camp bed next door, but I don't think either of us would have a good night. We're going to need that, I think.'

'Ben, I know. It's just . . . it feels a bit . . . odd. Don't you think?'

Ann comes round the side of the bed and gives the duvet a little tug.

'Sleeping in Alice's bed?'

She doesn't answer. She has her hand over her mouth, looking down at one of the pillows, which has the rounded indent of a head in its middle. Even Ben shudders. Ann reaches out and Ben watches as she pulls from the pillowcase a single long black hair, and holds it up to the light. It is a slow, thoughtful movement. Two nights ago, Ben thinks, my daughter slept in that bed as normal, and now she is shaven-headed, locked into a private and silent struggle with death. Ann pulls from her pocket a tissue and coils the hair into it.

'Ann . . .' he begins.

She is walking backwards and she sinks into a chair. Ben comes to crouch beside her. 'Ann, I know this is difficult, but I don't see what option we have.'

She clutches the tissue in both her hands.

'Alice wouldn't mind. You know she wouldn't. She'd prefer us to be here than in a hotel, wouldn't she?'

She looks at him. He can see she's thinking about this. 'Wouldn't she?' he persists.

'Maybe,' she concedes. She shifts in the seat, looks down at the chair and begins pulling clothes out from underneath her: socks, a short skirt, stockings, a red blouse. All Alice's. She drapes them one by one over the arm of the chair. 'Maybe if we changed the sheets . . .' She says.

The air of the bedroom is filled with flapping sheets. It feels to Ben like it could be the first movement within these walls for years, as if no one's lived in this room for a long, long time. Ann comes through the door with a pile of clean linen just as he is bundling the sheets up to take downstairs.

'What's that?' she says.

'What?'

'That.' Ann points at a patch of blue in his bundle.

Ben shrugs. 'It's a T-shirt. It was under one of the pillows.'

Ann stares at it, eyes narrowed. 'Alice doesn't wear anything in bed,' she says, almost to herself.

'Sorry?'

'She doesn't——' Ann breaks off, then comes forward and extracts the T-shirt out of the bundle like a conjuror pulling a string of coloured handkerchiefs from a hat. 'Alice never . . .' She stops again and, raising the T-shirt to her face, inhales. She has the kind of look on her face that people have when they are listening to a distant strain of music. Something closed to Ben is passing through her mind. He lifts the end of the limp T-shirt to his own face. Sniffs it. A sleep-soaked smell. Faint but distinct. Male. Ben and Ann look at each other, connected by the different ends of the T-shirt. Ben drops his.

'I don't think we should wash this,' Ann says quickly. 'Just in case,' she adds, and, folding it, puts the T-shirt down on top of Alice's clothes on the chair. Ben doesn't ask, in case of what. He gathers up the sheets again and goes downstairs.

A few strange weeks passed with the two of them tightroping above anxiety, circling around the subject in all their conversations. To Alice, it was like the limbo of waiting for exam results all over again: knowing that everything now hung in someone else's hands. John was optimistic and gloomy by turns. She knew he was calling his father and she knew he knew she knew. She also knew that the father kept his answerphone on and never returned John's calls. The weeks trickled past. It became mentioned less and less and he became more and more despondent.

One night, something happened: a train passed, or the curtains were filled by a wintry draught and then pressed flat, or someone shouted in the street outside. She was suddenly wide awake, jolted by something from sleep. The room seemed unnaturally still. John slept on beside her, his arm flung across her, his fingers entwined in her hair.

The certainty that his father intended to make him choose between them was there in her mind. He wasn't just sulking, as John kept determinedly claiming, he meant exactly what he said. He wouldn't return all those calls unless John could tell him that she was out of the house and out of his life.

Alice eased herself up on to her elbow, above him, and looked down at him. He had slid down off the pillow and his head was resting on the mattress. His arm felt heavy on her body. He must have sensed her sleeplessness or her gaze or something because he stirred. His eyes almost opened and he moved closer, burying his face between her breasts, muttering something. His arm came back to life and he drew her sleepily towards him. Then he stopped. For a few seconds he breathed against her body then he turned his head and looked up at her, eyes wide, fully awake. 'What?' he said.

Alice laid her palm against his cheek. 'I love you.'

He caught her hand in his. 'What is it, Alice? You've got a really scary look on your face.'

She bent and pressed her lips to his briefly, then said, 'I think it's a really scared look.'

He pulled her down towards him so that her face was very close to his and she was looking directly into his eyes. 'What's the matter?' he whispered.

She couldn't answer straight away. She didn't want to say the words.

'Alice, tell me. What's wrong? I've never seen you look so serious.'

She kissed him again. He kissed her back, but in a reserved and puzzled way.

'Your father,' she said, 'is going to make you choose between us.'

He began stroking the side of her body in long, slow sweeps of his hand, beginning at her neck, moving down the side of her breast, into the dip of her waist, over the curve of her hip and then up again. He did this three, four, five times and then he said, 'I know.'

She put her arms around his neck and they held each other very close.

'I can't do it, I can't do it, I can't do it,' he said.

'I don't want you to do it,' she said into his neck. 'I can't

239

bear for you to have to make that decision. I can't. It's a decision that no one should have to make. Ever.'

'I know,' he said again. 'I feel like a shuttle on a loom. All day I am passed from you to him in my mind. How can he expect me to make a choice, for me to say, "Well, I'll have you, but not you"? And even if I did say, "Yes, Dad, I'll give up my *shiksa* and be a good Jewish boy from now on," what kind of a relationship would he expect to have with me, knowing that he'd made me give you up? And how, in God's name, could he ever think I'd voluntarily give you up? It would be like saying, "Yeah, sure, Dad, you can cut off my right arm if you want to."'

He released her and she could look again into his face.

'I can't believe it's come to this. It's incredible in this day and age,' she said. 'My mother was right, you know.'

'Your mother?'

'Mmm. She said, with her usual bad-fairy tact, at my grandmother's funeral that your being Jewish would cause problems.'

'Oh, God. Alice, I'm sorry.'

'Don't be stupid. I didn't exactly go into this with my eyes closed, did I?'

'No, but you didn't expect all this either.'

'No, I didn't.'

'Do you know what he did last week?'

'What?'

'He sent me a copy of this Jewish youth magazine with lonely-hearts pages in the back. You can advertise for your perfect Jewish bride. He pinned this note on to it saying, "Have you thought about this?"'

Cars passed intermittently down Camden Road. He played restlessly with strands of Alice's hair and muttered, 'It's so ridiculous,' every now and again.

'What are you going to do, then?' she said after a while, addressing the region of his chest.

'To be very honest with you, I don't know. The way I see it, there are two options. Number one, I tell my father where to go and risk being cut off by him. Or, number two, I tell my father that everything's over between us, but we carry on seeing each other anyway in the hope that he'll come round eventually.'

She shook her head. 'That's not really an option, John, is it? We can't lie to him. He'd be bound to find out. There is,' she said steadily, still not meeting his eye, 'another option, though, isn't there?'

'No,' he put his hands over his ears. 'No. Never. Don't even say it, Alice.'

'Number three option,' she said, as if she hadn't heard him, 'is for us to go our separate ways.'

'But how could we?' He thumped the pillow with his fist. 'Alice, for fuck's sake, look at me, will you? Look at me,' he insisted. 'How could we do that?'

'I don't know,' she cried, 'but we may have to. You can't just . . . throw away your family like that. You just can't. I won't let you.'

He turned on to his back and glared at the ceiling. She held his hand between hers and examined it. This may be the last time we are in bed together, she caught herself thinking. 'Right,' she said, wanting to blot out that thought. 'I have a plan.'

'What? An Alice Plan?' He was reanimated, sitting up, his face filled with hope. 'Is it a solution?'

She laughed, in spite of everything. 'No, it's not a solution, more a means to a solution. You have a week to decide what you're going to do.'

'A week?' He took a deep breath. 'OK.'

'Starting from now. And — here's the part you really won't like — I go away.'

'No.'

'No? What do you mean "no"?'

'I mean, no, you're not to go away.'

'I have to. It's part of the plan.'

'But . . . but . . .' he floundered '. . . I need you to help me decide.'

'Bullshit. You need a bit of space and time on your own to think. Me being here will just cloud the issue.'

'No, it won't.'

'Yes, it will. So, I go away for a week. We don't call each other. There's no contact between us at all. You go and see your father and you talk to him. You have time to think about what it is you want, your beliefs, your priorities,' she waved her hand in the air, 'and so on. And then at the end of the week, you call me and tell me what you've decided.'

'I don't like the you-going-away part. What if you don't come back?'

'Well,' she said, 'then that would be option three decided upon, wouldn't it? And we'd both have to . . . learn to live with it.'

He was looking at her, she could see out of the corner of her eye, but she refused to return his look, in case she weakened in her resolve.

'OK. So, I stay here, see my father and decide between the three options.'

She slapped him on the arm. 'John! I declared option two null and void.'

'I know, I know. I'm only joking. But why can't I declare your going-away plan null and void?'

'Because.'

'Because what?'

'Because,' said Alice, climbing on top of him and pinning him to the bed, 'I said so. And, anyway, you know it's the only way.'

He looked up at her through her hair. 'You are right. As usual. But where will you go?'

'Where will I go? Home, of course.'

I caught the plane the next morning, splashing out on an air ticket because I was unable to face four and a half hours trapped in a train carriage. John cried at the airport. I'd never seen him cry before: it horrified me and I held him until after the last call for my flight. I had to run out on to the tarmac and up the metal steps to a peeved, waiting air stewardess.

I took it as a bad sign, of course. If he cried, I told myself, that means he thinks it's over. I saw Canary Wharf from the plane window. It looked tiny and flimsy, as if made from cardboard. If I'd shut one eye and raised my hand, I could have obliterated it with a thumbnail.

The flight took three-quarters of an hour. I ignored the safety demonstration, the offers of sandwiches and the peculiar lure of in-flight magazines, and sat slumped in my seat, staring out at the clouds. From the airport, I caught a bus to Princes Street. I'm no nationalist, but there is something about that first glimpse of the blackened tips of the Scott Monument and the green sweeps of the Gardens, the first lungful of that sharp, clean air that can always lift my spirits.

I pushed my way into a phone box outside Waverley Market and pulled the door closed behind me (just outside there was a man in a kilt playing bagpipes badly for the tourists). I lifted the receiver to my ear and dialled.

'Susannah? It's Alice.'

'Alice, where in God's name are you? It's twelve-thirty. You've got—'

'I'm in Edinburgh.'

'What? You are joking, I presume.'

I eased the door ajar with my foot. 'Listen to this,' I said, and held the receiver towards the blasting bagpipes. I could hear Susannah groaning. 'I can explain,' I said.

'Good. I'm listening.'

'But not right now.'

There was a pause.

'Ah,' she said, 'it's like that, is it?'

'Yeah.'

'OK,' she said thoughtfully, 'well, you can tell me all about it when you get back. When would that be, precisely?'

'Um . . . next week?'

'Alice, are you mad? What am I supposed to tell Anthony?'

'I don't know. You'll think of something. Tell him I'm ill. Tell him I'm doing research in Scotland. Anything.'

I heard her sigh. 'You owe me one for this.'

'Susannah, have I ever told you that I love you?'

'Yeah, yeah, yeah. Well, bring me some shortbread or haggis or whatever.'

'I will. 'bye.'

''Bye.'

I pressed the follow-on-call button and hesitated for a moment. John would be at work now, sitting at his desk by the window, with all of east London below him. I was aching to call him. Already. This was not a good sign. It was against the rules. I looked out of the phone-box window, up at the skyline of the Old Town. American tourists in inflated Puffa jackets and multiple scarves milled around outside shouting to each other as they waited for the tour buses. I turned my back on them and resolutely pressed in Kirsty's number.

'Kirsty?'

'Alice! How are you doing?'

'OK. Kirsty, can I come and stay?'

'Sure. When?'

'Like, now?'

'Now?' Kirsty repeated. 'Where are you?' she asked cautiously.

'Princes Street.'

'For God's sake, Alice, what are you doing here? What's happened? Are you all right?'

'I'm fine, I'm fine.'

Kirsty was silent at the other end of the line.

'Look, are you busy? Can I come now?'

'Am I busy?' Kirsty said, laughing. 'Of course I'm not busy. My days consist of either antenatal exercises or eating. Come now. I'll set off and meet you half way.'

Alice was writing an essay on Robert Browning. Pinned up in front of her was a calendar with black lines through the days of the year that had already elapsed. Boxed in red was the week of her Higher exams. The narrowing down of the clean white days between the red days and the encroaching black-lined ones made a crawling fear quicken in her stomach. This morning, when she was walking up to school, she'd felt the prickling smart in her throat and nose that meant hayfever, and hayfever meant summer and summer meant exams.

Alice bent her head over her work again. 'Compare and contrast,' the question read, 'the motivations of the Duke in "My Last Duchess" and those of the monk in "Fra Lippo Lippi".' Alice had four pages of notes and an essay plan. There was, she knew, a formula to these things: an introductory paragraph in which you should answer the question in shortened form and explain your argument, an expansion on your argument – using at all times as many quotes as you could, as well as, where possible, the words of the question – a final paragraph where you could try and crowbar in as many other insights you had about this text, if you had any, and then a summing-up, referring back to your introduction. It should be easy, it should be easy. But she couldn't quell these nerves. At night, she lay awake thinking over revision plans, subjects, notes, diagrams, links, multiple-choice answers.

She unscrewed the cap of the fountain pen she always used to write her essays. Her slanted writing had eroded the nib down on one side. 'Browning,' she wrote, 'was concerned with individuals absorbed by their own needs.' As she reached the end of the sentence, the ink at the beginning had already dried. The page of foolscap curled at the edges. She straightened it with her palm, and pressed her nib to the page again: 'In his poems "My Last Duchess" and "Fra—' She felt a movement of air in the room and saw her mother opening her bedroom door.

'Hello.'

'Hi,' said Alice, squinting because her eyes were adjusted to the cone of glare from her Anglepoise lamp, not the dark of the rest of her bedroom.

'How's it going?' Ann asked, coming forward and peering over Alice's shoulder at her work.

She swivelled round in her seat, trying to face her mother. 'Uh. OK.'

'Is that an essay? What's it on?'

'Robert Browning.'

'Oh.'

'He's a poet.'

'Yes. I know.'

Ann started picking up scattered clothes from the floor. Alice screwed the lid back on to her pen. She didn't want the ink drying up.

'How was school today?'

'All right.' Alice put her pen down on the desk and tucked her hands underneath her.

'What time do you want your tea?'

'Um. Don't mind. Any time.'

Alice started twirling her hair around her index finger, her mind still on her essay plan. Ann sat on the edge of the bed, crossing her legs. Alice watched as Ann started folding the clothes she'd picked up and tossing them on to the duvet beside her.

'Who is this boy who keeps phoning up, then?' Ann said brightly, as if it had just occurred to her to ask.

Alice stopped twirling her hair. 'What boy?'

'Oh, come on, Alice,' Ann said, irritation creeping into her voice for the first time, 'I'm talking about the boy who phones up here for you every night. Every single night.' She forced a smile, got her voice under control again. 'I just wondered who he was. That's all.'

Alice turned back to her work, shaking her hair loose so that it fell over her face. She stared at the page in front of her with the unfinished sentence, pretending to be thinking hard about it. Her pulse had speeded up so quickly she felt dizzy. Or maybe she was just hungry.

'It's him, isn't it?' Ann said.

Alice slammed down her hand on to the page, letting out an explosive sigh. 'Who?' she said, without looking round.

'Who? You know perfectly well who I mean. It's that – that Andrew Innerdale boy, isn't it?'

Alice didn't answer, still staring at her essay, her back hunched over the desk, fury swelling in her cranium.

'It is him, isn't it? I know it's him, Alice. I thought everything with him was . . . What's going on between you? Are you – are you seeing him, Alice? Are you? Are you going out with him?'

'No!' Alice screamed, her voice bouncing back at her off the wall to which her calendar was pinned. 'I'm not!'

'Then why does he phone up here all the time?'

Alice jumped up from her seat. She felt trapped: this was her room and her mother was in it. 'I don't know! Ask him, not me!'

'I just hope you're not giving him the wrong idea.'

'What the hell do you mean by that? How dare you? I'm trying to work here, Mum, I'm trying to write an essay. Why don't you just get out? Leave me alone.'

Ann was standing now as well. 'You must be giving him the wrong signals, Alice. Are you sure you're not encouraging him? Men don't phone like that without . . . provocation.'

Alice picked up the nearest thing to hand – her dictionary – and flung it at the wall. As soon as it left her hand, onion-skin pages fluttering in flight, she felt bad. It hit the wall with a dull clunk, and fell to the floor, pages crushed in concertina folds. Alice wanted to tell her mother about how he followed her to and from school, about the notes he left in her bag, about how he just appeared when she was walking through town or on the beach or to her friend's house, and about how all this was beginning to frighten her, that she didn't know how to handle it, that she didn't know what to do.

Ann was bending to pick up the dictionary when the phone began to ring downstairs. It rang three or four times. 'That'll be him again, won't it?'

'I don't know.'

The phone rang and rang. Was no one else in tonight? Alice didn't want to talk to him. It was the last thing she wanted, but she didn't want to be in this room any longer. She pushed past her mother and ran downstairs. Let it not be him, please, let it not be him. Ann followed her, taking the stairs two at a time.

'What is going on?' Ann demanded. 'Are you going out with him?'

'No!' Alice shouted. 'I told you! Go away! Leave me alone!'

They stood, facing each other over the ringing phone.

'Then why does he keep phoning? You must be leading him on. You must be.'

'I'm not! I'm really not! Go away!' Close to tears, Alice picked up the phone. 'Hello?'

'Alice? Hi. It's Andrew.'

Later I heard my father downstairs, his voice gentle, modulated: 'Ann, she's a young girl. What possible harm could—'

'Shut up!' my mother screeched. 'Shut up! You know nothing about this! Nothing!'

Alice lies on her back on Kirsty's bed, her head tipped back, watching her sister. Kirsty stands at the window with a hand mirror and a pair of tweezers, plucking her eyebrows in the blue-edged December sunlight. She is leaning all her weight on one leg, the swell of her stomach silhouetted against the net curtain. 'I've never understood why you do that,' says Alice.

'What?'

'Pluck your eyebrows.'

'What do you mean?'

'Well, you pull out all your eyebrows, hair by hair, walk round with swollen eyes for a day and then you just draw them back on again.'

'I don't pull them all out. Only some.'

'Still. It's a weird thing to do, don't you think?'

'Not all of us are blessed with naturally dark, arched eyebrows like you.'

Alice brings up her fingertip to feel her own eyebrows.

She smooths them first one way, then pushes her fingertip back against the natural lie of the hairs, feeling them stand up and bristle under her touch. 'What's it like?' she asks suddenly.

'What? Plucking my eyebrows?'

'No,' says Alice, turning over on to her front, 'that.' She points at Kirsty's belly.

Kirsty puts her head on one side and shifts her weight on to her other foot, thinking. 'It's like . . . it's like soap bubbles.'

'Soap bubbles?'

'Yes. You know how if you run a jet of water into soap bubbles, they froth and divide and multiply before your eyes. It's like that. All these cells are frothing and multiplying right in here. It's . . . quite amazing. That's the only way I can describe it.'

'Are you nervous?'

'I was. Incredibly. But I think when you get to this stage all your complacency hormones have kicked in and you don't give a shit about anything any more. I don't care now that I look like the side of the house or that I can only wear tents, or that my bottom is so huge that some days I'm convinced I'm carrying another baby in there as well, or that I've got stretch-marks on my stomach. It's nice, really . . . knowing that all that matters is this.' She straightens her dress over her stomach.

'Can I feel?'

Kirsty smiles. 'Of course. I don't know if you'll be able to feel much. I think it's sleeping at the moment.' She comes over to the bed and lowers herself, bending only at the knees, next to Alice. Alice puts the palm of her hand against the swell beneath Kirsty's dress. 'It feels so hard,' she exclaims.

'Of course it does. There's a whole person curled up in there.'

They wait, cocking their heads, as if listening out for a sound. Minutes pass.

'Can't feel anything,' whispers Alice eventually.

'Just wait,' Kirsty whispers back.

Alice begins to giggle. 'Why are we whisp—'

'Shush!' Kirsty interrupts. Alice feels a fluttering, a slight, rapid popping movement beneath her hand. 'There! Did you feel it?'

Alice laughs incredulously. 'Wow,' she says, 'wow,' and leans closer. 'Hello!' she shouts. 'This is your aunt Alice speaking. I'm looking foward to meeting you!'

Kirsty makes tea in the kitchen that she and Neil painted a pale apricot. Beyond the back door are the criss-crossing fences of tenement gardens. Frozen rows of washing cling to lines strung from tall wrought-iron poles.

'So,' says Kirsty, placing a mug of tea in front of Alice and fixing her with a steady blue-eyed gaze, 'are you going to tell me why you're here?'

Alice flips a teaspoon against her thigh and looks out at the grey Edinburgh sky. Steam curls up from the mug's rim and disappears into the apricot of the walls. 'I don't know where to start.'

'Is it John?'

Alice nods. Kirsty's face creases in concern and she grips Alice's hand in hers. 'Oh, Al, what's happened? I thought you were so in love when I saw you at the funeral. You both had a kind of Ready Brek glow around you . . . I don't know what it was . . . I've never seen you look at anyone like that before.'

'I know.' She shakes her head. 'I don't know what I'm going to do.'

Neil finished work later than usual that night. Rather than

risking the cold walk across the Meadows to their flat, he caught a bus from the Mound. As soon as he'd opened the outer door, he knew something was up. Instead of finding Kirsty sitting serenely on the sofa or lying in bed, the front of the flat was completely dark. Loud ambient music was blaring from the kitchen. Over it, he could hear a female voice – Kirsty? Beth? – shrieking, 'I don't care. I just don't care. Frankly, my dear, I don't give a damn,' followed by hysterical (female) laughter. Neil put down his briefcase, advanced up the hallway and came round the kitchen door.

Kirsty was sitting at the table with her head propped up on her elbows. Opposite her was Beth, still in her duffel coat, sitting on Alice's knee. There were two empty wine bottles on the table.

'Neeeeeeeil!' they shrieked in deafening unison on see-ing him. Neil's instinct drove him to clamp his hands over his ears.

'Do you know what?' said Alice, when the noise had died down, to no one in particular. 'You should never kneel for peace.'

'What are you talking about, Alice?' Beth asked.

'And do you know what else?' she continued. 'You should always look before you leap. Always.'

'Alice,' said Kirsty, 'shut up.'

Neil looked round at them all in amazement. 'What on earth is going on? It's like a coven of witches or something. And,' he said, turning to Alice, 'I won't even ask what you're doing here.'

'No,' Alice said, 'I wouldn't if I were you.' She shook Beth's arm. 'Beth, could you get off? I think I'm losing all sensation in my legs.' Beth got up and offered Neil a drink. 'That'll be the next thing,' Alice muttered to herself, 'I'll get gangrene and have to have my legs amputated. Before we know it, I'll be in a wheelchair for the rest of my life. I wonder what old Bollockbrain Friedmann would have to say about that. A cripple as well as a Kenwood.'

'What's she on about?' Neil asked Kirsty.

'It's Jewish rhyming slang, Neil,' Alice said, with a severe frown. 'Kenwood mixer – *shiksa*.'

'It's John,' Kirsty explained.

'Ah, I see,' he said, not really seeing at all.

The next day, Kirsty has a hospital appointment and Beth, who'd ended up staying the night next to Alice on Kirsty's sofa-bed, has to go to an early lecture on endocrinology. Alice walks arm in arm with Kirsty over the Meadows to the maternity hospital.

'Alice, you are going to go and see Mum, aren't you?' Kirsty says.

She sighs. 'I don't know if I can take the Spanish Inquisition just now.'

'Don't be so hard on her.'

'I'm not. And I'll have to put up with her "Well, I told you sos" and the passion-versus-judgement speech.'

'Just go. You can always come back to me if it gets too much for you to bear.' Kirsty raises herself on tiptoe and kisses her on the cheek. The two sisters hug. 'When are you going to hear from him?'

'Not until Saturday. We're not allowed to call each other. It's the rules.'

'Whose rules?'

'Mine.'

Kirsty shakes her head. 'I don't know, Alice. Do you never think that you sometimes make life hard for yourself?'

'Well, something had to happen, Kirsty. He wouldn't have made any decision if I hadn't forced him to. He'd have just let things drift, getting more and more unhappy.'

'I have to go,' Kirsty says, looking at her watch. 'Don't go back to London without seeing me again.'

Alice watches her crossing the hospital forecourt, her diminutive figure weaving in and out of the cars. Only when she's seen her obscured by the double glass doors does she shoulder her rucksack again and turn to go.

Alice sometimes worries that she might lose her grip on life. Like the fear that your hand might suddenly veer out of control when you are writing your signature for the millionth time on a credit-card slip, she can occasionally see how easily something in her could break and she'd be left spinning in a limbo of panic and disorder. To put off her appearance in North Berwick, she goes to the Chamber Street Museum, and wanders around the cases of dusty, taxidermed animals with marble eyes. She is mapping out John's day in her head: he'll be eating breakfast now in the kitchen on his own; he'll be leaving the house, walking down Camden Road; he'll be on the tube; he'll have arrived at work. Every step she takes around the museum is tracing one of his. At the huge whale skeleton hanging from the ceiling, she stops and leans on the balustrade, staring at the repeated arches of its ribs. She feels his presence so intensely that she wouldn't have been at all surprised to turn and see him standing next to her. How did this happen? How did she fall so in love with him that she feels her very sanity is threatened by the possibility of their parting? He might decide we have to finish, she keeps telling herself, and the weight of that thought seems to make her clumsy: as if she's become mysteriously lighter on one side, she stumbles when walking up the polished steps and navigating doorways proves difficult. She imagines all the little purplish bruises rising into the white of her skin like the heads of seals breaking the surface of the sea off North Berwick beach. At one point, she finds herself staring at a Grecian pot with the twists and coils of a jellyfish painted on it; she presses her palms together convulsively and whispers, 'Please, oh, please.'

Crossly, she bangs out of the museum doors and stands on the pavement. People sidestep her and she realises she must look very fierce and very mad. How could she have been so weak as to let this happen – to become this dependent on another person? She had always vowed to herself that she would never let her happiness depend on another. How can this have happened? She stomps down Chambers Street. He'll be in the office. She walks past a phone box, glowering at it, and then turns and walks past it again, just to test herself.

In the afternoon, when she has done everything she can think of to occupy her in Edinburgh, she walks down the slope into Waverley Station and catches the train to North Berwick.

'So what made you decide you needed a holiday?' her mother asks, as she serves her some mashed potato.

'Um, nothing really. I just felt like a break,' Alice mumbles, ignoring the look that passes between her parents.

'It's a bit sudden, isn't it?' Ann persists. 'Didn't work mind?'

'No, not really.'

'How is work going?' Ben asks.

'Fine. Yeah, good.'

'And how's John?' asks Ann.

'Er,' she finds with horror that she is very close to tears, 'he's OK.' She looks down at her vegetables and spears a floret of broccoli determinedly. You are not going to cry, you are not going to cry. Everything's fine.

'Is he going to be joining you? It would be nice to see him

again. I feel like we hardly met him properly at the funeral. You seemed in such a rush to get back to London,' Ann says, looking at Alice closely.

'Mmm,' she says, swirling the broccoli around her plate. 'He's . . . er . . . he's very busy with work and stuff. You know.'

Her mother is looking at her with an unnerving mixture of suspicion and concern.

'Well, that's a shame,' says Ben. 'You must bring him up another time. Show him round.'

'I will.' Alice tosses her hair off her face. 'So how are things here anyway? You've moved into Granny's room, I notice.'

'Yes, we have,' says Ann, with a little glow of pleasure. 'It's so wonderful to wake up to that view. I'm thinking of doing a bit of redecorating – maybe the living room and the kitchen. And the hall and landing as well. How are you finding it, living with John?'

'Fine.'

'Is it a nice house?'

'Yes.'

'So he's been living there for how many years?'

'Four.'

'Do you think you'll make many changes to it?'

'No. It's all . . . it's all fine.'

'And is everything,' Ann pauses, selecting her words, 'fine between the two of you?'

Alice bows her head over her plate again. 'Yes,' she says almost inaudibly.

'Well, that's good. Lucky, really. It was all so sudden, wasn't it, Ben? I mean, you'd hardly known him – what was it? – two months before you moved in. But things are OK?'

Her parents watch a tear roll down the curve of Alice's cheek, followed by another and another and another. Alice puts

down her fork and lays her head on her arms and starts to sob.
Ann tries to lift her hair out of the mashed potato and Ben goes
to stand behind her chair, patting her shoulders awkwardly.

Alice is surprised to wake the next morning in her old bedroom.
Then she remembers that several times in the night she woke
with the jolting sensation of being about to fall into a drop;
she'd been turning over, seeking the bulk of John's body, but
finding instead the edge of the narrow, single bed and the threat
of the floor beneath it.

The room is strange. Her mother has kept it like some
odd museum piece, exactly how Alice had it when she was
a teenager. Around the room are political posters for nuclear
disarmament, anti-apartheid, anti-vivisection and the banning
of fox-hunting. Robert Smith, Morrissey and, somewhat incon-
gruously, Albert Camus look down at her from the walls.
In the cupboard, Alice knows, will be clothes she hasn't
worn for six or seven years. Strings of hippie jewellery
hang over the dressing-table knobs; around the edges of
its mirror are photos of Alice and various schoolfriends at
parties, on the beach, in the sixth-form common room,
behind the cricket pavilion. Alice stretches out from where
she's lying and pulls at one of the poster's corners; the
Sellotape, yellowed and brittle, gives way and Albert Camus
comes floating to the floor. She gets up, stepping over him,
and pulls on a dressing-gown that no longer closes over
her chest.

The house empty, she pads around the rooms of the house
in which she spent eighteen years of her life. It's as though she's
in a slight time-warp, as if at any moment she might see Beth
walking in as a gawky adolescent, or turn a corner of the
house and find an enviably angelic nine-year-old Kirsty trailing
her dolls behind her in a pram. Alice catches sight of herself in

a mirror and thinks, how did I get here? How did I get to be this old?

This is the first time she's been here since Elspeth died and, unlike her room, she finds the house oddly cleared of all Elspeth's traces. Her bedroom is unrecognisable. All her books and magazines, which used to cover the table in the sitting room, have been stacked neatly in the bookcase. Ornaments and paintings have disappeared; tables and footstools have moved. The chair she used to sit in by the window to read or write letters has been re-covered in a rather hideous beige velvet and relocated to the corner of the room. Alice sits in it for a few moments and wonders what Elspeth's advice would have been over John. Would she have said hang in there or give up the ghost?

There's a note on the kitchen table from Ann, saying that she's gone out. Alice thinks about calling Beth to see if she's got any free time between lectures, then has a shower. She has just soaped herself all over when she hears the doorbell ring. Cursing, she rinses, winds a towel around herself, heaves up the bathroom window and cranes her head out to see who it is. Whoever it is is obscured by the wisteria that clings to the front of the house. Probably some awful friend of her mother's.

'Hello?' Alice shouts. The person carries on ringing the bell. The blast of cold air is making her shiver convulsively. 'Hello?' she shouts again, in a louder and crosser voice.

The gravel crunches and there, two storeys below, stepping back into the driveway, his face upturned to hers, is John. She is so astonished that she drops the towel covering her, giving what is half-way between a cough and a laugh. He looks up at her, his head on one side. 'Did you know that you've got no clothes on?' he says eventually.

'Yes, I did,' she says, trying not to smile. She doesn't reach for the towel, which is coiled around her ankles, holding instead his serious look. 'What do you call this, John?' she asks, pointing at him and the bag resting on the driveway at his feet.

'I don't know,' he says. 'What do you call it?'

'I call it breaking the rules.'

'What rules?'

'My rules.'

'There are no rules any more. I declare your rules null and void.'

'Do you now?'

He nods. 'Yes.'

'I'm not sure if you have the power to nullify, let alone voidify, the rules in the case of Friedmann versus Raikes.'

John scratches his head. 'Well, Ms Raikes, if I could refer you to the document drawn up on Sunday night between the two sides concerned, I think you'll find that I do, however, have the power to nullify all rules and especially all ultimatums with regard to the case of Friedmann Senior versus Friedmann Junior.'

There is a pause. Alice looks down at him, her body steaming in the cold air coming from the window. 'Is that true?' she says quietly. 'Do you mean it?'

'Yes.' He nods again. 'Now, are you going to let me in, Rapunzel, or do I have to climb up to you?'

'Don't do that. My mother'll be livid if you pull the trellis off the house. I'm coming down. Don't go away.' She slams the window shut, picks up the towel and runs downstairs.

Ann walks up the slope of Bank Street, stepping through the wet leaves fallen from her neighbours' tree. She's asked them many a time to sweep this section of the pavement, but they never do. She has always been saddened by the fact that they had to sell large portions of the garden to a property developer in 1975: what had been the croquet lawn and the lower garden were now ugly, box-like bungalows. Elspeth said they had to, or they'd need to sell the whole house and move. No one had wanted that.

As she turns into Marmion Road, she sees that Alice's curtains are still closed. Ann expels a sigh. Sleeping in late will not help matters. She feels a stab of pure hatred for John Friedmann, fuelled by a fierce maternal protectiveness and something else as well that she doesn't want to think about right now. She knew he meant trouble the moment she laid eyes on him at Elspeth's funeral, she just knew it. Dark-eyed simmering types were all very well but they always ended you up here – broken-hearted, crying and sleeping late. But Alice had refused to listen, of course. Ann has a mind to phone him up and give him what for: how dare he lure her daughter into being in love with him and then turn round and say, sorry, I'm Jewish.

She slams the front door behind her and feels a little better when the plates on the plate-rack running around the ceiling of the hallway rattle with the reverberation. She leaves her bags of shopping by the door and heads up the stairs to Alice's room. She is going to tell her: forget that man, he's no good, sometimes you just have to forget people, sometimes you just have to give them up and forget.

As she comes up the turning in the stairs, she sees something that makes her blink. Is she having some kind of vision? There appears to be a naked man standing on the landing. Ann blinks again. On second look, it is not just any naked man: it's that bloody John Friedmann with a towel wrapped around his waist. Him, in the middle of her house, in the middle of the afternoon. All but naked.

Ann is for a moment speechless. The two look at each other. Ann is satisfied to see that he looks suitably terrified. 'What,' she demands grandly, 'on earth are you doing here?'

He fiddles with the tiny towel. Ann finds herself, despite everything, giving his body a quick appraisal. She can, at least, see what Alice sees in him.

'Mrs Raikes,' he stammers, 'I—'

At that moment, Alice's bedroom door is torn open and Alice herself darts out on to the landing, completely naked. Ann raises her eyes to the ceiling in exasperation.

'Mum!' says the horrified Alice. 'What are you doing here?'

Ann advances up the stairs. 'What am I doing here? I live here. What I want to know is, what is he doing here?' Ann jabs a finger in John's direction.

'Mum, don't be rude,' Alice says, in a shocked whisper, as if she doesn't want him to hear. 'Everything's sorted. It's OK now.'

'Is that so?' Ann barks loudly and rhetorically at John. 'For the time being, I suppose. Meanwhile, you keep my daughter on a string so that you can reel her back in to you when it suits your religious conscience.'

'Mrs Raikes,' he begins, 'it isn't like—'

'People like you make me sick,' Ann continues, waving aside his interruption, 'how dare you think you can play around with my daughter's feelings. All this vacillating between Alice and your religion. It's so weak. Don't you think it's a bit late in the day to be thinking about this? I ought to throw you out of this house right here and now.'

'John!' Alice grabs him by the arm, making him clutch wildly at his towel, and pushes him towards her bedroom. 'Go in there. You don't have to listen to this.' When he has disappeared, she turns on Ann. 'Why are you doing this? You're so embarrassing. You don't have any idea what you're talking about. You can't speak to him like that.'

'I can speak to him any way I like. This is my house and you're my daughter. He's bad news, Alice.'

'He's not.'

'He is. I knew it from the first moment I saw him. Any man who doesn't know his own mind is not worth the effort.'

'How dare you? He does know his own mind. What the hell would you know about that anyway? I can't believe you, coming in here and shouting at John like some possessed harpy. I love him, Mum, does that mean anything to you?'

'Get rid of him, Alice. Make a clean break. It'll be easier for you in the long run. You have to believe me. The more you love him, the more he can hurt you. He'll break your heart and I can't bear to see that happen.'

'He won't. For your information, he's just told his father where to go.'

'Yes, but how long will that last? Alice, think about it.'

John reappears out of the bedroom, buttoning up a pair of jeans. 'Now, look,' he says calmly. 'I don't think we're going to get anywhere by shouting at each other. There's been enough shouting over this already. Alice, why don't you get dressed and then we all can go downstairs and talk about this properly?'

'No,' she says, 'there's nothing to talk about. We're leaving. We're catching the next flight back to London. I don't see why we should have to listen to this.'

Ann watches as he puts his arms around Alice's naked shoulders.

'Mrs Raikes,' he says, holding Alice to him, 'I'm so sorry. I'm sorry that I'm here uninvited in your house, I'm sorry that I've caused an argument and I'm more sorry than you'll ever know that I've done anything that's hurt Alice. But I told my father last night that I love Alice and that he is just going to have to come to terms with that. It's an end to all the vacillating. I promise.'

Ann glares at him. A memory is beating somewhere behind

a locked door that she won't open. John holds her gaze. Alice looks anxiously from one to the other.

'Who are you promising? Me or her?' Ann says, after a while.

'You, her, both, everyone, the whole family, the whole world. I'll sign it in blood, if you want me to.'

Ann feels a slight smile beginning to creep in at the corners of her mouth. The beating has stopped. 'I don't think that will be necessary.' She half turns to go back downstairs, then takes another look at them standing there. 'Alice, put some clothes on, for heaven's sake, and let's have lunch. John, you can come and help me while Alice gets dressed. You must be starving.'

When they get to the hospital the next morning, there are cards and flowers lined up on the window-sill. Ann reads them systematically, starting at one end and working her way to the other, holding each just long enough to absorb the picture on the front, read the message inside and decipher the signature. They feel flimsy and crushable in her hands. Some of the names she recognises — friends or colleagues she's heard Alice talk about — but there are lots she doesn't know at all. These ones affront her. Who are these people who sign themselves off to her critically ill daughter with 'lots of love and hugs', or send 'darling Alice' their 'very best wishes and prayers'? Someone called Sam — whoever he or she might be — has sent a huge bunch of lilies. As Ann is leaning over to read the small card stapled to their polythene shroud, she brushes against one of the protruding stamens. Grains of orange pollen burst into a rust-coloured stain on the sleeve of her white blouse.

Behind her, Ben's voice drones on. He is reading aloud an article about the Net Book Agreement. She turns, plucking at the stain. Ben has a newspaper spread out on the bed, over Alice's legs and middle. It is the paper John used to work for. This strikes Ann as an insensitive choice. The paper's lower corner, she notices, is resting on Alice's hand, in the V between her thumb and index finger. Ann is sure that feeling of a saw-toothed newspaper edge scratching at the skin of your hand would annoy Alice. Ann can feel the sensation in the corresponding part of her own hand. She can't believe that Alice can't move her hand out of the way, that Alice might feel it but is so trapped inside this non-functioning body that she's unable to move, *that Alice can't move*. Ben carries on outlining statistics, book sales figures, pros and cons for small businesses, comparisons with the US.

Ann seizes the paper and pulls it off the bed. There is a long tearing sound. 'Stop that,' she says, rubbing the skin between her thumb and index finger, 'just stop it . . . How do you know . . . She can't hear you anyway . . . Face it, Ben, she can't hear you.'

Her tears, running down her face and neck, start soaking into her clothes. She is surprised how salty they taste. Ben has his arm around her now. Ann peers over his shoulder at Alice who hasn't moved, who never moves, who − or so it seems to Ann today − will never move again.

Alice comes into the living room to find John hunched over his computer, the keys clicking in a rapid, staccato rhythm. She drifts past him into the kitchen; he grunts to acknowledge her presence but carries on typing without looking round. Alice opens the fridge door, yawning. She has spent most of the day reading and is feeling rather out of touch with reality, as if her own life has become insubstantial in the face of the fiction she's been absorbed in.

In the fridge is a tired-looking lettuce, half a pot of yoghurt and a paper bag of dried-out, etiolated mushrooms. She lets the door swing closed and sits down at the table. She feels ravenous but can't be bothered trekking round Sainsbury's. It doesn't look likely that John feels like shopping either. She drums her fingers on the table top and sighs, then gets up and approaches him on her bare feet. 'John,' she begins, just as she lays a hand on his shoulder.

He leaps up in the air as if she's electrocuted him. 'What are you doing,' he shouts, 'creeping up on me like that?'

She is so amazed that for a moment she can't speak. His face is flushed and he's jostled himself between her and the screen, as if trying to stop her from seeing what he's writing.

'I wasn't creeping up on you.' She gives him a nonplussed

smile and tries to see past him. 'What are you doing that's so top secret anyway?'

'Nothing.' He won't meet her eye. She starts to laugh.

'John, what is it? Let me see.' She tries to push him out of the way.

He resists and stands firm in front of the glowing screen. 'No. Alice, don't. It's nothing . . . It's just something . . . I have to finish.'

'Well, what? Go on, tell me.' She has fastened her arms around him. He tries to disentangle her fingers and push her away. 'It's not a letter to another woman, is it?' she asks teasingly.

'Don't be stupid.'

But at that close proximity, she has seen him wince, felt his body tense against her. After a few seconds when she registers nothing but a kind of stunned disbelief, she withdraws her arms and says, in what she hopes is a normal voice, 'I'm sorry, I didn't mean to disturb you. I just wanted to know if you felt like going out for something to eat. There's nothing in the house – well, unless you count some old vegetables – and I don't feel like shopping and I didn't think you did . . .' Alice is aware of a babbling noise that's her voice, and she shuts her mouth. The noise stops and she turns and goes out of the room.

She lies on the bed, staring up at the ceiling. John? Having an affair? The idea is so ridiculous she feels almost annoyed with herself for even entertaining it. But then why did he flinch when she asked – as a joke – if he was writing to another woman? Surely that was evidence enough that he was?

As she lies there, things start falling into a seeming chain of events: last week, for instance. She had arrived home before him and, finding there was no milk in the fridge, had gone out again to the corner shop. As she turned on to Camden Road she passed the phone box on the corner and had been astonished to see him in there speaking into the receiver, fifty feet from their house, his hand clamped over his ear against the noise of passing traffic. She'd tapped on the glass with the pound coin she was holding. Then what had happened? She tries to remember. He'd looked up, seen her and hung up. Did he speak into the receiver again before hanging up? Or did he hang up straight away? She remembers that she'd meant to ask him why on earth he was using the phone box when he was two minutes' walk from the house. Why hadn't she? He'd come out of the phone box and started kissing her, right there in the street. He'd been in a good mood, Alice recalls, and, with his hand up inside her shirt, she'd kind of forgotten about the fact that he'd been in the phone box. 'I've got to go and buy milk,' she'd protested, when he'd started pulling her in the direction of the house. 'Sod the milk,' he'd said, 'I want you at home, in bed, right now.' Why, why, why had she let the matter slip? He's been behaving oddly for a while now, she suddenly decides — obsessively checking and rechecking the answerphone messages, constantly asking her if she's got anything to post and then rushing out to the postbox late at night with mysterious missives. And he's always hurtling down the stairs in the morning when they hear the post drop through the door. He always says he's expecting 'freelance cheques' when she asks him what the rush is, but now she's not so sure.

She sits up crossly. Who on earth could it be? She runs through the list of their female friends, but can't think of a likely candidate. It must be someone at work. He has been doing a lot of late evenings. This is stupid. She must just ask him straight out. As she hears his feet on the stairs, she is beginning to feel the first tinges of anger and outrage. How dare he? Who is this woman? Does he love her? How long has it been going on?

He appears in the doorway and hovers there. 'Hi,' he says, with a forced jollity, 'are we going out, then?'

She watches him as he crosses to the window and begins fiddling with a cactus that she's put on the sill.

'This is a nice cactus. I like it. It's nice.'

She is still silent.

'Are we going out, then?' he asks again.

She shrugs. 'If you like.'

'Great. You all right?'

'Uh-huh.'

'Good. Good. OK. Shall we go?'

At the gate he takes her hand in a firm grip and sets off down the street. She has to keep breaking into a jog every three or four steps to keep up with him, but he doesn't seem to notice. He hums as he strides along. As they are going over the canal, Alice yanks on his arm. 'John!'

He stops and stares at her as if he'd forgotten she was with him. 'What?'

'Stop walking so fast. I can't keep up.'

'Was I walking fast?'

'Yes. Very.'

'I wasn't walking faster than I usually do.'

'You were.'

'What's the matter, Alice?' he asks, with exaggerated patience.

'What's the matter with me? Nothing. I want to know what's the matter with you.'

'Nothing.'

'OK. Fine. So nothing's the matter with either of us.'

'Fine.'

'Fine.'

He puts his arm around her shoulders and they continue like this to an Italian trattoria opposite the tube station.

after you'd gone

John is staring fixedly out of the window, flipping his menu between his hands like a wobble board. Two mini-cab drivers are having a row on the pavement: the smaller one keeps flicking the back of his hand against the taller one's shoulder. Alice applies lipstick in a small mirror. As she smooths the dark red mouth on to her face, she looks at him covertly, eyes narrowed. Is he or isn't he? He doesn't look any different. Surely having an affair would leave some kind of mark on him? She scrutinises his mouth and neck but sees nothing but the features of the man she loves. The thought of his body with someone else's makes her heart contract with agony. Even before she is aware of deciding to do it, she is drawing back her hand and by then it's too late – she's slapped him right across the face. 'Are you having an affair?' she shouts.

The effect is dramatic. The restaurant falls silent, just like it does in films. Everyone is staring at them. The waiter makes as if to come over to their table, then thinks better of it and makes a swift detour to rearrange the flowers on a table by the door. John is regarding her, aghast, his hand held to his face.

'What?'

'You heard.'

'Are you mad?'

'Answer the bloody question, John. Are you having an affair or not?'

'Alice, what on earth makes you think—'

'Tell me,' Alice hisses through gritted teeth, 'just answer me yes or no.' She grips her fork menacingly. He reaches over and tries to take hold of her hand. She snatches it away.

He sits back in his chair and looks her in the eye. 'No, Alice. I am not having an affair.' He turns to face the restaurant. 'I'm not having an affair,' he announces loudly.

Some people continue eating pointedly and don't look at them; others smile; someone at the back shouts, 'Good.'

269

He turns back to her. One side of his face bears the livid imprint of her hand. She bursts into tears and covers her face with her hands. He lifts his chair around to her side of the table, sits down next to her and gives her his handkerchief.

'Do you know what?' She sniffs and wipes her face.

'What?'

'You should never cry when you're wearing mascara.' She hands him back his handkerchief, streaked with black, and sighs.

John takes her hand between both of his. 'One thing about being with you, Alice, is that I never quite know what's going to happen next.'

'My mother used to say that to me when I was little.'

'What on earth made you think I was having an affair?'

'Well,' she says, suddenly accusatory, 'you were using the phone box outside our house that time, and then you wouldn't let me see what you were writing earlier on, and when I asked you jokingly if you were writing to another woman you flinched.'

'I flinched?'

'Yes.'

He shakes his head and laughs. 'Well, if you really must know, I was writing to another man. I was writing to my father.'

'Oh.' Alice feels all anger and suspicion drain out of her, leaving her feeling chastened and foolish. 'I didn't know you wrote to each other.'

'We don't. I write to him but he never replies.'

'How often do you write?'

'At first I wrote every couple of weeks or so. Now it's more like every couple of months. I phone him occasionally and leave messages on his answerphone.'

'What do you say?'

'I tell him what we've been doing. Not work – he gets the paper, I know that much. It's weird to think he probably reads the articles I write. I tell him what films we've seen, the places we go to, what I've been reading. That sort of stuff. And I ask him to get in touch.'

'And he hasn't?'

'No.'

'Not at all?'

'No. Not yet anyway.'

'John, I had no idea.'

'I know. I should have told you. I just didn't want you to get upset. After that time you left . . .' He tails off. 'It sounds very lame now. I should have told you.'

They eat. People smile conspiratorially at them as they walk past their table. Alice strokes John's cheek. The red mark fades. As they are leaving, the waiter wishes the *bello* and *bellissima* 'much happiness' and exhorts them to come back soon.

Later that night, they walk to the postbox together. She pushes the letter through the wide red mouth and listens to it drop on to the heap of uncollected mail. Impulsively, she hugs the postbox and kisses its cold metal. He laughs. 'He can't fail to write now.'

Ben hurried up the school steps, the cutting wind blowing open his coat. He'd left the house so quickly he hadn't even stopped to button it. He'd been a pupil at this school, and when he drove up and got out, he had to stop himself from going in at the boys' entrance, instead of the main central door for teachers and visitors.

At the reception – just on the right as he came in, in a room where language classes were held in his day – he spoke to a woman with dyed black hair. 'Hello. I'm Ben Raikes. Someone phoned me.'

'Oh, yes.' She got up and came round the desk. 'Come with me, please.'

As they walked down the corridor, she said, without looking at him, 'There's been an incident.'

'An incident?'

Her hair was tar-glossy with cardboard-grey roots. It hung like seaweed around her face. Her hips were so wide they strained the seams of her skirt.

'A disciplinary incident. Between your daughter and a sixth-former.'

'Which one? I mean, which daughter?'

'Alice.'

'Oh. What happened?'

'She hit him.'

In the headmaster's office was a boy holding a clump of bloodied tissues to his face, and Alice, slumped into a chair, stared at the ground in fury. The headmaster was a compact, lean, bald man. Ben had on occasion played golf with him. They would say hello to each other if they passed on the street, perhaps exchange a few pleasantries about their respective families or the weather, but there was no hint of that now. He sat behind his desk in full authority mode.

'I'm very sorry to have to call you up here like this.'

He was staring at the boy, so it took Ben a few moments to work out that he was talking to him. 'Oh. That's all right,' Ben said, then realising he should sound more serious, coughed and said, 'Well, under the circumstances '

'Yes!' the headmaster shouted, making Ben jump. 'Circumstances! Which one of you would like to explain to me what those circumstances are?' His gimlet gaze oscillated between the two teenagers. 'Alice? Andrew?'

He was answered by silence. Andrew's face was white with pain. Alice scuffed the toe of her boot against her bag, which was lying on the ground next to her. Ben saw that the knuckles of her right hand – clenched against her body – were red, grazed and swollen.

'You have broken Andrew's nose, Alice Raikes,' he announced. 'What do you say to that?'

Alice raised her chin, the blue and red streaks in her hair flicking over the back of the chair. She looked at the head-master, then at the boy, and said in a clear voice, 'I'm glad.'

The headmaster tapped his pen top against his thumbnail and looked at Alice as if he'd like to strike her. 'I see.' He forced the words out from between his clenched teeth. 'And would you mind explaining to your father and I why you're glad?'

There was a knock on the door and then in the room was a

273

tall, broad-shouldered man with longish dark hair. He looked around the room, taking in his son, whose face was covered with blood, the sullen Alice, the headmaster and Ben.

'Ah, Mr Innerdale. Thank you for coming. This is Mr Raikes.'

Ben held out his hand.

The man didn't meet his eyes as he took it, but turned quickly to his son. 'Are you all right, Andrew?'

'His nose has been broken,' the headmaster said, 'by this young lady here,' he extended a finger and jabbed it at Alice, 'who was, I believe, about to tell us her version of events and why it is she's rather pleased with herself. Alice?'

'He was chasing me.' Alice said. 'He pulled my jumper off me and wouldn't give it back. I was trying to get him to give it to me, then he . . . he kept . . . trying to . . . to push me over. So I punched him.'

The headmaster didn't seem to have taken in what she'd said at all. 'Is that correct, Andrew?' he said, as if an authority automatic pilot, swivelling his head in the boy's direction.

'Wait a minute,' Ben said, and the boy's father glanced at him. 'He was chasing you, did you say? And he pulled off your jumper? And tried to push you over? What do you mean?'

Alice shrugged. 'He was following me at lunchtime and I started running away and he ran after me. I was wearing my jumper round my waist. And he grabbed it. And,' she said, turning to him, accusingly, 'he hasn't given it back.'

'Fuck off,' the boy muttered under his breath.

'Fuck off yourself, weirdo,' Alice hissed.

Ben rubbed his forehead. Andrew's father put his hand on Andrew's shoulder, as if to restrain him.

'Right,' the headmaster shouted. 'That's it. No more explanations. It's clear to me there's a pair of you in it. As of now, both of you are in detention for a week. Andrew, give Alice back her jumper, Alice apologise to Andrew. And I want no more trouble. From either of you. Understood?'

They were silent, Alice's face set into an expression of defiant indignation.

'I said, understood?'

'Yessir,' Andrew mumbled, from behind his tissues.

'Alice?'

'Yes. Sir.'

Ben was the first to shuffle out into the corridor. Alice kept her head averted from Andrew.

'Have you got Alice's jumper, Andrew?' his father asked him.

Ben watched as Andrew, still holding the tissues to his face with one hand, unzipped his bag and drew from it a large black woollen sweater. The father took it, held it in his hands for a moment, then turned to Alice. 'Here you are, Alice,' he said.

Without a word, she took it from him and pulled it over her head. Her hair crackled with static, strands of it flying up as if she was connected to a van de Graaf generator. Andrew never took his eyes off her, Ben noticed. 'I'm sorry about . . . all that,' the father said to her. Then he led Andrew down the corridor. Alice rolled up the cuffs of her jumper. Ben stood watching them go.

Andrew never came back to the High School. His parents sent him to a private school in Edinburgh to finish his exams. Alice would see him sometimes in the distance, getting off the five o'clock train, dressed in the impeccable navy and white uniform of his new school. She never spoke to him again. If they passed each other on the High Street or in the Lodge Grounds, they didn't even make eye contact, as if they'd never met.

I've been hearing my father's voice. I know I'm not imagining it. It's not so much that I can hear what he's saying, but that I'm aware of the timbre, the speech patterns, the low volume of his speaking voice, murmuring regularly somewhere just outside me.

I cannot bear it. It makes me miserable. It makes me want to turn, sink, let the waters close over my head. I don't know what I'd say to him – to explain myself, to explain the whole thing.

It must have been a few weekends after they'd posted the letter. John had been checking the post every day, once in the morning and once in the evening, dialling 1471 if he came in and there were no messages on the machine, just in case – but nothing.

It was a Saturday morning and Alice was in the living room, eating an apple and reading a guidebook to Andalusia. John was upstairs somewhere. She could hear the stamp of his feet and every now and again she would shout something like, 'John, how do you fancy a few days in Seville?' or 'The Alhambra sounds amazing.'

John would always reply in maddeningly mild tones: 'Sounds good' was his stock response.

She got up and stood at the bottom of the stairs.

'John!'

'What?'

'Why aren't you excited about this trip?'

Infuriatingly, she heard him laughing. 'I am.'

'You don't sound it.'

'Well, it's just hard for me to be as excited as you are.'

'What do you mean?'

He appeared at the top of the stairs and looked down at her. 'What do I mean? Only that you've been scouring that guidebook in every spare moment you've had for the past two weeks, that you've practically almost packed your rucksack, you've been speaking Spanish for months now . . . Need I go on? You generate enough excitment for both of us.'

She was just about to give a cutting retort when she heard a gentle knocking.

'What's that?' he asked.

Alice went into the living room to see a delivery man in blue overalls tapping on the window. She and John opened the door. Two men were propping a gargantuan, bubble-wrapped rectangular parcel up against the side of the house. One of them consulted his clipboard. 'John Friedmann and Alice Raikes?'

'That's us,' said John. 'What is it?'

Alice squeezed whatever it was under the wrapping. It felt hard and cool.

'No idea. Sign here, please.'

'Who's it from?'

'Sorry,' they shrugged, 'no idea.'

It was flat, incredibly heavy and had 'fragile' stickers all over it. They speedily tore sheet after sheet of bubble-wrap off it.

'What on earth is it?' said Alice after a while, sitting down on the floor for a brief rest, panting.

'It must be a painting,' said John, looking down at it, his head on one side. 'It's the right shape.'

'Look,' she said, 'I can see gold. It's got a gold frame. Who do we know who'd send us a painting?'

'I don't know.' He seized an armful of the discarded bubble-wrap and tossed it into the air. It floated down on top of Alice, who lay flat on her back, watching it descend slowly towards her from the ceiling.

'This reminds me of a game my grandmother used to play with us,' she said from underneath a pile of bubble-wrap. 'Kirsty and I used to lie on the hall floor and my grandmother would stand on the landing above and throw the bedsheets to be washed on top of us. We loved it. We had to stop, though, because once a sheet caught a plate that was hanging on the wall. It fell and broke and a piece of it cut me, just here, next to my eye.'

John loomed into her vision above her, blurred by the plastic she was looking through. 'Where?' He lay down on top of her. There was a ricochet of bubbles bursting beneath them.

She giggled. 'Here,' she said, indicating her eye.

He kissed her through the rustling plastic, pinning her to the floor. She struggled, laughing and breathless. 'John, don't. I'll suffocate.'

He ripped away the sheets, diving down towards her, and then began pulling off her clothes.

'No, wait. I want to see what the parcel is.'

'We can do that later,' he said, standing up to pull off his trousers.

She peeled off her T-shirt. 'We should at least close the curtains.'

'Why?' he asked, lying down on top of her again. 'Who's going to be in our garden on a Saturday morning?'

'There might be some more removal men with more mystery packages for us.'

'Well, that's their look-out. If we want to have sex in the privacy of our own living room, that's our business.'

After they'd got dressed again, they pulled more and more layers off the package. A shiny surface began to emerge and John went to sit down on the sofa to watch Alice remove the final few sheets. It was a huge, gilt-edged mirror, decorated with ornate Gothic curlicues and fat, floating cherubs holding swathes of material over their genitalia. She stood back, amazed. 'My God. It's hideous.' She darted forward again and touched a smiling, golden cherub with her fingertip. 'Who would send us such a thing?'

He was staring at it, his head propped up on curled fists. 'It used to hang in my parents' bedroom. It's a family heirloom, brought over from Poland before the war.'

Alice crossed the room and clutched his arm. 'Your father's sent it?'

'It must be him . . . unless it was my uncle . . . No . . . it's definitely from him. That's very weird.'

She shook his arm again, perplexed by his sudden depression. 'But it's a good thing, isn't it, John? I mean, he's sent it to both of us.' She waved the delivery note in front of his face, which had her name next to his. 'Doesn't it mean he's kind of . . . well . . . accepted it?'

He got up and began pacing about. The bubble-wrap, beginning to take over the whole room, swirled about in the movement of air caused by his violent strides. 'I don't know, Alice. I don't know what he means by it.'

'Maybe you should call him.'

He stopped pacing and rubbed his hand over his head, thinking. 'Mmm. Maybe. I'm not sure I could. What would I say? I'm so angry with him for all this shit.'

'But you want to make things up with him, don't you? You know you do. Isn't it time to put all the shit, as you call it, behind you and swallow your pride? He's probably as frightened of speaking to you as you are of speaking to him.'

'Maybe you're right. But I don't know if I could handle a phone conversation with him yet. I mean, it's been almost a year.'

'Well, write him a card or something and ask him to meet you.'

'That's not a bad idea,' he said reluctantly. 'I could invite him over here. He could meet you then.'

She shook her head. 'I think you should get your relation-ship with him sorted first. I think meeting me may be a bit much for a first go. It'd be easier meeting him on neutral territory – a restaurant or café.'

'Yes. OK. You're right.' He sat down at his desk decisively and pulled a card out of his drawer. 'Dear Dad,' he said, his pen poised, 'thanks for the mirror. My girlfriend and I had a really good shag in all the wrapping.'

'I'm sure telling him that will really help matters.'

'Only kidding.'

He finished it and went out immediately to post it. He returned with an outsized picture hook and a new drill bit, bought from the grumpy hardware man across the road. He was whistling as he levered the mirror up off the floor, sending a rhombus of white light wheeling across the ceiling. He hung it in the hallway behind the front door. Alice watched anxiously as he heaved it on to the hook, balancing on two chairs, his legs straddling the gap.

What can I say about the time we spent in each other's lives? That we were happy. That we were barely apart. That, fleetingly, I would get that vertiginous, towering feeling of knowing another person so well that you could actually see what it would be like to be them. That I never felt incomplete before I met him but with him I felt finished, whole. What else? We lived in his house in Camden Town. I made him tidier, I painted the staircase blue, he eased my temper by laughing at me when I was in a rage. He cured my insomnia by reading to me in the middle of the night when he was half asleep. What else, what else? We flew a kite in Regent's Park and on a beach in the Isle of Wight with the Needles puncturing the horizon. We peered together down a vast telescope at a curved sliver of Venus, lit up by the sun, from an observatory on a hill in Prague. We sat on a beach in Sri Lanka during an electric storm, watching great Hammer-horror forks of lightning crack open the horizon, while phosphorescence glinted on the shoreline like cats' eyes. We made love on every available surface in the house, in numerous capital cities, in a cramped berth of a train going through Poland with the *provotznik* rattling the door handle, in a windmill in Norfolk, on a chilly Scottish golf course, in a darkroom and once in an Underground lift.

We got married three years after we first met. I didn't want to, not really. I agreed only because of pure attrition. John got it into his head that we should get married: he asked me and I said no, why should we, what's the point? Being the obtuse person he was, he then made a point of asking me to marry him at every available opportunity, often several times a day. 'Alice, what do you want for dinner and will you marry me?' he would say, or, 'What are you up to tomorrow? Why don't we get married?', or, whispered, 'Alice, it's your sister on the phone and by the way will you marry me, please?' This went on for months, I think. In the end I just said yes, all right, why not?

What else is there to say? That I loved him more than I ever thought it was possible to love anyone. That his father never spoke to him again.

That day, news of the bombing just seemed to seep through London like an urban form of osmosis. Even before newspapers could rush out stories on the explosion, rumours were spreading from person to person. I was at work. It was a Friday afternoon in winter. The sky was already darkening when Susannah returned from the Italian sandwich shop around the corner, shivering with the cold, struggling through the door with her hands full of steaming paper cups. 'I just heard,' she said breathlessly, her eyes wide. 'A bomb's gone off.'

I was at my desk, talking to Anthony. We stared at her.

'Where?' Anthony asked.

She set the coffees down on a desk and began unbuttoning her coat, not looking at me. 'Well . . . it might be a rumour. They weren't exactly sure.'

'Where did they say it was?' I said.

'This person didn't really know.'

'Susannah! Tell me! Is it Camden?'

'No. They said in east London somewhere.'

I remember staring at the buttons on her coat. They were a darker red than the material they were sewn into. If you had a paint the same red as the coat and mixed it with the slightest dab of black – no more than enough just to cover the tip of your brush – you would end up with the button colour.

I seized the phone. My fingers flew over the familiar pattern of the numbers. 'It's ringing.'

It rang for what seemed like a long time, until a woman's voice answered. 'John's phone.'

'Hi. Is John there?'

'No. He's out of the office. He's doing an interview I think.'

I laughed with relief. 'Of course, I forgot. Sorry. It's Alice here. We heard there might have been a bomb or something down your way.'

'God, news travels fast. There was a huge explosion about an hour ago maybe. I nearly jumped out of my skin. It was over the other side of the Docklands. It's absolute mayhem. Half a building's collapsed. The news desk is going mental.'

'I bet it is. Well, I'm glad you're all OK. Could you tell John I rang when he gets in?'

'Sure.'

I hung up. 'It's OK! He's at an interview.'

'Thank God for that.' Susannah slumped into a chair. 'So it's true, then?'

'Yes. In the Docklands apparently.'

'Bloody hell. Was anyone killed?'

'She didn't say.'

There was a silence between us for a moment. Then a phone rang and Susannah picked it up and began a conversation about writers' bursaries.

Later that night I watched the news with the cat curled on my lap. The camera panned up the sides of the devastated building, covered by now in green tarpaulin. Men in yellow hats and reflective jackets bobbed among the fallen beams in the ruins.

'No one has, as yet, claimed responsibility,' the reporter's voice intoned. 'Twenty-seven people are in hospital tonight, but miraculously there were no fatalities in today's bombing.'

Lucifer quivered and stretched in his sleep. It was nine-thirty. John still wasn't back. Life without him was such a ridiculous impossibility that I refused to let doubt make any impression in my mind at all. He was late. He was late. He was very late.

You slide back the aluminium bolt on the toilet door and step out. The fluorescent tubes of light overhead make the whole interior of the room gleam like an operating theatre: a lethally shiny floor, rows of melamine cubicles, steel wash-basins, metres and metres of blue mirror, white porcelain walls, which throw back a splintered, monochromatic blur of your reflection. At the basins, you dip your hands into the scorching, oxygenated water, glancing behind you in the mirror. Two teenage girls, one dressed in a thick red fake-fur jacket, walk the length of the mirror's frame, banging back cubicle doors to find two next to each other.

'Here's one,' the taller one says.

'Hold on, hold on,' says the other, adjusting the back of her left shoe by hooking her index finger into the rim of leather.

The soap from the dispenser is pink, with a pearlised sheen. Your hands will give off a cloying, sweetish smell after this. You rinse them. Strings of bubbles disappear down the steel eye of the plughole. The teenagers are having a shouted discussion about a dress. 'Flouncy!' one of them shrieks. The one in the red fur jacket, you think. 'Flouncy' is a horrible word. Makes you think of bunny rabbits or flowery pelmets. You turn to the hand-dryer, pushing the chrome button. The ends of your hair are lifted in the overheated stream. A middle-aged woman, laden with shopping-bags, breathing asthmatically, arrives at the wash-basins. You step closer to the dryer – why? To let her past? To allow her more room? Did the woman brush against you?

The front of the dryer has a small, square mirror stuck to it. It is smudged with fingerprints. You allow the depth of your eye's focus to zone in on these fingerprints for a second, maybe two, then you allow it to relax into the tiny mirror's distance. You must, at that moment, have shifted your weight from one foot to the other, because you are suddenly convinced that you've seen, flitting from one side of the minuscule square to the other, your mother. You blink, then lean forward because you are surprised. Your mother is here to see you as well? Kirsty must have phoned her to tell her you were coming. It is like peering through the viewfinder of a camera with a very powerful lens, trying to locate your subject. You catch a flash of fading blonde hair, but you have moved too far one way and have to duck the other way. There it is again – that flash of white-yellow, but this time mixed up with some dark-haired man who must be walking past. Then you stand rigid, staring at the reflection, which you now have perfectly framed in front of you. One of the teenage girls has raised herself up on the side of the cubicle, her elbows hooked over the edge and is talking down to her friend. The woman at the basins wheezes, her mouth open, her lungs labouring. Somewhere overhead a defective light-strip buzzes.

You turn, first your body, then your neck and head, then your eyes. You don't want to see this, you really don't. Behind you, you already know without looking, is a full-length one-way mirror. People washing their hands can look out on to the station concourse through the sickly brown glass. Beyond it, wading through tannin-coloured air, people stare up at the departures board, pick timetables out of display stands, drag luggage on little wheels, or sit around on rows of chairs, yawning. Right next to it, leaning against what they thought was just a full-length mirror, are your mother and a man.

You take a step towards them, then another. You are half a metre, perhaps less, away from them. You could press your fingers against the glass at the point where your mother's temple is resting. Or where his shoulder is leaning.

He is feeding her raspberries. In his hand, he holds a clear plastic tray of deep red-pink clusters. He eases the tip of his little finger into their soft, mossy innards and holds them out for her, one by one. She closes her mouth around them, you see her jaws work, her throat constrict, then his finger emerges, naked.

You recognised him straight away – North Berwick isn't, after all, a big place. But the thought that hurtles downwards through your mind takes a few seconds or so. You look at him, your eyes skim over his stature, his brow, his hair, his hands. It isn't so much a thought, more a conviction. Or a fact. That man is your father. There isn't the smallest splinter of doubt in your mind. As soon as you allow the thought, you know it as a truth. You are looking at your father. Your real father. The realisation seems to drop from a great height and refract like chromatography into a thousand unexpected rings of colour.

You are looking at him and then at her, and sweat is prickling under your hair and between your shoulder-blades, then you are slamming your way out of the toilets, through the barrier, across the marbled concourse. They mustn't see you, they mustn't see you. The balls of your feet and the joints of your knees hurt as you stride away, not looking back to where you know they are standing.

And as you walk, it seems to you that with every step someone is falling away from you. Ben. Kirsty. Beth. Annie. Jamie . . . You stop short. You stand still in the middle of the domed airiness of Waverley Station, looking about your feet like a person on a rapidly disappearing piece of sand. Then you take another step. Elspeth.

Through the café window, you can see your sisters. Kirsty is telling Beth some story, her hands curving and pointing. You walk through the café, navigating tables and chairs.

'I have to go now,' you say to them, and their faces turn to look at you.

The doorbell rings very early. It wakes Alice, and for a moment

she is utterly disorientated. The ceiling above her is not the
bedroom ceiling. A weak, greyish sunlight is illuminating the
room. She finds she is crumpled in an awkward position on
the sofa. She sits up and flexes her stiff neck. The doorbell
rings again. Early Saturday-morning TV is chattering at a low
volume in the corner; a red-haired man is hitting a woman
in dungarees over the head with an inflatable hammer. The
audience is laughing. Lucifer is sitting on the window-sill behind
the net curtain. He looks slightly fuzzy, his edges blurred by
the net. It occurs to her afterwards that he would have seen
the police before she did.

She is startled by their size. The man seems to fill the
room. The first thing he does is pick up the remote control
and turn off the TV. The woman stands in front of him. She
smells of cigarettes and overheated, crowded rooms. Her nails
are bitten down and varnished.

'Please sit down.'

Alice wants to laugh at this cliché, but she sits and so do
they. The man's radio, clipped to his shoulder, crackles and
shouts. He and the woman exchange a look and he switches
it off, looking ashamed. Alice stands up again.

'I'm sorry to tell you, Mrs Friedmann, that John is dead.'
As she says this, the policewoman gets up, comes over to her
side and takes Alice's hand in hers. A gentle downward pressure
is applied. She wants me to sit down, Alice thinks. She sits.
Familiar things suddenly look very strange. Her boots lie on
the carpet where she took them off last night, the long leather
tongue of one curled into the other. She stares at the table lamp
on John's desk, as if seeing it for the first time. It has a long,
beaded fringe around it and its shade is a tiny bit skewed.

'We found his body in the wreckage this morning.' Her
hand is stroking Alice's. 'He was in a newsagent's buying
a paper.'

'That's stupid. They get all the papers at his office,' Alice says. 'He'll have forgotten to pick one up on his way out. He's always doing that.'

'Right. I see.'

Alice starts jiggling her leg convulsively. 'Nimming', her mother calls it. 'It's Raikes.'

'Pardon?' The policewoman leans closer to her.

'It's Raikes,' Alice says, more clearly – maybe a little too clearly? She doesn't want to be rude. 'You called me Mrs Friedmann. I didn't change my name when we got married.'

'Oh.' The woman nods gravely. 'Sorry, Mrs Raikes.'

Alice shakes her head. 'No. Ms Raikes. But you can call me Alice.'

'OK, Alice.'

The man clears his throat. Alice starts. She'd forgotten about him. 'Is there anyone we can call for you, Alice?'

Alice stares at him blankly. 'Call?'

'Yes. Your family, a friend maybe?'

'My family live in Scotland.'

'I see. What about John's family? Maybe you'd like to be with them.'

Alice laughs – a short, mirthless bark that leaves her throat feeling raw and scraped. 'No.'

The woman struggles to keep the shock from her face.

Alice attempts to formulate an explanation. 'I've never . . . I've never met his father.'

The woman, having mastered her features, nods soothingly.

Alice turns to look her full in the face for the first time. 'He's dead?'

'Yes.'

'Are you sure?'

'Yes. I'm sorry.'

288

Rachel appears some time that day, and later Ben and Ann tiptoe into the bedroom where Alice is curled, prawn-like, on the bed. Ann drops darkened circles of tears on to the duvet cover beside Alice's dry, white face, calls her 'baby' and tries to get her to eat spoonfuls of soup that Ben brings up on a tray.

At some point Alice finds herself in the bathroom. It's the first time she's been alone all day. She leans her forehead against the cool silver of the mirror and looks straight into her own eyes. She feels disgruntled and weary, out of sorts somehow: the house is crowded and she wishes everyone would leave. With a kind of percolating horror, she suddenly becomes aware that what she is waiting for is for John to come back, as he usually would at this time of night. Her hands are resting on the basin. She looks down and sees his shaving brush on the shelf. Its bristles are still slightly damp from when he used it yesterday morning.

They are in the kitchen, sitting round the table. Rachel is saying, 'I saw him last week, it was last Saturday, he stood there at the cooker and made us dinner,' when Ann springs upright.

'What's that?'

A long, thin, keening sound scissors the air. It tapers off and then starts up with new strength, broadening into a sharp, animal scream.

'It's Alice.'

Ann rushes through the door, overturning her chair in her haste. They hear her pound up the stairs and then a loud hammering at the bathroom door starts. 'Alice! Let me in! Open the door! Please, Alice!'

And over it all that barely human cry floats out, undeterred.

part | three

Once again, Alice is struck by the fickleness, the blank, impassive callousness of mirrors. As she is passing from the sitting room into the hall, she catches sight of her reflection, as white-faced and large-eyed as a frightened ghost. It stops her short and she stands in front of the mirror, gazing at herself. Her eyes seem unnaturally bright and the skin around them bruised-looking and sunken. She has lost so much weight that her cheek-bones protrude sharply, giving her a worn, skeletal look. The golden-skinned carved cherubs on the frame mince and smile around her.

John must have seen himself a thousand times in this mirror – going out of the front door in the morning, on his way upstairs like she was just now. It must have an image of him locked away somewhere in its depths. Why, then, when what she wants more than anything else in the world is a glimpse of him, does it refuse to give her anything but her own, blank face? In more gloomy moments, she allows herself to imagine that he is standing just behind it, his face pressed up close to the surface, watching her passing beneath him, missing him, grieving for him, and no matter how hard he bangs on the glass, he cannot make her hear him.

She turns away and climbs the stairs. It's a hot, airless day and it feels as though it may thunder later. In the distance, she can hear the drone of slowly moving traffic on Camden Road.

Upstairs, Lucifer is asleep on the bed in a tight ball, his tail curled over his face. Alice runs her hand over the warmth of his fur and he makes a sleepy, unintelligible sound to acknowledge her.

She takes two deep, shuddering breaths, feeling the familiar, sickening waves of grief begin to roll over her. The first tears fall on the cat's fur before she curls up on the bed next to him. He opens his green eyes a crack and watches as she sobs, fingers pressed into her mouth. The bed shakes. From under her pillow, Alice pulls a T-shirt of John's, which still smells of him, and she crushes it to her face.

An English teacher at school once said to her, 'Alice, one thing I hope you never find out is that a broken heart hurts physically.' Nothing she has ever experienced has prepared her for the pain of this. Most of the time her heart feels as though it's waterlogged and her ribcage, her arms, her back, her temples, her legs all ache in a dull, persistent way: but at times like this the incredulity and the appalling irreversibility of what has happened cripple her with a pain so bad she often doesn't speak for days.

Later, she gets up and moves about the room, performing small tasks to look after herself: she dries her tears and throws the used tissues into the bin with a wet, sodden thud; she gets a drink of water, takes a paracetamol, lights her oil burner and straightens the duvet cover, tucking John's T-shirt carefully back under the pillow. She runs a bath and cries a little more when she is lying in the steam. The weekends are the worst: long clods of time on her own. His death has rendered everything else unimportant, so whatever she tries to fill her time with – books, films, seeing people – seems irrelevant and trivial.

She dries herself slowly with a thick towel. Her skin feels dry and parched, as if all the tears she's cried in the last four months have made it arid, dried it out. In her dressing-gown she goes downstairs and makes a sandwich. She eats it standing up, still not having the strength to eat at the table alone, forcing herself to swallow the lumps of bread that taste like ash. The house is utterly silent apart from the noise of her own half-hearted chewing. She wants to die.

Ben stood alone outside the ticket office, peering at his watch, on average, every three minutes. He didn't look at the red digital clock on the board, not entirely trusting it – his own watch was accurate, he knew that. He wound it every day. It was the first thing he did in the morning. They'd missed two trains now and he didn't want to miss this one, didn't want to spend another night in this city. He wanted to be at home again, wanted to have his daughter at home with them, sleeping upstairs in her old room, away from this place. What he wanted most of all, of course, he reminded himself, was for this never to have happened.

He saw Ann hurrying across the station and he stood straighter, extending his arm, waving. 'Ann! Over here!'

His lips felt cracked and he licked them. She didn't smile as she moved towards him. He searched her face, curious despite himself about what it must be like to have to identify a body. Ann had insisted that she did it – Alice was in no fit state, she'd told him, in a brief, whispered consultation they'd had in Alice's hallway that morning. Rachel had offered, but Ann said no, she was doing it. Rachel hadn't argued, and neither had Ben. What was it like, he wanted to ask. Was it definitely, definitely him? There'd been no mistake? Why had it taken so long and what did it . . . what did he . . . what in God's name did it look like?

Ann reached his elbow and seemed to be ignoring him, looking about her, twisting round and looking over her shoulder. 'Where's Alice?' she demanded. A muscle just below her eye kept twitching, making her eye jerk. Ben watched it, fascinated. 'How was it?' he asked, resting his hand on her arm. Was it awful, he wanted to say. I'm sorry if it was awful. She shook him off. 'Where is Alice?' she repeated.

Ben shrugged. 'She went to the newsagent's, I think.'

'For Christ's sake,' she exploded, 'how could you be so stupid?'

They found her standing in front of the newspaper stand, her hands held over her face. Hordes of people wove their way round her, some staring at her curiously. On the front page of every newspaper was a picture of the bombed building and headlines in fat, black letters: 'Bodies found in the wreckage', 'The undiscovered dead of the east London bomb'.

They each took one of her arms and guided her between them to the waiting train.

What are you supposed to do with all the love you have for somebody if that person is no longer there? What happens to all that leftover love? Do you suppress it? Do you ignore it? Are you supposed to give it to someone else?

I never knew it was possible to think about someone all of the time, for someone to be always doing acrobatic leaps across your thoughts. Everything else was an unwelcome distraction from what I wanted to think about.

I knew I should have cleared out his things. Anything that had touched his body was unbearable. His computer and fax machine I gave away to his friends. Two of them shuffled into the house, large and sheepish, picking up the boxes and taking them out to the car, slamming their car boots down on top of them. I think they felt obliged to stay for a while, so they sat with me at the kitchen table, swallowing rapid gulps of scalding tea, asking me hesitant questions, avoiding the subject of John. When it was time to go, they stood up with some relief.

On my way from the house to the tube station, I passed several charity shops and I kept steeling myself to take all his stuff in there. There was even one weekend when I opened the doors of our wardrobe resolutely, preparing to dispatch all his clothes to Oxfam on Camden High Street. But when I inhaled the scent of him that escaped from the folds and weave of the material, I knew I could never do it. I've never been able to think of those charity shops in the same way: how they must be full of the outflows of tragedy and loss.

Rachel rummaged in her bag for the sun cream. 'Alice.' She nudged the inert form at her side. 'Alice!'

Alice sat up and pushed her sunglasses on to the top of her head. 'What?'

'Put some of this on or you'll burn.'

Rachel watched her squeeze some cream on to her palm and smear it with her other hand over her shoulders and arms. They were sitting in the long grass on Parliament Hill. It was the first day of the year that had real heat in the sun. Above them, the stunt kites of the kite fanatics, who were attracted by the cross-breezes of this hill, zoomed and criss-crossed the expanse of blue sky.

'Tell me how you are,' Rachel said.

'I'm fine.' Alice didn't meet her eye, but fiddled with the top of the sun-cream bottle.

Rachel snatched it out of her hand. 'Don't bullshit me, Raikes. Fine? How can you be fine? You look like you haven't slept for a month and you must weigh about seven stone.'

Alice sighed and said nothing. The Bathing Pond glittered in the distance.

'You know,' continued Rachel, 'if you want to tell me to mind my own business or you want to talk endlessly about John, or if you want to scream and shout a lot, that's OK. Just don't tell me you're fine.'

Alice smiled faintly. 'OK. You really want to know?'

'I really want to know.'

'I'm dreadful.'

'How dreadful?'

'Just . . . dreadful . . .' Alice banged her balled-up fist into the grass. 'I miss him. I miss him. I miss him. He's gone. He's dead. I can't believe it, I don't want to believe it.' She broke off. Rachel hugged her and Alice cried into her shoulder. 'I'm sorry,' she said, between sobs.

'Don't be ridiculous.'

Alice pulled away and sat up straight, 'It's just all so . . . shit, Rach. I know it will get easier in time, but it's just so awful . . . and exhausting and relentless and . . . I just can't face life without him . . . I can't sleep at night because he's not there and I can't get up in the morning because he's not there and there just seems . . . no point in doing anything – in getting dressed, in going to work, in carrying on, in being brave because . . . he's not there. One day he was . . . and then he wasn't . . . and it's all so unfair, it's so unjust . . . And people say to me, oh, you're young, you'll get over it and you'll meet someone else, but the idea of being with anyone else is just hideous . . . It's a travesty . . . because all I want is him and I can't have him and never will be able to . . . I'm just so tired, Rach . . . I'm tired of carrying this weight around with me. I'm so used to being happy and now I've just got this huge, crushing weight of grief in my chest . . . and I'm so furious . . . I'm fucking furious that it was him and not someone else . . . and I'm furious with him . . . for leaving me . . . and I know it's ridiculous but I'm angry with him for not picking up a fucking paper in the fucking office like he should have done . . . and if he had, he'd be alive . . . he wouldn't have been in the newsagent's in the first place . . . He might even be here now on this rug with us . . . and that's just unbearable . . . that it was all so random and it could have been anyone but it was him . . .' Alice stopped at the sound of feet swishing in the grass. She wiped her face hastily with her hands. A woman and a small child walked past: the child dangled on the end of her arm and kept twisting back to look at them. 'Mummy, why is that lady crying?' Her clear, high voice was carried back to them.

The mother jerked on her small arm to pull her round and whispered something in her ear. 'But why?' she said again. The mother picked her up and carried her away; the fragile blonde head bobbed against her shoulder. Alice watched them, her shoulders slumped, her whole being drained and exhausted from her outburst. 'And that's the other thing,' she said dully.

'What?'

'John wanted a baby. He kept dropping hints and then eventually came out and said it. I laughed and said, no way mate . . . He was disappointed, but tried not to show it . . . We talked about it again, and I said maybe in a year or so, but I was just putting it off because I didn't really want one at all . . . and then he died . . . and do you know I want that baby so much now I just can't stand it . . . Sometimes I think I'm grieving for that child as much as I am for him . . . I was so stupid, so unbelievably, ridiculously, selfishly stupid . . . because if I had . . . I'd have it now . . . I'd have something lasting of his . . . I'd have John's child for ever . . . and instead I don't have the baby and I don't have him and it's just me rattling around in that house.'

'You never told me you wanted a baby.'

'Well, I didn't. Not then. I had no urge to have one at all – quite the opposite. I kind of always thought we'd have one eventually and that . . . we had all the time in the world to think about it . . .'

Alice fell silent and held her head in her hands. Rachel waited until the steady drip-drip of tears had abated. Just above their heads, the kites dipped and soared.

'Anything else?'

Alice blew her nose. 'I'm so sorry.'

'For what?'

'For going on like that.'

Rachel gave her a gentle slap on the leg. 'Yeah, you're so boring with your trivial problems. Look, don't you even dare to suggest that you shouldn't tell me these things. I want to do something to help, do you understand?'

Alice nodded. 'Thanks. You're good to me.'

'Oh, be quiet. Don't go all maudlin on me. Where's that wine you brought?'

Alice gripped the bottle between her knees and eased out the cork. It came out with a loud pop. Two of the kite fanatics turned round disapprovingly.

'Cheers!' Rachel shouted rudely. They turned away hurriedly. Rachel turned back to Alice. 'Can you imagine what it would be like to go out with someone who spent his whole weekend up here holding on to a piece of string?'

'Shush,' Alice smiled, 'they'll hear you. Anyway, it's really good, kite-flying. You should try it.'

'Don't tell me you do it too. I don't want to know.'

'I have done it. John gave me a kite.'

'Alice, I'm sorry, I didn't mean . . .'

'No, no, it's OK. It was . . . is, I mean – it's still hanging by the front door for all I know . . . It's a small red one with two strings. We used to fly it together sometimes. I loved it. I wasn't very good, though. I tended to get too excited and lose concentration, but it's an amazing feeling. Really exhilarating.'

Rachel rolled over on to her stomach and lit a cigarette. 'Well, I'll take your word for it.' She looked over at Alice. 'Hey, maybe that's what you need.'

'What?'

'A bit of exhilaration. Maybe you should fly your kite again.'

Alice shook her head. 'No. I don't think so.'

'Why not?'

'I couldn't imagine doing it without him.'

'I'm sure it would be OK. It might do you good.'

'There are some things you can't do on your own, Rach. Kite-flying's one of them. You need someone to stand there and throw it into the air, and I wouldn't want to put you through that. I know you'd hate it.' Alice handed her a glass of wine. 'What are we drinking to?'

Rachel held up her glass. 'To John.'

Before this, I used to try to work out how long I might live. Maybe I'd contract a terrible disease in my thirties and die. Or I could be struck down by lightning before I reached my forty-fifth birthday, or be in an air crash, or a car crash, or perish as the random victim of a madman.

But diseases, lightning and madmen aside, I could realistically live until I was seventy or eighty. Longer, perhaps. I couldn't believe I was going to live for all that time. I would find them incomprehensible – those fifty or so years stretching out before me that I would have to live without you. What was I going to do to fill them? It seemed cruel to me that I was so healthy, so alive, so seemingly indestructible when your life had been so easily and so randomly severed.

I was puzzled by those women in previous centuries dying of broken hearts, taking to their beds and just fading away. That's what I wanted: I desired nothing more than to lie down and let life ebb from me. I couldn't believe it when, every morning, I opened my eyes and felt it surging through me like sap through a tree – that aliveness, that undeniable force of existence. The beat of my heart, the swell of my lungs, the stiffness in my muscles that was telling me, despite everything, to get up, use my legs, stretch my arms.

And even now, after I stepped into the path of a car — a two-tonne hammer of steel, chrome and reinforced glass, travelling at a hurtling velocity — my body still clings to life, and I find myself suspended like Persephone between two states. I can't say which one I want. Death seems difficult and elusive to me.

Beth is having difficulty equating Alice, the person she saw only two days ago, with this inert life-sized doll in the bed. Her skin has a waxy, unreal look to it. They are told all the time in medical training, don't get emotionally involved with a patient, think of them as a bundle of symptoms, but how does it work if the patient's your sister?

The whole hospital smells of sickly antiseptic and reheated food — it's a smell she'll need to get used to. Her parents sit side by side on the only chairs in the room. They are quibbling about where to eat tonight: her mother just cannot bear the canteen food for one more night. Ben is saying that he agrees but he doesn't know anywhere to go in London.

'Why don't we ask someone if there's anywhere near here we could go?' Beth suggests.

They break off their discussion and look at her, as if surprised that she might have had a good idea.

'Yes, but who?' Ann says.

'We could ask the nurse,' Ben says.

'Which nurse?'

'The tall one.'

'I don't like the tall one.'

'OK. The younger one, then.'

305

'The younger one with bleached hair? Do you think she'd know? I'm not sure she would, Ben.'

Beth looks down at Alice, circling her wrist with her fingers. Alice's pulse moves under her hand. She's read that people in comas are often conscious of things being said and done around them. What would Alice think if she heard what was going on right now? She'd shout at them to hurry up and make a decision, for heaven's sake, it's not that important.

'Alice?' Beth whispers. 'Can you hear them? They're arguing about restaurants.'

Can Alice hear them? Her face is expressionless. She looks dead, Beth thinks, Alice looks dead. Beth has seen dead bodies, opened them up with a scalpel as if it were the handle of a zip that ran down their skin; she's had her hands inside the bodies of dead people, she's lifted the heart out of the body of a thirty-one-year-old man and it was heavy and she needed two hands. Alice looks dead to her, but she knows this can't be because she herself can see the ventilator moving and the ECG drawing the wave-like contractions of her heart in a green electronic pulse. But Alice has that bloodless, ceraceous look that Beth knows now. It makes a wave of panicky desperation hit her. She finds she wants to shake this figure on the bed.

'I've never liked Mexican food,' her mother is saying, 'you know that.'

The door opens behind Beth and she turns. Her parents are silenced. A slightly shabby doctor with a pen behind his ear is standing in the doorway. 'Hi,' he says. 'How are you all?'

'Hello,' Ben says, 'we're fine. This is my youngest daughter, Beth.'

The doctor comes into the room very slowly, and stands beside the bed, looking into Alice's face for a long time. Then he turns and looks at Beth. He's in his mid-thirties, maybe younger, and has dark rings under his eyes. 'Beth,' he repeats, in a thoughtful way, 'the medical student, right?'

Beth sees that he has his hand over Alice's in a rather intimate way, and wants to dash it away. How dare this man touch her sister? Alice would hate this man, suss him instantly as a pseud and a lech, and have nothing to do with him. Beth faces him, Alice between them, and puts on what Alice calls her Miss Jean Brodie voice: 'That's right. And you are . . . ?'

The man just nods. Ben shuffles forward. 'This is Dr Colman, Beth. He's been looking after Alice.'

Dr Colman offers Beth his hand. 'You can call me Mike.'

Beth snakes her way from the toilet through the tables in the hospital cafeteria to where her parents are sitting and slumps down into a seat opposite them. They have ended up eating here after all. The room is empty apart from the woman in a green overall behind the glass food counter and a couple of doctors talking in hushed tones over a trayful of food that neither of them is eating. Her father pours her a cup of tea from a dented stainless-steel teapot.

'What's with that guy Mike?' Beth asks.

'What do you mean?'

'Well, is he in love with her or something? Typical of Alice – people still falling in love with her despite the small fact that she's in a coma.'

'Don't be ridiculous, Beth.' Ann purses her lips and takes a sip of her cooling tea. 'He's a doctor. He's just doing his job.'

'Are you missing many lectures?' Ben says, trying to change the subject.

Beth adds milk to her tea and swirls it around with a plastic spoon. 'Some. I spoke to my director of studies yesterday after Neil came to get me. She said to take as long as I needed.'

'That was nice of her.'

'Yes. I suppose so.'

Ben squeezes his daughter's hand. 'She's going to be all right, you know,' he says.

'Do you think so?' Beth raises her eyes to her father's.

'Yes. I do.'

Beth swallows a mouthful of tea. It tastes thick and over-brewed.

Ben stands. 'I'm going to call a taxi and then we can go back to the house,' he says. 'You look very tired, Beth. I've put up a camp bed in Alice's spare room for you.'

Beth watches her father walk across the room to the row of telephones. Ann pulls a cigarette out of her bag and seems to be searching for a lighter. 'Mum! Don't do that.' Beth points at a sign. 'It's no smoking in here.'

'Oh,' Ann fumbles with the cigarette, dropping it under the seat, 'I forgot.'

Beth expects her to start feeling about for it around her feet, but she is leaning over the table, looking Beth straight in the face. 'Beth, tell me about Alice coming to Edinburgh.'

'There's not much to say, really,' Beth says, taken aback by her mother's sudden intensity. 'She came, and then she left.'

'Was she . . . Did she seem . . . upset when she left, do you think?'

'Um. Yes. She was, I think.'

'Do you know what had upset her?'

'No. Not at all. Kirsty and I were trying to work it out. She got up to go to the loo, was gone for about five minutes, then when she came back she was all strange and distant.'

'The loo?' Ann repeats. 'She went to the loo? Which loo?'

'God, Mum, I don't know. That big Superloo place, I think.' Beth thinks hard. 'In fact I'm sure it was the Superloo because she asked us if we had change.'

'Change?'

'Yeah. You need a twenty-pence coin to get in there.'

'What time was this?' Ann is no longer looking at her, but craning over her shoulder to look at Ben. He is speaking into the phone, his hand held over his other ear.

'Why are you asking about all this?'

'Why do you think?' Ann says, in a near-whisper. 'Because I want to know. Just tell me, Beth. What time was it?'

'Um . . . well . . . Alice's train got in about eleven. So this would have been – I don't know – quarter past, twenty past maybe.'

'Twenty past eleven? Are you sure?'

'Yes,' Beth says. 'But what's this got to do with anything?'

'Here's your father,' Ann announces in a loud voice, and Ben is loping back towards them, jangling the change in his trouser pocket.

I still cannot believe you have gone. Before this, I used to wake up and wonder for a split second why I had this weight of grief pressing down on my chest and why my pillow was wet. I used to forget because it was just absurd for me to be without you. Absurd.

But you did die. And for no reason at all.

A few days after you had died, the papers printed a photo of the man who planted the bomb that killed you. He died too and he was only young, younger than you. My family tried to make sure I didn't see the papers at that time, but I did see it and do you know I didn't hate him. I wanted to go to his mother and father and say, how do you feel do you feel like I do tell me how you feel?

Someone has put Annie on my lap. I am surprised by this. I don't remember anyone doing it. It must have been Kirsty. I turn my head to the right. Kirsty is sitting in the back of the car too, her face turned towards the window, our father between us. My mother is driving, her ringed hands grasping the wheel. She hates driving in London. Beth is next to her. I wonder vaguely where Neil is. I'm sure I saw him earlier with the new baby. Jamie.

I feel hot. I am wearing funny clothes. I had a bath this

morning and when I came back into the bedroom, my mother was standing by the window wrenching the labels off a new skirt and jacket with an angry flick of her arm, muttering, 'If you're going to meet those bastards I'm going to make damn sure you look good.' The material is black woven wool, the nap of it itching my skin, the jacket sleeves too short and the skirt an odd calf-length. It's tight around the knees and I have to take shortened steps when I walk. I feel old in these clothes.

I reach forward, my head touching Annie's, and turn the window handle a few times. The top of the window shudders down and a jet of icy air is sucked through the gap. Annie goes rigid in my arms, her almond-shaped blue eyes opening wide. I watch as she extends an arm upwards and sticks her tiny, pliable fingers into the gap. She snatches them back immediately, cradling her hand against her chest. I curl my own fingers round hers. 'Was it cold?' I ask her.

Suddenly everyone in the car has turned to me.

'What did you say?' 'What was that?' 'Sorry?' 'Pardon?' 'Did you say something?' they all say over each other.

I look down at Annie. Her hair, growing in wisps across her fragile skull, is so blonde it's the spun white of raw silk. Charts of blue threads run over her forehead. I can't remember when I last heard my voice. I clear my throat experimentally but then press my lips together. I allow myself to say his name inside my head: John. I try it again: he is dead.

Annie's eyes flicker to and fro at the streets we are passing through. Suddenly she lifts her arm again, the whole of her springy, compact body tensing in effort. Each of her knuckles is dimpled and she sticks out her index finger. 'Og!' she exclaims carefully, looking round at me for confirmation.

There is a pause.

'She's saying "dog",' says Kirsty. 'She can see a dog out there.'

I look out of the window. Not three feet from us, a couple are walking along the pavement. The man has slid his hand into the back pocket of the woman's jeans, but she is angry. Her face is frowning, turned towards his; she is speaking in short, emphasised jolts and with every expressive jerk, the arm attached to her by her jeans pocket twitches like a marionette's. Trotting beside them, a red lead held in his mouth, oblivious to their anger, is a brown, shaggy-coated dog.

The car moves off. I crane my head round to see them and as we turn a corner, they are still arguing. They have stopped walking and he has removed his hand from her pocket. They disappear from view. Annie has turned and is gazing intently at me. She doesn't see me very often. She presses the tip of her index finger against my chin. One of my tears catches it and rolls down her finger, over her hand and up her sleeve. She takes away her hand and peers in surprise up her jumper sleeve.

The car stops and everyone is getting out. I release the catch on the door and clutch Annie to me. I have to bend my knees awkwardly and stagger forward so as not to bump her head on the car door. I am aware of a sudden movement among the people standing about on the pavement and there is a muted slapping sound as feet hurry across the tarmac towards me. I am surrounded by jostling people, a stuttering volley of questions and bright flares of flashbulbs.

'Mrs Friedmann, do you have any comment on your husband's death?'

'Is it true that John was estranged from his family?'

'Mrs Friedmann, do you have any message for the bombers?'

'Alice, is that your baby? Is that John Friedmann's child?'

'Alice, can you look this way?'

I am shielding Annie's head with my hand. She is clutching the neck of my blouse so tightly in her fists that I feel I might choke and her rising screams are drilling into my ear. Then someone – a friend of John's from the paper who has appeared from somewhere – is shoving at these people and dragging me forwards, his hand gripping my arm. Then we are through some doors and Beth is there beside me and Annie is pulled away from me and my father is holding my hand. It is very quiet suddenly.

The coffin is a shock. He is in there, I tell myself inside my head, his body is just under that wood. It seems very important to examine it closely, run my hand along it, feel the grain of the wood against the striating lines of my hand. I am walking towards it and now I can see the large, wide-ended brass screws holding down the lid. There is a suffocating tightness across my chest. I am working out what kind of a screwdriver I would need to undo them and now I am getting closer, so close; I am putting out my hand ready and I can nearly touch it when I feel a restraining tug on my other hand. Puzzled, I look down and see that my father is still holding it. 'This way, Alice,' he is saying to me. 'Come and sit down.'

But . . .

'Come on,' he says gently.

I am so close. Another two steps and I could press my hand to it. Is it smooth? Would it feel warm? Could I lay my cheek against it? I look back at my father. It wouldn't be difficult to wrench myself from his grasp and take those two steps. Beyond him, I can see my family sitting down in the front row, looking at me, anxious. Neil is there too, with Jamie in his arms. And beyond them there is a mass of faces, so many faces – did John know this many people? – all looking at me but trying not to and I suddenly think that in those people, somewhere, must be John's father. I let my father lead me to the seat and I sit down between my parents. Maybe they'll let me touch it later.

I listen to myself breathing in and out, in and out, lungs

filling and then pressing out the air again into the atmosphere.
I imagine the air entering me as light filling a dark space. Then,
before I can stop it, I find that my thoughts are hurtling along
the familiar track of what it must be like trying to breathe when
you're pulling in only dust and old, stale carbon dioxide; or
trying to breathe at all when you are weighted down beneath
tonnes and tonnes of concrete and metal. Did he die straight
away or was he alive and conscious for hours, fighting for
breath, hoping to be rescued? The police couldn't tell me. I
feel again that tidal panic welling somewhere near my stomach
and I have to look hard at the person standing at the front
and concentrate on what he is saying to stop myself from
screaming.

It is Sam, John's friend from university, and he is talking
and talking and when he starts a sentence he spreads out his
hands, opening up his fingers like petals and when he finishes
the sentence he brings his hands back together. In and out, in
and out. I watch him but don't listen because I don't want
to hear because none of this is any good and none of it will
bring him back and nothing any of these people say will alter
the fact that he's lying there in that box and how I want just
to go and touch it. I hear Annie exclaim something and Kirsty
murmuring at her to shush, not long now, and poor Annie she
must be so bored. Then I hear Sam mention my name and it's
like a needle crunching on a scratched record and I am scared,
scared in case all these people want me to get up there and say
something because I don't know what I would say, what is there
to say now because all I want to do is just run my hand along it,
just once would be enough, and I would be really brave and not
cry and cause a scene in front of all these people, because that's
what my parents are worried about, I know that. In front of
his father.

His father. I twist round in my seat. I want to see him.

I scan the rows and rows of faces. I know all these people. Some of them give me a little smile and some of them nod. One person waves. I don't wave back – and I feel bad about ignoring them – but I just want to get a look at him. I just want to see who he is and I want him to look at me and think, that's Alice.

My mother is plucking at my sleeve and muttering 'Alice' in that way so I know she wants me to turn around and sit nicely, but I won't. Over the other side of the room, across the narrow aisle through all the seats is a group of people I've never seen before. John's family. I know it. Six or seven of them. There are four middle-aged men in dark overcoats. I realise that I'm looking for someone who looks like John, I'm searching for an older face that echoes his, but none of them do.

A woman from John's work is reading a poem. I can hear people sobbing in the room and beside me my father is supporting his forehead in his hand. It's funny because I used to tease John about how I thought that this woman fancied him. I am just about to turn round again to look at his family when there is a strange electronic whirring sound. Little wheels under his coffin are rotating and the coffin is moving slowly towards an opening in the wall that was hidden behind some curtains. Nobody told me this would happen.

I spring upright, my legs barely holding out, but immediately my parents seize hold of me and pull me back down.

'No!' I struggle. 'No, please, I just want . . .'

Both my hands are being crushed by my parents' and I watch in horror as his coffin trundles slowly into the hole and disappears. Then I wrest my hands free because I want to cover my face. I clamp both my hands over my eyes and won't take them away because I never want to look on anything ever again.

Rachel has her arm through Alice's and they are standing near the door. Lots of people are coming up to Alice — kissing her lightly on the cheek, shaking her hand, saying things which, once they are out of their throats and into the air, she can't recall at all. She looks at their mouths moving, nods a lot but doesn't speak. Rachel speaks and so does Alice's mother who is standing somewhere nearby but Alice can't see her. Someone puts into her hands a yellow plastic pot.

She stares at it blankly, her hands curled round its sides. Rachel's hand supports it from underneath. Rachel thinks she'll drop it. It has a tiny silver plaque on the front with the words 'John Daniel Friedmann' in a nasty italicised script. She is looking at this plaque, wondering if she can remove it when someone to her left says in a quiet voice, 'You must be Alice.'

She turns. It is one of the men in dark overcoats, offering his outstretched hand. She has to shift the pot into the crook of her left elbow to take it. His hand is warm and he holds on to hers for longer than she expected.

'I'm Nicholas,' he says, then adds, 'John's uncle.'

'Yes.' Alice tries out her voice cautiously. It sounds unnaturally high and cracked. She passes her tongue over her lips and draws in a deep breath. 'John's told me about you.'

'Alice,' he begins, 'we . . . that is, the rest of the family . . . want you to know how very sorry we are about . . . everything.'

Rachel is holding on to her very tightly. Alice nods.

'Also,' he glances involuntarily behind him at a man standing a few feet away, 'Daniel would like to know . . . if you don't mind telling us . . . where you're going to scatter those.' He points at the yellow urn.

Alice looks over his shoulder at John's father. He is shorter, stockier than she imagined, with grey hair cut very short. He is standing alone, gazing out of the doors at the crowds of people on the pavement outside and as she watches he draws the side of his finger across his eyelid in a slow movement full of weariness and grief. At precisely that moment, and just for a moment, she loves him. She actually loves him. It feels like the unfamiliar, cramping stretch of rarely used muscles. She even looks at her watch. At 3.04 p.m. I loved your father.

She unscrews the lid of the urn and looks inside. It is filled with a finely sifted, whitish powder. She dips her fingertips into it and rubs the grains between finger and thumb. They dissolve and flake under her touch. She screws the lid back on and pushes it into Nicholas Friedmann's hands. He is astounded. 'Are you sure?' he asks.

Ann, who has materialised at her side, is saying, 'Alice, you don't have to do that, you know. You might regret it. You don't have to do that.'

He is touching her sleeve hesitantly. Alice nods at him, twice. He walks back across the room and, saying something in a low voice, hands the urn to John's father. He cradles it in his hands and, just as Alice did, tilts it back to read the plaque. Then he looks over at her. Their eyes meet, briefly. She stands there thinking that he is going to come over and she is pushing down all the words that are crowding into her throat, but then he turns and, clutching the urn to him, goes out of the door and down the steps into the bright winter sun.

Ann hated North Berwick at first. Hated it. Hated that everywhere she went – into shops, on to the beach, into the park, into the library – everyone knew exactly who she was: 'You must be Ben Raikes's wife,' or 'You're the new Mrs Raikes,' or 'This must be Elspeth's daughter-in-law.' She would draw her coat around her, run her hand around the edges of the coins in her pocket, not knowing how to respond to these greetings. She was, she knew, at a disadvantage straight away, because she had no idea who anyone was, let alone have all sorts of inside information on them and their families going back four generations. People she'd not only never met before but would never want to meet would just stop her in the street and ask her questions as if they knew her: 'How do you like it here?' 'Do you play golf at all?' 'Why don't you call round for some coffee?' 'Where is it you're from anyway?' She couldn't be invisible. It was as if she was walking around with a big sign on her back. To her, the town, trapped as it was between the sea and the flat monotony of the agricultural fields, was a pit that seethed with gossip, circles of knowledge and people who clawed information from you. And they didn't like her, thought her a stuck-up Englishwoman – she knew that and she didn't care.

So she stopped going out after a while. Or would go out

in the winter dusk when she could keep her head down against
the driving wind, which always funnelled through narrow gaps
in the red sandstone buildings on the High Street, and no one
would recognise her. During the day, she would be left alone in
the house that was supposed to be her home but felt more alien
than anywhere else she had known. She would wander from
room to room, up and down the stairs, memorising where
certain objects were; she wanted to know where everything
was, how it all fitted together.

Then she had a baby and everything was better for a while,
and she even started venturing out more. She liked herself with
the pram, which was dark navy with squeaking silver wheels.
The people would look into it and not at her. After all, Kirsty
was blonde and pink and smiling. 'Like a wee angel,' they all
said, and Ann thought that because they liked Kirsty perhaps
they liked her better too. She felt in control for the first time
in her life: she had a baby, a husband and a house, which
admittedly wasn't hers but felt more like hers now she had
had a baby, and Elspeth had been nice and encouraged her to
paint the baby's room and plant as many flowers as she liked
in the garden soil. She would catch sight of herself in shop
windows – with coat, shopping-bag and pram – and would
think to herself: there is a smart young mother on her way to
buy something for her husband's tea. Her voice still sounded
out of kilter, foreign, alien when she asked for things in shops,
but somehow it mattered less now.

It was on one of these outings, when she was exploring
more and more, that she went into an antiques shop. In there
was a man with dark eyes and long lashes. Ann looked around
the shop and when she turned round, he had lifted Kirsty
right out of her pram without asking, and was holding her
to his chest. 'I have a boy almost her age,' he said. He had
an accent like Ann's. Kirsty looked tiny against the breadth

of his shoulder. Then came Alice, who had black eyes and black hair from the moment she was born. Ann felt like a photo negative next to her, and she couldn't wheel her about with confidence. She couldn't bear people's questions – however innocent – about this new baby. When she caught her reflection with Alice's pram in shop windows, it wasn't a young mother she saw, but an adulteress.

In the taxi back to Alice's house, Ben and Beth sit in the back, talking. Ann leans her head against the passenger window. It's getting dark earlier and earlier now. It will soon be a year since John died. Ann's breath appears in tiny beads of moisture on the glass propping up her head, vanishing as quickly as she inhales. On Saturday at eleven-twenty, or thereabouts, Alice was in the Waverley Station Superloo.

If Alice wakes up, Ann tells herself, the secret you thought was burnt and scattered on the Law with Elspeth's ashes could come out. She might not wake up. But then again, she might. As the taxi speeds through the night, and in the back seat Beth relates to Ben some story involving a dog and a frisbee, Ann imagines the scene: her and Ben standing around the bed. Alice stirring, stretching, opening her eyes. She looks at her, looks at Ben, her lips open and she says—

Maybe she wouldn't say anything. Maybe she didn't see anything at all. Maybe she was upset about something else entirely and it's just a coincidence that Ann happened to be there with—

And even if she did see, why would she automatically assume that the man has anything to do with her life, other than the fact that he's having an affair with her mother?

But Ann knows in her heart that Alice has that knack of instantly recognising the germ of any situation. Like someone else she knows. And Ann knows that if Alice wakes up, she is not the sort of person to let something like that lie. Alice would want to have it out with her. Probably straight away.

But what if she doesn't wake up. What then?

Alice dashes through the tube doors just as they are closing. It's about noon on a Saturday and the Northern line is relatively empty. As the train starts to rattle out of Camden Town Station, she makes her way down to the end of the carriage and sits opposite a middle-aged woman with a headscarf and a plastic bag full of children's toys. Alice will stay on the train until Kennington, where she will cross over to the northbound platform and catch another train which will take her back to Camden, where she will most probably go to the southbound platform and repeat the ritual.

Her tube-train riding has become a habit, something she would never admit to anyone. It's the only thing that makes her feel better – there is something about the anonymity of it, the lulling rattle of the train's movement, the aimlessness of it, that soothes her.

Today, the recollection of their last morning together is replaying over and over in her head, as if she's peering at it through the narrow slits of a zoetrope. When she'd woken up that morning, he had already got up and was in the shower.

She'd turned over into the warmth his body had left and cocooned herself under the duvet. I'll get up in five minutes, she'd told herself. She heard John thud downstairs and clatter about in the kitchen. Then he climbed the stairs again, pushed open the bedroom door and started crawling over the bed to her curled-up body. 'Time to get up, time to get up,' he'd crooned, and had kissed the back of her neck.

She'd shrieked when his wet hair met her bed-warmed skin. 'You're all wet, John.'

'I've made you some tea,' and he placed the mug on the bedside table before sliding in next to her under the covers. She'd turned over and they had lain in each other's arms for a while, looking into each other's faces.

'Do you know what I'm going to say now?' he asked.

'Yes.'

'What is it, then?'

'You're going to say, "Alice, it's eight o'clock."'

'No. Wrong. I'm going to say, Alice, it's eight-thirty.'

She gripped his arm. 'You're lying.'

He started laughing and shaking his head.

'It's just a ploy,' Alice continued, 'an evil ruse to get me out of bed.'

'I'm afraid not.' He dangled his watch in front of her face.

She pulled away from him and got out of bed. 'Oh, Jesus, I'm going to be so late. I blame you for this. You should have got me up earlier.'

He laughed and jumped off the bed, pulling on his trousers as she rushed into the bathroom.

When she had come downstairs ten minutes later, toast and cereal were laid out on the table for her. 'You're a wee angel,' she'd said to the top of his head, just visible over the newspaper he was reading. She ate rapidly, shovelling the hot toast into her mouth. John folded up the newspaper and laid it on the table next to him. 'What's your day going to be like?'

She'd pulled a face. 'Not great. We've got yet another

training day, for the new database they keep promising us, which never actually materialises. How about you?'

'Not too bad. I've got an interview this afternoon in Islington, but apart from that, not much else.' He yawned and stretched. 'Let's go away this weekend,' he said.

'Where to?'

'Don't know. I just feel like getting out of London. How about St Ives?'

'St Ives? Isn't it a bit far for a weekend?'

'Nah, you lightweight, it'll be fine. We can go to a little B-and-B, go for walks by the sea, see the new Tate Gallery, stay in bed all morning.' He got up and dumped his plate on the draining-board. When Alice had got back from her parents after his death it was still there, as he'd left it. It had taken her days to bring herself to wash it up. The knife had still held his fingerprints in smeary margarine.

'You're on.'

'I've got to go.'

Alice stood and walked with him to the front door. He put his arms around her waist and kissed her. 'See you tonight,' he whispered in her ear, 'goodbye, my love,' and then went out of the door, waving to her from the gate. She closed the door behind him and as she passed through the living room, she'd seen him through the front window, his head bent against the cold wind, caught in the act of zipping up his jacket. Then, like an actor exiting a movie screen, he was gone.

Tears are spilling down Alice's face, dripping off her chin on to her T-shirt. There's hardly anyone in the carriage, but she wouldn't care anyway. She attempts to wipe her face on her sleeves but they are already sodden. 'Would you like a tissue?'

It is the middle-aged woman opposite, leaning across the aisle, her face creased with sympathy, offering an opened packet of Handy Andies. Alice hesitates. 'Go on, love, you look like you need one.'

'Thanks.' Alice takes one, hoping that she will not try to say any more to her. After blowing her nose and wiping her face, she tucks the tissue into her jeans pocket and glances surreptitiously over at the woman again. Damn, she's still looking at her.

The woman clears her throat and leans forward again. 'You're crying about a man, aren't you?'

Alice looks at her in astonishment, then nods.

'I thought as much.' The woman tuts. 'Well, I can tell you this for free – he's not worth it.'

Alice lurches to her feet, pulling her bag up off the floor. She wants to shout, he's dead, he's dead and he was worth it, but she waits in silence by the door until the train jolts to a halt. As soon as the doors slam open, she steps off the train and loses herself in the crowd.

Alice goes shopping with Elspeth. She is allowed to hold the parcels. Some stuff goes in shopping bags, which knock Alice on the legs when she carries them. Food and cleaning products shouldn't be in the same bag, Elspeth says. Tins and cleaning products together is all right. Fruit shouldn't go in the string bag. It gets bruised. Alice knows that with a box of eggs she has to carry it in front of her in both hands. They come in grey, damp-feeling trays of half-dozens, which means six. Before buying eggs, Elspeth opens the box lid and pivots all the eggs around in their snug holders to check none have hairline cracks that are seeping liquids into the cardboard. When Alice is carrying them, she eases open the lid and turns them over again so that they all have their blunter ends facing down. Once, when she was doing this, they slid from her hands and broke on the pavement in a shock of yellow, shattered shell and viscous watery blur. Nevermindnevermind, Elspeth said, over and over again.

Today, they haven't bought much. A brown loaf swells the black netting of the string bag Alice is holding. Alice used to put this bag over her head and pull it down over her body with the plaited handles, folding her arm under the webbing. When she wore it like that she was Net Man. But that was a long time ago. Today Elspeth has met a friend of hers and they've been talking for ages outside the antiques shop. Alice doesn't like this friend very much: she has a powdery face, and when she kisses Alice, the stale, chalky smell makes her sneeze. Alice starts to jiggle ever so slightly on Elspeth's hand, and bends back the sole of her sandal under her foot. Without breaking off her conversation or even looking down, Elspeth twitches Alice's arm, which Alice knows means she is expected to behave. She extricates her fingers from Elspeth's, walks over to the window of the antiques shop, and presses her nose to it.

First of all, she is only looking at how tiny beads of moisture leave a ghostly negative of her nose and lips on the glass. Then she adjusts her eyes to peer into the shop. She has to make a tunnel with her hands to shut out the glare of the street. She's never been in here: it's dark, things hang from the ceiling, and there's a curved glass cabinet not far from where she is standing, heaped with beads, earrings, rings.

'Shall we go in and have a look?'

Alice brings her eyes back to the street and its reflection in the glass, and sees that Elspeth has come to stand next to her.

'Yes.'

The shop seems cold after the street. Alice stands next to a table that has a surface so polished she thinks that if she touched it, ripples would circle out from under her fingers to lap at its edges. She looks up and around the dark red walls: feathered fans, gold-edged paintings of East Lothian, a stuffed monkey with glassy eyes holding a platter, a slender-necked vase, blue-patterned plates gripped to the wall with little iron legs, a lampshade dangling strings of purple beads. Elspeth is talking to the shop lady in the back room, so Alice walks over to a chrome carousel of clothes. She knows these things from shopping with her mother, and she likes them. She gives it a shove to the left: the clothes swish on their hangers and there is the murmur of silk rubbing up against silk, a rustling, gushing, secret sound. Alice dives down to her knees and resurfaces in the middle of the carousel, surrounded by antique dresses and blouses and skirts and scarves. Alice runs her hand reverently down the insides of the clothes, the material giving her palm a cool frisson. She turns round and round, staring at each of them in turn, until dizziness starts to smudge her vision.

'You must be Alice.'

Alice looks up from under her fringe. She insists that it is cut straight across her forehead so it touches her eyebrows. She won't have it any shorter. If her mother, who cuts their hair by sitting all three of her daughters in turn on a stool in the kitchen, tries to cut it shorter, Alice screams until her lips turn blue. She once raged so much during a hair-cutting session that Ann stood her up and smacked her on the legs with the back of the hairbrush.

It is a man, looming above the top of the carousel, leaning with his elbows on the hangers. Alice can't quite make him out, but doesn't think she recognises him.

'Yes,' Alice says, from her crouched position, 'I am.'

He reaches in and Alice feels the hands of the stranger grip her underneath her arms before the floor falls away, and she is rising, rising towards the ceiling and a low red lantern covered with the writhing blue-green bodies of dragons. Then the floor is coming up to meet her again and she is set down in front of

327

the man. 'I thought you must be,' he is murmuring, surveying her face so closely that Alice glances towards the back of the shop to reassure herself that Elspeth is still there. Is she in trouble? The man is tall, with thick, powerful arms and hair that's longer than her father's. It reaches below the collar of his faded blue shirt. He's got canvas shoes on and no socks. One of the shoes is held together with a very short, knotted piece of red string.

'Is this your shop?' Alice asks.

'Yes.' He nods.

'Are all these things yours, then?'

The man laughs. Alice doesn't know why.

'Well, I suppose they are.' He crouches down at her level and puts his fingers around her upper arm. 'Tell me, what do you like best in here?'

Alice doesn't even hesitate, but points to the red dragon lantern. She loves their lithe, scaled bodies, their powerful tails and their fierce yellow eyes. 'What are those?' she asks, pointing at the strange, trailing, hair-like things that protrude from their jaws.

The man looks. 'I'm not sure.'

'It could be fire,' Alice steps closer, 'but I don't think so.'

'No. I'd agree with you there. I think they might be gills. I think these are sea-dragons.'

'Sea-dragons?' Alice repeats, turning to look at him. She's never heard of them.

He shrugs. 'Maybe you only get them in China.'

He sits down on a chair covered in deep red velvet. 'Do you know what I was doing when I saw you come in?'

Alice shakes her head.

'I was testing these,' he holds up a string of pearls, 'to see if they were real.' The man gets hold of Alice's wrist, opens up her fingers with his and coils the pearls into her palm. 'The best way to do this is to put them in contact with human skin. When real pearls are next to your skin they get warm and start to glow.' Alice and the man stare at the pile of white orbs in her hand. At the centre of the string, the pearls are at their biggest; at the ends they are impossibly tiny, seed-sized. Some of the man's hair falls over his face as they wait and they are so close together that some of it falls on to Alice's. She takes a small, shuffling step back, still watching the pearls for any signs of opalescent glowing. Suddenly, he has whipped them out of her hand again. 'Maybe that method's a bit time-consuming. The other way is to rub them against your teeth. Real pearls feel like sand. Open your mouth,' he commands.

Alice does so. She has a row of perfect, white baby teeth. The man rests his hand on her chin, looking her straight in the eye. With his other hand he rubs the largest pearl at the centre of the string against the enamel of her two front teeth.

Alice concentrates. There is a roughened, grainy feeling, a kind of scratchy rasp. 'They're real!' she says. 'They're real!'

The man laughs and nods. 'Good girl.'

Then he has placed her on a chair in front of a mirror, and is fastening the pearls around her neck. 'There. What do you think?'

They are too long for Alice, disappearing below the neckline of her T-shirt. The man stands staring at her in the mirror, one hand on her shoulder.

'You've got an English accent, haven't you?' Alice says. 'My mum's English.'

He nods very slowly, and looks as if he's about to say something when they both see Elspeth appear behind them in the mirror. 'Alice,' she says, 'come along now, we must be going.'

Alice gets down from the chair.

'Give the man back his necklace.' Elspeth turns her round and starts undoing the clasp at the back of her neck. The man is reaching in his shirt pocket for a narrow silver tin, from which he draws a thin cigarette. He presses down on a lighter from his trouser pocket, it sparks and he lights the cigarette. The air is filled with the faint scent of vanilla. Alice puts her hand up to the pearls to feel them for the last time.

'No, no,' he says, waving his hand and exhaling a spiral of blue smoke, 'I'd like her to keep them.'

'We couldn't possibly . . .' Elspeth is saying, and Alice feels the pearls flowing through her fingers as her grandmother pulls them off. Elspeth holds them out.

'No. Really. I want her to have them.'

'Don't be ridiculous,' Elspeth says, in that way that Alice always thinks is funny but serious at the same time, pushing them into his hand. 'Are you running a business or what?'

Elspeth turns away, holding Alice by the shoulders and propelling her towards the door. All at once, they are out on the street again and Elspeth has handed her the string bag with the loaf of bread to hold, and soon they are going up the hill, hand in hand, towards home.

Alice sits up and peers at the clock on the bedside table. She sighs shakily and rubs her face. It's only ten minutes since she last looked. She flings herself back against the pillow, which is damp and clammy. Maybe she should get up, but what's the point? She feels prickly-hot and kicks the duvet off her body impatiently. Car lights from the road criss-cross the dark ceiling.

She's been lying here in bed for four hours now and hasn't slept yet. She's so tired, so tired: she knows that if she could just sleep she'd feel better but her mind is whirring, whirring out of control like a bicycle freewheeling downhill. 'Please,

please, please let me sleep!' she says, through gritted teeth to
no one in particular.

She turns over on to her side and tries to breathe deeply
and concentrate on her favourite way of getting to sleep – a
fantasy that involves John coming into the room, sitting on the
edge of the bed and talking to her.

She has just got to the part where she imagines the tug on
the duvet from his weight as he sits down, when her eyes spring
open. Her whole body tenses and she pushes her nails into her
palms. Start again: she hears the door open, then his footsteps,
she can hear him breathing softly, he comes round the side of
the bed, she sees his sillhouette against the window . . .

She sits bolt upright. Her jaw is clenched so hard that the
sides of her head ache. 'No, no, no.' She grips handfuls of her
hair as she starts sobbing uncontrollably – great wrenching
gasps that make her cough and gulp for air.

For a week or so now, she's had this tiny, niggling suspicion
that she's been quelling, ignoring, pushing to the back of her
mind, refusing to acknowledge it.

She's forgetting his face. She can no longer bring to mind
an exact image of his features. His face, which she knew like
her own, is fading from her memory.

Alice blunders, panicked, from the bed and down the stairs.
In the sitting room she tears open drawers and pulls out box
after box of photographs. In her haste, she drops one and the
pictures spill over the carpet in an arc of shiny rectangles. She
falls upon them eagerly and snatches up pictures of John smiling
in Spain, in Prague, decorating the house, at their wedding, by
Camden canal. She lays them next to each other and kneels
down to examine them.

By the time she hears the electric rattle of the milk van
coming down the street, she is sitting motionless in the middle
of the floor, her knees drawn up to her chin, her hair hanging

in tangled clumps over her face. All around her is a sliding sea of photographs.

She takes a deep breath, closes her eyes and begins again at his hairline. She has his fringe, the creases on his brow, the curve of his temples, but after that, it's no use. She can remember isolated features perfectly – the jut of his eyebrows, the way his hair grew in whorls on the top of his head, the black depths of his irises, the precise grain of his stubble, the swell of his Adam's apple, the upward curve of his lips; but as soon as she tries to assemble them, the image blurs into a fuzzy mess.

How can this have happened? How can she have forgotten his face so soon? Is this how it will be – that he will gradually fade from her memory?

She feels cold. Her feet are chilly to the touch. She curls her hands around them, but doesn't get up and starts to rock gently back and forth. The sun moves in longer and longer triangles around the floor. The postman drops some letters through the letterbox. Sometime during the day, the phone rings but she still doesn't move when Susannah from work speaks to the answerphone: 'We were just wondering if you were coming in today, Alice.'

In late afternoon, she stops rocking, straightens up stiffly, slowly, walks through the photographs without looking at them and goes back to bed.

I padded cautiously on bare feet over the runnelled, slippery tiles of the changing room of the Oasis sports centre. The air was humid and hot and smelt stiflingly of talcum powder and deodorant spray. Women in various stages of undress lined the walls. The noise was a mixture of chatter, the hiss of showers, a fair amount of giggling, distant echoey shouts from the swimming-pool and a faint pound of music from an aerobics class somewhere. It was after five and all the

Covent Garden and Bloomsbury offices had emptied out their workers and it seemed that most of them were here, waiting for their step class, getting ready for the gym or struggling into swimming-costumes.

At the pool edge, I wound my hair into a knot on top of my head and pulled my goggles down over my eyes. The scene was immediately cobalt blue: swimming-capped heads of indeterminate sex bobbed up and down the lanes as instructed by the poolside notices – in an orderly clockwise fashion – except for one man who was ploughing up and down the middle of the slow lane in a violent butterfly crawl. Sedate swimmers flinched as he sprayed them in a flurry of foam. I frowned. I hate people who do that.

I lowered myself into the water, holding on to the aluminium ladder. The water was cold and my skin prickled with tiny goosebumps. When it reached my ribs, I released my hold and allowed myself to sink slowly, my palms lightly touching the smooth porcelain wall tiles, freefalling down into the turquoise water. My heart felt so weighted and heavy that I thought I might just sink to the bottom. All day at the office, I had been holding everything in while I spoke on the phone to the Arts Council, had a meeting with Anthony, showed a woman from a black literature project from Manchester round the library.

The blue disks of my goggles filled with stinging tears. Without rising to the surface to draw in air, I turned over in the water and kicked off from the wall. After two long strokes, my head broke the surface and I gasped for breath, but I pushed my body on blindly.

Five speedy lengths later, I crouched by the steps in the shallow end. My muscles ached and the blood was pounding around my body so fast that I felt dizzy. I had a sharp stitch under my ribs. Pulling off my goggles, I breathed deeply, drawing in large lungfuls of hot, chlorinated air, gripping the handrail.

'Hi.' A voice broke into my reverie and I turned to see a ginger-haired, tanned man with a goatee beard smiling at me with glittery white teeth. I recognised him as the man who was speeding up and down the middle of the slow lane. He had his hands on his knees, propping up his upper body.

'Hello.' I pretended to be adjusting my goggle straps.

'How are you doing?'

'OK,' I said, in the specially impassive, monotone voice I had perfected for times like this.

'I've seen you here before. You come here a lot, don't you?'

I shrugged without looking at him. I could sense that his body was large with swelling, hard muscles on the upper arms; it gave off a heat that I could feel on my cooling skin. I stared down at my fractured reflection in the choppy water. My legs were marbled with fractured light, stippled with bubbles. I willed him to go away, feeling my earlier tears hovering somewhere just below the surface, ready to break out at any moment.

'What's your name?'

I shook my head, unable to speak.

'Hey, are you OK?' He touched my arm. I flinched, covering the place he'd touched me with my hand. 'What's the matter? What did I say?'

'Please leave me alone.'

Without putting my goggles back on, I pushed myself away from the wall and swam with jerky, uneven strokes to the other end, where I pulled myself out of the water and reached for my towel, left folded up on a bench.

Later, I sat at the kitchen table, my feet curled around the chair legs, my chin resting on my hands. My skin smelt of the

tang of chlorine. My hair was still damp. I knew I should go
and wash out all the chlorine and dry it properly, but I didn't
have the energy. I also knew I should eat something, but what
was the point, what was the fucking point.

I sighed wearily and turned to look out of the back door into
the garden. The sky was just beginning to deepen into a darker,
indigo blue. Taking the key from a hook, I unlocked the door
and walked out into the garden. It had rained sometime that
afternoon, and the sodden trees were still dripping a steady,
despondent rhythm. There was a fresh, green scent of damp
soil, mingled with the sharp, sweet smell of rotting leaves.

I sat on the bench under the tree for a long time, watching
my neighbours' lights come on in their back windows, the damp
seeping slowly through the thin material of my skirt. At some
point, the cat came to join me, the question mark of his tail
appearing out of the gloom.

Above me, the branches of the trees were tossed and bent in
the gathering wind. The cat prowled around my ankles in a tight
circle, his back arched. Dark, deep blue clouds raced over the sky.
At a sound just behind me, I turned my neck, and as I did so, there
seemed to be a kind of slippage in me, as if electrical contacts had
been suddenly shifted and the crackle of a current was running
through me on a different route. I realised something. I realised
for the first time that all the unaccustomed disbelief and shock
had, without me really noticing it, eroded into hard fact: he will
never come again. He was dead. I had kept trying to make myself
believe it and now I knew it. My heart knew it, my head knew
it, my body knew it. He will never come again.

I sat there for a long time, feeling so numb, as if all sound
and sense had been switched off. What was left was a peculiar
kind of peace: I felt hollow, as if my body was filled with
nothing but smoke.

I looked up into the sky. The violet had sunk into a pitchy

dusk and birds sat higgled on the telephone wire that swept from the house opposite to the eaves of mine. 'Life goes on': so many people had said that to me. Yes, life fucking well goes on but what if you don't want it to? What if you want to arrest it, stop it, or even battle against the current into a past you don't want to be past? 'You'll get over it' – that was another. But I didn't want to get over it. I didn't want to become used to the fact that he'd died. That was the last thing I wanted.

I started up. It was darker. Lucifer followed me as far as the gate, which I slammed shut behind me. I bolted along the pavement, the echoes of my footfalls bouncing off the houses. I had no idea where I was going. All I was aware of was this hole, this gaping hole where my heart should have been. I read somewhere once that your heart is supposed to be the same size as your clenched fist, but this hole felt far bigger. It seemed to expand over my whole upper body and it felt cold, vacant – the cooling wind seemed to cut right through it. I felt frail and insubstantial, as if the wind could have blown me away.

Towards the tube station, the crowds of people thickened. I crossed the road, dodging the late-night traffic coming from the city centre and, to avoid a straggling group of people coming along the pavement towards me, I ducked into a side-street. I've no idea how long I walked for that night or where I went. I remember passing someone who called after me, 'Are you all right, love, are you all right?' and I must have passed by the fringes of Regent's Park because I do recall the strange braying of the zoo animals carried towards me by the breeze.

At one point I went into a twenty-four-hour supermarket. People were circling the shelves, filling wire baskets with ice-cream, wine and fruit, watched half-heartedly by a bored, underpaid teenager at the till. I wandered among them, mesmerised by brightly coloured packaging, notices of price cuts, lurid display stands. I trailed my hand over the shelves: hunks of yellow cheese, waxed fruit, cakes in shrink-wrapped plastic. When my hand encountered something soft, yet hard, I stopped. It was a ball of wool, bright red, its twisted skeins wound into a tightly packed cannon-ball. I weighed it in my hand. My hand was wet and slippery with wiped-away tears, but the wool sucked the moisture into itself, hoarding the salt water in its wound-up, labyrinthine strands.

I felt tense with desire for it. I could not walk out of the shop without it, but I had no money with me – I'd left the house so abruptly. I cast a careful side glance at the teenager at the till: he was staring out of the window at the tube station over the road. I looked about me. To my left, a woman was intently absorbed in a choice of different flavours of tinned soup. So I just did it. I stuffed it quickly up under my jumper. Then I headed for the exit, and looking back over my shoulder only once, I let the door spring closed behind me.

The thin wail of Jamie reached Kirsty through the leagues of her dreamless, zombiefied sleep. For a few moments, she could only open her eyes and stare at the darkened ceiling. Her limbs wouldn't obey her brain. Beside her, Neil turned over in his sleep, oblivious. How did he do that? How come his brain wasn't programmed into the children's sleeping patterns, as hers was? When Jamie's wail intensified to an outraged, hiccuping roar, she went into autopilot: sit up, swing legs off bed, stumble across debris of bunched-up socks, cardboard picture-books dissolving at the edges from too much toddler-sucking, discarded toys, a heap of maternity bras, feeding bottles and Neil's shoes over to the cot.

Tiny, reddened hands and feet were waving in the air. Jamie was lying on his back. When he saw her he filled his lungs for a mega-roar. Kirsty scooped up his stiffened frame on to her shoulder, muffling his cries, carried his warm, compact parcel of a body into the sitting room and sat down with him on the sofa. 'Now then,' she murmured, as she unbuttoned her nightdress, 'what's all this noise about?'

As soon as her nipple was in his mouth he was silent. His fingers closed possessively around one of hers and the only sound was of his gentle, fast, shallow breathing and his hungry, wet sucking.

after you'd gone

It was a warm night. Kirsty curled and uncurled her bare toes to the rhythm of his feeding and leant back into the cushions. She began to feel the numbing, addictive opiate of sleep soak into her. Her hands slackened, her fingers curling away from her palms and the knots in her spine relaxed. She slid slowly towards unconsciousness.

The next thing she remembered was the tingling feeling that there was someone else with her. Her head jerked upright, expecting to see a pyjama-clad Neil standing there in the dim light. The room was empty. Kirsty felt strange. Her heart was thudding. She had no idea how much time had passed. Jamie was asleep in her arms, the soft diamond of his fontanelle pulsing on the crown of his head.

Alice. Alice was awake. Somewhere. She just knew it. Kirsty hadn't managed to speak to her in weeks. Alice never seemed to be in or answering the phone when she called. Kirsty twisted her head around the room again, just to check her sister wasn't there, by some surreal coincidence, then she got to her feet, hefting the weight of the sleeping Jamie up on to her shoulder.

In the hallway, she crouched, Jamie on her lap, and dialled Alice's number. It rang once, then she heard Alice's voice, tight, strained: 'Hello?'

'Hi. It's me.'

She heard her sister take in breath and then break down in hysterical, gut-wrenching sobs. The tears trickled down Kirsty's face and fell on to Jamie's Babygro as she listened, the receiver clamped to her ear, to Alice's grief, pouring down the phone line, and she said gently, 'Alice, don't. Don't cry. Don't cry. Alice, don't.'

It went on for ten, fifteen minutes, maybe more. Round and round in Kirsty's head, as if fixed on a loop-tape, was the thought: my sister is five hundred miles away, all alone in her house and she is crying to herself in the middle of the night.

'Alice,' Kirsty said at last, 'why don't you phone us when you're feeling like this? I can't bear to think of you crying like this on your own.'

Alice began to speak in jolting, gasping snatches between sobs. 'I just can't do it . . . any more . . . Kirsty . . . It's like something . . . my whole life . . . has come unstuck . . . used to be . . . always was so happy . . . enjoyed life . . . and now nothing is worthwhile . . . Can't find anything . . . to make me feel better . . . Everything is pointless without him . . . I feel dead . . . can't feel anything any more . . . I'd rather be dead . . . Sometimes think I'm just going to lose it . . . Just feel dead inside . . . can't feel anything any more.'

When Kirsty finally replaced the receiver, she went back into the bedroom and lowered Jamie into his cot. Then she slid into bed and, pressing her cheek to the dip of Neil's spine, fell asleep with her arms around him.

The shop has a narrow double door. Only one side opens. Alice has to slide in sideways, her bag catching on the door handle.

'Hello again,' the woman behind the counter says brightly. Alice parts her lips in a soundless greeting, heading straight for the wide, box-like shelves that are stuffed with balls of wool, one colour to each box. Behind her, the woman carries on her conversation down the telephone: '. . . and I said to her at the time, if you have another child, that'll be you. I wouldn't take any notice of what he wants. The best thing to do is be content with the one kid, get to a good surgeon, get it all whipped out and get yourself sewn up properly. But you know what she's like . . .'

Alice listens to her breathing to shut out the woman's voice, reads the closely spaced words of a pattern, squeezes the balls of wool between her fingers, brushes their strands against her cheek to check their softness and selects pair after pair of long, lithe, silver needles of varying circumferences and lengths. Then she carries the lot to the till. The woman says into the phone: 'Sorry, got to go. Yes . . . yes . . . I'll call you later.' She turns to face Alice and rings up her purchases on the till with pink-varnished fingernails like candied petals. 'Your husband's a lucky man, having someone who can knit all these nice clothes for him,' she says, pushing the things into a plastic bag, making the needles clatter against each other.

Alice twists the thin, platinum band that encompasses the fourth finger on her left hand. 'Yes,' Alice says, and has to clamp shut her mouth to make sure she doesn't say anything else. It frightens her, how close she is to yelling something at this woman's over-made-up, over-cheerful face.

Outside, clutching her new needles to her chest in the middle of the crowded market, Alice has to lean against the wall to recover. She feels light-headed, as if she's run up several flights of stairs.

She can't go back to work now. She just can't. She knows she should call them and tell them she's going home, but she only thinks of this when she's already on the tube to Camden Town. And by then it's too late. She'll make something up when she goes in tomorrow. She'll say she was ill or something.

At home, she lies down on the bed for a while, still in her coat, still clutching the plastic bag and her keys. When the light starts draining from the sky outside, she sits upright, wedging a pillow between the wall and her back and draws everything out of the bag, laying it all out on the bedclothes. She spreads the pattern across her knee and pores over the first ball of wool, searching for its end. Then she begins to knit, the needles pressed cool into the grooves at the base of her palms, their heads clicking together, the skein of wool slipping through her fingertips, being woven, twisted, looped into an ever-growing mesh of complex stitches. The rhythm of it is a marvel to her: in, round, through and off; in, round, through and off. The vocabulary that comes with it is solid, short, unequivocal: purl, plain, cable. When one row is finished, the weighted needle is passed into the other hand and the newly freed one dives into the first, new stitch.

When she first started she'd been crap, of course. Dropped stitches were like an insidious virus, unravelling the work from the middle. These efforts she threw away. But once she'd been doing it a week or two she no longer dropped stitches and soon she could do it without looking. There is something so satisfying in wearing something you have made. As her arms move in the comforting, regular rhythm, she looks down at the interlocking stitches that are covering her arms: I made every one of those.

When there is a long, heavy beard of stitches hanging from one needle, she stops. She lays it aside, sits on the edge of the bed, her legs dangling to the floor, and stares unseeingly out of the window. At times – often when she's been in the house for a few days on her own – she flies into a private and bitter rage, like nothing she's experienced since she was a child: what on earth do you do if, at the age of twenty-nine, you've lost the only person you know you can be happy with? Today, though, she's not being bitten at by anger. Today, she just wants him back, she just wants him back and it hurts more than she can ever say.

She sits there, hands tucked under her, her feet swinging, scuffing at the floor. She feels nothing for anyone – apart from him. Of course. Always him. She is welded together; hard, brittle. Nothing and no one touches her. She is immovable as stone and just as cold.

When she'd called her at work that morning, Rachel had said that if she didn't come she'd never speak to her again, so at about eight Alice went round the deserted office switching off the lights and shutting down the computers. She applied some make-up in the loo mirror, spiking her lashes with mascara, painting on a bright red smile, and walked down the five flights of stairs. Before leaving, she tidied the competition leaflets in the stand beside the front door.

It was a warm evening. Neal Street was thronged with people. She walked past them all and past all the neon-lit shops. The bar where Rachel said she'd be was just off Seven Dials, in a basement reached by spiral metal steps. As she descended, she could see Rachel sitting at a table near the back with another woman. They were talking animatedly.

'Alice! You came!' Rachel stood up and gave her a hug. 'This is Camille.' The woman smiled a slow, sympathetic smile and turned her pale milky-blue eyes on Alice. 'Alice, it's so good to meet you,' she said, in a low, confidential sort of voice. 'Rachel's told me all about you. How are you now? Feeling any better yet?'

Alice stopped struggling out of her jacket and looked in surprise at Rachel, who was staring at the table, a slight blush staining her cheeks.

'I'm fine, thank you,' Alice said bluntly. 'How are you?'

'Fine, fine.' Camille smiled radiantly.

Alice felt disembodied; it was incredibly hot and noisy after the balmy air of the street. The people at the bar were shouting and straining for the bartenders' attention. Cigarette smoke rose in blue-edged plumes from each table and everyone's faces looked florid and somehow desperate, as if the crucial thing was to be seen to be having a good time. She looked across the table at Rachel, who was listening to something Camille was saying, and felt as if she knew her as well as she knew this Camille person. Was this really her friend? It seemed like years ago that they'd known each other. Alice stared down at her hands in her lap, gulping at her drink to try to open up her throat. She looked up and focused again on the two faces opposite her, attempting to tune into their conversation.

'So, where did you go? What was he like?' Rachel was saying. She saw Alice was looking at them and leant towards her, 'Camille's just split up with someone she was with for — how long was it, Camille?'

'A year and a half.'

'A year and a half, and last night she went out with this bloke – her first date since she split up with her ex.'

Alice tried to look interested.

'Well, he took me to this bar in Islington.'

'Which one?' Rachel asked.

'The one across from the tube station, called Barzantium, something like that.'

'I know it. And? Go on.'

'We had cocktails, talked a bit and he told me all about this theory he has.'

'Which was . . . ?'

'Well, Mañuel says—'

'Wait a minute,' Rachel interrupted. 'He's called Mañuel?'

'Yeah.'

'What kind of a name is that?'

'His parents are South American or something. Look, do you want to hear his theory or not?'

'Yes, sorry. Go on.'

'Mañuel has this theory that if your relationship's ended or whatever you shouldn't, like, go into hibernation – which is what I've been doing a bit, he said. What you should do is start seeing someone else as soon as possible. It's the only way to get over it.'

'Why?'

'He says there's no point in dwelling on all that pain, that what you need is a transition person, a kind of human anaesthetic.'

Rachel snorted. 'A human anaesthetic, my arse. Let me

345

guess, Mañuel wasn't by any chance magnanimously offering to be your human anaesthetic, was he?'

'No, no, it wasn't like that. He said people needed something to kick-start them, to sort of get them back out there.'

'Sounds suspiciously like a desperate chat-up line to me,' Rachel said, leaning back and swigging her drink. 'What do you think, Al?'

'A human anaesthetic?' Alice repeated, still with this out-of-body sensation.

Camille looked vacant, confused. Rachel was horrified, slamming her drink on to the table, suddenly falling over herself. 'Alice . . . I don't think Camille meant . . . It's different for you . . . I mean . . . Christ, Alice, I'm sorry . . . I can't believe we were just talking about this in front of you like that . . . It was really stupid, and— -'

Alice got up and pulled her jacket off the chair. 'I think I'm going to go.'

As she was crossing Shaftesbury Avenue, she heard feet hitting the pavements behind her, and Rachel caught up with her, grabbed her by the arm. She stopped, but didn't look at her friend.

'Alice. I'm so sorry.'

'It's fine, Rach. It's really fine. Honestly. I just didn't feel like . . . being there any more.'

'Well, I can't say I blame you. I think I win the Crap Friend award.'

'No, you don't,' Alice said. 'Don't talk shit.'

'Well, I'd rather talk shit than human anaesthetics.'

Alice looked at Rachel, and they both burst out laughing. Rachel threw her arms round Alice's ribcage and hugged her hard. 'God, Alice, I can't stand it.'

'Can't stand what?'

'Can't stand that I can't understand what it's really like for you.'

'Well, you do a pretty good job.'

'No,' Rachel shook her head, 'I don't. Not at all. But then there isn't anyone else in the world who can really understand what you're going through.'

Alice hadn't even thought of the answer she came out with before she said it, and it surprised her so much that it kept churning over and over in her head: 'There's his father.'

It wasn't hard to find the address. She'd searched through John's files in the spare room, and discovered at the back of a box an exercise book with a faded red cover. Written in the flyleaf, in a rounded adolescent version of his handwriting, was 'If lost, please return to:' and then the address.

In her lunch-hour, Alice had gone into a stationery shop and bought a special new pad of writing-paper. It was thick blue cartridge paper with raised ridges. If you held it up to the light, the secret stamp of the manufacturer would be illuminated. This was real, grown-up writing-paper. For serious letters. When you opened the cover, the first page was a striped one with thick black lines to guide your pen in straight, neat rows.

Alice slid the guiding lines under the first blue sheet and squared it up. Then she filled her fountain pen, dipping the gold nib into the thick black liquid, squeezing the dropper and releasing it. She wiped the nib on her trousers – they were black anyway, so what did it matter.

In the top right-hand corner, she wrote her address. The pen nib scratched against the grain of the paper. Under it she wrote the date, and leant back to look at her work. Was the address the first thing you read when you got a letter you weren't expecting? She doubted it. If it were Alice getting this letter, she'd shuffle quickly through the pages to the end and examine the signature. Maybe she didn't need the address after all.

Alice tore off the sheet, half crumpled it, then superstitiously put it into the drawer next to her. She didn't want anything to fuck this up.

'Dear,' she wrote, then stopped. What should she call him? She had no idea. 'Daniel' was too casual, too intimate, but did 'Mr Friedmann' make her sound like an Inland Revenue inspector? She gripped her pen tighter. She could leave it until last, fill it in when she'd finished.

'I wanted to write to you', she began. 'Wanted'. Sounded too past tense. She still wanted to, after all, which was why she was writing. Alice peeled off that page, tossed it in the drawer after the first one, and sat there, staring at the new blank page.

What exactly did she want to say? All she knew was that, since that evening with Rachel, every minute of every day she'd been thinking about writing this letter, wanting to get in touch. But she couldn't say that to him. Maybe she should write down the reasons first, in rough, and then write the letter.

Alice pressed her nib to the page. Ink leaked out into a tiny, circular stain, before her pen glided quickly across the ice-blue expanse. 'Because I want to talk to you.' Then: 'Because I'm angry with you.' 'Because I loved your son.' Half-way through shaping the letters to 'Because John is dead now, he's dead,' she told herself to stop, that she promised herself she wouldn't do this, that she wouldn't get like this while she was trying to write to his father. And when she felt the tears coming, running down her face and down her neck, soaking her jumper, she was so cross with herself that she rubbed at them roughly with her sleeves. Then she saw that tears had splatted on to the paper, making it buckle, blurring the ink into a watery mess. She tore off the page, sobbing now, and discovered that the page underneath had absorbed the water, and the one underneath that, and the one underneath that. Alice ripped off sheet after sheet, shoving them into the drawer, until she found a flat, clean one, and she put her pen to it and tried to calm herself and think of more reasons, tried to start again because she knew that if she didn't get a grip on herself now, in a few minutes' time it would be too late. But she found that all she could write, over and over, was his name and after a while she had to give up and just let herself cry and cry, her head resting on her arms, her body curled round his desk.

It's strange to think of my body lying somewhere. I think about it and how it looks. I think about how I know every mark, every pore, the creases of my palm, the scars from childhood, the small, pigmentless chickenpox circles and the tattoo on my shoulder-blade. I think about the day I had it done – a swelteringly humid day in Bangkok where I woke on the mattress I was sleeping on in a cockroach-ridden hotel. The bedsheet was tangled around my damp limbs, the roar of the traffic from the road, nineteen floors below, already audible, and I thought, I'm going to get a tattoo today. I went out into the burning air, pushing my sunglasses on, sweat already crawling down the groove of my back like slow insects, the mixture of pollution and heat fizzling in my lungs. I walked through the streets, past people eating in noodle bars on the pavements, past rows of vegetable stalls in narrow, shaded streets, under racks and racks of washing drying on bamboo poles outside people's windows, through lanes of roaring traffic, past people selling fake designer watches, through a park where old men in black trousers and white vests did the slow, mesmeric movements of tai ch'i or played each other at chess, past shops selling tiles and taps to a small tattoo parlour

I'd seen a few days before. It was grimy from the outside and the photos of people with reddened skin, proudly displaying their new markings nearly changed my mind. Inside, I pulled my T-shirt down from my shoulder. 'Here,' I said.

The man spanned my shoulder-blade with his hand, his dry fingers whispering against my skin. 'But a Chinese dragon,' he said, 'maybe not suitable for you.'

I turned to face him. 'It's what I want.'

He shrugged and swabbed my back with antiseptic. In the corner, a radio blared out the chiming, syrupy chords of Cantopop. He hummed along as he inked out the dragon. I watched him fill the tattoo gun with bottle-green ink. 'Are you sure?' he asked, the gun poised, buzzing, above my shoulder.

'I'm sure.'

It didn't hurt, or rather it was a strange kind of pain, like the way ice can burn. When it was finished I twisted and turned with my back to the mirror, looking over my shoulder. It was green, with golden eyes, a red tail and red tendrils coming from its mouth.

'I love it. Thank you,' I said, smiling, 'thank you,' and I plunged back into the roar, the heat, the bustle of the street, a secret dragon on my shoulder.

Ben gets up first. Ann can hear him and Beth having breakfast downstairs – plates and cutlery clashing together, the modulated murmur of their conversation. Ann knows she should get up and go down as well, but that kitchen is so small. She cannot bear the idea of the three of them banging into each other while boiling kettles, looking in Alice's cupboards for teabags, working out how the toaster works, opening and slamming the fridge, searching for margarine. There is something about eating the food Alice bought for herself that makes Ann queasy.

Ann sits up and leans her back against the wall. She hasn't slept well. The bed smells unmistakably of Alice, and Ann spent a lot of the night staring down at the peaks and troughs made by her and her husband's body in the duvet, trying to remember which side of the bed Alice slept on.

Ben has half opened the curtains. Ann can see out to the houses opposite. They seem incredibly close, their windows a stone's throw from where Ann is lying. How does Alice stand it, being that overlooked? She must feel constantly watched.

Ann looks about the room and is disconcerted to realise that from where she is lying, in the centre of Alice and John's huge bed, she can see herself and most of the bed in the mirror opposite. She turns her head and sees that the wardrobe mirror throws back a side angle of the bed; and a cheval mirror on the right-hand side of the room completes this 180-degree view. Ann is puzzled and is wondering why anyone would want to see themselves asleep when the reason for this arrangement hits her. Blood leaps to the surface of her cheeks and she is faced with three replicas of herself, blushing in her nightie, her hand covering her mouth. She gets up quickly.

In the bathroom, she tries not to look at that repulsive lizardy thing in the tank. Ann had been hoping it might have died since she was last here. But it's still there, as always, hanging in its water, feet splayed, staring at her with tiny, stupid-looking eyes. Its skin is the translucent pinkish-white Ann associates with illness, and she is disgusted to find that you can see its internal organs and blood vessels just under the surface. She thinks about having a bath, but the thought of that thing watching her throughout rather puts her off.

Ben calls up to say that he and Beth want to go to the hospital, and does she want to come with them. Ann shouts down that they are not to worry about her, that she doesn't want to hold them up, that she'll catch a taxi later.

After they've gone, Ann revels in the stillness, the solitude. She's never been able to cope with being with people twenty-four hours a day. On the floor in the bedroom is Alice's little backpack. Ann sits on a chair and pulls it open, looks inside: pens, sunglasses, a flyer for a reading by some novelist at the South Bank, Alice's Filofax, a personal attack alarm with the word 'Galahad' embossed in silver, a small plastic sheep (Ann peers at this in surprise, holding it up by one of its back legs. It has horns and lurid pink udders. She finds it distasteful, and puts it down quickly), a monthly tube pass issued at Camden Town station that expires next week (the headshot of Alice makes her flinch), a lipsalve (worn down on one side), foil-wrapped paracetamols. Ann lays all these things out at her feet and stares at them, as if playing that memory game where someone will remove one object and she'll have to say which one. Then she picks up the Filofax and opens it. Not much is written in it. On 24 April, Ann learns that her daughter had a staff meeting at 3 p.m. On 27 May, Alice and Rachel went to see the 7.30 p.m. showing of something called *Time of the Gypsies* at the Riverside Cinema. Nothing is written in for last weekend. In November, Alice has drawn a line through a weekend and written 'Norfolk?' As Ann reaches the back, a pair of rail tickets fall out: to Edinburgh, via any reasonable route. One outward, one return. Standard class. Adult one, child nil.

Ann shoves everything back into the rucksack and stands up. Without registering to herself what she is about to do, Ann opens Alice's wardrobe. Clothes are racked along the rail evenly – Alice's on one side, John's on the other. Ann touches them with her hand. Metal coat-hangers clack together. John's shirts are lined up, two or three to a hanger, his trousers and jeans folded over each other on the spar beneath. Alice's side – which takes up over two-thirds of the rail – is more elaborate, a mix of velvets, silk, embroidery, sparkly cardigans, lace dresses. At the bottom, shoes are mixed up – a trainer nestles between a pair of black sandals; a ridiculously high strappy shoe rests on top of a heavy, mud-rubbed boot. At the point where Alice's clothes meet John's, a red slip dress hangs next to a blue cotton shirt, slightly crumpled. It makes Ann cry, their clothes hanging together like this, it makes her cry a lot. And she's not sure who she's crying for: for her daughter, yes, the thought of whose death makes her feel like a glove pulled inside out on itself; for John who should never ever have died when Alice loved him so; and a part of her cries for herself, whose clothes would never hang like this with anyone's.

The sitting-room door opened slowly and Alice crept in, clutching a pillow to her chest. It was late morning, but she hadn't yet opened the curtains so the room was in half-light. The ringing of the phone stopped abruptly as the answering-machine clicked on: 'Alice? It's Rachel. I know you're there so pick up the phone.'

Alice didn't move but stared, unfocused, at the ceiling.

'Come on, Alice, pick up . . . OK. So, this is the . . . what? . . . sixteenth or seventeeth message I've left for you. Is your machine working? Have we fallen out without me noticing? Are you still alive?'

Alice heard her friend pause and sigh. The tape hissed gently. 'Right. Have it your way. I'll call again later.'

It was only after she had hung up and the tape had finished its little ritual of winding and rewinding that Alice backed out of the room and closed the door behind her.

Rachel bangs on the door again with the hardest bones of her knuckles.

'Who is it?' Alice's voice comes from behind the door.

'It's me. Open the door, for fuck's sake.'

There is a pause then she hears the flicking, clicking slide of a lock being drawn back. The door swings open. The two women stare at each other, Rachel with her hand on her hip, her mouth pursed. Rachel is puzzled, but can't quite say why. Alice looks different – well, even. Her eyes look brighter and she has more colour in her cheeks.

'So?' Rachel enquires.

'So what?'

'So, what's going on?'

'Nothing.' Alice looks at her defiantly. 'What do you mean?'

'You don't call me, you ignore my messages. Alice, it's been almost three weeks since I last saw you.'

'Has it?' she says vaguely, her eyes following a car going down the road.

Rachel sighs, seeing this is going to get them nowhere. 'Can I come in, then?'

'Um.' A shadow of panic passes over Alice's face, then she relaxes her grip on the door jamb. 'I suppose so, yes.'

'Thanks,' Rachel mutters, as she steps into the hall.

Alice drums her fingernails on the side of the kettle as she waits for it to boil. Rachel sits at the table, looking about her for something to say.

'Is that a new cardigan?'

'What?'

'That.' Rachel points at a red woollen cardigan draped over the back of a chair. 'Is it new?'

Alice picks it up quickly, refolds it and puts it down in exactly the same place. 'Yes.'

'It's really nice. Where did you get it?'

Alice, with her back to her, mumbles something unintelligible.

'What?'

'I said, I made it.'

'You made it? Really? Seriously?'

'Yes.'

'What . . . ?' Rachel is amazed. 'You knitted it?'

'Yes. Why is that so surprising?'

'Well, I didn't know you could knit for starters.'

Alice places a mug of tea in front of Rachel and sits down. 'I've been teaching myself.'

'That's a bit weird. What for?'

'What for? What do you mean "what for"? Why does anyone knit?'

'Well, I don't know. Old people like my grandmother knit to give themselves something to do. But you hardly need to fill your time.'

'I like it.'

'What? Knitting?'

'Yes.'

'Alice, do you know how sad that sounds? Is this what you've been doing instead of calling me – spending your evenings in, knitting?'

'Maybe. What's wrong with that?'

'What's wrong with that? Alice! For God's sake . . .' Rachel breaks off her tirade and gazes at her friend across the table. In the bright sunlight streaming in through the kitchen window, she's just seen that Alice's new, healthy complexion is due to a layer of carefully applied make-up.

Knowing she needs to say something and not yet sure what it is, Rachel gets up and, from the seat by the door, she lifts up a work-in-progress by the needles. It's a large, bottle-green sweater, or will be, when Alice has finished the ribbing round the bottom. Holding it up to the light, Rachel stares at its intricate web of stitches. This one slightly disturbs her but she's not quite sure why. She turns back to Alice, still sitting at the table. 'This one's a bit big for you, isn't it? Who's it for?'

Alice looks up and the expression of horrified anger that

distorts her face astonishes Rachel. 'Don't touch that. Put it down.' Alice darts across the kitchen and tears it from Rachel's hands.

Rachel watches as Alice winds the knitting protectively into itself. There is something about the colour of that sweater, the feel of it, the V-neck that unfailingly brings John to mind. She is knitting that sweater for John, Rachel thinks, she is knitting her dead lover a sweater.

'Al,' Rachel begins, chewing the inside of her lip, 'are you all right, I mean, how are things?'

Alice nods before speaking. 'I'm fine.'

Alice dials the number, checking it in the open book beside her, waits, hears the click of connection, then the ring. She imagines the telephone, it'll be a black, old-fashioned one with a cradle, maybe by the front door or on a window-sill, vibrating with her ringing. She imagines him hearing it – he's reading perhaps, or washing up, or watching TV – looking up, putting down whatever he's doing and crossing the room or coming downstairs – slowly because he had a slightly laboured gait, didn't he – reaching for the receiver.

Alice hangs up. She waits for a while. She gets up and walks around the room twice. She rearranges her plants by the window, turning their outward sides towards the light, pulling off any etiolated leaves and crushing them in her palms. Then she sits next to the phone again. Redials. This time she waits longer, listening to the faraway ring. The telephone dings as he picks it up, but before he can speak, Alice puts down the receiver. She has no air in her lungs. There's a needling, numb sensation all down her spine and up into her scalp.

Alice gets out of the taxi. The street is narrow and curves in an S-shape. Tall privet hedges obscure the gardens and houses from the pavement. House numbers are twisted into the wrought iron of the gates, which are dwarfed by the green mass of the hedges. As she walks along, she meets no one, no cars pass her. The sound of traffic from the busier three-lane main road behind her fades away. The houses are different, more suburban, set back from the road, detached with garages separating them from their neighbours. As the number nears, something like excitement flutters in Alice's chest.

There is a straight, flagstone path, bisecting the lawn, from where Alice is standing to the front door. A sprinkler jets arcs of water over a flower-bed: part of the path is darkened by the spray. This is where John grew up, Alice thinks, where he returned to every day from school, where he came that last time to tell his father about me. The windows are dark, giving out only reflections of the garden. Curtains are drawn over a room downstairs. It is big, Alice decides, she cannot imagine what it would be like to live in it on your own. By the gate is a rosebush. Overblown red roses that would have been perfect a week ago have let their petals droop and fall. Alice looks down to see that the pavement beneath her feet is strewn with them. There is a faint, sweetish odour of crushed petals. It reminds her of . . . of wreaths . . . and . . . Alice looks away, looks at the house, looks up at the sky, looks at the trees. The front door opens and the shape of the man that comes out and turns to lock the door behind him is blurred with Alice's sudden tears.

She darts away from the gate and hides round the corner of the neighbouring driveway, her fist pressed into her teeth. Has he seen her? What would she say? She's not prepared now, she's not prepared at all. She can't organise her thoughts, can't think of what to say now. Peering round the rockery, she sees him come out of the gate and pull it closed. He is holding a striped shopping-bag with wire handles that he transfers to his other hand to shut the gate. Then he walks off.

Alice pulls up the hood on her sweatshirt, horrified to realise as she does so that it is one of John's. How could she be so stupid? She spends a few seconds panicking, trying to work out how long John had had it, and was there any way that Daniel might recognise it. Then she steps out on to the pavement and follows, keeping a stretch of road between them, her eyes fixed on his back, the polished heels of his shoes.

He walks along the street and turns right, heading down the hill towards the shops and tube station she passed on her way in the taxi. He walks slowly and unevenly, his back a little bent, and Alice thinks how much older than her parents he seems. He pauses outside a delicatessen with barrels of apples outside. She ducks behind a phone box until he moves on again At the crossroads he waits with two or three other people for the traffic to stop. She loiters in the doorway of the bank. Would he recognise her if he saw her? Would he know her if she was to approach him? How would she introduce herself? When he has crossed the road, the traffic-lights still bleeping, she dashes across at the last minute, just as he is climbing the steps to the public library.

It is quiet and dark in the library. The hallway has a red stone floor and blackened wooden panelling. There is a smell of lots of books – that unmistakable, moistureless, throat-catching odour. Through glass swing doors, she sees him go up to the returns desk, taking from his striped bag three books. He places them one by one on top of each other on the desk and waits in line, shunting them along beside him as the queue moves.

Alice pushes through the doors and stands behind a book stack filled with children's books. 'Hello, Mr Friedmann,' she hears the librarian say. He is fumbling in the inside pocket of his coat, pulling out a glasses case. Nodding, he mumbles something Alice cannot hear, then turns and walks across the room.

Alice shifts her position. She knew he was retired. Is this what he does all day? He takes off his coat and settles it over the back of a chair. Then he sits and adjusts a pair of half-moon spectacles on his nose. He opens one of the newspapers impaled on wooden sticks and starts to read.

Now would be a perfect time. She tugs at the drawstring running through the rim of her hood. If he looked up, straight ahead of him, he'd see her eyes watching him through the shelves. She walks around the edge of the room, nearly tripping over a mother reading to a toddler balanced on her lap. She gets so close to him, close enough that if she leant over and stretched out her arm she could tap him on the shoulder. Then what? He would turn, look up into the face of this woman wearing his dead son's sweatshirt, and then what?

One of his hands is curled around the back of his neck, the other rests, limp, on the table. From where she is standing, Alice can see through the lenses of his glasses: the newsprint distorts and stretches beyond them. She just has to reach out, or say something, that's all it would take. A surge of adrenalin pulses through her body, making her head ring. She's going to do it. She's going to do it right now. Right now.

At that moment, another librarian, a middle-aged woman, pale beneath a rash of freckles, appears on the other side of the table to Alice and Daniel. 'How are you, Mr Friedmann?' she trills.

He jumps. Looks up. His hand on the table tenses, his nails scratching against the newspaper. 'I am well,' he replies, 'thank you.'

And Alice cannot bear this, she really cannot. It makes scalding tears brim without warning into her eyes. Surface tension holds them there for a second – making the librarian leaning over the table, his back, the paper, the book stacks beyond them all swim before her as if the scene is melting

360

— then they spill down her face. His voice. IIis voice is so like John's. It is John's. It has a slight Polish edge to it, but the tone, the inflection, the pitch are identical. It could have been him speaking, it could have been his voice sounding out into this library. But it wasn't and she cannot bear it.

Her feet move beneath her, carrying her around the edge of the table, past the librarian who is staring at her now, so she puts her hands up to cover her face and has to negotiate the rest of the building though the gaps between her fingers. Once outside, she runs and runs, bolting past people on pavements, dodging cars; she runs, and runs so far and without seeing anything, that when she stops she has no idea where she is.

Beth, wearing only a T-shirt, encounters her mother in the sitting room. She has woken late, her head feeling muzzy. Her mother has an apron on (Beth wonders where it came from and if her mother brought it with her – it couldn't possibly belong to Alice), and rubber gloves, and is gripping a duster in one hand and the head of the vacuum cleaner in the other. Beth knows that this can only mean one thing: Ann is preparing for a germ genocide.

'Morning,' Beth says warily.

'Hello.'

'What are you up to?'

'I've just got to do some cleaning.' Ann marches over to the desk and starts sorting papers into vague piles, dusting the area cleared. 'This place is, frankly, a health hazard. I don't know what your sister was thinking of.'

'Mum, I don't think you should––'

'I mean, *really*.' Ann yanks open a drawer and begins pulling out bits of scrumpled-up blue paper and dropping them into a rubbish bag.

'Mum, don't.' Beth goes over and peers at the bits of paper in the bin. Some have unintelligible writing on them. 'You shouldn't do that. Alice wouldn't like it. You can't throw her stuff out like that.'

Ann moves off and starts pushing at the sofa. 'Help me with this, Beth, will you? I wouldn't like to think when this was last vacuumed under.'

Beth is considering trying to stop her doing this as well, but is deciding that her mother isn't easy to deflect when in cleaning mode and that vacuuming is probably the least harmful thing she could be doing, when the phone begins to ring.

'Phone,' Beth says.

Ann stops unravelling the flex of Alice's vacuum cleaner. This is the first time the phone has rung since they've been here. Beth isn't wearing enough to be wandering around the house this late in the morning, so Ann moves through into the hall and picks up the receiver.

'Yes?'

'Hello.' It's man's voice. Oldish. Middle-aged sounding. Hesitant. 'I'm not sure if I have the right number.'

'No,' Ann says, a bit thrown, 'no, I mean, it's not . . . Alice isn't . . . here.'

'I see.' He sounds uncertain. Ann feels irritated. Don't take all day, for heaven's sake. 'Maybe you could give her a message for me.'

Ann is silent. Who is this person who doesn't know? She isn't sure how to phrase it – is he a friend? A colleague? The gas man?

'If you could tell her that . . . that I saw her last week, I saw her in the library. And I tried to . . . I came out after her, but she ran away too fast. I looked everywhere, but I couldn't find her. If you could tell her . . . I meant to call . . . a long time ago, but . . . I never did. And now I've been meaning to call all week, but I still didn't, so . . .' He trails off, then inhales audibly, summoning courage, 'I think what I really want to say is that . . . I would very much like to . . . talk to her. I would like to see her.'

'Who are you?'

'My name is Daniel. Daniel Friedmann. I am John's father.'

Ann sees a man in bright-white sunlight, walking down the steps with John's ashes, and Alice's face watching him. Fury, unexpected and potent, surges upwards in her.

'I see,' Ann says. She looks up and sees her face thrown back at her by the large gold mirror hanging in the hall. 'Well, Daniel Friedmann, this is Alice's mother. I can't give Alice your message, I'm afraid. Do you want to know why?'

'Oh. I—'

'Alice was hit by a car. She's in a coma. You have a habit of leaving things too late, don't you? Alice is in a bloody coma. And she's probably going to die. What do you say to that?'

Ann slams down the receiver, cutting off the line, then drops it so that it dangles somewhere near the floor.

Ann slips through the heavy double doors into Intensive Care. There's hardly anyone around and anyone she does pass doesn't give her a second look.

In Alice's room she pulls a chair up close to the side of the bed so that she's close to her daughter's face. Ann moves her handbag off her lap and pushes it under her chair. She lays her hand over Alice's – surprisingly warm and tense – then removes it quickly. She wonders what happened to Alice's hair when they cut it all off. Would it have been incinerated? Ann shifts her chair even closer to the bed and leans towards Alice's ear. 'Alice,' she begins, 'I want to tell you something.'

At at movement beyond the window, Ann stops. A nurse is passing, holding the arm of a man of indeterminate age. His skin is sallow, puckered, the texture of brown paper, and he walks with the laboured steps of an astronaut. His head lolls to one side. 'Very good,' the nurse is saying brightly, 'that's farther than yesterday already.'

Ann's gaze flicks back to her daughter, then back to her lap. She picks a few hairs off her coat, letting them drift into the airless atmosphere of the room, then leans forward again. 'I loved him,' she whispers. The hospital hums around them. 'I really did. I want you to know that I always—'

The door opens and Ben walks in. He is carrying two cups and three books. He pushes the door closed with his foot. 'Hello,' he says, 'I got you tea.'

Ann sits back in her chair. 'Thanks.'

'Is tea all right?' he asks, as he hands it to her.

'Yes. Fine.'

'Or would you rather coffee?'

'Coffee's fine too.'

'I got coffee for me. But you could have it if you wanted.'

'I don't mind. Either.'

'Oh. Tea or coffee, then?'

'I said I don't mind. Whatever you want.'

'I don't mind either.'

'Ben,' Ann clears her throat, 'Ben, I need . . . to talk to you.'

Ben has his back to her. He is putting the books down on the bedside table. He rests his cup on top of them, then turns to Alice. 'Hello,' he says, in his special I'm-talking-to-my-daughter-in-a-coma voice. 'How are you today?'

Ann marvels for a moment at her ability to be irritated by him, even at a time like this. 'Ben? Did you hear me?'

He still doesn't react, rubbing Alice's arm with his hand.

'Ben! I'm talking to you. Or trying to.'

He half turns. 'Ann, if this is about dinner tonight, Beth and I were talking about it, and—'

'It's not about dinner.'

'Oh.' He sits.

'Ben,' Ann begins, 'I need to tell you things . . . about Alice. You see, if Alice wakes up—'

'When,' Ben corrects her.

'If,' Ann insists, 'if she does, then . . .' Ann finds her hands are slippery with sweat. She laces her fingers into one another. 'We need to have talked about this first.'

Ben jumps up. 'I think I'll have coffee after all.' He picks up the cup. 'Are you sure you're happy with tea?'

'Will you shut up about the bloody tea?'

He jerks his head as if she's slapped him. For a moment, this room where people only ever talk in hushed tones seems shocked by her raised voice – pulsing with silence, waiting. Then the ventilator is released, Alice's chest falls, and the spell seems broken.

'The thing is,' Ann begins, in a lower voice, 'I'm not sure that Alice is—'

'Don't,' Ben murmurs. Ann looks at him over the mound of Alice's body. He has his hand spread over his forehead, covering his eyes.

'Don't what?'

'Don't say it. I don't want you to say it.'

'You don't know what I'm going—'

'Yes, I do,' he interrupts, 'of course I do,' and he is taking his hands away from his face. 'You must think I'm a fool.'

'Ben . . . I . . .' Control seems to have slipped from her grasp. She feels as if something is curdling inside her, something very cold, pulling substance away from the edges of her body, leaving her as just a shell of skin stretched over bone. Ann gets up, stumbles from her chair, holds on to the window-sill, knocking over several of Alice's cards by her movement. How does he know? Did he see them ever? Did Elspeth tell him, after all?

366

'How long have you known?' she asks, her back to her husband.

'I've always known.'

'Right from when she was born?'

'Yes,' he sighs.

'How?' Ann is incredulous, appalled. She turns round to face him.

He almost laughs. 'You never did understand how North Berwick works, did you? Everybody knows everything. And there are always people who'll tell you, and,' he winces at some hidden recollection, 'people who'll take pleasure in telling you. But when Alice was born, and I held her . . . I held her in the hospital when she was about two hours old, do you remember? And she was wailing and screaming and fighting. You were really tired, and I took her in my arms down the corridor away from you so that you could sleep, and I looked down at her and I realised that what I felt for her was no different, no less fierce or less intense or less protective, than what I'd felt for Kirsty, and I told myself: Ben, don't listen to gossip, either she is yours, or she's as good as, and in the long run will it really matter? And the doubt hurt, God, it hurt sometimes — especially as she got older and it was more and more obvious — but whenever it threatened to overtake me I just kept telling myself that being a father is about more than just DNA. She is to me what Beth and Kirsty are.'

'Why . . . why did you never say anything before?'

'Why? Because . . . because what was the point, Ann? I knew, you knew. It would have been . . . vindictive . . . to . . . to drag it all out into the open. Alice and her sisters — what kind of an effect would it have had on the three of them? And Elspeth . . . it would have broken Elspeth's heart. You know how they were with each other. Elspeth would have hated you for it. Why would I have wanted all that?'

Ann looks down at her feet. 'Ben, I think she does know. Alice, I mean. I think she's found out.'

Ben uncrosses his legs, shifting his foot up on to his knee, gets hold of his ankle. 'What do you mean?' he asks.

'I mean . . . in Edinburgh . . . when she came up . . . I think she saw . . .'

'You and him?'

Ann nods.

'You are . . . ?' Ben flounders for the words, the lines in his forehead and around his eyes deepening. 'Still . . . ?'

Ann nods again.

Ben bites his lower lip, swallows, his eyes slide away from his wife, back to the figure on the bed. 'I see.'

The most depressing thing about these cases for Mike is that after a certain amount of time, people give up on them; the patient gets relegated to a smaller room, off a more distant ward; the question of quality of life is raised, euthanasia discussed; donor transplant is mentioned, gently at first, to the relatives.

The hospital corridors move under him, then he turns right down the long glass walkway. There are still some tests he can run. He could put her in for a new brain scan, take another lumbar puncture. But he tells himself that he must decide if there's any point, must set down, in his head at least, a cut-off date.

Ahead of him is a middle-aged man that Mike's been kind of trying to overtake ever since he walked through the doors of this wing of the hospital, but there have been so many people and wheelchairs and beds coming the other way Mike feels he can't barge past him. The man walks just that bit slower than him so that every now and again Mike has to take three or four mincing, foreshortened steps so as not to tread on the back of his shoes.

To his dismay, he sees that the man is going through the double doors to Intensive Care. Mike sighs and then reminds himself that it's not much farther now anyway. Two nurses pass. Their eyes rest on the bloke in front of Mike, and rest on Mike for slightly longer.

The man stops outside Alice's room. Mike is so unprepared for this that he nearly falls over him, turning his head and reading – at the same time as the man – 'Alice Raikes' on the little white sign on the door. The man is leaning his weight against the door, going in, closing it behind him. Mike steps up to the window, covered in those mirrored slats that give you back sections of your face interspersed with narrow glimpses of the room beyond. He sees the man pull a chair up to the bed and sit down.

I am somewhere. Drifting. Hiding. Thoughts running around tracks, random and unconnected as ball-bearings in the circuit of a pinball machine. I am thinking about the party at which John and I didn't meet, how we must have circled each other round the room like moths at a light-bulb. I am thinking about my grandmother and how she told me that she made her own trousseau. I am imagining her cutting through the flimsy sheen of coral silk, the weight of the dressmaking scissors leaving red welts in her thumb and finger; folding the fraying edges into themselves, hemming them with infinitesimal, slanting stitches, sewing on to them the long webs of lace. I am thinking of the garden in North Berwick and my mother pocking at the soil with a trowel, pulling up weeds and shaking their tangled roots to divest them of any particle of earth they might have dared to think they could take with them. I am thinking this and all this and nothing, when I hear someone somewhere saying, 'Hello there, Alice.' Just like that. Three words propelled into my atmosphere. And I know that voice. I know it so well. It's John. And he is speaking to me. And suddenly it feels like the moment before thunder: the air around me seems to vibrate and darken, and I am not in control any more, I'm being driven towards something, or through something, through what feels like a small, narrowing gap, and for a moment I wonder if this is it, if the time is now, if I'm dying, and part of me is laughing, scoffing at all that bullshit we are fed about tunnels and light because it doesn't feel like that at all, not at all, but I'm not really laughing very much because I'm concentrating too hard to see if he's going to speak again. If I had antennae they'd be quivering, stretched out to their limit, straining for sound, and then I hear it again: he is clearing his throat, and I want to cry and shout, where have you been, you bastard, how dare you leave me like that. But then I hear, 'I have been meaning to come and see you for a long time. A very long time.'

It's not him. It's not him and it feels like my heart is breaking all over again.

But I do know who it is. He is speaking again, saying things about how he's left everything too late and can I forgive him, and I don't know if I can and I am wondering about this when I feel that his voice seems close to me, very close indeed, so close that I can almost feel his breath moving at the side of my head; then I realise that all this time I am being carried forwards, or up, and I'm not sure if this is what I want and I'm panicking now, unsure if I should be trying to tread water or swim back down against this force, but it seems there's nothing I can do, my head rushing rushing towards some surface I didn't know was there or that I'd forgotten was there, and I'm gasping now, my lungs tight and airless, strings of bubbles streaming from my mouth like pearls.